SUPER EDITION
WARRIORS
SKYCLAN'S DESTINY

WARRIORS

THE NEW PROPHECY

POWER OF THREE

OMEN OF THE STARS

EXPLORE THE
WARRIORS WORLD

Also by Erin Hunter

SEEKERS

SUPER EDITION

WARRIORS

SKYCLAN'S DESTINY

ERIN HUNTER

HARPER

An Imprint of HarperCollinsPublishers

SkyClan's Destiny

Copyright © 2010 by Working Partners Limited

Series created by Working Partners Limited

Manga text copyright © 2010 by Working Partners Limited

Manga art copyright © 2010 by HarperCollins Publishers

Library of Congress Cataloging-in-Publication Data

Hunter, Erin.

   SkyClan's destiny / Erin Hunter. — 1st ed.

     p.   cm. — (Warriors)

   Summary: Leafstar struggles to maintain control of her Clan as she
figures out how SkyClan can survive in the gorge.

   ISBN 978-0-06-169994-8 (trade bdg.)

   ISBN 978-0-06-169995-5 (lib. bdg.)

   [1. Cats—Fiction.   2. Adventure and adventurers—Fiction.   3. Fantasy.]   I. Title.

PZ7.H916625Sky 2010   2009053451

[Fic]—dc22   CIP

                                         AC

Typography by Hilary Zarycky

10 11 12 13 14 LP/RRDH 10 9 8 7 6 5 4 3 2 1

❖

First Edition

Special thanks to Cherith Baldry

ALLEGIANGES

SKYCLAN

LEADER
LEAFSTAR—brown-and-cream tabby she-cat with amber eyes

DEPUTY
SHARPCLAW—dark ginger tom

MEDIGINE GAT
ECHOSONG—silver tabby she-cat with green eyes

WARRIORS
(toms, and she-cats without kits)

PATCHFOOT—black-and-white tom

PETALNOSE—pale gray she-cat
APPRENTICE, SAGEPAW

SPARROWPELT—dark brown tabby tom

CHERRYTAIL—tortoiseshell-and-white she-cat

WASPWHISKER—gray-and-white tom
APPRENTICE, MINTPAW

SHREWTOOTH—skinny black tom

EBONYCLAW—striking black she-cat
APPRENTICE, FRECKLEPAW

BILLYSTORM—ginger-and-white tom
APPRENTICE, SNOOKPAW

HARVEYMOON—white tom

MACGYVER—black-and-white tom

ROCKSHADE—black tom

BOUNCEFIRE—ginger tom (Clovertail's son)

TINYCLOUD—small white she-cat (Clovertail's daughter)

APPRENTICES (more than six moons old, in training to become warriors)

SAGEPAW—pale gray tom (son of Petalnose and Rainfur)

MINTPAW—gray tabby she-cat (daughter of Petalnose and Rainfur)

SNOOKPAW—black-and-white tom

FRECKLEPAW—mottled light brown tabby she-cat with spotted legs

QUEENS (she-cats expecting or nursing kits)

FALLOWFERN—pale brown she-cat (mother to Hunchfoot's kits: Rabbitkit, Creekkit, Nettlekit, and Plumkit)

CLOVERTAIL—light brown she-cat with white belly and legs (expecting Patchfoot's kits)

ELDERS (former warriors and queens, now retired)

LICHENFUR—gray mottled she-cat

TANGLE—ragged tabby tom loner

CATS OUTSIDE THE CLAN

EGG—cream-colored tom loner

HUTCH—dark brown kittypet (formerly Shortwhisker)

OSCAR—black kittypet

BELLA—tabby-and-white kittypet with amber eyes

ROSE—elegant brown-and-cream Siamese kittypet with slanting blue eyes

LILY—Rose's sister

STICK—brown tom with yellow eyes and a torn ear

CORA—black she-cat

COAL—black tom

SHORTY—brown tom with amber eyes and half a tail

SNOWY—white she-cat

PERCY—dark gray tabby tom

RED—dark ginger she-cat

DODGE—dark brown tabby tom

SKIPPER—ginger-and-white tom

HARLEY—gray-and-brown tabby tom

MISHA—cream-colored she-cat

ONION—silver-and-black she-cat

NUTMEG—tortoiseshell-and-white she-cat

VELVET—silver kittypet

ANCIENT SKYCLAN

CLOUDSTAR—pale gray tom with white patches and very pale blue eyes

BUZZARDSTAR—ginger tom with green eyes (deputy when SkyClan left the forest)

FAWNSTEP—light brown tabby she-cat (medicine cat when SkyClan left the forest)

BIRDFLIGHT—light brown tabby she-cat with long fluffy fur and amber eyes

FERNPELT—dark brown tabby she-cat

MOUSEFANG—sandy-colored she-cat

NIGHTFUR—black tom

OAKSTEP—gray tabby tom

SPIDERSTAR—dark tabby tom (last leader of Ancient SkyClan)

HONEYLEAF—ginger tabby she-cat (last deputy of Ancient SkyClan)

BRACKENHEART—brown tabby tom (last medicine cat of Ancient SkyClan)

SWALLOWFLIGHT—black tom

SKYWATCHER—dark gray tom with pale blue eyes (lived in the gorge before Modern SkyClan was formed)

RAINFUR—light gray tom with dark gray flecks (killed in the battle with the rats)

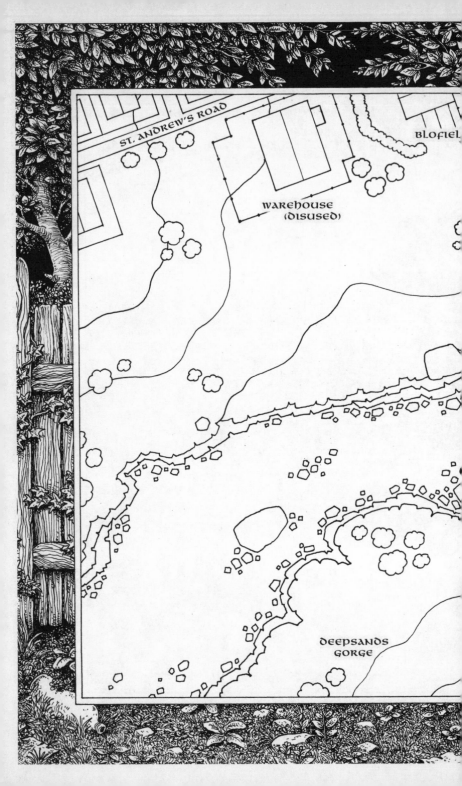

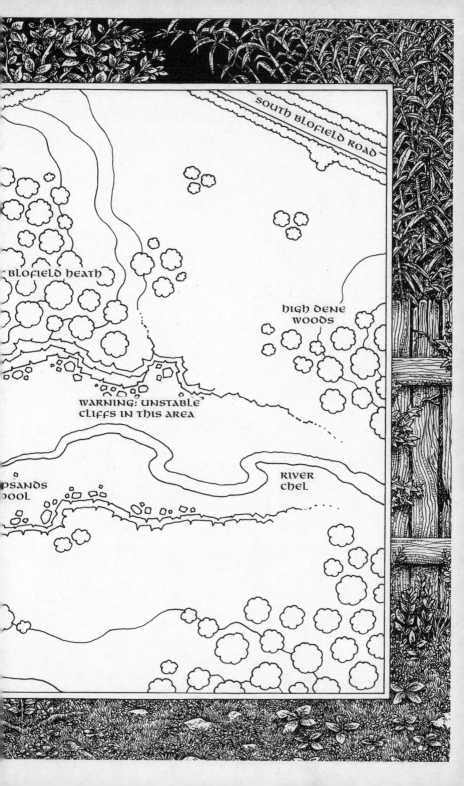

PROLOGUE

❧

The sun was going down, casting deep shadows over the gorge. A chilly breeze ruffled the surface of the river and whirled the last few shriveled leaves through the air. The only sound was the murmur of water that surged from a black hole in a pile of boulders, coiling into a pool before winding away into the darkness beneath the cliffs.

A dark tabby tom appeared at the top of the gorge, outlined against the sky. He paused for a moment, tasting the air. The dying sun shed bloodred light over his pelt, touching a patch on his shoulder where the fur had been torn away. After a few heartbeats the tabby tom signaled with his tail and began to pick his way down a narrow track that zigzagged across the face of the cliff. Seven other cats followed him: A white she-cat stumbled awkwardly on three paws, the fourth a mass of blood-soaked fur held close to her chest; a long-legged black tom edged downward nervously, one eye closed and sticky with blood; a young ginger tom limped with both ears shredded. Not one of the cats was free of wounds.

As the eight warriors padded painfully down the trail toward the water's edge, four more cats emerged from a cave a little farther along the gorge. The first was a young brown tabby tom who sprang quickly down the rocks to the foot of the boulders. His paws worked anxiously in the sand as he waited for the warriors to arrive. The other three were elders who stumbled after him on shaky legs.

"Well, Spiderstar?" one of them rasped as the leading cat reached the bottom of the cliff. The elder's muzzle was gray with age, and every one of his ribs was visible beneath his thin black pelt. "What happened? Did you win?"

The dark tabby tom paused for a moment, then padded forward to touch his nose to the older cat's ear. "What does it look like, Nightfur?" he murmured in reply. "Brackenheart," he added to the young brown tabby, "I hope your den is well stocked with herbs. We're going to need them."

Before the medicine cat could reply, the long-legged black tom pushed up beside his Clan leader, his lip curling in contempt. "Of course we didn't win. This battle was lost before it was even begun."

A ginger tabby she-cat, who had brought up the rear as the battle-scarred cats made their way down the cliff, bounded up and glared at the black tom. "You can't say that, Swallowflight! We had to fight. SkyClan still has its pride!"

It was the white she-cat who replied, shaking her head sadly. "Pride in what, Honeyleaf? We can't feed ourselves because the rats have chased off all the prey. No kits have been born in moons. The only ceremonies we have now are to send our Clanmates to our ancestors."

The ginger she-cat's head whipped around, her green eyes

narrowing to slits. "Look, Frostclaw—"

"Will we hold ceremonies for Sunpelt and Fallensnow?" the young warrior with the shredded ears interrupted. His voice was trembling with grief.

"We will, Rowanfur." Spiderstar dipped his head to the young cat. "Their spirits are free now to walk among the stars."

"What?" A gray tabby elder rose shakily to his paws. "Sunpelt and Fallensnow are *dead*? Then where are their bodies? We must sit vigil for them and then bury them."

"Oakstep, we had to leave them behind," Swallowflight spat out with a lash of his tail. "We were too busy fleeing to save our own pelts to carry our fallen Clanmates." He turned away, his head bowed as if he couldn't bear to go on looking at the others.

Frostclaw padded up and sat quietly beside him, pushing her nose into the black tom's matted shoulder fur. "Swallowflight, there was nothing else we could have done for them. No cat could blame us."

"She's right," Brackenheart meowed quietly. "Our Clanmates hunt with StarClan now. They'll understand."

Spiderstar nodded, his eyes dark with pain and loss.

"But if you had brought them back we could have buried them!" Oakstep protested. "Where is the honor in leaving them to be picked over by the rats? Sunpelt and Fallensnow should never be crow-food!"

Every paw step an effort, he started to hobble up the trail that led to the top of the gorge. Before he had gone more than a few fox-lengths, Spiderstar darted in front of him and forced the grief-stricken elder to stop.

"We have lost enough Clanmates tonight," he mewed. "Let us pray for their spirits as they join StarClan."

Swallowflight's ears pricked, and he turned to look at his Clan leader. "StarClan? Do you think they are really watching over us?" His whiskers twitched with disgust. "If they cared about us at all, they would never have let the rats come."

Honeyleaf whirled to face her Clanmate. "StarClan has given us the warrior code, and with that comes the courage and skill to defeat our enemies. SkyClan is not defeated yet!"

Silence greeted her words. It was several heartbeats before Spiderstar spoke, his voice aching with sadness. "Honeyleaf, you're wrong. We are defeated. I cannot bear to lead my Clanmates into one more battle, to watch them starve through another leaf-bare, afraid of every noise, every stirring leaf. We have become prey." He heaved a sigh from the depths of his chest. "The rats have won. SkyClan is no more."

A chorus of protest broke out at the Clan leader's words. The third elder, a sandy-colored she-cat, hauled herself to her paws and padded up to face him, her whiskers twitching.

"That can't be right, Spiderstar," she growled. "I was a kit when we lived in the forest, when the Twolegs stole our territory and the other Clans forced us to leave. Some cats thought SkyClan was finished, but we found a new home for ourselves, here in the gorge. If losing our home didn't beat us, neither should this battle."

"Mousefang's right." Oakstep padded to his Clanmate's

side. "We can't give up now."

"Show us these rats and *we'll* fight them," another elder, Nightfur, added.

"I never knew the forest, but I honor your memories of it." Spiderstar dipped his head to the three old cats, respect in his eyes. "No cat doubts your courage, my friends, but there's nothing that any of us can do. There are too many rats."

"Then there has to be another answer!" Honeyleaf burst out. "Spiderstar, I've tried to be a good, brave, loyal deputy, to you and to SkyClan. I've worked my paws off, and I've never been afraid to fight. I didn't come this far just to watch our Clan die!"

Spiderstar reached out to touch the she-cat's shoulder with the tip of his tail. "You have been the best deputy a cat could wish for," he told her. "And you would have led your Clan with the same honor and courage. Every cat knows that."

"What do you mean, 'would have'?" Honeyleaf drew her lips back in the beginning of a snarl; her neck fur bristled up. "I—"

"This is all a load of mouse dung." Nightfur cut off what the deputy was about to say. "How are we supposed to survive as loners if we can't survive as a Clan?"

For a few heartbeats no cat answered; they exchanged dismayed glances with one another, as if the old black tom's words had suddenly made them realize that they were facing a future without the support of their Clan. Even Honeyleaf subsided, her fur settling flat again and only her tail-tip twitching.

"I . . . I've been taking food from Twolegs now and again,"

Frostclaw admitted, lowering her head and giving her mangled paw a lick. "It doesn't taste too bad, if you're hungry."

"What?" Honeyleaf's ears pricked. "Food from *Twolegs*? That's completely against the warrior code!"

Frostclaw blinked at her guiltily and didn't try to defend herself.

The young ginger tom, Rowanfur, padded up to her and pressed himself against her side. "So what?" he meowed defiantly. "I've been taking food from Twolegs, too. I'd rather do that than starve. I reckon they'd take us into their dens," he added, his voice shaking a little. "I think they're sorry for us, seeing how thin we are. If we went to live with them, we'd have shelter and we'd be safe from the rats."

One or two of the other cats nodded and murmured agreement.

Honeyleaf stalked into the middle of the group, raking them with an icy glare from her green eyes. "Kittypets? You want to be *kittypets*? SkyClan warriors will never do that! It would be the greatest shame of all!"

"That's true!" Swallowflight agreed with a lash of his tail. "I'd rather die than go crawling to Twolegs for food!"

None of the other cats could meet the deputy's accusing stare. At last, Mousefang asked quietly, "Brackenheart, have you had a sign from StarClan? Can *they* tell us what to do?"

The young medicine cat padded forward, his eyes downcast. "I feel nothing but sadness and guilt coming from our ancestors," he confessed. "Guilt for taking us away from the forest, and sadness because SkyClan is coming to an end."

"What?" Oakstep's eyes stretched wide with horror. "Has even StarClan given up on us? I remember when Cloudstar led us away from the forest," he went on when no cat answered him. "He said we should never look to the spirits of our warrior ancestors again, and he was right. We should never have listened to StarClan. They have done nothing for us!"

By now the sunlight had almost gone, and warriors of StarClan were beginning to appear in the darkening sky. But none of the cats in the gorge looked up at their frosty glitter. Instead, they huddled together at the bottom of the cliff, where the rocks retained a little warmth from the sun, and there was shelter from the chilly wind.

"Then this is the end," a black-and-white tom meowed. "Rowanfur, will you show me where to get Twoleg food?"

"Of course," the ginger tom replied. "Any cats who want to can come with me and Frostclaw."

A gray she-cat got up and padded to his side. "I'll come, too. There'll be food and warmth with the Twolegs. The warrior code can't feed or shelter us. It's just words."

"I never thought I'd hear a SkyClan warrior say that!" Honeyleaf hissed, horrified. "The warrior code lives in all of us, when we hunt and fight and give thanks for the life of a Clan cat."

The gray she-cat whipped around to face her. "I do not give thanks for this life! It is over!"

Honeyleaf slid out her claws, and for a heartbeat it seemed as if the two she-cats would turn on each other, screeching and clawing. Then the Clan deputy turned her back.

"Well, *I* won't turn into a mewling kittypet," she insisted, her bristling fur showing how furious she was. "If we can't stay here, I'm going farther up the gorge, away from the rats. There might be better hunting there."

"I'll come with you," Swallowflight meowed. "We'll survive better if we hunt together."

All three elders sat silent as the warriors discussed where they would go. At last Mousefang raised her head to meet Spiderstar's sorrowful gaze. "I want to stay here," she stated flatly. "I'm too old to find a new place. This is where I belong."

"Me too," murmured Nightfur, giving the old she-cat's ear a lick. "The rats don't come here. There's water, and we can still find the odd mouse or beetle."

"It's not like we have much time left," Oakstep added.

Once again Spiderstar dipped his head. "I will stay with you," he meowed. "I will see that each of you has an honorable ending, to give thanks for your loyalty."

Nightfur nodded, his eyes full of grief and loss too deep for words.

"I'll stay, too," Brackenheart added. "This is where I can make the best use of my medicine cat skills . . . before I am no longer a medicine cat."

He rose to his paws, glancing around at the remnants of his Clan, gathering their attention as a queen gathers her kits into the shelter of her tail. Then he looked up at the sky, staring unblinkingly at the cold light of his warrior ancestors.

"May StarClan light your path, Fallensnow, and yours, Sunpelt, as you walk the skies to join them," he meowed. "May you find good hunting, swift running, and shelter when you sleep."

The cats around him murmured their agreement with the words spoken for each fallen warrior.

Spiderstar heaved a deep sigh. "May StarClan light a path for all of us. We still live on, but our Clan has died."

No cat responded. Their eyes shone in the starlight, full of fear and despair, as they stared at the cat who had been their Clan leader. Spiderstar did not meet their gaze, as if he was too overwhelmed by shame at the destruction of the Clan he had led for so many seasons.

Brackenheart remained silent for a heartbeat, then gave his pelt a swift shake, as if he had just pulled himself out of icy water. "Come," he mewed. "It's time I looked at your injuries."

With a wave of his tail, the young brown tabby led his wounded Clanmates to his den, where he stopped the worst of their bleeding with cobwebs, and made poultices of marigold against infection. For Honeyleaf and the other cats who were leaving to explore farther up the gorge, he made up bundles of traveling herbs.

"May StarClan walk with you," he meowed as they left.

Honeyleaf bounded away without replying. Brackenheart followed her out of the den, and sat beside Spiderstar to watch his Clan separate for the last time. The moon had drifted from behind a patch of cloud, shedding a frosty light over the rocks and the river. The dark outlines of the departing cats slipped up the trail to the top of the gorge, and were lost to sight. Only

Spiderstar, Brackenheart, and the three elders were left.

"Let's move our nests into the elders' den," Brackenheart suggested quietly to Spiderstar. "That way we can take care of them until they don't need us anymore."

Spiderstar nodded, looking around the empty gorge. It was still littered with the lives of so many cats, with memories like shadows clinging to each rock and crevice.

"I wonder . . ." He sighed. "Will a Clan ever live here again?"

"I think they will. One day, cats will return here and find a way to succeed where we have failed." A deeper echo sounded in Brackenheart's voice, a strength that came from pride and courage and unflinching loyalty to the warrior code. "This is the leaf-bare of our Clan. Greenleaf will come, but it will bring even greater storms than these. SkyClan will need deeper roots if it is to survive."

CHAPTER 1

Floodwater thundered down the gorge, chasing a wall of uprooted trees and bushes as if they were the slenderest twigs. Leafstar stood at the entrance to her den and watched in horror as the current foamed and swirled among the rocks, mounting higher and higher. Rain lashed the surface from bulging black clouds overhead.

Water gurgled into Echosong's den; though the SkyClan leader strained her eyes through the stormy darkness, she couldn't see what had happened to the medicine cat. A cat's shriek cut through the tumult of the water and Leafstar spotted the Clan's two elders struggling frantically as they were swept out of their den. The two old cats flailed on the surface for a heartbeat and then vanished.

Cherrytail and Patchfoot, heading down the trail with fresh-kill in their jaws, halted in astonishment when they saw the flood. They spun around and fled up the cliff, but the water surged after them and carried them yowling along the gorge. Leafstar lost sight of them as a huge tree, its roots high in the air like claws, rolled between her and the drowning warriors.

Great StarClan, help us! Leafstar prayed. *Save my Clan!*

Already the floodwater was lapping at the entrance to the nursery. A kit poked its nose out and vanished back inside with a frightened wail. Leafstar bunched her muscles, ready to leap across the rocks and help, but before she could move, a wave higher than the rest licked around her and caught her up, tossing her into the river alongside the splintered trees.

Leafstar fought and writhed against the smothering water, gasping for breath. She coughed as something brittle jabbed inside her open mouth. She opened her eyes and spat out a frond of dried bracken. Her nest was scattered around her den and there were deep claw marks in the floor where she had struggled with the invisible wave. Flicking off a shred of moss that was clinging to one ear, she sat up, panting.

Thank StarClan, it was only a dream!

The SkyClan leader stayed where she was until her heartbeat slowed and she had stopped trembling. The flood had been so real, washing away her Clanmates in front of her eyes. . . .

Sunlight was slanting through the entrance to her den; with a long sigh of relief, Leafstar tottered to her paws and padded onto the ledge outside. Down below, the river wound peacefully between the steep cliffs that enclosed the gorge. As sunhigh approached, light gleamed on the surface of the water and soaked into Leafstar's brown-and-cream fur; she relaxed her shoulders, enjoying the warmth and the sensation of the gentle breeze that ruffled her pelt.

"It was only a dream," she repeated to herself, pricking her ears at the twittering of birds in the trees at the top of the gorge. "Newleaf is here, and SkyClan has survived."

A warm glow of satisfaction flooded through her as she recalled that only a few short moons ago she had been nothing more than Leaf. She had been a loner, responsible for no cat but herself. Then Firestar had appeared: a leader of a Clan from a distant forest, with an amazing story of a lost Clan who had once lived here in the gorge. Firestar had gathered loners and kittypets to revive SkyClan; most astonishing of all, Leaf had been chosen to lead them.

"I'll never forget the night when the spirits of my ancestors gave me nine lives and made me Leafstar," she murmured. "My whole world changed. I wonder if you still think about us, Firestar," she added. "I hope you know that I've kept the promises I made to you and my Clanmates."

Shrill meows from below brought the she-cat back to the present. The Clan was beginning to gather beside the Rockpile, where the underground river flowed into the sunlight for the first time. Shrewtooth, Sparrowpelt, and Cherrytail were crouched down, eating, not far from the fresh-kill pile. Shrewtooth gulped his mouse down quickly, casting suspicious glances at the two younger warriors. Leafstar remembered how a border patrol had caught the black tom spying on the Clan two moons ago, terrified and half-starving. They had persuaded him to move into the warriors' den, but he was still finding it hard to fit into Clan life.

I'll have to do something to make him understand that he is among friends now, Leafstar decided. *He's more nervous than a cornered mouse.*

The two Clan elders, Lichenfur and Tangle, were sharing tongues on a flat rock warmed by the sun. They looked content; Tangle was a bad-tempered old rogue who stopped in the gorge now and again to eat before going back to his den in the forest, but he seemed to get on fine with Lichenfur, and Leafstar hoped she would convince him to stay permanently in the camp.

Lichenfur had lived alone in the woods farther up the gorge, aware of the new Clan but staying clear of them. She had almost died when she had been caught in a fox trap, until a patrol had found her and brought her back to camp for healing. After that she had been glad to give up the life of a loner. "She has wisdom to teach the Clan," Leafstar mewed softly from the ledge. "Every Clan needs its elders."

The loud squeals she could hear were coming from Bounce-paw, Tinypaw, and Rockpaw, who were chasing one another in a tight circle, their fur bristling with excitement. As Leafstar watched, their mother, Clovertail, padded up to them, her whiskers twitching anxiously. Leafstar couldn't hear what she said, but the apprentices skidded to a halt; Clovertail beckoned Tinypaw with a flick of her tail, and started to give her face a thorough wash. Leafstar purred with amusement as the young white she-cat wriggled under the swipes of her mother's rough tongue, while Clovertail's eyes shone with pride.

Pebbles pattering down beside her startled Leafstar. Looking up, she saw Patchfoot heading down the rocky trail with a squirrel clamped firmly in his jaws. Waspwhisker followed him, with his apprentice, Mintpaw, a paw step behind; they both carried mice. Leafstar gave a little nod of approval as the hunting patrol passed her. Prey was becoming more plentiful with the warmer weather, and the fresh-kill pile was swelling. She pictured Waspwhisker when he had first joined the Clan during the first snowfall of leaf-bare: a lost kittypet wailing with cold and hunger as he blundered along the gorge. Now the gray-and-white tom was one of the most skillful hunters in the Clan, with an apprentice of his own. He even had kits, with another former stray named Fallowfern.

SkyClan is growing.

As their father padded past, Waspwhisker's four kits bounced out of the nursery and scampered behind him, squeaking. Their mother, Fallowfern, emerged more slowly and edged her way down the trail after them; she still wasn't completely comfortable with the sheer cliff face and pointed rocks that surrounded SkyClan's camp.

"Be careful!" she called. "Don't fall!"

The kits had already reached the bottom of the gorge, getting under their father's paws, cuffing one another over the head and rolling over perilously near to the pool. Waspwhisker gently nudged the pale brown tom, Nettlekit, away from the edge.

But as soon as their father turned away to drop his prey on the fresh-kill pile, Nettlekit's sister, Plumkit, jumped on him. Nettlekit swiped at her, as if he was trying to copy a battle move he'd seen when the apprentices were training. Plumkit rolled over; Nettlekit staggered, lost his balance, and toppled into the river.

Fallowfern let out a wail. "Nettlekit!"

Stifling a gasp, Leafstar sprang to her paws, but she was too far away to do anything. Fallowfern leaped swiftly from boulder to boulder, but Waspwhisker was faster still, plunging into the pool after his kit. Leafstar lost sight of them for a few heartbeats. She watched the other Clan cats huddled at the water's edge—all except for Shrewtooth, who paced up and down the bank, his tail lashing in agitation. Leafstar purred with relief when she saw Waspwhisker hauling himself out of the river with Nettlekit clamped firmly in his jaws. The tiny tom's paws flailed until his father set him down on the rock. Then he shook himself, spattering every cat with shining drops of water. Fallowfern pounced on him and started to lick his pelt, but Nettlekit struggled away from her and hurled himself straight at Plumkit.

"I'll teach you to push me in the river!" he squealed.

"I did not push you! You fell in, so there!" Plumkit yowled back. She crouched down and leaped forward to meet her littermate in midair. The two kits tussled together in a knot of fur while their parents, looking frustrated, tried to separate them.

Leafstar glanced over her shoulder at the sound of paw steps approaching from farther down the gorge and saw Echosong with a bundle of herbs in her mouth. The young medicine cat's soft fur shone in the sunlight, reminding Leafstar that not long ago she had been a kittypet. But now she moved confidently over the stony ground, her pads hardened by her time in the gorge, and she had the lean, muscular strength of a Clan cat.

Echosong looked up at her Clan leader. "Greetings, Leaf-star!" she called, her voice blurred by the herbs.

"Greetings!" Leafstar meowed back to her. "We'll start the warrior ceremony soon."

Echosong acknowledged her words with a wave of her tail, and vanished into her den near the bottom of the cliff to add the herbs to her store.

"Are you ready?"

Leafstar started as a voice spoke at her shoulder, and spun around to see her deputy, Sharpclaw, standing behind her. She hadn't noticed his silent approach. "Oh, it's you," she meowed. "You frightened my fur off, creeping up on me like that!"

The dark ginger tom narrowed his eyes in amusement. "Nothing frightens your fur off, Leafstar." With a glance at the sky, he added, "It's sunhigh. When are you going to start the ceremony?"

"I'm waiting for the others," Leafstar explained.

Sharpclaw's amusement vanished and he flicked his tail. "You should carry on without them," he meowed impatiently.

Leafstar twitched one ear in surprise, and saw a defensive look come into her deputy's eyes.

"We never know when they're going to turn up," he persisted. "And there are three young cats down there ready to burst with excitement."

Glancing at the Rockpile again, Leafstar saw that he was right. Bouncepaw and Rockpaw were circling each other as if they were about to start battle training, while Tinypaw bounced up and down on the spot, too anxious to sit still.

Their shrill mews floated up to Leafstar.

"Very well." Leafstar dipped her head. "We'll start now."

With one more glance at the top of the gorge, she led the way down the trail to the Rockpile. As she and Sharpclaw approached, their Clanmates parted to let them through. Leafstar bunched her muscles and sprang to the top of the rocks, while Sharpclaw took his place at the base, not far from the fresh-kill pile. From the Rockpile, Leafstar looked down at her deputy's broad shoulders, and felt a stab of gratitude for his courage and loyalty.

He's a good deputy. Firestar advised me well.

Leafstar raised her head and let her yowl echo throughout the gorge. "Let all cats old enough to catch their own prey join here beneath the Rockpile for a Clan meeting!"

Sagepaw shot out of the apprentices' den and raced down the trail to join his littermate, Mintpaw, at the foot of the Rockpile. They settled down, tails twitching, not far from Sharpclaw and Waspwhisker. Sagepaw's mentor, Petalnose, emerged from the warriors' den and padded down to sit beside her apprentice. Patchfoot sat beside Clovertail, who was heavy with his kits; the she-cat leaned over and touched his ear with her nose, but her attention stayed fixed on the three apprentices.

Leafstar suppressed a sigh when she saw how Shrewtooth edged away as the other warriors approached. He peered around nervously as if he thought the gorge was full of enemies and then skittered down to the very edge of the stream, where he sat, darting anxious glances around him.

He's lived in the warriors' den for three moons, Leafstar thought, her claws kneading the rock in exasperation. *Doesn't he know by now that no cat will bite his tail off?*

She wondered—not for the first time—what had happened in Shrewtooth's past to make him so troubled, but she didn't have time to worry about him right then. The black tom would confide in her when he was ready, and meanwhile she had a warrior ceremony to conduct. Glancing around, Leafstar saw that almost all the Clan had assembled. She wondered briefly what was keeping Echosong, but in the same heartbeat the young medicine cat appeared from her den, the sweet scent of herbs drifting up from her pelt. She sat down beside Petalnose and looked expectantly up at the Rockpile.

"Cats of SkyClan," Leafstar began, "today we gather for one of the most important ceremonies in the life of a Clan: the naming of new warriors. Bouncepaw, Tinypaw, Rockpaw," she added with a wave of her tail, "come and stand here beneath the Rockpile."

The three young cats rose to their paws and padded forward, eyes sparkling and whiskers twitching with anticipation. Clovertail gave Rockpaw a final lick as he passed her, though a tuft of black fur still stood straight up on his head, while one of Bouncepaw's ears was folded back on itself. His littermate Tinypaw gave it a quick flick with her tail to turn it right side out.

Their three mentors also rose and stood together a couple of tail-lengths away. Leafstar looked down at them, the solemnity of the moment surging over her like a wave. She knew that even if she led her Clan for season after season, she would never fail to feel the wonder of presenting new cats to StarClan. Besides, these three cats were special: the first warriors of SkyClan who had been born in the gorge.

"Patchfoot," Leafstar began, "has your apprentice, Bouncepaw, learned the skills of a warrior? Has he studied the warrior code and understood what it means to every cat?"

The black-and-white tom glanced proudly at his apprentice as he replied, "Yes, Leafstar."

"And so has Rockpaw," Cherrytail added.

Leafstar dipped her head in acknowledgment; she wished Cherrytail had waited to be questioned in her turn, but Rockpaw's mentor looked almost as excited as her apprentice, and there was no point in scolding her.

"Sparrowpelt," Leafstar went on, "are you satisfied that your apprentice, Tinypaw, has learned the skills of a warrior and the importance of the warrior code?"

"Yes, Leafstar," Sparrowpelt replied. "She is ready to become a warrior."

With a purr of satisfaction, Leafstar leaped down from the Rockpile and stood in front of the three young cats. Their eyes stretched even wider as their leader raised her head and addressed StarClan.

"I, Leafstar, leader of SkyClan, call upon my warrior ancestors to look down on these three apprentices. They have trained hard to understand the ways of your noble code, and I commend them to you as warriors in their turn."

A shiver went through Leafstar as she remembered the

ranks of starry cats who had stood around her when she received her nine lives and her name. *Are they watching me now? Will they protect these young warriors until it's their turn to walk among the stars?*

"Bouncepaw, Tinypaw, Rockpaw," Leafstar went on, "do you promise to uphold the warrior code and protect and defend this Clan, even at the cost of your lives?"

Bouncepaw gave a huge gulp and replied, "I do."

"I do." Rockpaw's voice rang out clearly.

Tinypaw blinked; her eyes were deep blue pools as she too replied, "I do."

"Then by the powers of StarClan I give you your warrior names. Bouncepaw, from this moment you will be known as Bouncefire. StarClan honors your energy and your loyalty, and we welcome you as a full member of SkyClan."

Leafstar rested her muzzle on the top of Bouncefire's head, and the young ginger tom licked her shoulder. Then he took a couple of paces back to stand with the other warriors.

"Rockpaw," Leafstar went on, "from this moment you will be known as Rockshade. StarClan honors your courage and your strength, and we welcome you as a full member of Sky-Clan."

The black tom closed his eyes briefly as Leafstar rested her muzzle on his head, then licked her shoulder and withdrew to stand beside his brother. Tinypaw was left alone in front of her Clan leader; Leafstar could see that the little white she-cat was quivering with anticipation.

"Tinypaw," she meowed, "from this moment you will be

known as Tinycloud. StarClan honors your intelligence and enthusiasm, and we welcome you as a full member of Sky-Clan." She rested her muzzle on Tinycloud's head and felt the rasp of her tongue before she moved away to join her litter-mates.

"Bouncefire! Rockshade! Tinycloud!" The whole Clan raised their voices to welcome the three new warriors. Leaf-star looked on proudly as her Clanmates crowded around to offer congratulations.

"Tinycloud!" The white she-cat's voice rose indignantly above the rest. "I'm *not* tiny anymore. I thought I'd be big enough to have a different name."

A murmur of amusement ran through the cats around her. Clovertail padded up to her and gave her a comforting lick on her ear. "You'll always be tiny to me," she purred.

Leafstar could see that the small white cat still wasn't convinced; Bouncefire and Rockshade both looked thrilled with their new names, but there was a shadow of hurt in their sister's eyes.

The Clan leader slipped through the crowd of cats until she stood in front of Tinycloud. "Your name may be tiny but your spirit is not," she murmured. "One day the name of Tinycloud will be honored by your Clanmates, and all the Clanmates to come."

Tinycloud stared at her. "Do you really think so?"

Leafstar nodded. "It's up to you to do great things that will be remembered forever. Your name has nothing to do with what you choose to do."

"I'll do my best to be a great warrior," she promised earnestly.

Leafstar touched Tinycloud's shoulder with the tip of her muzzle. "I know you will."

While she was still speaking, Waspwhisker's four kits bundled past and crowded around their mother, Fallowfern.

"We want to be apprentices!" Nettlekit announced.

Fallowfern stroked him gently with her tail. "One day you will be," she promised. "But not yet. You're too young."

"No, we're not!" Nettlekit's sister, Plumkit, pushed forward to face her mother. "We're three whole moons old!"

"But to be an apprentice you have to be six moons," her mother reminded her.

Plumkit's eyes clouded with dismay.

"But that's forever!" her brother Rabbitkit wailed. "We don't want to wait that long."

"That's right," the fourth kit, Creekkit, added. "We want to learn how to be warriors *now*!"

Fallowfern gazed at Leafstar over the heads of her kits. Her eyes were half-amused, half-helpless. "What do I do with them?" she asked.

Leafstar twitched her whiskers. "They'll be apprenticed soon enough," she mewed. "Then their mentors will have to deal with them."

Fallowfern heaved a long sigh. "I can't wait!" But Leafstar saw that her gaze was full of affection as she watched the wriggling kits.

Nettlekit popped his head up. "Plumkit pushed me in the

river!" he complained. "I was all wet for the ceremony."

"Did not!" Plumkit protested. "You were showing off and you fell in."

"That's enough," Fallowfern mewed sharply. "Nettlekit, Plumkit, I don't want to hear another squeak from either of you."

Plumkit glared at her brother. "Clovertail, he says I pushed him!" she wailed, padding up to the light brown she-cat. "And I didn't! He was just showing off. He should know he can't do that fighting move yet."

"I know." Clovertail bent her head to lick the dark gray kit's ear. "Accidents happen. And there was no harm done. Nettlekit is fine."

Leafstar was impressed by Clovertail's soothing words. She remembered what the she-cat had been like when she first joined SkyClan—lazy, spoiled, and selfish, and interested in Clan life only for the protection it offered herself and her kits. But since then she had become like a mother to all the cats, always ready with comfort and advice. She would never be a great hunter or fighter, but she kept the nursery clean and well ordered.

And I don't know how Fallowfern would manage without her, looking after that rowdy lot!

"Come on," Clovertail urged, gathering the four kits together with her tail. "Let's go back to the nursery, and I'll tell you all about the time Firestar came to the gorge."

"Yes!" Creekkit exclaimed, his eyes gleaming. "That's the *best* story!"

As Clovertail and the kits headed up the trail, Leafstar gazed proudly at her Clan. Sharpclaw was sitting in a patch of sunlight, grooming his dark ginger fur with long, smooth strokes of his tongue. The three new warriors were bunched together in an excited huddle, while their former mentors chose prey from the fresh-kill pile and settled down to eat it.

Petalnose waved her tail at Waspwhisker. "Come on, let's give our apprentices some battle practice."

"Great!" Sagepaw yowled, and raced off up the gorge. His sister, Mintpaw, took off after him in a whirl of dust, followed more slowly by the two mentors.

Leafstar let out a sigh of pride and satisfaction. Her Clan had survived the long leaf-bare, and the battle with the rats was fading from memory.

But we'll never forget Rainfur. The gray tom, Sagepaw and Mintpaw's father, had fought valiantly on behalf of the Clan he had belonged to for such a short time. He would always be remembered as the first warrior to give his life for the newly restored SkyClan.

And now SkyClan is strong in the gorge, thanks to Firestar and Sandstorm.

Leafstar's thoughts drifted back through countless seasons, to the Clan who had lived there before and left their claw marks in the warriors' den. She wished so often that she could know more about them. The last remnant of that long-ago Clan was Skywatcher, the old gray tom who had been nicknamed Moony, ridiculed and called mad by the cats who were now Leafstar's loyal warriors. He had nurtured the memory of SkyClan like a tiny flame, until Firestar came to fan it into brilliant, blazing life. Leafstar raised her head to gaze at the Skyrock, where the Clan gathered at the full moon. *There are so many of us now that some cats have to sit on the main part of the cliff.* She caught her breath as she made out a faint gray shape against the drifting white clouds.

Skywatcher!

Warmth filled the Clan leader as she realized that the old cat had come back to see the ceremony for the first warriors who were born in the gorge. She raised her tail in greeting, hoping that all the SkyClan ancestors were looking down from StarClan, and were proud of their descendants, and those who had decided to become Clan cats.

"We will honor you always," she murmured, her gaze still fixed on Skywatcher's faint outline. "And we will do everything we can to keep your Clan alive."

CHAPTER 2
❧

"Invasion! Invasion!"

Leafstar spun around at the panic-stricken yowl, her claws sliding out as she prepared to defend herself and her Clan. Sharpclaw and the warriors around the fresh-kill pile sprang to their paws, their fur bristling. A few tail-lengths farther down the river, Shrewtooth stood stiff-legged on a rock, his eyes wide with horror as he gazed upward. His mouth hung open from where he had just screeched a warning; now he looked too frightened to say anything.

Three cats had appeared over the lip of the gorge and were trotting down the trail. The leader was a black she-cat, closely followed by a ginger-and-white tom and a younger tom with a black-and-white pelt.

"That's Ebonyclaw, Billystorm, and Snookpaw," Cherry-tail meowed. "Why is that mouse-brained tom making such a fuss?"

"He nearly made me jump out of my fur," Sparrowpelt grumbled.

Leafstar relaxed with a sigh. "Shrewtooth, it's okay. It's just the daylight-warriors!"

The jumpy black tom stared at her, then flicked his gaze

back toward the cats who were rapidly making their way down the rocks. At last he seemed to recognize the newcomers. "Sorry," he muttered, ducking his head to Leafstar. "The sun was in my eyes. I got confused."

"He's permanently confused, if you ask me," Cherrytail muttered.

Sharpclaw let out a hiss of annoyance and went back to grooming his pelt. He seemed to be ignoring the approaching cats, though Leafstar spotted the tip of his tail twitching back and forth. She opened her jaws to speak and then thought better of it. Instead, she padded over to the bottom of the cliff to welcome the newcomers as they leaped down the last couple of tail-lengths.

"Hi, Leafstar," the black she-cat meowed. "Are we in time for the ceremony?"

Leafstar shook her head. "I'm sorry, Ebonyclaw. We held it at sunhigh."

"Oh, no!" The young tom's voice rose in a wail. "We missed it! I've been looking forward to it for nearly a moon."

"We called for Harveymoon and Frecklepaw," Ebonyclaw explained. "But they were shut in." She shrugged. "I guess we waited too long."

Leafstar didn't turn to look, but she could feel Sharpclaw's gaze boring into her back like a fox's fangs. She knew he didn't approve of allowing kittypets to join the Clan and go back to their Twoleg nests at night. But she wasn't about to start that argument again. SkyClan needed the daylight-warriors.

They help us keep the fresh-kill pile well stocked. And the Clan is still small; we can't afford to turn any cat away.

"Never mind, Snookpaw," Ebonyclaw went on. "There'll be other ceremonies."

"But I wanted to see *this* one." Snookpaw padded over to the three new warriors. His eyes shone with admiration as he spoke to Bouncefire. "I wanted to be the first to call you by your warrior name. And now I don't even know what it is!"

"It's Bouncefire," the young warrior told him, seeming to swell with pride.

"That's a great name!"

"And we're Tinycloud and Rockshade," Tinycloud added.

Leafstar stifled a *mrrow* of amusement when Snookpaw completely ignored the young white warrior.

"I bet you're the best warrior in the Clan," he went on to Bouncefire. "I wish you could be my mentor."

"Hey!" The ginger-and-white tom strolled over to the younger cats and gave Snookpaw's shoulder a friendly shove. "What's wrong with the mentor you've got?"

"Sorry, Billystorm." Snookpaw gave his chest fur a couple of embarrassed licks. "You're a great mentor, too."

Before Billystorm could reply, excited squeals broke out from farther up the cliff, as Nettlekit, Plumkit, Creekkit, and Rabbitkit scrambled out of the nursery and headed down the trail, slipping and tumbling over their own paws in their haste.

"StarClan must be looking after those kits," Ebonyclaw commented, "or they would have broken their necks long ago."

"Billystorm!" Rabbitkit mewed as he plopped down from the top of the last rock and scrambled over to the ginger-and-white tom. "Watch us do the moves you taught us yesterday!"

"I'm the best fighter!" Nettlekit boasted.

"No, I am!" Plumkit gave her brother a shove.

"They're too young to be taught fighting moves," Fallowfern meowed, her neck fur beginning to bristle. "Nettlekit nearly drowned today when they were play fighting."

"That's right." Patchfoot padded over to stand beside the pale brown she-cat. "You shouldn't encourage them, Billystorm. Half the time you're not even here. You don't see the trouble that they get into."

Billystorm dipped his head politely to the kits' mother. "I'm sorry if there was an accident, Fallowfern. But hawks and foxes won't stay away from them just because they're young. They may as well know some defensive moves."

"What would you know about hawks and foxes, *kittypet?*" Cherrytail hissed from the other side of the fresh-kill pile.

Leafstar wasn't sure if Billystorm had heard; he gave no sign of it. But she thought it was time to step in. *The full Clan cats and the daylight-warriors have to get on together. A divided Clan cannot survive.*

"We can't blame Billystorm for Nettlekit's accident," she meowed, padding up to stand beside the group of cats. "Kits play all the time, and they don't watch where they're putting their paws. If they're not play fighting, they're pretending to stalk like foxes or fly like owls. I hope you'll all be more careful from now on," she finished, gazing down at Nettlekit and his littermates.

Nettlekit nodded vigorously, his eyes stretched wide at being addressed by his Clan leader.

"And can Billystorm keep teaching us?" Plumkit begged.

"If he wants to," Leafstar agreed. "And provided your mother says yes."

All four kits hurled themselves at Fallowfern, who staggered under the impact.

"Please!"

"We'll stay away from the river!"

"We promise."

"Well . . ." Fallowfern still looked reluctant. "I suppose so. . . ."

Squeaks of delight came from the kits. They immediately started wrestling, pummeling one another with soft paws.

"Billystorm, look at me!"

"No, watch *me*! I'm going to bite Rabbitkit's throat out!"

"That's enough for now," Leafstar mewed. Spotting Sharpclaw padding up to her, she added, "It's time to set the patrols."

Sharpclaw gave her a curt nod. "I'll lead a patrol to check the borders on this side of the gorge. Cherrytail and Patchfoot, you can come with me. Sparrowpelt, you can lead a border patrol on the other side; take Bouncefire and . . . yes, Ebonyclaw, since your apprentice isn't here today, you might as well go with them."

Leafstar's whiskers twitched; there was a definite edge to

her deputy's words when he spoke to the daylight-warrior, as if he didn't think she was much use to the Clan.

He might think that, Leafstar thought. *But that's just his opinion. He doesn't have to be so obvious about it.*

Ebonyclaw had understood the barb in Sharpclaw's comment, Leafstar could see, but she just dipped her head politely to the deputy, and went to stand beside Sparrowpelt and Bouncefire.

"What about me and Tinycloud?" Rockshade asked, his eyes shining. "We want to do our first patrol as warriors."

"I haven't forgotten you," Sharpclaw meowed, sounding much more friendly as he addressed the gorge-born cats. "We need more fresh-kill. . . . Try the woods farther downriver. Shrewtooth, you can go with him."

The black tom gave a nervous jump. "Right, Sharpclaw."

"And Billystorm—"

"I'd like Billystorm and Snookpaw to join the other mentors and apprentices at battle training," Leafstar interrupted.

Sharpclaw nodded. "Fine. Then that's every cat. Let's go."

"Just a moment." Echosong padded up with a courteous flick of her tail to Sharpclaw. "I need a cat to help me collect herbs. May I have Tinycloud?"

"But that's an apprentice task!" Tinycloud objected, her neck fur fluffing up in dismay. "I'm a warrior now."

"And warriors do what they're told," Sharpclaw growled.

"But—"

"It needs doing, Tinycloud," Echosong interrupted gently. "And what if a fox or a badger attacks me while I'm out of the gorge? I'll need a warrior to protect me."

"Oh . . ." Tinycloud's eyes brightened and her neck fur lay flat again. "Then I'll be glad to come, Echosong. I'll make sure you're safe!"

Leafstar watched the various patrols dispersing. *It must be just like this in the forest where Firestar lives. We're a real Clan, just like them.*

"Sharpclaw," she murmured, before her deputy could leave. "Just a quick word."

Sharpclaw cast a glance to where the other members of his border patrol were waiting a little farther up the gorge. His tail-tip twitched, but he waited for his Clan leader to continue.

"Was it necessary to sneer at Ebonyclaw like that?" Leafstar asked.

"I didn't—" Sharpclaw began to protest, his eyes sparking with anger, then broke off with a sigh. "All right. I was a bit sharp, and I'm sorry. But these kitty-warriors ruffle my fur."

Leafstar flattened her ears and felt her neck fur start to bristle. "*Kitty-warriors*, Sharpclaw? Don't you think that's a bit insulting?"

Sharpclaw met her gaze steadily. "I'm just trying to be accurate. What would you call them? They don't live here in the gorge. They turn up when they feel like it. How can they follow the warrior code when they go home to their Twolegs every night?"

"We've been through this already, Sharpclaw." Leafstar

sighed. "Too many times. You know my thinking on this. We're a small Clan, and if we give these cats the chance to experience the way that warriors live, they might decide to join us permanently."

"It can't be too soon for me," Sharpclaw snorted. "Even their names are half kittypet! Snookypaw . . . please!"

"*Snook*paw," Leafstar corrected him. "He doesn't think that Snooky sounds like a warrior."

"And Snook does, I suppose?"

Leafstar gave him a half-exasperated, half-amused nudge. "If their names are all you've got to complain about, they're doing well. Go on, your patrol is waiting for you. And just be a bit kinder to Ebonyclaw next time. She's one of the keenest cats we have."

"She's a kittypet!" Sharpclaw twitched his whiskers. "She wears a collar, for StarClan's sake!"

"And look at the way she's tucked moss around it," Leafstar countered. "She's doing everything she can not to scare off prey. So don't discourage her, okay?"

"All right, Leafstar." Sharpclaw blinked at her, the anger gone from his green eyes. "I might think your brain is full of bees, but I'll do as you say." Turning, he padded away and joined his patrol.

Leafstar saw that Fallowfern was herding her kits back up the trail to the nursery, ignoring their protests. "You can play with Billystorm later. Right now it's time for your naps."

"I'll still be here, kits!" Billystorm called after them.

Leafstar waved her tail to beckon him and Snookpaw, and

led the way up the gorge, following in the paw steps of Sharp-claw's patrol. By now the sun had disappeared behind swelling black clouds and a chill breeze stirred up the dust.

Rain before sunset, Leafstar thought.

A few tail-lengths farther on, the cliff curved inward, leaving a wide, sandy space between the rocks and the river. Petalnose and Waspwhisker were seated at one side of it, watching their apprentices. Mintpaw was crouched in the middle of the sandy area, her tail lashing as if she was about to pounce on a piece of prey. Sagepaw stalked forward, then suddenly ran at her, flashing out his claws to rake her along one side. But Mintpaw was too fast; she rolled toward him, ducked under his outstretched paw, and hooked his hind legs out from under him. Springing to her paws, she left her litter-mate scrabbling helplessly in the sand.

"Well done!" Leafstar called.

Mintpaw gave a little bounce of excitement when she realized that her Clan leader had seen her successful move.

"Yes, very well done," Waspwhisker meowed. "But next time follow it up. While he's floundering about in the sand, you could get in a couple of good blows."

"And next time, Sagepaw," Petalnose added, "try feinting to one side before you attack on the other. That way you get your opponent confused."

"I want to try that!" Snookpaw mewed eagerly as he and Billystorm reached the edge of the training area. "Can I?"

"Sure," Billystorm replied. "Let's watch Sagepaw and Mint-paw do it a couple more times first."

"Yes." Sagepaw sat up, spitting out sand. "I'm gonna *get* you next time, Mintpaw!"

"Yeah, and hedgehogs will fly!" his sister retorted.

Leafstar settled down beside the mentors, her tail wrapped over her paws, and watched the training session. Very soon all three young cats had mastered the new move. They still had a lot of training to do before they would be ready for their warrior names, but they seemed to grow stronger and faster every day.

"I want to practice what you showed us yesterday," Snook-paw meowed, scratching furiously to get sand out of his ear. "Where we leaped up on the rocks. That's such a great move!"

Leafstar pricked her ears with interest; she hadn't seen that move yet. "Show me," she invited.

Snookpaw and Sagepaw faced each other, each one maneuvering to get closer to the rock wall. Suddenly Sagepaw leaped up the cliff, twisting his body, clung there for a heartbeat, and launched himself down on top of Snookpaw, who failed to back off quickly enough. Snookpaw let out an indignant yowl as he battered at his opponent with all four paws, trying to thrust him off.

"Again!" he insisted, struggling to his paws.

"Okay, if you want more sand in your pelt," Sagepaw agreed.

The two young cats squared off again. This time Snook-paw was first to leap up the cliff, but when he hurled himself down again he was a heartbeat too slow, and landed hard on the ground.

"Missed!" Sagepaw squealed.

Undaunted, Snookpaw spun around and scratched hard at the sand with his hind paws, sending a shower of it over Sagepaw. "Now who has sand in their pelt?" he taunted.

"Hey!" the gray apprentice protested.

"Snookpaw, that's enough," Billystorm warned.

"But it's part of the move," Snookpaw explained, trotting over to his mentor. "If I could get sand in my enemies' eyes, they couldn't see to claw me."

"He has a point," Leafstar purred. "It's a good move for fighting here in the gorge."

"True," Billystorm admitted. "But don't overdo it when you're training, okay, Snookpaw? We don't want Echosong spending all day getting sand out of apprentices' eyes."

"Okay." Snookpaw gave his mentor a cheerful nod.

Leafstar was impressed by the young cats' enthusiasm. Here in the gorge, there wouldn't be the kind of battles with other cats that Firestar and his Clan had to face from their rivals. But there could still be clashes with rogues and loners, or overly curious kittypets from the Twolegplace.

Not to mention that the rats might come back. And there are foxes and badgers in the woods. Leafstar was determined that all her cats would be able to defend themselves and their Clan.

"I want to try it now," Mintpaw meowed, bounding up to stand by Snookpaw. "I—"

She broke off with a startled squeal as a snowflake landed right on top of her head. Looking up, Leafstar saw that the black clouds had covered the sky, and more flakes of snow were drifting down onto the sand.

"Snow!" Patchfoot exclaimed, wrinkling his nose in disgust. "It's supposed to be newleaf!"

"I think that's enough training," Leafstar decided as the snow began to settle on her fur and whiskers. "Let's get back to the camp before we're all soaked."

Even though the camp was only a few fox-lengths down the gorge, the snow grew thicker, a white screen that hid even the cliff on the opposite side of the river. The track beneath their paws was churned into mud. Before the dens came into view, every cat's pelt was plastered to their body by the melting flakes.

Reaching the camp, Leafstar peered through the snow and managed to make out Shrewtooth and Rockshade racing back up the gorge with a couple of scraps of sodden prey in their jaws. Sparrowpelt's border patrol was only a few fox-lengths behind.

"Back to your dens!" Leafstar gasped. "Billystorm, Ebonyclaw, go with them. You'll have to stay until this is over."

"Come on," Mintpaw meowed to Snookpaw. "You can shelter in our den."

Rockshade veered toward the cliff with the other warriors behind him, clawing their way up a trail that was suddenly treacherous and slick with melting ice. Leafstar spotted Echosong and Tinycloud hurrying into the medicine cat's den, and Fallowfern carrying a wriggling kit back into the nursery by its scruff. More cats appeared from the top of the gorge: Sharpclaw and his patrol were returning to camp.

Leaping rapidly down the trail, the Clan deputy reached Leafstar and the other cats on the ledge outside the warriors' den.

"Snow!" the deputy exclaimed, shaking white flakes from his head with a disgusted snort before padding inside the den. "As if we didn't get enough of it in leaf-bare."

"So let's not stand around complaining," Leafstar meowed, following him inside. "Come on, all of you—into shelter."

"It'll be a good chance to do some cleaning out," Sharpclaw meowed as the other warriors crowded into the den after their leader. "It's starting to stink as if a fox died in here."

"Yuck!" Cherrytail exclaimed, slapping her tail over her nose.

"Good idea," Leafstar agreed, though all she could pick up was the overwhelming scent of wet fur from the cats milling around. "We can pull out the old moss and rub snow on the walls to clean them."

"And I'd like to investigate those caves farther up the gorge," Sharpclaw suggested. "We've been meaning to do it for nearly a moon. They could be useful for storing food, or extra sleeping dens."

"You mean, go out there again?" Shrewtooth asked, his eyes wide and nervous. "In this snow? What if we fall off the cliff? What if we freeze to death? What—?"

"What if a giant hedgehog spears you on his prickles?" Cherrytail asked, giving the black tom a shove that was only half impatient. "I never knew a cat could worry so much!"

"Well, I think cleaning up is a good idea." Petalnose spoke

up. "I'll go over and help in the nursery, if it's okay with you, Leafstar."

"Good idea. Thanks, Petalnose."

The gray she-cat slipped out into the snow, which was already starting to ease off. Leafstar stuck her head out to watch her go, then turned back to speak to her warriors. "Sharpclaw, if you can supervise the clean-up here, I'll take some cats and check out the unused caves. And I'd be grateful if some cat could clean my den out while I'm gone."

"I'll do that!" Sparrowpelt offered. "It'll be so clean you won't recognize it."

Leafstar gave the warrior a nod of gratitude. "Okay, Rockshade and Bouncefire can come with me. And you, Billystorm. We'll pick up the apprentices from their den on the way."

"Er . . . Leafstar." Billystorm gave his chest fur a couple of embarrassed licks. "I really think I should be going. I'm worried about getting snowed in. My housefolk won't know what's happened to me, and—"

"I don't think you're bothered about your housefolk at all," Sparrowpelt interrupted indignantly. "You just don't want to do the cleaning up."

"That's not true!" Billystorm sounded equally outraged; his neck fur started to bristle.

"So stay." Rockshade took a pace forward to stand beside Sparrowpelt. "The snow is easing off already."

"It might start again," Billystorm argued. "I don't want to get stuck here. Remember when there was that really strong wind last leaf-bare, and all the kittypets stayed overnight until it was over? My housefolk were really scared. I'm sure they thought I was never coming back at all."

Sparrowpelt slid his claws out and opened his jaws to reply, but Leafstar silenced him by lifting her tail. "Okay," she meowed to Billystorm. "If you need to go, then go. We'll see you again tomorrow."

"Thanks, Leafstar." The ginger-and-white tom sounded relieved. His embarrassed gaze swept around the remainder of the cats; then he turned and slipped out of the den.

"Do you need to go too, Ebonyclaw?" Leafstar asked.

The black she-cat started. "Oh—no, Leafstar. I'll stay. I'll help with the clean-up."

"Well done," some cat murmured from the back of the crowd.

"I don't think we should let Billystorm back tomorrow," Sparrowpelt announced, his eyes still sparkling with indignation.

"Right," Rockshade agreed. "He only wants to be involved in the fun stuff. When there's work to do, he goes back to his housefolk."

Leafstar suppressed a sigh. She knew she needed to head off quarrels between the full Clan cats and the daylight-warriors. She wanted every cat to be accepted as equal, but Billystorm wasn't helping.

Before she could intervene, Sharpclaw stepped forward and faced the two warriors. "What happens to Billystorm is Leafstar's decision, not yours. Now let's get on with what we have to do."

Sparrowpelt and Rockshade exchanged a glance. "Right, Sharpclaw," Rockshade muttered.

"Mind you," Sharpclaw murmured into Leafstar's ear when the two warriors had turned away, "they've got a point. When Billystorm comes back we should find him some extra tasks. We don't want these kitty-warriors getting the idea that they can have an easier time than the full Clan cats."

Leafstar felt her neck fur begin to bristle as her deputy used the insulting term again, but she forced it to lie flat again. This wasn't the time to start an argument.

Sharpclaw paused to give his ear a scratch with one hind paw, then added, "If they want to be part of the Clan, they'll have to understand that tasks are shared equally."

"You're right," Leafstar replied. She was grateful for her deputy's support, when she knew that he really agreed with Sparrowpelt and Rockshade. "Maybe if we get them all involved in organizing the new dens, they'll feel more like staying in the gorge."

Sharpclaw gave her a disbelieving look and twitched one ear. "Yeah, maybe."

Leafstar decided there was nothing to be gained by discussing the problem anymore. Instead, she waved her tail to beckon Rockshade and Bouncefire. "And you, Ebonyclaw," she meowed. "You can come with me instead of Billystorm."

Ebonyclaw blinked, obviously surprised and pleased to be picked out by her Clan leader, and followed Leafstar out of the den with the two young toms. Outside, the snow had almost stopped, only a few stray flakes still drifting down. But the trails were treacherous with snowmelt and the wind still swept across the rocks, nearly strong enough to blow a cat off the cliff.

"Watch where you're putting your paws," Leafstar warned.

She led the way down the trail to the apprentices' den to collect Mintpaw and Sagepaw, and was pleased to see Snookpaw peering out when she reached the entrance to the cave. *He stayed, too.*

"Come on," she meowed to the apprentices. "We're going to start clearing out the caves farther up the gorge."

"Great!" Sagepaw shot out past Snookpaw and onto the trail, nearly losing his balance when his paws struck a lump of ice. "What do you think we'll find in there?"

"Bird bones and dust," his sister replied, emerging more sedately. "Mouse-brain!"

Sagepaw raised a paw as if he was about to swipe his sister across the ear, then stopped when he saw that Leafstar had her eye on him.

"Let's go," Leafstar meowed, before the apprentices could start tussling. "It's cold, so we can warm ourselves up with some exploration."

Once they reached the bottom of the gorge, she picked up the pace until the cats were bounding along, muscles stretching and tails streaming out behind them. Their panting breath made white clouds in the cold air. The new caves were a couple of fox-lengths before the training area, now white with a light covering of snow. Looking up, Leafstar spotted four narrow openings, two close to the bottom of the cliff, and two others higher up.

Ebonyclaw approached the nearest gap and stuck her head and shoulders inside. "It's really small," she reported, her disappointment obvious even though her voice was muffled.

"Ebonyclaw, come out," Leafstar ordered.

The black she-cat backed out of the cave and turned an inquiring look on Leafstar.

"What did you forget?" the Clan leader asked.

Ebonyclaw looked puzzled.

"She should have listened and sniffed first," Rockshade meowed loudly.

Leafstar gave him an annoyed look. *He's right, but I shouldn't have given him the chance to embarrass Ebonyclaw. I need to be more careful.*

"You never know what might be lurking inside," Leafstar explained. "There could be a fox or a badger, or even a bees' nest. So you have to watch out when you're going into a confined space."

"Sorry." Ebonyclaw hung her head and scraped one forepaw on the ground in front of her.

"So why don't you have a look at this other cave and show us how to do it the right way?" Leafstar indicated the second lower cave with a flick of her tail.

Ebonyclaw padded up to the cave and halted a tail-length in front of it, opening her jaws to taste the air. After a few heartbeats she turned to Leafstar. "I can't hear or scent anything. There's nothing alive in there."

"Go and look, then."

Ebonyclaw approached the cave and slid cautiously inside, to reappear a moment later. "It's empty, Leafstar. But I think it's also too small to be much use."

Leafstar took a look in both the lower caves. Ebonyclaw was right. They were too cramped to make comfortable dens; they didn't go back far enough, and the roofs were low. Snail trails crisscrossed the stone floors with silver lines, and farther back leaves and debris were heaped against the walls.

"We'll clean them out later," she decided. "They might do for storage."

Outside, Bouncefire was staring up at the other two caves. "I can climb up there," he announced. "Do you want me to take a look?"

"We'll all take a look," Leafstar replied. "Follow me, and be careful. There's no proper trail leading up there."

The route up to the next cave was a hard scramble. Leafstar had to push herself up using cracks in the rock for paw holds, hauling herself over boulders and edging along narrow ledges. Glancing back she saw that the other cats were managing to follow; Rockshade grabbed Mintpaw by the scruff and dragged her up a slanting rock when the short-legged apprentice couldn't reach the next crack.

If we want to use this cave as a den, we'll have to make a better way of getting to it.

But when she reached the entrance to the cave and checked to see if it was safe, Leafstar was encouraged to see that it was much bigger than the two lower ones. Its roof arched at least a tail-length above her head, and she couldn't see the back wall, it was so choked with debris.

Bouncefire scrambled panting onto the ledge beside her, and immediately let out a huge sneeze. "Dust!" he gasped.

"Right," Leafstar mewed, feeling a spark of amusement at the young cat's surprised look. "So let's get on with clearing it out."

She started by clawing at an old bird's nest, which instantly came apart in her paws, sending up another cloud of dust and setting her sneezing, too. She heard a *mrrow* of laughter from Bouncefire as he set to work beside her.

The other cats arrived to help, pulling out twigs and leaves and bones of long-dead prey and sending it all cascading over the lip of the entrance into the gorge below. At last Leafstar began to get a better idea of how big the cave was: a wide space stretching deep into the cliff, dry and shielded from bad weather.

"This could be good," she wheezed as she blinked through a haze of dust. "Plenty of room, and it will be comfortable once we bring some moss up here."

"Safe, too," Ebonyclaw pointed out. "Nothing could sneak up on us."

Leafstar gave her an approving nod. She might spend her nights in a Twoleg nest, but the black she-cat was smart and thought like a warrior. *Maybe we shouldn't try to make an easier trail. It'll be safer to leave it as it is.*

"Let's take a breather," she mewed, sitting where she could look out of the entrance at the climb they had just managed. "You've all worked really hard."

Her Clanmates flopped down around her and began to groom dust and bits of debris out of their pelts.

"Leafstar, will you tell us more about the old SkyClan?" Snookpaw asked, sounding unusually shy. "I've heard the other cats say there was another Clan here a long time ago. Is it true?"

"Completely," Leafstar answered, trying to recollect everything that Firestar had told her about the first SkyClan. She settled herself more comfortably on the sandy floor of the cave. "Long ago, the first SkyClan lived in a forest, with four other Clans. But they had to leave when Twolegs stole their territory to build a Twolegplace."

"There are *other* Twolegplaces?" Mintpaw gasped, her eyes stretched wide in wonder.

"Oh, yes, lots of others. Anyway, SkyClan traveled for a long way, and at last they came to the gorge and made their camp here. They lived in the dens where we live now."

The three apprentices glanced at one another, their eyes wide, as if they expected to see the spirits of those long-ago cats padding in through the cave entrance.

"But then the rats came," Leafstar went on. "They killed many of the old SkyClan cats, and drove out the rest. Some of the warriors went elsewhere, and some of them became loners or kittypets. And some—just a few—held on to the memory of SkyClan until Firestar came and brought it back to life."

Sagepaw heaved a long sigh. "That's so great! Do you think that we could be descended from those old SkyClan cats? I wish I was!"

"And me!" Rockshade put in.

"Me too!" Mintpaw added, while Snookpaw blinked but said nothing.

"You might be," Leafstar mewed, though privately she had her doubts. Firestar had told her that the old SkyClan cats had long legs for jumping and hard pads for walking on rocky surfaces. Mintpaw and Sagepaw didn't have either of those, and neither did Rockshade or Bouncefire.

But Snookpaw could be a SkyClan descendant, she thought. *He's good at leaping and fearless when he climbs trees. And Ebonyclaw's legs are long and strong.*

"Every cat around here could have links to the old Clan," she continued, careful not to single out the daylight-warriors. "Which means that every cat has the right to be our Clan-mate."

"I'm a SkyClan cat!" Rockshade announced, crouching down as if he intended to take a flying leap out of the cave. "I can jump and climb really well."

"So can I!" Mintpaw chimed in, her eyes gleaming. "And my legs are really strong."

Leafstar suppressed a sigh. *Are they going to start measuring each other's legs now?*

"I'm strong, too. Unlike some I could mention," Rockshade growled.

He means the daylight-warriors, Leafstar realized. "SkyClan cats come from many different places," she reminded the young black tom. "They should all have a chance to belong here."

"I guess so," Rockshade mumbled, though Leafstar wasn't sure he really agreed.

Ebonyclaw and Snookpaw exchanged a glance, but neither of them spoke.

Inwardly, Leafstar admitted to doubts of her own. *I wish I could be sure how to handle this. I want a Clan where every cat will be welcomed and valued for the skills they can bring. Instead, all my warriors seem to be pulling in different directions.*

When Firestar and Sandstorm left, all the SkyClan cats had lived in the gorge day and night, dedicated warriors like the Clans in the forest where Firestar lived. He'd had no way of knowing that cats from the Twolegplace would want to join SkyClan on their own terms, spending days in the gorge and nights with their housefolk, well fed and cozy and safe from foxes. None of Firestar's advice about leading a Clan had prepared Leafstar for having Clanmates who seemed to be split in two.

Can I really hold them together?

CHAPTER 3

Leafstar opened her eyes to see moonlight slanting in through the entrance to her den. A voice had roused her from sleep, but now all was silent except for the whispering of the river at the bottom of the gorge. She rose to her paws, arched her back in a long stretch, and shook scraps of moss from her pelt. Slipping out of her den, she padded down the trail until she reached the edge of the water.

At the foot of the Rockpile, the three new warriors were keeping vigil, each one sitting upright with their tails curled neatly over their paws. In the moonlight they looked like cats carved out of ice or stone, and they didn't acknowledge the nod Leafstar gave them as she passed.

She headed for the new dens, her paws gliding silently over the white drifts of snow that still lingered in the shade of the rocks. The boulders glistened with frost, as if leaf-bare had returned to the gorge, but the brown-and-cream tabby didn't feel cold. Instead, her body felt warm and curiously light, like a leaf spinning idly in a warm breeze. Scrambling up the rocky cliff face, Leafstar reached the largest of the new dens and padded inside, shaking the snowmelt from each of her paws in turn.

I was right, she thought. *This* will *make a good den. It's sheltered from the wind, and it will be hard for enemies to reach the entrance—if they suspect we're in here at all.*

"Your cats will be safe here."

Leafstar spun around at the sound of a voice behind her. Another cat stood outlined in the entrance to the cave, black against the silver moonlight. Catching her breath, Leafstar drew in a sweet but unfamiliar scent. Not until the strange cat stepped forward did she recognize the graceful tortoiseshell-and-white figure of Spottedleaf.

The medicine cat who walks with StarClan. Firestar's friend. What is she doing here?

Spottedleaf paced forward, her pelt glittering with starlight, until she was close enough to brush against Leafstar's fur. Her scent wreathed around them. "Greetings, dear friend," she murmured.

"Am I—am I dreaming?" Leafstar asked hoarsely. She still wasn't used to dead cats walking into her mind and talking to her as if they were still alive.

Spottedleaf dipped her head. "To your Clanmates, you are asleep in your den. Didn't you notice how the new warriors didn't even blink when you walked by?"

Leafstar shrugged. "I thought they were obeying the rules of the first night vigil."

"I don't doubt that they are," Spottedleaf murmured. She looked around, pricking her ears. "SkyClan must be doing well if you need new dens," she observed.

"I . . . we were just exploring," Leafstar explained. "Wondering what these caves could be used for. We have new kits in the Clan, and more on the way, but we haven't spilled out of our old dens yet."

Spottedleaf's glowing green eyes searched Leafstar's face. "Is all well with your Clan?"

"Everything's fine," Leafstar replied carefully. She wasn't going to share her concerns about Billystorm and the others with this cat who was almost a stranger to her. *She isn't part of our Clan.* "How are Firestar and Sandstorm?"

"They're both well," the StarClan cat replied. "They have two kits—little daughters."

"That's great!" Warm pleasure flooded through Leafstar. "When you see Firestar, tell him how happy I am for them."

"I will." To Leafstar's surprise, Spottedleaf didn't seem as pleased as she would have expected at the thought of Firestar's litter. Once again, she fixed her green gaze on Leafstar. "You have the hardest task of any Clan leader," she meowed. "You must build a Clan from cats who know nothing of the warrior code."

Leafstar hadn't expected Spottedleaf to begin discussing her Clan, and she wasn't sure she welcomed it. *We do know the warrior code. Firestar taught the first of us, and we're teaching the rest!*

"I do my best," she pointed out.

"And you are doing well," Spottedleaf told her. "But there is a long way to go before your future is secure."

Leafstar stiffened. What did Spottedleaf know that she wasn't sharing? Had she seen the tension among the SkyClan warriors earlier? She opened her mouth to defend her Clan-mates, but Spottedleaf was beckoning her to the cave entrance with a wave of her tail.

Looking out, Leafstar saw several unfamiliar cats in the bottom of the gorge. At first her fur started to bristle at the idea of strangers invading the camp. Then she realized that pale starlight glimmered from the fur of the newcomers, and their bodies were so faint that they were almost transparent; Leafstar could make out the jagged shapes of rocks behind them through their shadowy forms. As she watched, some of the cats padded away in different directions. Three more melted into the shadows of the elders' den, leaving only two behind, sitting together at the entrance of Echosong's cave.

"Who are they?" Leafstar whispered, icy claws pricking her spine.

Spottedleaf didn't reply. Instead, the voice of the bigger cat, a dark brown tabby tom, floated faintly up from the gorge. "Will a Clan ever live here again?"

The other cat, a paler brown tom, dipped his head and murmured something Leafstar couldn't catch. She sensed great sadness clinging to the pelts of both cats, like the scent of rank herbs.

Then the smaller cat raised his head, gazing upward as if he spoke directly to Leafstar. "This is the leaf-bare of my Clan." Now his words rang clearly in Leafstar's ears, echoing through the seasons that separated her from the long-ago cat. "Green-leaf will come, but it will bring even greater storms than these. SkyClan will need deeper roots if it is to survive."

"Is that a warning?" Leafstar whispered over her shoulder, trying hard to keep her voice steady. "Maybe a prophecy?" She remembered her dream of the night before, the uprooted trees and bushes hurled down the gorge by the foaming torrent where her cats were drowning. *Was that dream a prophecy, too?*

No answer came from Spottedleaf, and when Leafstar turned toward her the cave was empty. Shivering as if she had fallen into icy water, Leafstar looked out at the gorge again. The moon shone down on empty rocks; the shadowy cats had vanished.

A heartbeat later, Leafstar opened her eyes to find herself curled up in the mossy nest inside her own den. Watery dawn light seeped in through the entrance. She blinked in confusion, the words of the small brown tom still echoing in her ears.

What did he mean by "greater storms"? And how can cats have "deeper roots"?

"Mouse-brain! There'll be more prey if we go downstream!"

"No, we should cross the stream and hunt in the forest."

"You're both wrong! We should climb the cliff and try the trees at the top. There are plenty of squirrels there."

Leafstar sighed as the bickering reached her den; she recognized the voices of Tinycloud, Rockshade, and Bouncefire. Heaving herself to her paws, she stumbled to the entrance of her den, struggling to tear her mind away from the clinging cobwebs of her dream. When she peered out the entrance,

Leafstar spotted the Clan's three newest warriors crouched together at the bottom of the Rockpile.

Bouncefire's voice rose in a wail. "If you would just *listen* . . ."

Leafstar headed down the trail to break up the argument, but before she reached them Sharpclaw appeared, bounding down the rocks from the direction of the warriors' den. Leafstar halted on a boulder at the foot of the cliff and watched her deputy deal with the quarrel.

"What's going on here?" His voice was as rough as a pawful of claws scraping across rock. "You're supposed to be keeping vigil, not waking the rest of the camp with your caterwauling."

"It's dawn. Our vigil's over," Rockshade pointed out.

"And we want to go hunting," Tinycloud added.

Sharpclaw raked all three of them with an icy glare from eyes like chips of green ice. "Funny, I always thought it was the Clan deputy who set the patrols. Am I wrong?"

The young cats hung their heads. "No, Sharpclaw," Bouncefire muttered.

"Good." The Clan deputy flicked his tail. "Rockshade, you can come with me and do the border patrol on this side of the gorge. Bouncefire, Patchfoot is leading a hunting patrol; go find him and tell him I said you're to go with him."

"What about me?" Tinycloud asked.

"Cherrytail is leading the other border patrol. You can go with her. And make sure that I don't have to talk to you about this kind of squabbling again."

Leafstar gave her deputy a nod of approval as he spun around and stalked away. Pleased that she hadn't needed to intervene, she headed along the bottom of the cliff toward the medicine cat's den.

From behind her, she overheard Tinycloud's voice. "At least I can stay away from Echosong's den today. If she catches me, she'll have me fetching herbs again."

Leafstar almost turned back and ordered the white she-cat to do just that, but she didn't want to countermand Sharpclaw's orders. *I'll make sure she helps Echosong again soon, though*, she decided. *Every cat has to understand how important the medicine cat is to the life of the Clan.*

When Leafstar slipped through the outer cave into Echosong's inner den, the young medicine cat had her back to her as she bent over the herbs that were stored in cracks at the back.

"Juniper berries, yarrow, tansy . . ." she murmured to herself. "No, that's not tansy, it's coltsfoot. . . ."

"Greetings, Echosong."

At the sound of her leader's voice the silver tabby jumped and whipped around, her green eyes wide. When she saw Leafstar she relaxed, puffing out a breath. "Leafstar, you startled me!"

"Sorry." Leafstar padded forward to touch noses with the medicine cat, enjoying the sweet, crisp scent of herbs that clung to her fur.

"I'm glad you're here," Echosong went on. "I—I had something that might have been a dream last night. At least, I know it was a dream, but I'm not sure if it was important."

Leafstar felt a tingle beneath her pelt. She'd intended to ask the medicine cat about her dream, too: a coincidence, or something more? "Tell me what happened," she prompted.

Echosong paced across the outer den and sat down in the entrance, beckoning with her tail for her Clan leader to sit beside her. "I woke up—or at least I thought I woke up—and I heard quiet voices outside my den. When I looked out, I saw two cats. One was a big dark tabby, and the other was smaller and paler brown. Starlight was glimmering in their fur, but they looked so faint and far away."

Leafstar's belly clenched. Echosong was describing the two cats she had seen in her own dream. "Did they say anything?" she asked warily.

Echosong nodded. "The big tabby said, 'It is time to leave. Our last duty is completed.' They started to pad away, up the gorge. Then the smaller cat stopped and turned, and I felt as if he was looking straight at me. He said, 'This is the leaf-bare of my Clan. Greenleaf will come, but it will bring even greater storms than these. SkyClan will need deeper roots if it is to survive.' What do you think he meant, Leafstar?"

Leafstar's heart was thumping as if it were about to burst out of her chest. It was a moment before she could reply. "I don't know. But it must mean something. Because I had the same dream last night."

Echosong sprang to her paws. "The exact dream?"

"Near enough. Except I dreamed that I went to the new dens up the gorge, and that's where I saw the two cats.

Spottedleaf was there, too."

Briefly Echosong looked envious. "I wish I'd seen her. There's so much I need to ask her about herbs."

"Maybe Fawnstep will visit you tonight for another training session. After all, she was a SkyClan medicine cat," Leafstar suggested. She was still a little suspicious of Spottedleaf's appearance in her dreams. Surely Spottedleaf's loyalties were to ThunderClan? *Why is she so interested in my Clan?* Leafstar flicked her tail-tip, trying to control her frustration. "But right now, we need to figure out what those cats in the gorge were talking about. It . . . it sounded like a prophecy, didn't it?"

"Yes, it did," Echosong agreed quietly.

"The small tabby was warning us," Leafstar murmured, anxiety prickling in her fur as if ants were running through it. "He talked about worse things to come for SkyClan."

The young medicine cat shuddered. "What could be worse than the rats?"

"And 'deeper roots,'" Leafstar went on. "Whatever that means."

"Maybe we should eat roots?" Echosong guessed.

Leafstar shook her head. "What good would that do? Unless they're a source of medicine that we haven't discovered yet. . . . Besides, I had another dream the night before. Floodwater was pouring down the gorge, uprooting everything in its path, flooding into our dens and sweeping us away. I think the two dreams are connected."

Echosong nodded thoughtfully. "One of our Clanmates might have a better idea about what the dreams meant," she suggested. "Should we call a meeting and tell them?"

Something inside Leafstar flinched away from the thought of confessing to the rest of the Clan that the leader and the medicine cat couldn't figure out what their ancestors were trying to tell them. Was Firestar plagued by these kinds of doubts? Maybe she should give StarClan another chance to explain.

"No, we won't say anything to the rest of the Clan yet," she meowed. Echosong looked surprised. Leafstar added, "Not because they're not involved, but because we might get more dreams that make the prophecy clearer. After all, what could we tell them now? That something bad is going to happen? That will only make them panic."

Echosong tilted her head to one side. "If that's what you want, Leafstar," she murmured.

Leafstar tried not to bristle at the hint of doubt in the medicine cat's tone. "It's what is best for the Clan," she insisted. "And if we have any more visions, we'll discuss them in private until we can figure out what our ancestors are trying to tell us."

CHAPTER 4

Leafstar padded up the gorge toward the new caves, enjoying the sensation of sunlight on her fur. A few days had passed since the snowfall, and the weather had turned unexpectedly warm for so early in newleaf.

As she approached the new dens, a twig sailed out into the air from the cliff face and clattered onto the ground by Leafstar's paws; she had to jump aside to avoid it.

"It's a snake!" a voice yowled from above her head. "I killed it!!"

Gazing upward, Leafstar spotted two of the daylight-warriors, Harveymoon and Macgyver, on a ledge outside the fourth of the new caves, which so far no cat had cleared out. As she watched, Macgyver scooped up a pawful of dry moss and threw it at Harveymoon; it hit the white tom in the chest and spattered all over his fur.

"I'll get you for that!" Harveymoon meowed, leaping on top of Macgyver.

For StarClan's sake! Leafstar thought, annoyed, as she began to scramble up to the ledge. *Fallowfern's kits have more sense!*

The toms sprang apart as Leafstar bounded up the last

couple of tail-lengths and joined them on the ledge.

"What d'you think you're doing?" she growled. "I thought you were here to help, not behave like a couple of kits."

Before either of them could reply, Sharpclaw emerged from the cave. His dark ginger pelt was clumped and streaked with dust and his green eyes sparked with irritation. "I've had to put up with this all morning," he told Leafstar, turning a furious glare on Harveymoon and Macgyver. "You're being disloyal to your Clan when you behave so stupidly. Don't you care about the honor of being a warrior? You haven't done a stroke of work, and you're making it harder for every other cat."

"It's not like we'll have to sleep in these caves," Harveymoon pointed out. "So why should we have to clear them out?"

Sharpclaw let out a long hiss of anger, and even Macgyver's eyes widened in shock. Harveymoon glanced uneasily from one to the other; Leafstar could tell that he hadn't realized how insolent the words sounded until they were out of his mouth.

Ebonyclaw and her apprentice, Frecklepaw, had appeared at the mouth of the cave, peering around Sharpclaw, and Leafstar spotted Rockshade and Sparrowpelt in the shadows behind them. She realized that every cat was waiting for her to do something; behavior like this couldn't be ignored. The fact that it was warriors from Twolegplace causing the trouble somehow made it much worse.

"Clan cats don't fool around when their Clanmates are working," she told Macgyver and Harveymoon. "And they certainly don't talk like that to the Clan deputy—or any other cat. Warriors treat one another with respect." She felt as if a stone were lodged in her belly as she added, "It's not as if this is the first time. You couldn't be bothered to turn up for the warrior ceremony, and on your last two hunting patrols you never caught a thing." She took a deep breath and went on, "You're both banished from the camp until the next full moon. Perhaps by then you'll have decided whether you really want to be part of SkyClan."

Macgyver and Harveymoon crouched down as their leader scolded them, their ears flattened. As she pronounced their sentence they exchanged a shocked glance.

"We're sorry, Leafstar," Macgyver meowed. "We didn't think. Please let us stay."

"We'll work really hard," Harveymoon promised. "Sharpclaw, I'm sorry I said what I did. I didn't mean it."

"'Sorry' catches no prey," Leafstar responded. "It's too late for that."

"But I promised to join Waspwhisker and Mintpaw on a hunting patrol after sunhigh," the white tom protested.

"And I was going to help Sagepaw check the elders for fleas," Macgyver put in. "Tangle is halfway through telling us a story about a fox, and I really want to hear the end."

"You should have thought of that sooner," Leafstar meowed. She couldn't weaken now, not with Sharpclaw's stare scorching the fur on her back. "We'll welcome you back at the next full moon, if you are ready to behave like proper warriors while you're here. But now you have to go."

Harveymoon opened his jaws to argue again, then seemed

to think better of it. Despondently the two cats scrambled down the cliff face to the bottom of the gorge and headed toward the Rockpile with their heads bowed and their tails drooping.

Watching them, with Sharpclaw bristling at her side, Leafstar wondered if she was doing the right thing by allowing kittypets into her Clan at all. Could this be the "greater storm" that the dream-cat had warned about? Leafstar shoved the thought away; a couple of flea-brained toms didn't deserve a prophecy all to themselves.

But I can't go on ignoring Sharpclaw's doubts about the daylight-warriors. I have to stand up for my deputy.

Before Harveymoon and Macgyver had gone more than a couple of tail-lengths, they met Cherrytail and Bouncefire bounding around a spur of rock on their way to the new caves. In the still air, their voices floated clearly up to Leafstar.

"What's the matter with you two?" Cherrytail asked, halting in front of the dejected toms. "You look as if you've lost a squirrel and found a beetle."

"It's worse than that," Harveymoon muttered.

"What, then?" Bouncefire demanded.

"We were fooling around," Macgyver admitted; he sounded genuinely ashamed. "And then this flea-brain"—he gave Harveymoon a shove—"was really rude to Sharpclaw. So Leafstar has banished us from camp until the next full moon."

"That's terrible!" Bouncefire squeaked, wide-eyed.

"It sounds as if you asked for it," Cherrytail meowed tartly.

"You must have bees in your brain if you think you can come here and just fool around."

"Cherrytail's right." Leafstar jumped as Ebonyclaw spoke quietly behind her from the mouth of the cave. "It was all their fault. Don't feel bad about it, Leafstar."

"That's right," Frecklepaw added; she was a leggy light brown tabby, and she looked scared stiff at speaking directly to her Clan leader.

Leafstar touched her shoulder gently with her tail-tip. "Thank you, Frecklepaw."

More cats pushed their way out onto the ledge to watch the two daylight-warriors leave. Billystorm and Snookpaw joined Ebonyclaw and Frecklepaw, with Tinycloud just behind, while Shrewtooth crept out last of all. Leafstar blinked in surprise; she hadn't realized how big this cave was.

"It's a pity they couldn't stay," Tinycloud mewed sadly. "There won't be as many of us to fill the fresh-kill pile."

Billystorm and Snookpaw glanced at each other, murmuring agreement.

"And there won't be as many mouths to feed," Rockshade pointed out, swiping his sister over the ear with one paw. "Besides, how much prey did those two ever bring in?"

"What about enemies?" Shrewtooth crouched at the front of the ledge and peered along the gorge. "Will there be enough of us to fight them off?"

Rockshade rolled his eyes. "What enemies, mouse-brain? There's only us."

Leafstar's heart grew heavier as she heard her Clanmates

arguing. *Will this Clan ever learn to work together?*

"Thanks for supporting me." Sharpclaw broke in on her thoughts. "It was the right decision."

"I didn't do it for your sake!" Leafstar snapped, surprising herself with her sharp tone. "This problem isn't over yet."

Sharpclaw looked surprised, too, his green eyes flashing at her, but he said nothing. Leafstar wondered if she should apologize, but she couldn't think of the right thing to say.

Apologizing is all I do these days, when I'm not being baffled by something going on in the Clan.

Giving her deputy a brusque nod, she headed down into the gorge. At the foot of the cliff she met Cherrytail and Bouncefire; Harveymoon and Macgyver had disappeared.

"We're looking for Billystorm and Snookpaw," Bouncefire meowed. "We're supposed to be doing a border patrol."

"They're up in the caves," Leafstar told them.

"Great! Er . . . Leafstar," Cherrytail went on, "we spoke to Harveymoon and Macgyver. Do you still want us to patrol the border, or should we hunt instead?"

Leafstar remembered the few miserable pieces of prey that had remained on the fresh-kill pile when she passed it on her way up the gorge.

"You'd better hunt," she decided. *Border patrols can wait. Right now, it feels as if all SkyClan's problems are inside its borders, not outside.*

Leaving Cherrytail yowling for Billystorm and Snookpaw at the bottom of the cliff, Leafstar headed for the elders' den. Just as she reached the end of the trail that led up the cliff face, she met Sagepaw.

"Can you go to help Sharpclaw with the new caves?" she mewed. "Some of his cats are going hunting, and there's still a lot of work to do."

Sagepaw blinked in disappointment. "Sure, Leafstar. But I was just going to check the elders for fleas."

"You *want* to check the elders for fleas?" Leafstar mewed.

Sagepaw gave his chest fur a couple of awkward licks. "Well, Tangle was telling this really great story. . . ."

Leafstar let out a soft purr of amusement and gently flicked the apprentice's ear with her tail. "There'll be plenty of chances to listen to Tangle," she promised. "Now you need to go and help Sharpclaw."

"Okay." Sagepaw dipped his head and bounded along the gorge toward the new caves.

Leafstar watched him go, then padded up the trail that led to the elders' den. "Greetings, Lichenfur, Tangle," she meowed as she poked her head inside.

"Where's that pesky apprentice?" Tangle growled without returning her greeting. "He was supposed to be sorting out my fleas." The old cat vigorously scratched his rumpled tabby pelt. "They're driving me mad."

"I'll do your fleas, Tangle," Leafstar offered, slipping right inside the den. "Sagepaw is busy."

Lichenfur raised her head from the nest of moss where she was curled up. Her amber eyes were wide with shock. "Do other Clan leaders search their elders' pelts for fleas? I didn't know that."

The barb in her voice was unmistakable, like a thorn hidden in a bed of moss. Leafstar guessed the old cat thought she was inviting criticism by taking on tasks that were beneath her rank. She bit back a sharp reply.

"I wouldn't ask any of my cats to do something I'm not prepared to do myself," she responded mildly. "And I have no idea what other Clan leaders do. But if you want to lie here with fleas in your pelts, I can go away and leave you in peace."

"I suppose it's all right," Lichenfur admitted grudgingly.

Tangle just grunted; Leafstar assumed that was agreement. *I bet elders are the same wherever they are.*

"What's this I hear about you sending those kittypets away?" Lichenfur asked as Leafstar settled down beside Tangle and started to probe deep into his ragged fur.

Leafstar blinked, surprised even though she knew how fast gossip traveled within the Clan. "How do you know about that?"

"Petalnose met Harveymoon and Macgyver on their way out," Tangle explained. "And she came to tell us."

And the whole Clan will know about it by now, Leafstar thought, pouncing on a flea and cracking it between her teeth.

"I'm not sure I did the right thing," she admitted. "There seem to be so many arguments at the moment, and I'm afraid I've just added to them."

Tangle twisted his neck to look up at her with bleary amber eyes; Leafstar thought she could make out a trace of wisdom lurking in their depths. "Whatever you decide," he rumbled, "you have to be strong. The path SkyClan walks is shadowed, and you're the one leading us along it."

Lichenfur snorted. "Cats are supposed to be able to see in the dark, and I for one don't want a blind leader."

Leafstar tensed at the hostility in the elder's tone.

Tangle gave her a nudge. "Ignore her," he whispered. "She sat on a thistle all night."

Leafstar nodded, warmed by the grumpy old cat's support. *But how many more of my Clanmates think that I'm a blind leader?* she wondered.

Leaving the elders, she turned her paws in the direction of Echosong's den. It would be a relief to discuss Harveymoon and Macgyver with the young medicine cat and ask her advice. She hadn't gone more than a couple of paw steps, when she heard a scrabbling sound from above; grit and scraps of debris pattered down onto the trail. The shriek of a terrified cat echoed through the gorge.

Looking up, Leafstar saw Sagepaw dangling from the cliff face above the highest of the new caves, clinging to the rock by the tips of his claws.

"Help!" he screeched. "Help me!"

CHAPTER 5

Before Leafstar could move, Sharpclaw shot out of one of the lower caves and began clawing his way upward, closely followed by Patchfoot. In the same heartbeat, Petalnose emerged from the nursery and flung herself across the rock face toward the terrified apprentice, scrambling precariously along a trail that was so narrow it was almost invisible against the sandy cliff.

Leafstar began to climb, too, her paws pounding over the rocks, but she was much farther away than her deputy.

"Hold on!" Sharpclaw ordered, his voice crisp and calm. "Don't move!"

Petalnose let out a panic-stricken wail. "StarClan help him!"

The rock was crumbling beneath Sagepaw's claws. Leafstar's belly lurched as she saw him slide a tail-length down the cliff. She spotted Ebonyclaw and Rockshade peering out of the cave below, but Sagepaw was just out of reach of their paws.

"I'm slipping!" he gasped. "I can't hold on!"

"Yes, you can. Keep still." Sharpclaw was only a couple of fox-lengths below the apprentice now, the only cat close enough to have a hope of reaching him. His powerful hind legs pushed upward from a crack in the rock and he lunged toward Sagepaw, but before he could fasten his claws into the young cat's fur, more of the rock flaked away under Sagepaw's paws.

The apprentice let out a shriek; his paws flailed as he tried to dig his claws into the powdery surface. Leafstar gazed in horror as his small body plummeted down. Off balance, Sharpclaw barely saved himself from following.

Sagepaw's shriek was cut off as he struck a jutting boulder, bounced off, and fell the rest of the way to the foot of the cliff, landing with an ugly thud. He lay motionless on the trail between the cliff and the river.

With a cold weight gathering in her belly, Leafstar turned and scrambled down to join him. Landing lightly beside him, she bent her head to sniff his pale gray fur.

"Is he dead?" Petalnose hurtled down the cliff and flung herself onto the ground beside her son. Every hair on her pelt bristled with horror. "StarClan, don't let him be dead!"

Sagepaw lay stretched out in the dust at the bottom of the cliff. His eyes were closed, but relief flooded through Leafstar when she saw his flank twitch.

"He's not dead," she murmured, pressing her muzzle against Petalnose's shoulder.

Patchfoot jumped down and shot one horrified look at the motionless apprentice. "I'll fetch Echosong," he meowed, and raced away.

Petalnose crouched beside Sagepaw and started to lick the

fur on the top of his head. "Wake up, Sagepaw," she pleaded, her voice quivering. "It's my fault," she added, raising wide blue eyes to her Clan leader. "I should have been watching him."

Leafstar could understand the gray she-cat's guilt. Sagepaw was Petalnose's son and her apprentice; no wonder she felt responsible for his accident.

I remember Firestar telling us that forest cats don't mentor their own kin. Maybe they have a point.

"It's not your fault," she reassured Petalnose, resting her tail-tip on the distraught cat's shoulder. "He's an apprentice, not a kit. You can't have your eye on him all the time."

Petalnose didn't respond, just went on covering the young cat's head with frantic licks.

Leafstar glanced over her shoulder at the sound of soft thuds behind her, and saw Sharpclaw, Sparrowpelt, and Shrewtooth heading toward her. Rockshade, Tinycloud, and Ebonyclaw leaped down just behind them. They crowded around and gazed down at the motionless apprentice.

"I'm sorry." Sharpclaw lashed his tail, clearly angry with himself. "If I'd been just a bit quicker . . ."

"You did your best," Leafstar told him. "No cat can—"

"He's dead!" Shrewtooth let out a loud wail, his neck fur bristling out. "Sagepaw's dead!"

Petalnose gasped, her blue eyes stretching wide with horror.

"No, he's not," Leafstar snapped. "And he's not going to die. Shrewtooth, instead of terrifying every cat, go find some moss and wet it in the river."

Shrewtooth stared at her; he opened his mouth to let out another wail, then shut it with a snap. "Sorry," he muttered, scuffling at the ground with his forepaws. "I—I guess I'll go and do that, then."

He dashed off. Leafstar bent closer over Sagepaw's body, encouraged to see that his breathing seemed to be more steady. She saw that one of his legs was stretched out at an awkward angle. *Something's wrong there. Please, StarClan, don't let it be broken!*

To her relief, she heard the quick pattering of paw steps approaching from farther down the gorge and Echosong appeared at her side, with Patchfoot just behind.

"Keep back, all of you," the medicine cat mewed briskly. "Petalnose, you can stay, as long as you can keep him calm and not make him more scared."

Petalnose gulped and sat upright, forcing the fur on her neck and shoulders to lie flat. Leafstar was impressed by her self-control, but the bleak look in her blue eyes showed how much she was suffering.

"Echosong, please save my son," she begged.

Pity for the gray she-cat stabbed through Leafstar like a thorn. Petalnose had already lost her mate, Rainfur, in the battle against the rats. *StarClan, you couldn't be cruel enough to take her son, too!*

For a few heartbeats Echosong studied Sagepaw, running her paw lightly over his fur. He stirred under her touch and tried to raise his head.

"Rainfur?" he whispered.

"No, it's me, little one," Petalnose purred, bending her head to lick his ears.

"That's good." Sagepaw's voice was muzzy. "I thought I was in StarClan." He scrabbled at the ground in an effort to sit up, then sank back with a sharp yelp of pain.

"Keep still," Echosong told him, resting a paw on his shoulder. "You've hurt your leg, and I need to look at it properly before I can fix it."

Her voice was steady, but Leafstar wondered how confident she really was. The Clan had been lucky to get through leaf-bare without any bad accidents, and Echosong had never needed to treat an injured leg before.

"Tinycloud," Echosong meowed, glancing over her shoulder to where the other cats had withdrawn into a worried huddle. "Go and fetch me some poppy seeds."

Tinycloud nodded, her eyes wide, and trotted off.

"Rockshade." Echosong beckoned with her tail. "Come here and lie down in the same position as Sagepaw."

Looking mystified, the young tom did as she told him, settling himself in the dust beside the injured apprentice. Echosong ran her paws over Rockshade's outstretched leg, then did the same to Sagepaw's. She felt Rockshade's leg again, pushing it in each direction with one paw resting at the top where it joined his flank. She touched Sagepaw's leg at the same place, and the apprentice let out a squeak of pain.

"I think I understand," she meowed, nodding. "Thank you,

Rockshade, you can get up now. Sagepaw's leg isn't broken," she went on, "but it has come out of place. I need to put it back."

"Can you do that?" Petalnose whispered.

"Yes." Echosong sounded tense but brave. "But it will hurt. I'm sorry, Sagepaw."

"I'll be okay," Sagepaw mewed. He blinked gratefully as Shrewtooth returned with a mouthful of dripping moss and set it down beside him. "Thanks, Shrewtooth."

While the apprentice was lapping the moss, Sparrowpelt padded up with a stick in his jaws and dropped it next to Sagepaw. "Bite down on that," he advised. "It'll help when the pain comes."

Sagepaw nodded. "Can we do it now, please?" he asked Echosong, unable to hide the fear in his voice. He gripped the stick in his jaws and held it tightly.

Echosong motioned with her tail for the other cats to stand out of the way. Leafstar stepped back with them; only Petalnose stayed close, crouched beside her son with their pelts brushing.

The medicine cat bent over Sagepaw. "I'm sorry, I'm going to have to use my teeth," she meowed. She planted her forepaws firmly on the young cat's haunches, and gripped his leg in her jaws. Then she gave a massive wrench; Leafstar heard the click as Sagepaw's leg went back into place.

The stick splintered in Sagepaw's teeth. Dropping the fragments, he let out a shriek. Petalnose gasped as she bent over him and pushed her nose into his fur.

Then Sagepaw raised his head. "Hey, it doesn't hurt so much!"

Echosong's eyes glowed with a mixture of relief and triumph, while her Clanmates murmured their congratulations. Leafstar could see how impressed they were. Petalnose didn't say anything, but her purrs almost drowned out the voices of the other cats.

"Well done," Leafstar meowed. "I'm proud of you, Echosong."

Echosong dipped her head, giving her chest fur a couple of embarrassed licks. Then she turned and spotted Tinycloud, who was hovering close by with a poppy seedhead in her jaws. She beckoned the white warrior over with a flick of her ears and took the seedhead from her. Carefully she shook out two seeds in front of Sagepaw.

"Lick those up," she instructed. "You'll need to come back to my den and rest, where I can keep an eye on you. The poppy seeds will dull the pain and help you sleep."

"Thanks, Echosong." Sagepaw swallowed the seeds with one lap of his tongue, then tried to struggle to his paws.

"Don't you dare try to walk!" Petalnose meowed. "I'll carry you."

"I'm not a kit!" Sagepaw protested.

"You'll always be my kit, little one." Gently Petalnose picked up Sagepaw by his scruff and began to carry him toward Echosong's den, staggering slightly under his weight but careful not to let his injured leg knock against the ground. Echosong padded alongside.

Leafstar watched them go.

"We're lucky to have Echosong," Sharpclaw remarked with satisfaction.

"We certainly are," Sparrowpelt meowed. "Thank Star-Clan!"

Leafstar murmured agreement. "But what I'd like to know," she went on, "is what Sagepaw was doing, climbing so high up the cliff. He was well away from any of the trails."

Sharpclaw shook his head. "I have no idea."

Leafstar glanced around the rest of her Clanmates, and spotted Patchfoot scrabbling uncomfortably at the ground with his forepaws. "Patchfoot?" she prompted.

"I—I'm sorry, Leafstar," the black-and-white tom stammered. "I think it might have been my fault."

A growl began deep in Sharpclaw's throat, but Leafstar motioned him to silence with a wave of her tail. "Explain," she meowed.

"Well . . . I think Sagepaw was trying to prove he was descended from the old SkyClan cats. He was trying to show how good he was at jumping and climbing."

"And why is that your fault?" Sharpclaw asked tartly.

"I—I teased him about it," Patchfoot confessed, his eyes full of guilt. "I said he wasn't a real SkyClan cat. But I never thought he would do something like that, Leafstar, honestly I didn't!"

"I believe you," Leafstar told him. "No cat would expect him to do anything so stupid."

But while she reassured Patchfoot, anxiety rose inside her

like floodwater. This wasn't the first time she had noticed how much her Clanmates cared about their ancestry. The day after the snowfall, she had heard Cherrytail boasting to Echosong about her strong legs and tough pads. *No cat should care so much about being descended from the ancient SkyClan cats. Maybe they all are, but there's no way of telling. It shouldn't matter to any of them.*

"I'm really sorry," Patchfoot went on, blinking in relief that his Clan leader wasn't angry with him. "I'll never do it again."

"Make sure you don't," Leafstar replied, nodding to dismiss him.

She watched him set off up the cliff again, back toward the cave where he had been working, while Sharpclaw chivvied the other cats back to their duties. *I need to make them understand that we're all one Clan. The ancestors that matter are those in StarClan, who watch over us as if we were all their kits.*

The hunting patrols were returning, adding their prey to the fresh-kill pile. Leafstar watched Tinycloud bound up to Mintpaw as she returned with Cherrytail's patrol.

"Mintpaw, Sagepaw has had an accident!"

Mintpaw let her prey fall and stood with her jaws open in horror as Tinycloud described how Mintpaw's littermate had fallen from the cliff.

"But he's going to be fine," the white she-cat finished. "Echosong was great. She put his leg back in the right place, and now he's resting in her den."

"Then he'll need to keep his strength up," Mintpaw declared, grabbing the biggest squirrel off the fresh-kill pile and hauling it in the direction of Echosong's den.

Leafstar waited until all the cats had gathered around the fresh-kill pile and chosen something to eat. They huddled in small groups; those who had witnessed Sagepaw's accident were passing on the news to those who had been out of the camp.

As the talk died down, Leafstar leaped up onto the Rock-pile and raised her voice in a yowl. "Let all cats old enough to catch their own prey gather here beneath the Rockpile for a Clan meeting."

Most of the cats were already there, crouching near the fresh-kill pile or on the bank of the stream. Fallowfern's kits scrambled out of the nursery with their mother behind them, trying to make sure they didn't fall off the trail as they bounded downward.

"Remember what happened to Sagepaw!" Fallowfern warned, but the kits didn't pay any attention, plopping down happily onto the path by the waterside and lining up in a row with ears pricked and eyes shining with curiosity. Fallowfern sat down beside them, stretching out her tail around them.

Leafstar looked around to see if any cat was keeping watch; it was easy to feel trapped and vulnerable when every cat was at the bottom of the gorge, and a few moons ago she had ordered that some cat should always guard the camp during meetings. She nodded in approval when she spotted Wasp-whisker bounding away to take up a position on a boulder halfway up the trail.

Lichenfur and Tangle emerged from their den and padded slowly toward the Rockpile, settling down on a flat, sun-warmed stone that jutted out over the water. Mintpaw appeared from Echosong's den to join her Clanmates, while Echosong and Petalnose sat in the den entrance where they could listen and still keep an eye on Sagepaw.

"Cats of SkyClan," Leafstar began when they were all assembled. "First of all, there's no need to worry about Sagepaw. He's going to be fine, thanks to Echosong."

"Echosong! Echosong!" the Clan yowled; several of the cats jumped to their paws and waved their tails.

The young medicine cat dipped her head in embarrassment at the sound of her Clanmates' enthusiastic praise.

Leafstar raised her tail for silence. "There's something else I need to say to you," she went on. *StarClan, give me the right words,* she prayed. "This is our Clan, and we should all be proud of it, and proud to belong here. This is our home now. We protect the borders, we hunt the prey, and we train new warriors. If there are echoes of the old SkyClan among us, such as the ability to jump and climb well, they are no more important than what each cat brings to the new Clan."

Patchfoot was looking uncomfortable again, his gaze fixed on his paws; one or two of the others seemed uneasy as well. Leafstar sank her claws into the boulder underneath her. *I was right. It's time to root out this obsession with SkyClan blood.*

"I look down at all of you," she continued, "and I see cats who have done everything they can to make our Clan strong. Clovertail has raised healthy kits who are now SkyClan warriors. Shrewtooth, your sharp hearing means that enemies will never sneak up on us."

The black tom started with surprise that his leader had singled him out for praise, and Sparrowpelt, sitting beside him, gave him a friendly shove.

"Sharpclaw is the best deputy a Clan leader could wish for, and Echosong is a truly gifted medicine cat." Leafstar paused and let her gaze sweep across the assembled Clan. "But there is no need for me to go on naming names. I am proud to have *all* of you as my Clanmates, and SkyClan would be diminished without a single one of you."

The cats below her glanced at one another; she saw Lichenfur lean over and mutter something into Tangle's ear.

"But Firestar chose me and Cherrytail first," Sparrowpelt pointed out, "because we inherited our climbing and jumping skills from old SkyClan."

"That's right!" Cherrytail agreed, nodding.

"No, he didn't!" Fallowfern argued, her neck fur beginning to bristle. "From what I heard, he chose you because you were nearest. You have no more right to be part of the Clan than my kits."

Cherrytail sprang to her paws, only to sink down again when Leafstar raised her tail in warning.

"What Fallowfern said is exactly what I mean," she went on, struggling to keep her voice even. "No cat has more claim to SkyClan than any other, no matter who their ancestors were. As Clan cats, StarClan is here for all of us."

"Leafstar is right." Sharpclaw rose to his paws to address

the rest of the Clan. "A place in the Clan is earned by loyalty, duty, and courage."

Leafstar had no time to feel warmed by her deputy's support before she saw him cast a dark glance at Billystorm, Ebonyclaw, and the two daylight-warrior apprentices.

Before she could say anything else, she was interrupted by a yowl from Waspwhisker. "Intruders!"

The gray-and-white tom, still on watch halfway up the cliff, had sprung to his paws and was gazing across the gorge to the cliff on the other side. The rest of the Clan spun around, their neck fur bristling, and stared at the top of the rocks. Leafstar spotted a cat peering over the cliff, only its brown-furred head visible. Within a heartbeat it was joined by another, then a third and a fourth.

A low growl came from Sharpclaw's throat. "How did they get so far inside the borders without us noticing?"

"We should have been on border patrol," Bouncefire explained helpfully, "but Leafstar told us to hunt instead."

Leafstar winced at the querying look Sharpclaw shot at her. What the young warrior said was true, but when so few strange cats ever came into the territory, she had thought it was more important to stock the fresh-kill pile.

This would *happen the one time there's no patrol!*

Resentment stirred inside Leafstar at the thought of defending herself to her deputy, so she didn't respond to what Bouncefire said. "Patchfoot," she meowed instead, "fetch the strangers down here. Cherrytail and Sparrowpelt, go with him."

The three cats ran a short way down the gorge and crossed the river by a line of stepping-stones. Patchfoot led the way back up the gorge and they vanished around a bend in the cliff. The four cat heads vanished, too, pulling back from the edge.

"You're trespassing on SkyClan territory!" Leafstar heard Patchfoot's voice raised in a stern yowl. "Come down and meet our leader!"

The SkyClan cats waited in tense silence, in which the sound of paw steps running down the cliff could be heard. A heartbeat later the patrol reappeared with Patchfoot in the lead, while Cherrytail and Sparrowpelt flanked the four intruders. The SkyClan cats escorted the newcomers across the river, all the way to the foot of the Rockpile. The other cats drew back to let them pass. Leafstar's eyes narrowed as she saw her Clanmates' bristling fur and extended claws. *Let's hope we can end this peacefully.*

She jumped down from the Rockpile and confronted the four strange cats. The tallest of them, a long-legged brown tom with yellow eyes and a scraped pelt, let his gaze travel slowly around. To Leafstar's surprise, he didn't look scared at being surrounded by a Clan of hostile cats. Instead, he looked . . . *satisfied.*

Turning to Leafstar, he gave her a nod. "It looks like Firestar found you after all," he meowed.

CHAPTER 6

❧

Leafstar stiffened. "How do you know Firestar?" she demanded. *"Are you from ThunderClan?"*

The brown cat snorted. "No, we're not from any Clan. But we met Firestar and his mate, Sandstorm, when they were on their way to find some cats who needed a new home. Is this it?"

He let his gaze travel around the gorge again, and Leafstar could tell he wasn't impressed. She had to concentrate hard to keep her neck fur lying flat and her voice sounding proud and confident.

"Yes, Firestar found us and this is our home. I am Leafstar, the leader of SkyClan."

"And what are *your* names?" Sharpclaw prompted, coming to stand beside Leafstar.

Leafstar realized that she should have asked that before she offered the strangers any information. But the mention of Firestar's name had shaken her off balance.

"My name is Stick," the skinny brown tom announced. He flicked his tail toward a black she-cat. "This is Cora."

"I'm Shorty." A brown tabby tom with the end of his tail

missing took a step forward and dipped his head politely.

"Coal." The last cat, a black tom, shouldered his way forward. "We come from a Twolegplace farther downstream. We helped Firestar and Sandstorm when they were separated by a flood."

"Why are you here?" Leafstar asked. "Are you looking for Firestar? He and Sandstorm left us long ago."

Stick glanced at his companions; his tail-tip twitched and Leafstar sensed he was ordering them to leave the talking to him. "We often talk about Firestar and Sandstorm," he replied. "And we've always been interested in learning more about Clans."

Sharpclaw's gaze flicked from one cat to the next. "You took quite a risk coming in search of them," he pointed out. "It doesn't sound as if you knew much about Firestar's plans."

The scrawny brown tom shrugged. "The risk paid off."

Sharpclaw exchanged a wary glance with Leafstar. She could tell that he was impressed by the strangers' courage, though he still wasn't inclined to trust them. Leafstar felt uneasy, too, and guessed from the hesitant glances they were sharing that her Clanmates felt the same. Creekkit looked up at her mother, Fallowfern, and asked in a penetrating whisper, "Who are those cats, and what are they doing here?"

Fallowfern gently covered the kit's mouth with her tail, but Leafstar knew that the question had to be answered. "Yes, why are you here?" She addressed Stick, since he seemed to be the leader. "You're welcome to visit, of course. . . ."

Cora stepped forward; her eyes were gentle and

unthreatening. "We believe we could learn a lot from you," she explained. "How to hunt, how to guard our territory—"

"Yeah, we did a brilliant job of that today!" Cherrytail muttered.

"And how to protect our kin," the black she-cat finished, untroubled by the interruption.

Leafstar was flattered by the respect in Cora's tone. "We're only just starting out ourselves," she admitted. "We still have a lot to learn, too. We—"

"We'd be glad to teach you what you want to know," Sharp-claw interrupted, his tail-tip twitching. Turning to Leafstar, he added, "We can always use extra help with hunting, right?"

Leafstar heard a gasp from one of her Clanmates, and noticed one or two uneasy looks at the deputy's tone; it almost sounded as if he was telling his Clan leader what to do. But for now she had to make it clear to every cat, including the visitors, that she was in charge. *I'll have a word with him about that later.*

"Of course," she meowed calmly. "Four extra cats—"

A loud wail from Echosong's den interrupted her. "My leg hurts!"

Leafstar realized that Sagepaw must have woken up. Echosong, who had been sitting at the entrance of her den, immediately vanished inside, with Petalnose hard on her paws.

"What's that?" Cora asked, looking shocked. The other newcomers were wide-eyed, too, their pelts beginning to bristle.

"Nothing to worry about," Leafstar reassured them. "One

of our young cats had an accident earlier, but our medicine cat is taking care of him."

"A medicine cat?" Coal echoed. "You mean you have a cat who looks after you when you're hurt or ill? I'd like to learn more about that."

Leafstar's pelt was still prickling with pride in the way Echosong had dealt with Sagepaw's injury. Surely there was no harm in sharing her skills with these visitors? "Yes, you can do that," she told Coal. "Why don't you go down to Echosong's den and watch what she does? Tinycloud, go with him and tell Echosong I said it was all right for Coal to be there."

The young white warrior dipped her head and waved her tail to beckon Coal. "Thank you," he mewed to Leafstar, and padded off after Tinycloud. Leafstar noticed that Tinycloud managed to keep a tail-length ahead of the black tom, as if she didn't want him getting too close to her.

Leafstar also noticed that Sharpclaw was staring at her with narrowed eyes, as if he was questioning her decision to let Coal into the medicine cat's den.

Stop being so sensitive! she scolded herself. *Sharpclaw is a good deputy. He was the one who said we should let the visitors see how we live in the first place.*

Stick, Cora, and Shorty were looking expectantly at Leafstar. It was like being faced with three new apprentices. Did they really want to learn what Clan cats did? Leafstar tried to think of any reason why she couldn't use the offer of free help in exchange for some hunting and fighting tips. With Harveymoon and Macgyver back in Twolegplace, there was room for some extra paws. Checking the fresh-kill pile, she saw it was still well stocked, so there was no point in sending them out on hunting patrols right now.

"Would you like to join a training session with our apprentices?" she suggested. "We all train together, because even warriors have to practice their battle skills."

At the front of the gathered cats, Mintpaw gave an excited wriggle. "That would be great!" she exclaimed. "I can show them my best move."

"You mean the one where you get sand in your face?" Snookpaw teased. "Sure, we'll show them that one!"

Stick glanced at Cora and Shorty, then nodded to Leafstar. "I think we'd all enjoy that," he meowed.

"Then let's go."

As soon as Leafstar spoke the three apprentices raced off up the gorge toward the flat training area just beyond the bend in the cliff. Fallowfern's kits jumped up and pattered after them, only to be herded gently back by their mother.

"But we want to train, too!" Nettlekit protested.

"That's right," Plumkit added. "We know lots of battle moves!"

"You're not even apprentices yet," Fallowfern pointed out. "You're too young."

"Mouse dung!" Rabbitkit lashed his tail while Creekkit let out an annoyed hiss.

"Never mind, you can have your own practice by the pool," their mother consoled them. "Just as long as you don't fall in!"

The four kits let out squeaks of excitement and launched themselves toward the flat stretch of pebbles at the water's edge, with their mother trotting rapidly behind them.

The warriors headed up the gorge after the apprentices, with Sharpclaw in the lead. Waspwhisker came down from his lookout post while Tinycloud and Petalnose emerged from Echosong's den and bounded up to them. "Wait for us!" Tinycloud panted.

As Leafstar was preparing to follow, Billystorm paused beside her.

"Do you think some of us ought to hunt?" he asked, too softly for any other cat to hear. "There'll be four extra mouths to feed tonight."

Leafstar felt a stab of embarrassment that one of the daylight-warriors had needed to point this out. "Oh, thanks." She also felt encouraged that the ginger-and-white tom had come up with the suggestion. Ever since Billystorm had caused an argument by leaving on the day of the snow, he had worked hard, as if he was trying to make up for a bad decision. "Do you want to lead a patrol?"

"I can't," Billystorm pointed out. "I have to supervise Snookpaw's training."

Leafstar nodded. "You're right; that's more important. Patchfoot," she called, "will you lead a hunting patrol? Take Cherrytail, Shrewtooth, and Rockshade with you."

Rockshade halted and glanced over his shoulder. "Do I have to?" he complained. "I wanted to join the training session."

"When your Clan leader tells you to, then you have to," Billystorm meowed sharply.

Rockshade gave him a glare as he fell in behind Shrewtooth and Cherrytail. "What would a *kittypet* know about it?" he muttered into Cherrytail's ear, just loud enough for Leafstar and Billystorm to hear.

Leafstar opened her jaws, preparing a stinging rebuke, but Billystorm shook his head and she stayed silent.

"It doesn't matter," the ginger-and-white tom mewed. "Scolding him will only make him worse. Let's go and see what those apprentices are doing."

By the time Leafstar and Billystorm reached the training area, Sharpclaw was dividing the other cats into two groups.

"Sparrowpelt, you lead this one," he meowed, "and Waspwhisker, you can lead the other."

Leafstar padded to the edge of the broad stretch of sand where Cora, Stick, and Shorty were sitting.

"Do you do this all the time?" Cora asked, wide-eyed.

Leafstar shook her head. "Usually we train in smaller groups, or mentors practice battle moves with their apprentices. But Sharpclaw likes to work on bigger exercises now and again."

"What do you want us to do?" Billystorm called to Sharpclaw, padding over to join his apprentice.

"You see this thorn tree?" Sharpclaw flicked his tail toward a dead and twisted tree that stood a few tail-lengths away from the edge of the training area. "Whichever cat touches the trunk first wins for their patrol."

"I can do that!" Mintpaw leaped to her paws and bounded off in the direction of the tree, only to skid to a halt as Sharpclaw raised his tail to stop her.

"It's not going to be as easy as that, Mintpaw," the Clan deputy warned with a glint of amusement in his eyes. "While you're trying to reach the tree, the other group will be trying, too. What do you think will happen?"

Ebonyclaw took a step forward. "They'll try to stop us?"

Sharpclaw gave her a curt nod, while Leafstar felt pleased that one of the daylight-warriors had given the right answer.

"You'll need to think about attack and defense," he went on, addressing all the cats. "It's not just about getting there first; you have to stop the other group beating you to it. Can you think of any moves that would be useful?"

"Claw their ears off!" Tinycloud meowed loudly.

Sharpclaw merely flicked one ear, while Bouncefire muttered, "Mouse-brain!"

Frecklepaw raised her tail. "We could choose one cat to run for the tree," she suggested. "And then the others could get in the way when the other group tries to stop her."

"Good idea!" Ebonyclaw praised her apprentice before Sharpclaw could comment.

"Or we could create a diversion," Sparrowpelt meowed. "If one cat yowled, 'Fox!' its teammates could dash for the tree while the other cats were looking for it."

"That would have been a great idea," Sharpclaw

commented drily, "if you hadn't just told every cat what you're going to do."

Sparrowpelt shrugged. "You asked for suggestions."

"So I did." Sharpclaw twitched his whiskers. "Okay, I'll give you a moment to decide what your team will do, and when I say 'now,' start racing."

Leafstar watched as the two groups huddled together, whispering urgently while casting suspicious glances at their rivals.

"This is going to be really useful for us," Stick remarked. "It's the sort of thing that would help us get to a bit of prey before another cat."

"Or a good sleeping place," Shorty added.

Leafstar nodded, remembering back to when she had been a loner, without a Clan to support her or a den that she could really call her own. "Life's much better when you're not on your own," she murmured, half to herself.

Cora opened her jaws to respond, but just then Sharpclaw yowled, "Now!"

The two groups of cats exploded outward like seeds from a gorse pod. Tinycloud let out a screech and raced for the tree, ducking around Waspwhisker's outstretched paws, but before she got within reach she was bowled over by Bouncefire. The two littermates rolled over together in a whirl of flailing paws and tails.

Ebonyclaw and Frecklepaw worked as a team to weave their way past Petalnose, who didn't seem to know which cat to attack first. Leafstar thought they had a clear run to the tree, until Billystorm came charging up, swatted Frecklepaw aside with one blow of his paw, and shouldered Ebonyclaw away. Petalnose wrapped her paws around the black she-cat's neck and dragged her over onto her back.

Leafstar heard Cora gasp, and saw her and Shorty wince as the battling cats tumbled into the dust, attacking one another with piercing caterwauls.

"It's all right," she reassured them. Pride warmed her from ears to tail-tip as her Clanmates showed off their strength and courage. *And Sharpclaw knows exactly how to get the best from them.* "All claws are sheathed when they're training. And they have to learn to land lightly and get back onto their paws before an enemy can strike a death blow."

"That's a good move," Stick pointed out, angling his ears to where Sparrowpelt had just intercepted Waspwhisker a couple of tail-lengths from the tree, hooked his paws out from under him, and leaped on top of him, pummeling him around the ears with his forepaws. "I'll have to remember that one."

Sharpclaw, who was standing nearby, dipped his head to acknowledge the loner's praise. "Our young cats learn that move almost as soon as they're apprenticed," he meowed. "We can teach you, if you want."

"We're here to learn," Stick responded.

Leafstar realized that she hadn't seen Snookpaw in the middle of the combat. Glancing around, she spotted the tip of a black paw poking out from the bottom of a heap of boulders between the fighting cats and the tree.

A heartbeat later, Snookpaw appeared, creeping along the

ground in his best hunter's crouch. The other cats were too preoccupied to notice him. A tail-length from the tree he sprang into the air and landed just beside the trunk as if he was pouncing on prey.

"I did it!" he yowled triumphantly, stretching his paws up the trunk to score his claws down the bark. "I won!"

The tussling cats broke apart, Waspwhisker's group spinning around to stare at the apprentice, while Sparrowpelt's patrol wore identical smug expressions, as if they'd just caught a plump thrush.

Sparrowpelt licked his paw and drew it over one ear. "Well done!" he told Snookpaw. "I knew they'd never spot you sneaking up like that if we kept them busy."

"Mouse dung!" Bouncefire exclaimed. "I never thought of that!"

Billystorm bounded over to his apprentice and stretched his tail over the young cat's shoulders. "Good job," he meowed.

"Yes, very well done." Sharpclaw's voice had an edge to it, as if he wasn't pleased that a daylight-warrior had taken the most important part in his group's strategy. "Let's try something else, shall we?"

He gestured with his tail for the cats to gather around him. Leafstar saw that two long, striped hawk feathers lay beside his paws; as the cats approached he pushed them forward.

"This time," he began, "you have to take one of these feathers right up to the top of the thorn tree. The cat who gets there first wins."

"Then we should have a feather each," Tinycloud objected.

"No," Sharpclaw explained patiently. "This is still an exercise for patrols. You have to decide whether you send one cat up the tree with the feather, or try to do it all together."

Sparrowpelt nodded. "I get it." He beckoned with his tail to summon his patrol to the other side of the sand.

"Would you like to join in?" Leafstar asked the visitors.

The thee cats looked at one another, then nodded; Leafstar thought that Cora and Shorty both seemed slightly reluctant.

"Good," Sharpclaw mewed. "Stick and Cora, you join Waspwhisker's patrol, and Shorty, you go with Sparrowpelt."

The visitors moved off, but before he joined his group Stick halted and glanced over his shoulder. "Don't you ever join in?" he meowed to Leafstar.

"Sometimes," she replied, surprised by what seemed like a challenge. Flicking her tail at Sharpclaw, she added, "Let's do it."

Her deputy nodded. He padded over toward Waspwhisker's patrol, leaving Leafstar to join Sparrowpelt.

"What do you think we should do this time?" she meowed quietly, dipping her head to Sparrowpelt to show him that he was still in charge.

"They'll expect us to do something sneaky," the tabby tom began, "so I suggest we go straight for it. Petalnose, you take the feather and climb as fast as you can. The rest of us will try to keep Waspwhisker's patrol out of your fur."

Petalnose nodded. "Sounds good to me."

Leafstar tensed as she waited for Sharpclaw to give the signal to start. Energy coursed through her muscles. *I haven't felt like this in moons*, she thought. *I love training with my Clan.*

"Now!" Sharpclaw yowled.

Grabbing the feather in her jaws, Petalnose raced for the tree, veering around Mintpaw as the apprentice tried to stop her. Leafstar realized that all of Waspwhisker's patrol, except for Mintpaw and Bouncefire, were heading for the tree. Sharpclaw was in the lead with the feather.

Leafstar flung herself into the crush, slamming into Ebonyclaw and carrying the black she-cat off her paws. She ducked underneath a blow from Stick, realizing that the scrawny loner had good instincts even without training. The blow she had avoided could have been better aimed, but he was strong, and not afraid to challenge a Clan leader.

Petalnose and Sharpclaw reached the tree at the same moment. Petalnose flung herself up the trunk, but Billystorm grabbed Sharpclaw's tail in his jaws as the deputy sprang upward and dragged him down again. Sharpclaw passed the feather rapidly to Frecklepaw before battering at Billystorm with all four paws to break his grip.

Bouncefire jumped on Cora as she tried to reach the tree; Leafstar saw how the she-cat let herself go limp under his paws, then heave herself up and throw him off.

Nice move. Bouncefire should have been expecting that!

With a loud screech, Mintpaw dashed up to Shorty and swiped a paw across his face. The tabby tom stumbled, off balance, but managed to stay on his paws. He wasn't fast enough to catch Mintpaw, though; the gray apprentice whirled around and headed off Sparrowpelt as he tried to break through to support Petalnose.

By now, Petalnose was halfway up the tree and climbing well. Frecklepaw, Ebonyclaw, and Waspwhisker were scrambling up together a little way below, passing the feather from one to the other, while Sharpclaw had thrown off Billystorm and was racing to overtake Petalnose.

Leafstar paused, looking up. It didn't seem as if anything could stop Petalnose now. But just before she reached the top of the tree, the branch she was clinging to gave way with a loud crack. Petalnose swung there for a couple of heartbeats, dangling from the broken half of the branch as it gradually tore away from the tree. Then she plummeted downward, scrabbling at the thorny branches in an attempt to break her fall. She dropped the feather, which fluttered gently down and landed just in front of Leafstar's paws.

Frecklepaw, who held the other feather, had slid downward as she tried to avoid Petalnose. Ebonyclaw and Waspwhisker were too far away to take the feather from her, and began clambering through the branches to reach her.

Tinycloud and Sparrowpelt were helping Petalnose to her paws. With a swift glance to make sure that the she-cat wasn't hurt, Leafstar snatched up the feather and leaped into the tree. Thrusting herself up from branch to branch, she suddenly realized that Sharpclaw was crouched above her, his muscles tensed to fight once she came within reach.

I've got to get past him. If we start tussling up here, we'll both fall out of the tree.

She feinted to one side; Sharpclaw moved to intercept her,

and his paws slipped on the branch. With a hiss of annoyance he struggled to keep his balance, and Leafstar slid past him on the other side. Digging her claws into the topmost branch, she waved her tail and let out a triumphant yowl, managing not to let go of the feather. Down below, she could see her Clanmates circling at the foot of the tree with a mix of frustration and excitement in their eyes.

Sparrowpelt's triumphant shout drifted up to her. "She did it! Leafstar won!"

CHAPTER 7

"We won!" Sparrowpelt waved his tail as the cats poured back down the gorge toward the camp. "Snookpaw, you crept up to the tree like a shadow!"

The apprentice blinked in embarrassment and let out a pleased purr.

"We'll go hunting tomorrow," Billystorm promised him. "And you can try out that crouch on real prey."

"It was just bad luck that we lost," Waspwhisker meowed; Leafstar was relieved to see that none of his teammates was looking angry that Sparrowpelt's group had beaten them in both exercises.

"Yes, you just wait till next time," Mintpaw murmured, her eyes gleaming.

"Did you see me trip up Tinycloud?" Bouncefire boasted. "She never saw me coming!"

"I got in some good blows over your ears, though," his sister retorted, giving him a flick on the shoulder with her tail. "You're lucky my claws were sheathed!"

"Frecklepaw, you did well, too." Ebonyclaw brushed her tail against her apprentice's shoulder. "You were a strong part of our group."

"It was fun," Frecklepaw replied, her eyes shining. "Can we do it again some time?" she asked Sharpclaw shyly.

The deputy nodded. "Of course. It's the best way of keeping our skills sharp."

To Leafstar's surprise, Sharpclaw sounded quite friendly as he spoke to the apprentice, as if he'd forgotten for now that she was a daylight-warrior. *Training like this brings us closer together.*

Even the visiting cats seemed more at ease among the warriors now. "You could try racing up the cliff," Stick suggested, pausing to scan the rock face stretching above him. "We could give you some tips there; we're used to climbing walls in our Twolegplace."

"I'll think about it," Leafstar promised, though privately she wasn't sure it was a good idea. The memory of Sagepaw's fall was too vivid in her mind.

Or does that mean we ought to do more climbing practice? she wondered. *I'll have to discuss it with Sharpclaw.*

"Or we could show you different ways of dealing with dogs." Shorty scraped the ground with his front claws. "You must see plenty of them, with a Twolegplace so near."

Sharpclaw gave him a long look. "Thanks. That could be very useful."

"And what to do about monsters," Cora put in. "Or young Twolegs." She sighed. "Sometimes I think we spend our whole lives dodging something."

"You wouldn't have to if you were in a Clan," Tinycloud meowed, her tail proudly raised. "Clan cats look out for one another."

"There's one thing that puzzles me," Stick went on, as if

Tinycloud hadn't spoken. "In our Twolegplace, we hunt at night, and sleep in the day."

"But you're awake all day," Shorty mewed. "Somehow it doesn't seem right for cats."

"Firestar said this is how the other Clans live," Leafstar answered. "It's easier to hunt and patrol our borders in daylight."

"And fight, if we have to," Sharpclaw added; there was the hint of a challenge in his voice. "We could hunt by night if we wanted to, but we prefer it this way."

Leafstar spotted Shorty rolling his eyes at Cora, and heard him mutter, "Weird, or what?"

She didn't bother to argue with them. SkyClan hunted by day and slept by night because that was the way Firestar and Sandstorm had taught them. She couldn't see that it mattered. As Sharpclaw had said, there was no reason why they couldn't hunt at night, and sometimes two or three warriors would go out on patrol after dark, especially if the night was fine and the moon shone brightly.

Rounding the last spur of rock, Leafstar saw the Rockpile and the camp ahead of her. Patchfoot and his hunting patrol were padding along the stream, their jaws laden with prey. Tangle and Lichenfur were already crouching beside the fresh-kill pile, sharing a plump pigeon, while Clovertail and Fallowfern lay stretched out at the water's edge with Fallowfern's kits scrambling all over them.

As the other cats gathered around the fresh-kill pile, choosing pieces of prey for themselves, Coal emerged from

Echosong's den and bounded up to join them.

"Stick, you *have* to go and meet Echosong!" he announced. "She's amazing! She has herbs to cure every illness you can think of, cobwebs to stop bleeding, ointment for cracked pads. . . ."

"Echosong is great!" Bouncefire chimed in. "She looks after every cat in the Clan."

"Are you going to set up your own Clan?" Tinycloud asked Stick, tipping her head to one side. "Is that why you've come here?"

All four visiting cats looked shocked, their eyes wide and their fur beginning to bristle.

"Never!" Stick exclaimed.

"You should," Tinycloud insisted. "In a Clan you've always got other cats to watch your back."

"We share prey," Rockshade added. "No cat goes hungry."

"And we learn how to look after ourselves and our Clanmates." Mintpaw stretched out her front paws and unsheathed her tiny claws. "Dogs and foxes had better watch out!"

"We help one another," Ebonyclaw mewed softly, while her apprentice Frecklepaw nodded. "We're friends."

Leafstar's chest swelled with pride as she heard how confident her Clanmates sounded. *SkyClan is strong!*

Stick shook his head. "We have our own way of life."

"That's right." Leafstar thought that Cora sounded regretful, but there was no hesitation as she backed up the scrawny brown tom. "We can learn from one another, but we don't want to decide that one way of life is better than all the others."

"Just what are they doing here, then?"

The muttered words came from behind Leafstar; she looked over her shoulder to see Lichenfur glaring at the visitors from narrowed amber eyes. Leafstar glanced back at the visitors, but none of them seemed to have heard; Sharpclaw invited them to take prey from the fresh-kill pile and they settled down to eat.

"It's no surprise that other cats want to learn from us," Rockshade pointed out to the mottled gray elder. "We're so strong and fierce!"

"And skilled!" Bouncefire put in.

Lichenfur batted crossly at a pigeon feather that had got stuck to her nose. "And how did they hear about us, hmm? Squirrels passing whispers through the trees?"

"They said that Firestar and Sandstorm told them," Rockshade flashed back at her.

The gray she-cat grunted. "Maybe."

A light touch on her shoulder distracted Leafstar; she turned to see Tinycloud standing beside her, the tip of her tail still resting on Leafstar's pelt. "Leafstar, may I have a word with you, please?"

"Of course." Tipping her head to show Tinycloud she should follow, Leafstar picked her way among the feeding cats to a quiet spot near the cliff face. "What is it?"

"I know how important the medicine cat is to a Clan," Tinycloud began, "and I like helping Echosong. I've learned a lot from her, but I really, really want to be a warrior, and I feel that I'm missing out on training." She dug her claws into the ground. "*Please* can I go back to ordinary warrior duties now?"

The small white cat was so earnest and solemn that Leafstar had to bite back a purr of amusement. "Of course," she meowed. "Just as long as you remember that if Echosong needs help, it's the duty of every warrior to respond, for the sake of the Clan."

Tinycloud nodded seriously, then scampered off, skidding to a halt beside her littermates. "Watch out!" Her voice was an excited squeak. "I'm back in training!"

Gazing after her, a sudden pang of concern banished Leafstar's amusement. *Echosong needs to start training an apprentice.* She wasn't exactly sure when a medicine cat usually started to train an apprentice, but it made sense to start sooner rather than later. *We depend so much on Echosong. What would we do if we lost her?*

Tinycloud obviously didn't have the passion she would need to live the life of a medicine cat. *It's going to be hard to find an apprentice,* Leafstar thought. *A medicine cat gives up so much for her Clan.*

Mintpaw and Sagepaw were desperate to be warriors like their dead father, Rainfur, and Leafstar knew that Clovertail would have the same ambition for the kits she was carrying now. *Maybe one of Fallowfern's kits will show a skill for healing.* Leafstar swallowed a hiss of frustration. Echosong was young and healthy; worrying about her replacement seemed like one worry too far right now.

The sun was sinking down below the top of the cliffs, and

shadows began to creep across the gorge. As the cats finished eating, Sharpclaw began to sort out the evening patrols.

Billystorm padded across to Leafstar, with Ebonyclaw, Snookpaw, and Frecklepaw just behind him. "Is everything all right?" he asked, concern in his green eyes.

Leafstar took a breath, ready to tell the ginger-and-white tom what was on her mind, then stopped herself. *I'm the Clan leader; it's my job to sort out these problems on my own.*

"Yes, everything's fine," she replied.

Billystorm looked as if he didn't quite believe her, but all he said was "We'll be off now, unless there's anything else you want us to do."

"No, we're all set for tonight. We'll see you again in the morning."

Billystorm dipped his head and turned to go, then checked and looked back at his Clan leader. "I think you did the right thing about Harveymoon and Macgyver," he meowed. "Being part of SkyClan means that they have to respect the warrior code—and you—above anything else." He hesitated, then added, "If they don't show respect, then they don't deserve to be here."

Gratitude for the tom's support warmed Leafstar from ears to tail-tip. It meant a lot to her, especially coming from another daylight-warrior. *Billystorm knows it's a real privilege to be part of SkyClan.*

"Thank you," she murmured. "Good night, and may Star-Clan light your path."

"Good night," Billystorm responded, and padded away to

the bottom of the nearest trail, waving his tail to beckon Ebonyclaw and the two apprentices.

Leafstar rose and arched her back in a long stretch. The evening patrols had left, and the huddle around the fresh-kill pile was thinning out. Padding over to join the cats who remained, Leafstar saw that the four visitors were looking around curiously.

"Why are those cats leaving?" Shorty asked, pointing the stump of his tail at Billystorm and the other daylight-warriors, who had climbed halfway up the trail. "Are they part of a patrol?"

"They're kitty-warriors," Tinycloud meowed, adding hastily as she caught Leafstar's eye, "I mean, *daylight*-warriors. But they do all the same things as real warriors."

The visitors looked confused and Cherrytail explained, "Billystorm and the others still have housefolk, and spend part of their time in Twolegplace, living as kittypets." Her whiskers twitched in faint contempt. "Sometimes they come out at night, sometimes in the day."

"And you still let them join in with everything?" Stick asked, his surprise evident in his voice.

Leafstar felt her pelt beginning to rise defensively, and choked the feelings down. "SkyClan is young," she meowed. "We need all the help we can get to keep the fresh-kill pile stocked and the borders strong."

"But your borders won't be strong if half your warriors are eating kittypet slop in a Twoleg nest," Cora pointed out. Leafstar wondered how much her air of innocent inquiry was genuine. If the visitors wanted to cause an argument, they were going about it in exactly the right way.

"SkyClan would have no trouble defending itself without the extra Clan members," Sharpclaw meowed. There was a hint of warning in his voice.

Narrowing her eyes, Leafstar watched the four visitors, but there was no sign of hostility from any of them. Stick merely nodded and murmured, "Interesting."

There's something they aren't telling us, Leafstar thought. *They haven't come here just to ask questions about Clan life.* She exchanged a glance with Sharpclaw, and saw her suspicions reflected in her deputy's green eyes. *So I'm not imagining this! Sharpclaw thinks there's something odd about these strangers, too.*

Leafstar felt as if her paws were slipping on the frozen surface of a river, with nothing to cling on to. She couldn't find any fault with the visitors so far—they had been polite, interested, and willing to join in the battle training—but she felt unsettled and vulnerable with their presence in the camp. Had it been a mistake to let them take part in the training session? Had they learned anything they could use against SkyClan?

I wish they hadn't come.

The last of the sunlight had gone, and the first warriors of StarClan were appearing in the sky. A chill night breeze whispered along the gorge and ruffled Leafstar's fur.

Sparrowpelt parted his jaws in a huge yawn. "I'm off to my nest," he announced, rising to his paws.

"Yes, it's time," Fallowfern agreed, sweeping her tail around to draw her kits close to her. "Come on, back to the nursery!"

Petalnose padded up to Leafstar and murmured in her ear, "Where are the visitors going to sleep?"

"There's not enough room for all of them in the warriors' den," Sparrowpelt pointed out. "We'd be sleeping on top of one another!"

"Maybe one of the new caves?" Petalnose suggested.

Leafstar thought for a moment, then nodded. "Yes, but I don't want them in there on their own. Some of our warriors should go with them."

Though she had spoken softly, Patchfoot overheard her and shot her a keen glance. "Why, don't you trust them?"

Not as far as I could throw the Rockpile, Leafstar thought, but she wasn't going to admit it, even to her own warriors. "No, I just want them to feel that SkyClan welcomes them," she replied.

"I don't mind sleeping in one of the new dens," Patchfoot meowed.

"Neither do I." Bouncefire sprang to his paws. "We'll get to try them first!"

"I'll go, too," Sparrowpelt offered, with another huge yawn. "But let's do it now, okay?"

"Thank you." Leafstar dipped her head. "It'll be a good opportunity to see if the new dens will work for us."

"I want to sleep there, too!" Nettlekit announced, his tiny paws kneading the ground.

"So do I!" Plumkit pattered up to Leafstar. "We'll all go!"

"No, you won't." Fallowfern stretched out her tail and drew her little daughter back. "You can't leave the nursery yet."

Nettlekit leaned over to whisper into his sister's ear. "We'll sneak out when she's is asleep."

Fallowfern's ears twitched. "Don't even try," she mewed without looking around. "I hear everything, even when I'm asleep."

Gathering her kits together, she led them off to the nursery, with Clovertail plodding behind, her belly heavy with her unborn kits. "But I'm not tired!" Nettlekit wailed, stumbling over his paws as he headed for his nest.

"It's too late to start gathering fresh moss," Patchfoot pointed out. "Let's move some over from the warriors' den; we can collect more in the morning."

"Good idea," Sparrowpelt agreed. "Come on," he added to the visitors. "We'll show you what to do."

Stick, Shorty, and Coal followed the SkyClan warriors up the trail to the main den, but Cora lingered behind with Leafstar. For a while the two she-cats sat close together, watching the warriors as they carried balls of moss out of their den, showing the visitors how to carry it across the cliff face toward the biggest of the new dens. In the twilight their pelts smudged together, so that it was hard for Leafstar to distinguish her own cats from the visitors.

She jumped when Cora spoke.

"We haven't come to cause you harm," the black she-cat murmured. Her voice was distant, as if there was more that she did not say.

Leafstar dipped her head, watching the cats as they eddied between the dens. "I hope not," she whispered.

CHAPTER 8

A *paw prodding him in the* side woke Stick. "Wha . . . ? Get off!" he growled.

He had spent the night hunting and prowling the streets of Twolegplace; it felt as though he had only just closed his eyes. His muscles still ached with tiredness.

The paw prodded Stick again, harder this time. Opening his eyes a crack, he saw Cora curled up close to him, and Snowy's white tail poking out from behind a nearby garbage can.

Shorty was standing over him, his amber eyes worried. "It's happening again," he meowed.

Stick scrambled out of his shallow nest among the tree roots and shook scraps of dead leaf from his pelt. "Where?"

Shorty angled his ears toward the far side of the patch of rough ground behind the Twoleg nests. "Follow me." He led the way to the far corner near a gate in the Twoleg fence. "It's Dodge, Skipper, and Misha," he added, glancing over his shoulder at Stick.

Stick felt his neck fur bristle. "They shouldn't be here."

Drawing closer, he soon spotted Dodge. The huge brown

tabby tom stood stiff-legged, his back arched and all his fur fluffed out. A low growl came from his throat. Just behind him stood Skipper and Misha, their eyes gleaming and their lips drawn back in a snarl.

Pinned up in the angle of the fence were Coal and Percy. Stick's heart thumped as he realized they were alone. "Where's Red?" he muttered to himself.

A few scraps of food lay at his friends' paws: a couple of scrawny mice and a bone dragged out of a Twoleg garbage can.

"But it took us all night to get this!" Coal was protesting as Stick and Shorty bounded up.

"Are you too idle to hunt now, Dodge?" Stick snarled.

The brown tabby tom spun around; his eyes glittered with hostility. "We have an agreement, remember? Sunrise belongs to us."

Stick turned to look at the horizon where the sun would come up. A jumble of Twoleg rooftops was outlined against a sky that was barely turning pale with the first light of dawn.

"You're splitting whiskers," he hissed. "It's still dark."

Ignoring him, Dodge took a menacing step forward. "If you can't keep to the rules, I'll force you to."

Stick curled his lip. "I've had enough of your threats. We were here first!"

Dodge nodded to Misha. The cream-colored she-cat padded forward. Then without warning she sprang forward. Percy let out a shriek as her claws scored down the side of his face, slashing at his eye.

Yowling with fury, Stick hurled himself at Dodge and knocked him onto the ground. The brown tabby tom let out a screech and battered at him with all four paws. Stick could hear hisses and thuds behind him as the other cats clashed, and a thin wail from Percy, who was trying to stagger away with blood streaming from his face.

There was a crash as a Twoleg door was flung open. Twoleg yowling split the air, along with the barking of dogs. Scrabbling on the ground under Dodge's weight, Stick saw the nearby gate swing open and two dogs ran out. Their tongues lolled and they let out a flurry of high-pitched barking as they bounded toward the cats.

Dodge and his two followers scrambled to their paws and streaked away, their belly fur brushing the ground. The dogs hurtled after them.

Stick limped over to the fence where Percy had come to a stop, blinded and dazed. Beckoning Shorty with his tail, Stick gripped Percy's scruff and the two toms half dragged, half carried him into hiding behind a stack of wood.

"Hurry!" Coal urged. "The dogs are coming back."

Stick crouched in the shadow of the wood. He could hear the padding of the dogs' paws, their panting breath and their snuffling as they nosed around the wood stack. But they were too big to squeeze their way behind it and get at the cats.

"Help me! Please help me!" Percy wailed, his uninjured eye wide with terror. "I'm going to die!"

"No, you're not," Stick told him bluntly. "You've lost an eye, that's all."

Percy let out another wail.

"Don't make such a racket," Cora meowed; the black she-cat was wriggling her way along the back of the stack to crouch close to Percy. "Here, let me clean you up."

She began to lick away the blood from his rumpled gray pelt, and his agonized wails sank to faint whimpering.

Stick could no longer hear the dogs. Peering around the edge of the stack, he saw the Twoleg holding the gate open and the dogs trotting back inside. Dodge and the other cats had vanished. Gazing across the rough ground, Stick couldn't see any other cats except for Snowy, who had fled up a tree when the fight started. Now she clung to a branch, staring down with frightened blue eyes.

Stick looked over his shoulder at the cats crouched behind the wood. "Where's Red?"

"I have no idea," Coal replied. "She started hunting with us, but then she went off on her own."

"How could you let her out of your sight?" Stick snapped, digging his claws into the ground. "I told you, no cat should be alone just now."

Coal shrugged. "You can't stop Red that easily."

"I'm going to look for her."

But before Stick could move, Cora looked up and flicked out her tail to rest it on his shoulder. "Red's full grown now," she pointed out. "She can take care of herself."

Stick shook off Cora's tail. "It's my fault," he growled. "If she had been raised by her mother . . ."

"It's not your fault Red's mother isn't here," Cora snapped.

"Look, with any luck Dodge will feel he's won enough battles for today. If Red's not back by sunhigh, we'll go and look for her."

Leaving the others with Percy, Stick slid out from behind the wood stack and raced across the rough ground to leap onto the roof of a shed. From there he looked out over the place he had always called home. The milky light of dawn uncovered thin grass and scrubby trees, surrounded by Twoleg fences and dens.

I know every hiding place, every puddle, every corner where mice make nests.

But now everything had changed. The familiar alleys and rooftops hid an enemy: Dodge and the cats he had brought with him to steal this place from those who had lived here forever. Cats who would rather fight than hunt, who enjoyed inflicting fear and pain. Cats who prowled around looking for trouble.

And Red is out there. . . .

CHAPTER 9

"*We may not have rival Clans* on our borders, but there are always enemies out there!" Patchfoot announced as he beckoned his patrol with his tail. "We have to make sure the border markings are good and fresh."

Leafstar watched as Billystorm and Ebonyclaw padded up to join the black-and-white warrior at the foot of the Rockpile. Their apprentices bounced eagerly behind them. It was the day after Sharpclaw's training exercises, and the Clan leader was pleased to see her Clanmates so enthusiastic about regular tasks.

"I've never reset the markers before," Frecklepaw meowed. "This is really exciting!"

Snookpaw lashed his tail and fluffed up his neck fur. "Those foxes and rogue cats had better watch out! We'll see off anything that tries to set paw on SkyClan territory."

Amusement prickled Leafstar's pelt and she let out a soft purr of pride. *I hope these apprentices decide to stay with the Clan. They'll make fine warriors.*

She noticed Cora and Shorty standing a few tail-lengths away, sharing bemused glances at the talk of border markers.

"Would you like to join the patrol?" Leafstar invited. "If there's trouble, we could do with a few more paws."

Cora hesitated, then gave a restrained nod; Shorty kneaded the ground with his front paws, his eyes gleaming. "Let's go!" he mewed.

Leafstar padded up to Patchfoot with the Twolegplace cats following. "Okay if we join you?"

Surprise flickered in Patchfoot's eyes as he dipped his head. "Of course, Leafstar."

He led the way up the trail, winding back and forth across the face of the cliff. Leafstar enjoyed the feeling of the breeze blowing through her pelt and the warmth of the stone under her pads. *It's good to be out of the camp. I haven't patrolled the borders for ages.*

When the patrol reached the top of the cliff, Shorty pushed forward until he could squeeze between Patchfoot and Leafstar as they weaved through the undergrowth. "What do you do if you meet a fox?" he puffed. "How can you practice fighting one?"

Leafstar flicked her ears to Patchfoot, indicating that he should answer.

"We practice the usual battle moves," the black-and-white warrior meowed. "They work on anything . . . foxes, other cats—"

"Badgers!" Snookpaw put in, waving his tail wildly.

"If you spot a badger, you tell a senior warrior right away," Billystorm warned him, flicking his tail sharply over his apprentice's ear. "Do *not* try fighting one on your own."

Leafstar nodded. "Even senior warriors wouldn't tackle a badger without plenty of backup," she meowed. "And you'd have to be pretty stupid to attack a fox alone. That's why we train apprentices to fight as a team."

"We'd like to learn that," Shorty commented, glancing over his shoulder at the other Twolegplace cat. "Wouldn't we, Cora?"

The black she-cat twitched her whiskers. "It would be useful."

"And what would you do if you found a strange scent on the border?" Shorty went on eagerly.

"The first job would be to protect the camp—" Leafstar began.

"We'd follow the scent and track down the intruder," Ebonyclaw meowed at the same moment.

"Huh?" Shorty glanced from one to the other, looking baffled.

Ebonyclaw seemed to realize that she had interrupted her Clan leader, and had given advice that directly contradicted her. She slapped her tail over her jaws and took a step back. "Sorry," she muttered through a mouthful of fur.

Leafstar took a pace toward her and rested her tail-tip on the embarrassed she-cat's shoulder. "We're both right," she purred. "Protecting the camp and tracking down the intruder are equally important. What we did first would depend on the number of warriors available."

"And apprentices!" Frecklepaw squeaked, her eyes gleaming.

* * *

The patrol prowled on through the undergrowth, setting scent markers as they went. With a *mrrow* of satisfaction Leafstar skirted the boulder where Firestar had set a marker when he first defined the SkyClan borders. The Clan had grown since then, and Leafstar had expanded the territory by setting the next marker on an ivy-covered tree stump several fox-lengths farther from the edge of the gorge. The change had brought a wide stretch of prey-rich woodland inside Sky-Clan's borders.

Patchfoot was heading for the Twolegplace when he suddenly halted; his jaws were open to taste the air and the fur on his neck began to rise. Leafstar stopped beside him and tasted the air for herself.

No! It can't be! Panic jumped in Leafstar's throat. *Not now, when the Clan is doing so well!*

The rest of the patrol was milling around confusedly, not knowing why Patchfoot and Leafstar had halted.

"What is it?" Frecklepaw called; the young cat sounded scared, and she flattened her ears as she gazed around as if she expected a fox to leap out of the undergrowth.

Shorty stepped forward to Leafstar's side and took a good sniff of the air. "Hey!" he exclaimed. "Even though we're on a border patrol, we're still allowed to hunt, right?" When none of the others replied, he glanced around, puzzled. "You do eat rats, don't you?"

The name of her Clan's worst enemy plunged Leafstar back into the memories she had tried so hard to forget: narrow rat faces with cruel eyes, snakelike tails, sharp claws, the over-whelming stench of rotting things. She felt once again the powerless surge of fury as the rat swarm rushed over her and her Clanmates, drowning them in a choking brown tide. She struggled to escape the barn; she gazed once more at Rainfur's body, bleeding from countless bites.

"Oh, wow! Rats! Just like in the stories!"

Frecklepaw's awed whisper brought Leafstar back to the present. She dug her claws into the ground to stop herself from fleeing back to the camp, chased by scenes she would never forget.

"Is something wrong?" Cora prompted, padding up with concern in her eyes.

Leafstar swallowed, forcing herself to speak calmly. "Sky-Clan had a lot of trouble with rats a couple of seasons ago," she explained. "We—"

"There were more rats than you could count!" Frecklepaw interrupted. "Cherrytail told me about it. They wanted to kill all the cats and take the gorge—"

"That's enough." Leafstar's voice was curt. *If the rats are back, we have troubles enough, without an apprentice frightening the whole Clan.* "We need to work out what to do."

"Maybe we should go back to camp," Ebonyclaw suggested, shuffling her paws.

Leafstar could see Patchfoot nodding; she would have liked nothing better than to agree, to turn her back on the problem and flee to the safety of the dens. *But that's not why StarClan made me Clan leader.*

"We need to check this out first," she meowed firmly, "and find out where the scent is coming from." To Cora and Shorty she added, "We won't hunt today."

Leafstar took the lead, creeping through the undergrowth with the patrol hard on her hindquarters. The scent of rat grew stronger, along with Twoleg scent and the stink of crow-food. The undergrowth around them became thicker and thicker, until it was hard to force a path through the stems; tendrils of bramble snagged the cats' fur and leaves clogged their ears and eyes, leaving them stumbling blindly.

Just when she thought they would have to turn back or risk getting lost, Leafstar crawled under a low-growing hazel branch and emerged into a clearing. In front of her rose a huge pile of Twoleg waste: bulging, shiny black pelts, some of them split and spilling out their contents onto the ground; squared-off red and gray stones like the ones Twolegs used to build their dens; huge things almost as big as monsters made of wood and some sort of soft pelt. The disgusting smells rolled out of the heap until they filled the air like fog.

"That . . . that's truly horrible," Leafstar whispered.

The other cats were pushing up behind her, and Leafstar stepped forward a couple of paces to let them into the clearing. For a few heartbeats they stood staring up at the mountain of waste.

"It's Twoleg stuff," Snookpaw declared, his voice full of contempt. "Why do they have to come and dump it here, in *our* territory?"

Ebonyclaw padded forward and sniffed at one of the huge things made of wood and pelts. "Why do they want to get rid of this?" she asked, bewildered. "It's a sofa!"

"What's a sofa?" Patchfoot growled, eyeing the object suspiciously.

"Twolegs keep them in their dens," Snookpaw explained, unable to hide his glee that he knew something his Clanmate didn't. "And that thing there's a chair. The Twolegs sit on them." He licked one front paw. "They're pretty comfortable, actually."

"Chairs, bricks, cushions . . ." Shorty was stalking around the outer edge of the pile. "Some Twoleg has cleared out the whole of their den!"

"There's chicken here." Cora had padded closer to the pile and was sniffing something that had spilled out of one of the black pelts. "Any cat want some?"

"You'd eat that?" Patchfoot gasped. "It looks as if it's been dead for a moon!"

"Where we come from, you'd be glad of it," Cora replied, gulping down some of the pale crow-food.

Leafstar was appalled, though she tried to hide it. *These cats must be starving!* She crept closer to the mound. With every heartbeat she was more outraged that Twolegs would leave a disgusting heap like this in the middle of the forest, destroying the territory with its stink and filth.

She was just stretching out her neck to sniff one of the soft pelt-things, when she heard the scuttle of tiny paws coming from inside the heap. The wedge-shaped head of a rat poked out from a gap beneath a piece of wood, its eyes glittering with hostility.

Startled, Leafstar leaped back. Even though the rat vanished at the same time, she couldn't tear her eyes away from the dark hole where it had appeared. Now she could hear the sounds of more rats inside the pile, squeaking and chewing and rustling with sharp yellow teeth and pointed paws, their naked tails flicking and coiling like tiny snakes. . . .

The whole heap is infested with them!

"We'd better get back to camp and report this," Patchfoot meowed at her shoulder.

"You're right," Leafstar replied, striving to make her voice as steady as his. "We must call a Clan meeting and decide what to do."

"But it's no big deal, surely?" Shorty protested as the patrol began to move off. "What's wrong with a few rats?"

"I don't see why we can't hunt them," Cora put in. "The Clan would eat well for days with the prey from here."

Leafstar didn't stop to argue. Cats who hadn't survived the terrible battle at the edge of Twolegplace would find it hard to understand why every hair on her pelt was prickling with horror.

As she sprang down the last couple of tail-lengths into the camp, Leafstar spotted Sparrowpelt returning with his patrol; they had been renewing the scent markers on the other side of the gorge. Sharpclaw was padding along the trail beside the river with his hunting patrol behind him; all of them carried fresh-kill.

Leafstar bounded across to intercept Sharpclaw as he headed for the fresh-kill pile. "I want you to round up all the senior warriors," she meowed. "Every cat who was here when we had the battle with the rats."

Sharpclaw cocked his head to one side. "Trouble?"

Leafstar nodded tensely. "I'll tell you when we're all together. Make sure Clovertail and Echosong come as well. We'll meet in my den."

"Can I come, too?" Stick asked, rising from a flat rock on the edge of the stream and bounding over to them.

"Sure you can," Sharpclaw replied, just as Leafstar was opening her jaws to refuse.

The Clan leader flashed an annoyed look at her deputy. *This is Clan business! We're not even including the daylight-warriors, and it affects them.* But she couldn't argue with Sharpclaw in front of Stick, so she gave the Twolegplace cat a curt nod and headed toward the trail that led up to her den.

By the time she reached it her Clanmates were beginning to arrive. Cherrytail and Sparrowpelt padded through the entrance together, dipping their heads to their leader before sitting side by side with their tails wrapped around their paws. Patchfoot appeared, looking grim, and a few heartbeats later Clovertail followed, with Petalnose at her side. Clovertail's belly was bigger than ever, and she was panting from the effort of the climb.

Sharpclaw and Stick were the last to appear, just behind Echosong, who slipped into the den and crouched beside the wall, her eyes fixed on Leafstar.

"That's every cat," the deputy announced. "What's all this about?"

Leafstar explained what the patrol had found as quickly as she could, trying to make the Clan see and smell the hideous pile of rubbish in the forest.

"Rats!" Cherrytail exclaimed, exchanging a horrified glance with her brother Sparrowpelt. "Don't say we have to go through all that again!"

"No, no, we can't!" Petalnose's voice rose in a piteous wail, and Leafstar knew that she was remembering the death of her mate, Rainfur. "We must all stay away from them—as far away as we can."

She sat with her head bowed; Clovertail pressed up against her side and gave her ear a comforting lick.

Stick listened to the she-cats with a puzzled look in his eyes. When Petalnose had fallen silent, he turned to Leafstar. "What's all the fuss about?" he meowed. "It's only a few rats."

"Only a few rats!" Patchfoot echoed, rolling his eyes.

"We've had problems with rats before," Sharpclaw told the visitor, describing how a vast family of rats had attacked the cats in the gorge until their only option had been to take the battle to them and wipe them out.

"One of our warriors died," he finished, "and all of us were injured. We can't let these rats get strong enough to attack us again."

The Twolegplace cat looked thoughtful. "We're used to hunting rats for food," he meowed. "Maybe we can help."

Leafstar was about to thank him and assure him that the Clan could cope, when Sharpclaw forestalled her. "That would be great. What do you think we should do?"

That's the second time Sharpclaw has made the decision for me. Leafstar twitched her tail irritably. *But maybe we should listen to what Stick has to say.* "Go ahead," she told him.

"Okay, suppose this is the rubbish heap." Sharpclaw pulled out several clawfuls of moss and bracken from Leafstar's nest and piled it up in the middle of the den. "The rats are in the middle, right? I suggest we take a patrol—as many cats as we can spare. Some of us should circle the pile and find the entrances where the rats go in and out. Then we block up most of them—"

"Why not all of them?" Cherrytail interrupted, lashing her tail with excitement.

"Because we don't want the rats trapped inside there," the brown tom explained. "We want them *gone*. We want them to think they have a chance to escape. So we leave a couple of entrances unblocked, and put our best fighters just outside." With one paw he poked two holes in the heap of bracken. "One or two cats climb over the dump to frighten the rats and chase them out. Then when they run out"—Stick slid out his claws—"no more problem."

He stared around at the SkyClan cats, his gaze focused and confident. Leafstar realized he was sure his plan would work. *And it just might,* she thought. *It's worth a try.*

"We could try pulling the heap apart, too," Stick went on. "That would drive the rats out."

Patchfoot wrinkled his nose. "Yuck!" he spat. "Have you seen that dump? It's *disgusting*!"

Stick shrugged. "You don't have to do that. But it's a way of finding food."

"You eat rats?" Sparrowpelt asked, his eyes stretched wide with dismay. "I'd sooner starve."

"So would I," Cherrytail agreed. "Just thinking about it makes me sick."

"Where I come from," Stick mewed drily, "you'll eat any sort of fresh-kill. I've often been thankful for a good plump rat."

Leafstar looked at her Clan, feeling ashamed and a bit guilty that they were being so picky. *We've never been really hungry,* she thought. *Maybe the time will come when rats won't seem so disgusting.*

"Right," Sharpclaw meowed, rising to his paws. "Stick, will you organize some training patrols to prepare for the attack? We weren't properly prepared last time; that's how we lost Rainfur."

A stab of anger pierced Leafstar like a claw. *Have I said that we'll go with Stick's plan?*

"Are you saying Firestar didn't know what he was doing?" she challenged, rising to confront Sharpclaw. "He's the cat who created this Clan out of nothing, or have you forgotten that?"

"That's not the point," Sharpclaw retorted, with a single lash of his tail. "I respect Firestar, but he didn't have Stick's experience with rats. And experience is what we need here. This time things will be different."

Leafstar gazed at the ginger warrior, shocked that he seemed to be rejecting everything that Firestar had done for SkyClan. Sharpclaw's green gaze met hers boldly. *Sooner or later, I'll have to talk to Sharpclaw about what's appropriate for a deputy and what isn't. But not now.*

Suppressing her anger, Leafstar dipped her head. "Stick, we'd all be grateful for your help. Sharpclaw will help you organize patrols."

"Fine." Stick turned to go, with Sharpclaw following.

The other warriors made their way out of the den after them, until only Echosong remained. Her eyes were calm and sympathetic as she padded up to Leafstar and brushed her pelt against her leader's.

"The Clan will face new challenges which we have to deal with on our own," she mewed. "Firestar didn't have time to teach us all he knew."

Leafstar guessed that Echosong was trying to say that Sharpclaw was still a loyal Clan cat. But it troubled her that Sharpclaw seemed to have more respect for Stick than he did for Firestar.

Firestar did everything for us. None of us know anything about Stick.

Thinking back, Leafstar had always known that there was tension between Firestar and Sharpclaw, especially when she had become leader and Sharpclaw was only deputy.

"Do you think Sharpclaw blames me for taking the leadership of SkyClan?" she asked Echosong.

The young medicine cat regarded her gravely. "You didn't *take* anything," she reminded her. "StarClan sent me a sign—a vision of dappled leaves to represent your name, Leafdapple. Firestar and I knew that our warrior ancestors had chosen you."

"But does Sharpclaw know it?" Leafstar muttered, half to herself.

"That's not the problem now." Echosong's voice was firm. "Every cat has to focus on getting rid of the rats."

Her certainty soothed Leafstar, though she still wondered if she had made the right decision. *Sharpclaw didn't give me time to think!* "Maybe we should let the rats stay and use them for fresh-kill," she suggested.

Echosong shook her head. "No, you were right with your first instinct. We should get rid of them as fast as we can." She paused to give her white chest fur a couple of licks. "Rats are SkyClan's oldest enemy," she meowed. Her green gaze seemed to travel out of the den and back into the distant past when the first cats of SkyClan had made their home in the gorge. "They are not prey. They are rivals for everything that Sky-Clan needs to survive."

When Leafstar climbed down from her den she spotted Mintpaw, Snookpaw, and Frecklepaw struggling to carry sticks and bramble tendrils up the gorge past the Rockpile.

"What are you doing?" she called.

Mintpaw dropped her bundle to answer. "Stick is building a waste pile in the training area. It's going to be *huge*! He says it'll help us learn how to fight the rats."

"I've got to see this," Leafstar meowed.

She padded alongside the apprentices; rounding the spur of rock that separated the camp from the training area, she stopped dead in surprise. An enormous mound of twigs, bracken, brambles, and other debris covered the middle of the open space.

How did Stick build something that big so quickly?

Most of the Clan cats were watching from the edge of the training area. Billystorm and Ebonyclaw were sitting under the overhang of the cliff, while Rockshade, Bouncefire, and Tinycloud crouched in the shadow of the mound; the young warriors were quivering with excitement, as if they could see their enemies in front of them and were ready to pounce. Shrewtooth, however, was hanging back, shifting uneasily from paw to paw. Cherrytail and Sparrowpelt were huddled together with Patchfoot at the far side of the area; Leafstar could hear that he was telling them more about the place where they had found the rats, in all its disgusting detail.

Meanwhile, Stick and Shorty stood beside the heap, their heads close together. Sharpclaw waited a fox-length away, listening intently.

"It should still be a couple of tail-lengths higher," Shorty decided. "And it was more . . . more close-packed. You could climb up it and it would take the weight of a cat."

"It would take too long to build something like that," Stick argued. "This will do to work out our plans. Well done," he added to the apprentices as they staggered up and dropped their burdens at the edge of the pile. "That's enough for now. Can you make some of this bracken into bundles about the size of rats?"

The apprentices got to work while Leafstar padded across the training area to join Sharpclaw.

Her deputy turned toward her, his eyes gleaming. "With the help of our guests, we'll soon show the rats they're not welcome here."

"We'll turn them into crow-food," Snookpaw growled. "Stick knows just what he's doing."

"Right!" Mintpaw exclaimed as she clawed a bunch of bracken into a rat-shape. "Maybe if he'd been here before, my father wouldn't have died."

Leafstar shook her head; she didn't believe that any cat could have changed the result of the first battle, however much they knew about rats. *You can't understand if you weren't there,* she thought.

Hearing a sigh, she glanced over her shoulder to see Petal-nose standing close by, her eyes full of sorrow at the mention of her dead mate. Leafstar eased back until she stood at her side.

"Rainfur didn't make any mistakes," Petalnose whispered to her leader. "He died fighting for his Clan."

"He was a fine warrior," Leafstar agreed, touching her nose to Petalnose's ear.

"Now they're talking as if he was stupid," Petalnose went on, her voice quivering with grief. "As if he went out unpre-pared to tackle an enemy that was too strong for him."

"Every cat who was there knows that isn't true," Leafstar comforted her.

Petalnose let out another long sigh, and leaned her head briefly against Leafstar's shoulder.

Leafstar watched Stick patting the last of the twigs and brambles into place. "That looks great," she mewed, not wanting to seem as if she begrudged praise for the visitors' help. "But the Clan still has mouths to feed. Some cats need to go on a hunting patrol. Sparrowpelt, will—"

"No," Sharpclaw interrupted, "every cat has to stay here for Stick's battle training."

Leafstar felt her claws slide out. *Who exactly is Clan leader here?* "We need to restock the fresh-kill pile," she declared firmly. "Stick can hold another training session in the morning."

"But we don't want to hunt," Cherrytail objected. "We want to learn to fight rats."

"Yes, that's more important than our next meal," Sparrowpelt agreed.

Leafstar raised her tail to cut short a full-scale argument, but before she could speak again Billystorm stepped forward.

"I'll lead a patrol if you like," he offered. "Ebonyclaw will come with me, and our apprentices. Shrewtooth, will you come as well?"

"Glad to!" the black tom gasped, looking relieved to be away from the terrifying preparations for battle.

Leafstar blinked gratefully at the kittypet. "Thanks. Go anywhere you like, but stay away from the rats."

"We'll hunt on the other side of the gorge," Billystorm promised, waving his tail to gather his patrol together.

Leafstar watched him lead his cats away, then turned back to the training area, where Stick was gathering the rest of the Clan together for the training session to start.

"I want to be the first cat to attack a rat," Mintpaw insisted, her fur bristling as she angled her ears at the rat-shaped bundle of bracken she had made. "Rainfur was my father, and this is my chance to avenge his death!"

"I want to fight, too." Sagepaw's disconsolate voice came from behind Leafstar; she turned her head to see the injured apprentice limping around the spur of rock with Echosong beside him. "It's not fair!"

"And us!" All four of Fallowfern's kits bundled up to the edge of the training area, scampering ahead of their mother. "We'll kill lots of rats!"

"No, I told you, you're only allowed to watch," Fallowfern meowed.

Leafstar stifled a purr of amusement. Her earlier panic was being replaced by a warm glow of pride as she watched her Clanmates rise to the challenge of the rats.

Is this what it takes to unite us as one Clan? Did StarClan *send the rats?*

CHAPTER 10

Leafstar reached the top of the gorge and crept into the under-growth, flinching as thorns scraped along her pelt. The moon had already set, but the stars shed enough light to show her, as she glanced back, the dark outlines of her Clanmates slipping onto the cliff top. The first glimmer of dawn had yet to show itself above the rocks.

Five sunrises had passed since Patchfoot's patrol had found the mound of Twoleg waste in the forest. Every cat had practiced Stick's battle moves until they could do them in their sleep.

And I have. Each night Leafstar's dreams had been full of thin faces and glittering, malignant eyes, the squeaking of rats and the stench of blood. *Now is the time to end it.*

A cool night breeze rustled the leaves above her head as Leafstar headed toward the rat heap. Sharpclaw and Stick had pressed up beside her, the other warriors following. Every cat kept low, gliding along the ground, their paw steps making no more noise than raindrops dripping from branches after a shower.

Suddenly a sharp snapping noise broke the silence. Leafstar

jumped, her heart beginning to pound.

Sharpclaw whipped around. "What was that?" he hissed.

Every cat had halted, their neck fur bristling, their gazes flicking warily to the shadows. Shrewtooth looked frozen with fright.

"Sorry." Bouncefire's voice came from the darkness at the back of the patrol, sounding embarrassed. "I stepped on a twig."

"Great!" Sparrowpelt grunted. "Now the rats know we're coming!"

"It doesn't matter," Stick assured him. "All the rats will do is hide deeper inside their nest. And they'll soon find out there's nowhere safe in there."

As Leafstar's heartbeat slowed, she waved her tail as a signal for the patrol to move on. She could feel the tension in the air now, like the sparks before a storm broke.

This is the first time I've led my Clan into battle. StarClan, please give us strength and bring all our warriors home safe.

The first faint light of dawn was filtering down into the forest. Leafstar's nose twitched as the breeze carried a foul stench toward her. A few fox-lengths ahead, the waste pile was just visible through the trees, pale in the half-light. Even if the rats had heard the patrol approaching, there was no time to change their plans.

This is it.

Leafstar signaled with her tail for the patrol to halt and turned to face her Clanmates. Sharpclaw turned with her; his eyes blazed with a green light and his dark ginger fur bristled.

Leafstar could almost taste his desire to avenge the death of Rainfur.

"You're sure you remember the plan?" he demanded, his gaze raking over the patrol. "We block most of the holes, then frighten the rats so they try to escape through the holes we've left open. And then . . ." He bared his teeth, giving Stick a glance to make sure he had repeated the loner's plan accurately.

Stick replied with a curt nod. "They won't know what hit them."

Leafstar began to feel more confident as she listened to her deputy and saw the determination in his eyes. *We can win this battle!*

She could see tension mounting even higher in the listening cats, in their twitching tails and flexing claws. Fear-scent came from the senior warriors, those who had battled the rats before, in spite of their struggles to hide it. The younger warriors picked it up, too; Shrewtooth was visibly trembling.

It's time to get on with this, Leafstar decided. *Before some cat starts to panic.*

"Sparrowpelt, you led a patrol here yesterday," she mewed softly. "Did you locate the exits from the heap?"

The young tabby tom nodded. "We didn't want to get too close," he explained, "in case the rats spotted us. But we think there are three gaps on the far side from where we are now, one on each side, and two in front—one up high where that piece of wood is poking out, and the other low down, underneath the Twoleg sofa."

Peering through the trees, Leafstar could make out the two front holes Sparrowpelt had mentioned: dark cracks leading into the center of the dump. She forced herself to stay calm as she thought of rats pouring out of them.

"We'll leave these two exits open," she meowed, relieved that her voice stayed steady. "Patchfoot, Tinycloud, and Petalnose, you go around the back and block the exits there. Cherrytail, you deal with the one on that side"—Leafstar gestured with her tail—"and Bouncefire, you take the one over there. When the holes are blocked, stay beside them, in case any rats try to force their way out."

She paused briefly, letting her gaze travel across the cats standing in front of her. "Sharpclaw, you're in charge of catching the rats as they come out of the front."

Her deputy didn't speak, but his eyes glittered and he gave a single lash of his tail.

"Waspwhisker, Sparrowpelt, Rockshade, Stick, Coal, and Shorty, go with Sharpclaw."

"And what about the rest of us?" Mintpaw asked, fluffing up her fur as if she wanted to make herself look twice her size. "We want to fight rats, too!"

"In a moment you'll have all the rats you want," Leafstar promised. "You and Cora and Shrewtooth will come with me, once the exits are blocked. We'll prowl over the heap and chase the rats out so Sharpclaw's patrol can deal with them."

Mintpaw's eyes glowed. "I'll *terrify* them," she hissed, extending her claws.

Dawn light was strengthening as Leafstar padded around

to the back of the heap, following Tinycloud, Petalnose, and Patchfoot. On the way they passed Bouncefire, who was struggling to push a chunk of wood up the side of the heap, toward a gap between two shiny black pelts. Leafstar gave him a nod of approval as she crept past, silently thanking Stick for all the practice in the gorge. Her confidence grew with every paw step as she saw how focused and determined her warriors were. Pride stabbed through her as she watched her Clan working together.

Then she remembered the fight with the rats in the barn, and her confidence ebbed as she pictured the hordes of evil creatures who had poured out from their hiding places with only one thought in their narrow skulls: *Kill cats!* Her breath choked in her throat as she recalled the horror of being overwhelmed in a tide of brown bodies, drowning in their reek and their stifling fur. She had barely fought her way out then.

Are there enough of us here? Maybe I should have brought the daylight-warriors, too.

She hadn't included them, because the attack had started too early for them to arrive from their Twoleg nests. Now she wondered whether it would have been better to wait.

But Sharpclaw didn't include them in the practices, so maybe he didn't think they'd have the strength to tackle the rats.

Shaking her head to clear it, Leafstar told herself that it was far too late to call up reinforcements. She halted and gazed up at the mound.

Great StarClan, it's big!

She had checked out the waste pile several times before,

but she had never come as close as this. The towering heap seemed to fill the whole sky, and its reek was all around her. It looked far more difficult to climb than the pile of sticks they had used for practice in the gorge. Rustling and scraping and the high-pitched squeaks of rats came from deep inside it, and Leafstar suppressed a shudder.

Beside her, Petalnose, Patchfoot, and Tinycloud were collecting sticks and lumps of wood and stone to block the three exits on this side. Cora padded up to her.

"Should we be climbing up now?" she murmured. "We need to be ready."

Leafstar nodded. She beckoned to Mintpaw and Shrewtooth, who were waiting a few tail-lengths away, and began to claw her way up the pile.

The stench grew stronger and flies buzzed around Leafstar's head as she climbed. Every hair on her pelt stood on end. Sometimes the heap felt sticky underpaw, and she tried not to imagine what might be clinging to her fur. *I don't look forward to licking that off, whatever it is!* Sometimes the pile gave under her weight, and she imagined it collapsing altogether, pitching her down into the rat-filled darkness. She could still hear the tiny rat noises; to her relief their enemies hadn't yet realized that they were under attack.

Leafstar had nearly reached the top of the pile when she heard the beginning of a yowl of alarm, quickly cut off. Glancing over her shoulder, she spotted Mintpaw a tail-length below her, clinging by her forepaws to a jutting piece of wood while her hind paws dangled in the air, her tail waving wildly.

"Sorry!" the apprentice squeaked, meeting Leafstar's gaze. "I slipped."

Scrabbling with her hind paws, she managed to haul herself up again. Leafstar tensed, all her senses alert for the rats to start pouring out before they were ready, but there was no change in the busy scratching and squeaking just beneath her paws.

"It's okay," she murmured, with a nod to Mintpaw. "They didn't hear you. Try to be more careful."

A fox-length below Mintpaw, Shrewtooth had frozen with his paws splayed out across one of the squashy Twoleg pelts and his eyes glazed with terror. Before Leafstar could speak, Cora scrambled up beside him.

"Come on," she whispered. "You're doing fine."

As Shrewtooth managed to put one quivering paw in front of the next, Leafstar felt grateful for the Twolegplace cat's level head and steady courage. *This would be a lot harder without Cora and her friends,* she admitted to herself.

At last Leafstar found a firm paw hold on a squared-off piece of stone, and let her gaze travel around the clearing. At the bottom of the pile, just below her, she could see Patchfoot, Tinycloud, and Petalnose, each braced against the blocked exits. Farther around, Bouncefire was in position; she couldn't see Cherrytail on the far side. The curve of the mound cut off her view of Sharpclaw and his patrol, but she had to assume that they were ready.

The SkyClan leader let her gaze sweep around one last time. Then she threw back her head and yowled, "SkyClan, attack!"

Her voice echoed through the forest, and the mound came alive beneath her paws. The rats' voices rose in squeals of mingled panic and fury. Leafstar could hear their frantic scrambling underneath her paws, and felt the stone she was standing on shift.

A rat's head popped out of the hole that Tinycloud had blocked, trying to force its way past the barrier of sticks and brambles. The small white warrior slashed it twice across its nose with one forepaw, and the rat vanished again.

"Well done!" Leafstar called out as Tinycloud shoved the sticks back into place. "Force them back! Sharpclaw and his cats will do the killing."

Petalnose was hissing furiously at two rats who were trying to escape through her exit, and Patchfoot darted across to help her. The sight of two enraged cats terrified the rats, who slid back into the mound without a blow being struck.

Reassured that her warriors knew what to do, Leafstar scrambled up to the very top of the heap, digging in her claws and yowling to frighten the rats out of the mound and into the claws of the waiting fighters. She caught glimpses of Cora and Mintpaw doing the same, while Shrewtooth perched on a spiky and battered Twoleg object with his pelt bristling and his jaws gaping in a spine-chilling shriek. The mound lurched under Leafstar's paws; new gaps were starting to open up. A wiry rat body broke into the open a couple of mouse-lengths from her nose, fleeing down the side of the heap before she could swipe at it. A sharp squeal from below, abruptly cut off, told her that another cat had been waiting for it.

Mintpaw appeared, clawing her way over the top of a Twoleg chair, her lips drawn back in a threatening snarl. Suddenly the chair gave way, sinking deeper into the waste, carrying the apprentice down with it into a gaping hole. Mintpaw let out a terrified screech, scrabbling vainly at loose debris as she sank into the depths of the mound.

Leafstar leaped forward and grabbed the she-cat's scruff before she disappeared altogether. Digging in her hind claws, she hauled Mintpaw upward. Two or three rats followed; one of them snapped at Mintpaw's tail. Leafstar, with her teeth still sunk in the apprentice's scruff, had no way of attacking, but the apprentice kicked out with her hind paws and caught the rat across the side of its head. It toppled off the mound in a flurry of waving paws and tail and vanished.

"Thanks," Mintpaw gasped as her Clan leader set her down on a more solid part of the heap.

"You did well with that rat," Leafstar panted.

From where she stood now, Leafstar could look down and see the battle at the front of the mound where the exits had been left open. Horror cramped her belly when she saw Sharpclaw and his patrol surrounded by a surging mass of rats. Every cat was spattered with blood.

StarClan, please let it be the rats' blood and not their own!

Stick's plan had been for two warriors to attack each rat, but the rats were too many, and too fast, for that. They squealed and scrabbled as the SkyClan warriors pounced on them, but there were always more to replace them. Leafstar spotted Rockshade just below her, struggling with a massive rat.

His paws slashed at the rat's flanks, but the creature had its teeth fastened in his shoulder, and Rockshade couldn't throw it off.

With a yowl of rage, Leafstar launched herself down the heap, her paws barely touching the side. With one swipe of her paw she tore the rat's throat open and it sagged to the ground, releasing its grip on Rockshade.

Leafstar flinched as blood came welling out of the wound she had made. *This is wrong; we should kill only to eat.* But she knew too well that if she and her Clan didn't succeed in wiping out the rats, they would become prey themselves.

"Thanks!" Rockshade grunted, whirling to block another rat as it fled from the heap toward the safety of the trees.

Leafstar reared up on her hind paws as she felt tiny claws fastening in her back fur. The rat fell off and scrambled away, squealing in terror, only to run straight into Sparrowpelt's paws.

A huge female rat crashed into Leafstar's haunches, with Shorty hard on its tail. The two cats battled side by side; still reluctant to kill, Leafstar found herself sheathing her claws as she gave the rat a blow on the side of the head.

"No!" a furious voice yowled from behind her.

Glancing back, Leafstar saw Sharpclaw; her deputy's dark ginger fur was soaked with blood, and there was a wild light in his eyes.

"Show no mercy!" he snarled. "Kill or be killed!"

He's right, Leafstar thought. Her claws slid out again, and she snatched at the she-rat's throat, while Shorty bit down on its neck from the other side. The rat squeaked and died, while Leafstar shared a brief glance of satisfaction with the Twolegplace cat.

The battle surged around her in a wave of fur and teeth. She winced with disgust as her paws slipped on blood-soaked grass. The air was filled with the reek of blood and the shrieking of cats and rats. Leafstar leaped and twisted and struck out instinctively, fighting to escape from her nightmare of glittering eyes and sharp fangs. She wasn't aware of her Clanmates any longer, only the wiry brown bodies that fell beneath her claws.

The rat under her paws stopped struggling. Leafstar spun around to face the next enemy and saw Cora standing in front of her. The Twolegplace cat's ear was ripped and there were toothmarks along her jaw; she stood still, her chest heaving. Beyond her, more cats were standing like islands in a lake of dead rats.

"It's over," Cora panted.

"No more rats." Sharpclaw made his way to Leafstar's side, his paws shoving aside rat bodies as he approached.

Leafstar looked around. Heaps of dead rats lay around her, and blood-smeared trails through the bracken and long grass at the edge of the clearing showed where a few of the rats had dragged themselves into the trees to die. The waste heap was torn apart into smaller piles, with separate bits of debris scattered all over the clearing.

The rats won't be able to use that as a refuge anymore.

The shrieking had given way to heavy silence, broken only

by the wheezing breath of Waspwhisker, who lay on his side a few fox-lengths away. Mintpaw was heading toward him, scrambling over the bodies of rats to reach her mentor's side.

"He's hurt!" she wailed.

Leafstar picked her way through the dead rats to reach her injured Clanmate. Waspwhisker was bleeding from a deep scratch down his flank; the wound stretched under his belly almost to his tail.

The gray-and-white tom lifted his head and blinked pain-filled eyes. "I'm fine," he rasped. "Just give me a couple of heartbeats to rest."

"You need more than that," Leafstar meowed, dipping her head to give Waspwhisker's ear a lick. "We'll help you back to camp and let Echosong take a look at you."

"I finished off the rat that did it," Waspwhisker murmured, lying down again and closing his eyes.

The rest of the cats gathered around him. All of them had some sort of injury—scratches, torn claws, nicked ears—though none as bad as Waspwhisker's or Cora's. Leafstar felt the sting of a scratch on her shoulder; she had never even noticed the rat who gave it to her.

"We won," she announced.

None of the cats responded; Leafstar met Sharpclaw's gaze, both cats acknowledging silently that this was not the time for celebration.

"Let's go back to camp," she meowed.

CHAPTER 11

❧

"*Waspwhisker, lie down here in the* sun," Echosong directed. "You too, Cora. The rest of you, go and wash yourselves in the pool below the Rockpile. Come back here when you're clean."

By the time the Clan returned to camp the sun was peering up over the top of the rocks, though patches of deep shade still lay in the bottom of the gorge. Leafstar and Cherrytail had helped Waspwhisker down the trail to the medicine cat's den; though the warrior kept insisting he was fine, he was exhausted by the time he collapsed in the patch of warmth just outside Echosong's cave.

Cora sat beside him and started licking his pelt to clear up the blood around the wound.

"Wash ourselves?" Patchfoot echoed disbelievingly as Echosong gave her last order. "In the pool?"

Murmurs of protest came from the cats behind him.

"I don't like getting into water," Petalnose complained. "Can't I just lick myself clean?"

"And it's dangerous," Shrewtooth added, casting a nervous glance to where the water surged into the pool from beneath the rocks. "Some cat might drown."

"I can't believe you expect us to get wet all over," Sparrowpelt grumbled.

"But that's what I said." Confronted with so many injuries, Echosong was trying to work efficiently, but Leafstar could hear a slight edge to her voice as she faced the protesting warriors. "I can't treat a wound if I can't see it, and you need to get rid of the stench of rat."

Sharpclaw flicked his ears irritably. "Come on. We'd better get on with it."

He led the way toward the pool and slowly lowered himself into the water, looking as if it felt worse than a rat bite. Reluctantly, the rest of the cats followed him.

Sagepaw limped out of Echosong's den, halting with a squeak of dismay at the sight of so many injuries. "You're *all* hurt!" he mewed, his eyes stretching wide.

"Yes, but you should have seen the rats," his littermate, Mintpaw, replied with grim satisfaction. "They won't bother us anymore."

More agitated squeaking filled the air as Fallowfern's kits tumbled down the trail, followed by their mother and Clovertail.

"Come back!" Fallowfern called, as the kits pelted toward Waspwhisker. "Don't get in Echosong's way."

The kits ignored her, climbing all over their father, who by now was barely conscious. He gave a grunt of pain, and Cora tried to thrust the kits back with one paw. "Don't do that," she told them. "You're hurting him."

"But we want to help!" Nettlekit protested.

Leafstar was heading over to intervene, when she spotted Shorty returning from the pool, shaking water from his pelt. He snaked his tail over Waspwhisker's back and gathered in the four kits. "Come with me, and I'll tell you all about the battle," he promised.

Instantly the kits bounced off their father and crowded around him.

"Did you kill lots of rats?"

"Was there lots of blood?"

"Will you show us your battle moves?"

Fallowfern padded up with concern in her blue eyes. "Be careful; you might frighten them," she murmured to Shorty.

The Twolegplace cat touched her shoulder reassuringly with the tip of his tail. "Don't worry. I won't tell them anything too scary."

Fallowfern gazed after Shorty as he herded the kits toward a flat rock near the water's edge, then followed Clovertail, who was speaking to Echosong.

"Tell us what we can do to help," the light brown she-cat meowed.

"Thanks, Clovertail. You could take over from Cora and get Waspwhisker cleaned up. Cora's wounded, too, and she needs to rest. And it would be a big help if you could fetch them both some water."

"I'll do that," Fallowfern mewed instantly, darting off toward the river.

Leafstar let her gaze travel around the gorge, making sure that all the injured cats were ready to be treated. Tinycloud, who had only a few shallow scratches on one side, was slipping in and out of Echosong's den, fetching her the herbs she asked for, no longer reluctant to help the medicine cat. Sharpclaw had washed off the blood from his own pelt and was making sure that the rest of the Clan did the same, firmly dunking Shrewtooth in the pool as the black tom shivered on the edge, then hauling him out again.

Reassured that no cat needed her help, Leafstar padded down to the pool and slid into the water. After the first cold shock she enjoyed the lap of the waves against her scratches, and the sight of rat blood streaming away from her fur. Relaxing, she looked up and saw three cats appear at the top of the gorge and begin scrambling down the trail: Billystorm, Ebonyclaw, and Frecklepaw. They picked up the pace when they spotted their injured Clanmates, and skidded to a halt among the cats waiting for Echosong.

"What happened?" Billystorm demanded. "Did you fight the rats?"

Frecklepaw's eyes stretched wide in horror at the sight of Waspwhisker, now lying on his side with his eyes closed. "Is he dead?" she whispered.

"Yes, we fought the rats," Patchfoot meowed proudly. "We set off before dawn this morning, and we ripped their pelts off. And no cat is dead. Waspwhisker will be just fine."

"Why didn't you let us know when the attack would be?" Ebonyclaw hissed with a lash of her tail. "We could have been useful!"

At the sound of anger in the black she-cat's voice, Leafstar hauled herself out of the pool and padded over to her. "We didn't leave you out because we don't value your help," she mewed, touching her nose to Ebonyclaw's ear.

Ebonyclaw twitched away from her. "Then why weren't we told?"

"We needed to use cats who were ready to leave at any moment," Sharpclaw put in, thrusting his way through the cats to Leafstar's side. "Including during the night."

"We could have been here if we'd been warned." Billystorm didn't sound as angry as Ebonyclaw, but he was clearly offended. Turning to Leafstar, he added, "Are you hurt?"

"Er, I'm fine, thanks," Leafstar replied, startled by the change of focus. "Just a scratch on my shoulder."

Billystorm leaned closer to give the wound a sniff. "That's more than 'a scratch,'" he commented. "You need some herbs. I'll fetch them for you—what should I look for?"

"Marigold!" Frecklepaw chirped. "I know what it looks like. I'll get it," she offered, racing toward the medicine cat's den. A moment later she returned with a mouthful of leaves, chewed them up carefully, and plastered the pulp onto Leafstar's injury.

"Echosong said you should make sure to let her have a look at it," she told Leafstar when she had finished. "Just in case I didn't do it right."

"I'm sure you did," Leafstar responded, flexing her shoulder. "It feels better already."

Frecklepaw's eyes sparkled. "I like watching Echosong," she admitted.

"Then you'd better go and see if you can help her some more," Leafstar meowed. "With so many warriors to treat, she'll be glad of an extra pair of paws."

"Thank you!" Frecklepaw dashed off again with her tail straight up in the air.

Leafstar let out an affectionate purr, then turned back to Ebonyclaw and Billystorm. Both cats were shifting their paws awkwardly, as if they felt out of place among so many battle-scarred warriors.

"I guess we could go on a hunting patrol," Billystorm suggested, with a glance at the black she-cat. "We need to restock the fresh-kill pile."

"Thanks, good idea," Leafstar meowed, though she felt uneasy as she watched them go. Two was a very small number for a patrol. Perhaps the Clan needed Harveymoon and Mac-gyver more than she had realized; she hoped they wanted to come back when their banishment was over.

The pain of Leafstar's scratch was ebbing, but she thought she had better let Echosong check it out, and then see if there was anything she could do to help. As she approached the medicine cat, she saw her instructing Frecklepaw, who was pressing a pad of cobweb against Rockshade's wounded ear.

"That's right," Echosong prompted. "Make sure all the edges are sealed. Good. Now you can collect another pawful of cobweb and treat that bite on Cherrytail's hind leg. Make sure the wound is really clean first."

"I will, Echosong," Frecklepaw mewed.

Meanwhile Echosong started patting marigold pulp

along Waspwhisker's scratch. "Tinycloud, fetch Waspwhisker a poppy head," she directed the white warrior. "Give him three seeds and no more. Now, Bouncefire, let's have a look at you."

Leafstar was impressed by the way the young medicine cat could think of three things at once, and treat the wounded warriors without keeping them waiting for long. Before she could find out if Echosong had a task for her, Sharpclaw came limping up; a nasty bite on his leg needed attention but the light of battle still gleamed in his eyes.

"They fought well," he meowed.

Leafstar wasn't sure who he meant. "The new warriors? Yes, they—"

"No, the Twolegplace cats," Sharpclaw interrupted. "We owe our victory to Stick—you know that, don't you?"

"He helped us a lot," Leafstar began, "but every cat—"

Sharpclaw interrupted again. "Any Clan would be lucky to have them as warriors."

Leafstar felt faintly surprised. "You think they should stay? They've only been here for a quarter moon," she pointed out. "And they haven't said anything about their plans."

Sharpclaw twitched his ears. "Maybe they're waiting for an invitation to join us," he suggested.

"Maybe." Somehow Leafstar wasn't so sure.

"We owe you a lot," Sharpclaw mewed to Coal, who padded up at that moment; Leafstar wondered how much the black tom had heard of their conversation. "Without you and your friends, we never would have defeated the rats."

Coal shrugged. "It's the least we could do in return for your shelter."

Leafstar's paws tingled with uneasiness. *Why are you here?* she wondered yet again. *What do you want, to make you risk your own pelts in battle, just because we let you stay here in the gorge?*

CHAPTER 12

The sun had gone down, leaving the uneven line of Twoleg roof-tops outlined against a scarlet sky. Stick clambered up a pile of Twoleg waste, pushing aside pieces of debris, his nose twitching. Last time he'd been here, the pile had been teeming with rats. Now all he could find were stale scents and droppings.

"Not a whisker," Cora spat, looking down at him from the top of the heap. "Some other cats must have cleaned the place out already."

"Dodge!" Stick hissed.

"We can't be sure of that," Cora pointed out. "There are other cats living here; any of them could have taken the rats."

"I know it's Dodge," Stick growled. "He doesn't want us living here, so he's trying to starve us." He jumped down from the mound, swiping bad-temperedly at an empty Twoleg box as he landed, and stalked away.

Before he had taken more than three paw steps, he glimpsed a flash of orange out of the corner of his eye. Spinning around, he saw Red sitting in the shadow of a wall.

"Where have you been?"

Red's neck fur fluffed up. "Around."

"Well, stay close by in future."

The flame-colored she-cat sprang to her paws. "Why?" she challenged. "I can look after myself."

"There are some dangerous cats around," Stick growled.

To his surprise Red bounded forward and pushed her forehead against his shoulder with an affectionate purr. "More dangerous than you?" she meowed, looking up; her eyes were glimmering with amusement. "Surely not!"

For a moment Stick wanted to cover her ears with licks as he used to when she was a kit. But those days were long gone. When he didn't say anything, he saw the amusement fade from Red's eyes.

"I'm going to see how Percy's getting on," she mewed, turning and stalking across the patch of waste ground.

Stick watched her go, sadness twisting in his belly.

"You won't tame that one so easily."

Stick jumped as he realized that Coal had padded up behind him. "I don't want to tame her," he responded gruffly. "I want to keep her safe."

"She's old enough to keep herself safe," Coal pointed out.

"She needs a mother."

Coal touched his tail-tip briefly to his friend's shoulder. "You've done the best you could."

"But it's not enough, is it?" Stick replied. "It won't ever be enough."

Stick padded across the waste ground, in the opposite direction from the one Red had taken. At the edge of the open space he leaped onto the fence and began walking along the top, balancing easily. The Twoleg gardens were deserted in the gathering night. Though lights showed in some of the dens, the shadows lay thickly where Stick prowled.

Stick's whiskers quivered and he opened his jaws to taste the air. *Rabbit!* His belly rumbled and water flooded his jaws, but he knew that this scent came from a rabbit in a Twoleg cage.

I'd be in more trouble than it's worth if I tried to catch it.

As Stick padded along the fence top the smell grew stronger. A new taint mingled with it: the scent of fear. Stick wondered if young Twolegs were trying to play with the rabbit again; he knew that the rabbit didn't like it. Then a terrified shriek rose from the garden just ahead. Stick froze. This wasn't because of clumsy young Twolegs. The rabbit was being *hunted*!

Stick bounded along the fence top until he came to the garden where the rabbit lived. Halting in the shade of a holly tree, he looked down at the shiny mesh cage in the middle of the smooth green grass. The black-and-white rabbit crouched close to the ground, while Misha and Skipper circled the cage. Their pelts bristled and their teeth were bared in a snarl. On the far side of the grass, the Twoleg nest was dark and silent.

"Stop it!" Stick called out. "That rabbit isn't prey."

Misha and Skipper halted and stared up at him.

"Oh, really?" Misha sneered. "You'd hunt it fast enough if you weren't scared of the Twolegs."

"I'm not scared!" Stick growled.

"Prove it!" Skipper challenged. "Help us catch this rabbit."

"No." Stick began to back away along the fence. *No good will come of this.*

But before he could leave, Skipper ran at the cage and rocked it upward with one massive shoulder. The rabbit shrieked again and shrank back into the corner farthest from the gap. Misha pressed herself to the ground and reached under the cage with one paw to drag the creature into the open.

The rabbit crouched on the grass, trembling, as first Misha, then Skipper darted at it, lashing out with their paws to rip its ears. Tufts of black-and-white fur drifted over the grass, and Stick spotted a dark stain beginning to spread on the rabbit's shoulder.

"Kill it cleanly, at least," he growled.

Misha looked up at him, her cream-colored pelt pale in the gathering darkness. "Make us."

She turned back to the terrified rabbit, motioning Skipper to stand aside. The rabbit tried to run; Misha let it cover a few tail-lengths before pouncing on it again and cuffing it around the head.

The rabbit let out a long, high-pitched wail and struggled as both cats returned to the attack. Its powerful fear-scent flooded over Stick and his belly growled with hunger. He slid his claws in and out, scoring the wooden fence. All his instincts were telling him to leap down and join in, to claim his share of the prey, but he knew what the result would be.

We can't afford to make enemies of the Twolegs.

Finally the rabbit collapsed, limp with shock, its chest heaving with fast, panting breaths. Stick couldn't bear to watch any longer. Leaping down from the fence he raced across the grass and shouldered Skipper away from the quivering creature.

"What do you think you're doing?" the ginger-and-white tom demanded.

"I'm going to put the poor thing out of its misery," Stick snarled.

"Don't think you get to share," Misha spat. "This is *our* prey."

Ignoring her, Stick lifted one paw to deliver a killing blow. At the same moment Skipper and Misha both threw their heads back and let out bloodcurdling yowls. A window in the Twoleg nest lit up; yellow light flooded over the grass. The door of the nest crashed open and loud Twoleg voices came from inside.

Stick glanced around. Misha and Skipper had vanished, leaving him alone in the middle of the lighted patch of grass, crouched over the shivering rabbit. The Twoleg yowling grew louder. A huge male Twoleg appeared in the doorway, brandishing a bristly wooden pole. His mate and two Twoleg kits followed him out, wailing, as he charged at Stick.

The rabbit scrambled to its paws and took off. Stick spun around and fled for the fence. Something sailed over his head and crashed into the bushes a tail-length away. Without looking back he scrambled to the top of the fence and ran along it, past the waste ground and down into the alley. The Twoleg yowling died away behind him.

Stick stood still, his heart thumping. He shivered at the thought of the Twoleg stick landing across his back, cracking his spine. *We keep our heads down around Twolegs. And now this happens.*

"Enjoy your fresh-kill, loser?"

Stick spun around as he recognized Skipper's voice. He and Misha were sitting farther down the alley in the shadow of some garbage cans, calmly cleaning their paws.

"I didn't hurt that rabbit, and you know it," Stick snarled, padding toward them. "You set me up."

"You set yourself up." Misha drew her paw over one ear.

"Maybe it'll teach you not to interfere in the future," Skipper sneered. He rose to his paws and padded forward until he stood nose to nose with Stick.

Stick tensed. He was here alone; if they attacked, he would be torn apart. He'd seen what Misha was prepared to do to another cat.

But Skipper stayed relaxed, and his voice was almost friendly, though Stick saw hostility gleaming in his narrowed eyes. "I've seen Red around a lot lately," he remarked. "Next time, it might be a tuft of her fur that's left beside a dead Twoleg pet."

"Leave Red out of this," Stick growled. "And don't make threats you can't keep."

"Oh, they're not threats." Misha spoke from behind Skipper, arching her back in a long, luxurious stretch and showing her sharp teeth in a yawn. "They're *promises.*"

CHAPTER 13

❧

Leafstar padded up to the fresh-kill pile and dropped her squirrel onto it. "We hunted well today," she observed.

Patchfoot nodded as he deposited his own prey—a mouse and two shrews—on the pile. Shorty had caught two mice, and Shrewtooth was pleased with himself for once, for chasing a rabbit and bringing it down.

The sun had risen above the gorge, but it was so early that dew still clung to the grass. The cats who had not been chosen for the dawn patrols were beginning to emerge from their dens. Sparrowpelt bounded down the trail, halted briefly at the bottom to give one ear a good scratch, then headed for the river to drink. Waspwhisker clambered down after him, slower and more awkward because of the wound from the rat battle. Leafstar padded across to meet him as he reached the foot of the trail.

"How do you feel?" she asked. "Is that scratch healing well?"

"I'm fine, Leafstar," the gray-and-white tom replied. "I'm just fed up with being stuck in the gorge. Please can I go out on patrol today?"

"Not until Echosong says you can," Leafstar told him, narrowing her eyes as she examined his wound. It still looked raw, and she guessed it wouldn't take much for it to open up again.

Waspwhisker slid out his claws and gave the ground in front of him a frustrated scrape. "I was afraid you would say that."

"Just be patient," Leafstar advised him. "It's only a few days since the battle."

"It feels like moons," Waspwhisker retorted gloomily; following Sparrowpelt to the water, he crouched down to lap.

Leafstar let her gaze travel around the gorge as more cats appeared. She could almost taste the sense of pride and strength that her warriors shared, united by the victory over the rats. They stalked confidently out of their dens, as if they were showing off their healing wounds.

We'll be back to full strength soon, Leafstar told herself with a purr of satisfaction.

Several cats appeared at the top of the gorge and began running lightly down the trail: Cherrytail was returning with her border patrol. The young tortoiseshell leaped down the last few tail-lengths and bounded up to Leafstar.

"We checked out the waste heap," she reported. "There was no sign of rats, and all the scents were stale."

"That's good news," Leafstar purred.

"Everything was quiet," Coal added, padding up behind Cherrytail. "We picked up the scent of a loner, but it seemed to lead straight out of the territory again."

Leafstar's whiskers twitched. "A loner? Where was this?"

"Between the rubbish heap and the Twolegplace," Cherrytail replied, flicking her tail to show Leafstar the direction. "Coal's right. The trail seemed to veer into our territory for a few fox-lengths and then head out again."

"Maybe the scent markers put it off," Coal suggested.

"You could be right." Leafstar gave one paw a reflective lick. It didn't seem as if the loner was a threat, but there was no harm in staying alert. "All the same, we'll keep an eye on that part of the territory, just in case it comes back."

The border patrol chose fresh-kill from the pile and settled down to eat. Leafstar found a flat, sun-warmed stone and sat with her tail wrapped around her paws, watching her Clan as the gorge stirred into full wakefulness.

The Twolegplace cats no longer stood out from the rest of the Clan: Coal was gulping down a sparrow and chatting to Cherrytail about that morning's patrol; Cora had joined Waspwhisker and Sparrowpelt at the water's edge, where Echosong was checking on Waspwhisker's wound; Shorty was telling yet another story to Fallowfern's kits, while Sharpclaw and Stick were prowling up and down near the foot of the Rockpile, discussing hunting techniques.

All four of the newcomers took part in their share of patrols, brought in a good amount of fresh-kill, and were gentle with the oldest and youngest members of the Clan. Leafstar was especially relieved that Sharpclaw and Stick were getting on so well. Her deputy's brusque manner could be off-putting, and he hadn't made any close friends within his own Clan.

I'm still sure there's something Stick's not telling us, she thought. *But he's fair and loyal to his friends, and I appreciate that.*

Loud meows from the top of the cliff announced the arrival of the daylight-warriors. Frecklepaw skidded down the trail in a cloud of sand, well ahead of the others, and came to a panting halt in front of Leafstar.

"I promised to prepare some herb poultices for Echosong before the first training session," she gasped. "Is that okay?"

Before Leafstar could reply, Echosong came bounding up. "Well done, Frecklepaw," she meowed. "You've got here really early." Blinking at Leafstar, she added, "It's all right if I borrow her for a while?"

Leafstar nodded, a bit surprised that Frecklepaw seemed to prefer helping the medicine cat to hunting or battle practice.

"Good," Echosong went on briskly. "Frecklepaw, I need a poultice of daisy leaves; Lichenfur has been complaining of back pain. And you'd better do some burdock root. I think a few of the rat bites will need another dose."

"Right, Echosong," Frecklepaw meowed happily, racing off toward the medicine cat's den.

Echosong watched her go, then headed to the waterside for a drink. Leafstar followed her and hesitated for a moment as the medicine cat lapped.

"Do you trust Frecklepaw to work without you to keep an eye on her?" she asked eventually.

The young silver tabby turned to her, scattering shining drops from her whiskers. "Oh, yes. Frecklepaw knows what she's doing. She—"

Echosong broke off at the sound of her name being called. Frecklepaw had popped her head outside the den.

"We're really low on tansy," she reported. "And if Lichenfur has a bad back, she'll probably need some."

"You're right; thanks for spotting that," the medicine cat replied.

"I could look for some while I'm out training," Frecklepaw offered.

"That would be really helpful," meowed Echosong.

With a happy *mrrow* Frecklepaw disappeared inside the den again.

"She's learned a lot," Leafstar meowed, impressed.

Echosong nodded, then turned back to the river, crouching down to lap a few more mouthfuls of water. In a couple of heartbeats she stood up again, swiping her tongue around her jaws to catch the last drops. "I need to think about finding an apprentice," she remarked.

"You mean Frecklepaw?" Leafstar had just seen for herself the young cat's enthusiasm and competence, but she wasn't sure that she was the right choice for Echosong. "Can a medicine cat live part of the time with Twolegs?"

"I don't know," Echosong admitted. "But Frecklepaw has natural talent, and she enjoys the work. She learns quickly, too."

Leafstar still wasn't convinced. "Has StarClan sent you any signs about this?" she asked.

Echosong shook her head. "I don't think I need a sign, when Frecklepaw is perfect for the job."

Leafstar couldn't agree. This was far more difficult than accepting kittypets into the Clan as warriors. A medicine cat needed to have a special link with StarClan; Leafstar didn't know if their ancestors would accept a cat who was not a full member of a Clan. "I'll think about it," she promised.

Echosong dipped her head in acceptance, but Leafstar could see she wasn't happy with her reply. "I'd better get on." The medicine cat spoke more curtly than usual.

"Yes . . . fine." Leafstar flinched at the tension that had sprung between them. "Send Frecklepaw out as soon as you can. She's supposed to be hunting with Ebonyclaw."

Echosong nodded and stalked off.

Leafstar watched her go with an unaccustomed feeling of helplessness. She had grown used to being challenged by Sharpclaw over her decisions about the daylight-warriors; she hadn't expected the same challenge from a cat she regarded as her closest friend in SkyClan.

"Full moon tonight!" Tinycloud gave an excited little bounce. "Rockshade, I'll race you up to the Skyrock!"

Leafstar, coming across the two young warriors on her way down from her den, was about to remind them that they weren't apprentices any longer. The trail that led up to the ledge under the rim of the gorge was narrow, and there was a dangerous jump from there to the Skyrock itself. As warriors, they should know better than to take stupid risks.

But before she could speak, Cora looked up from where she was sunning herself with the other visiting cats. "What's the Skyrock?" she meowed.

"That, up there." Rockshade raised his tail to point at the flat ledge jutting out over the gorge. "The whole Clan meets there when the moon is full."

"Why?" Coal asked, getting up to join the younger warriors. "Can't you meet down here in the gorge?"

"It has to be a special place," Tinycloud explained. "And up there we're closer to StarClan—that's the spirits of our warrior ancestors."

Coal exchanged a mystified glance with Shorty. "Warrior ancestors? What are you meowing about?"

Leafstar stopped to listen but stayed in the background, interested to know what the visiting cats would think about the idea that the spirits of their ancestors watched over them. *Or do they? Maybe it's only Clan cats who go to StarClan when they die.*

"Every moon we hold a Gathering on the Skyrock," Tinycloud began. "We tell StarClan what has been happening in the Clan, and we discuss stuff."

"Er . . . sounds interesting," Stick mewed, looking mystified.

"Back in the forest where Firestar lives," Rockshade went on, "there are four Clans. They meet at the full moon, too, and exchange their news, and there's a truce so they're not allowed to fight one another."

"We can't do all of that, because we're only one Clan," his littermate meowed, sounding rather disappointed. "But we still Gather. It's what Clan cats do."

The Twolegplace cats were silent for a moment.

"So . . . you go up to the top of the cliff to talk to dead cats?" Shorty meowed at last.

"No, that's not exactly what we do," Tinycloud objected, with a glance at Rockshade; she sounded confused, as if she wasn't sure what else she could say to make the visitors understand what a Gathering was.

"I guess you have to be there . . ." Rockshade began.

Leafstar padded forward, deciding that it was time to intervene. "Tinycloud, Rockshade, go find Sharpclaw. He'll be organizing the hunting patrols. Off you go."

The warriors bounded off at once, looking distinctly relieved.

"You'll find out all about the Gathering later," Leafstar reassured the other cats.

"Oh, are we invited?" Cora asked, sounding pleased.

"Every cat comes," Leafstar told her. *And if you're going to join this Clan,* she added to herself, *you'll have to learn about StarClan sooner or later.*

Leafstar padded in the paw steps of the two young warriors, toward the center of the camp. She glanced over her shoulder as she heard Billystorm call her name.

"Leafstar, could you give me a couple of moments, please?"

Billystorm was padding down the trail with his apprentice Snookpaw just behind. "I . . . er . . . I want you to check out the hunting move I've been teaching Snookpaw," he explained. "I'm not sure he's got it quite right. Could we go to the training area?"

"Sure." Leafstar felt faintly uneasy. Billystorm looked as if he had more on his mind than a hunting move. *More trouble between the daylight-warriors and the Clan cats?* she wondered.

When they reached the training area, Billystorm waved Snookpaw into the middle of the empty space. "I've been showing Snookpaw how to leap onto a rabbit's back and roll it over before it can run. Snookpaw, show Leafstar."

The apprentice dropped into the hunter's crouch and crept up on his imaginary rabbit. Leafstar watched approvingly as he waggled his haunches and leaped into the air, coming down on all four paws and flipping himself onto his back as if he was gripping the rabbit in his claws.

"That looks fine to me," she meowed. "Snookpaw, you might want to keep your legs tighter to your body as you roll. That way, you'll keep a firmer hold on the rabbit."

"Thanks, Leafstar." Snookpaw scrambled to his paws and shook sand from his black-and-white pelt.

"Why don't you practice that a few times?" Billystorm suggested. "We'll watch you."

The apprentice nodded and crouched down again, creeping low across the open space.

"You've taught him well," Leafstar commented. "Now, what is this *really* about?"

Billystorm looked guilty. "I wanted to know," he began, "whether the visitors have said anything to you about their plans."

That was the last question Leafstar had expected him to ask, yet on reflection she realized she shouldn't be surprised.

The whole Clan must be speculating about what the Twolegplace cats want.

"No," she meowed, annoyed that she sounded defensive. "They haven't told me anything."

"Maybe you should ask them." Billystorm hesitated, and then went on, "I've seen them leading patrols of SkyClan cats in Twolegplace."

Leafstar's belly lurched and she felt her neck fur beginning to bristle. "That's not possible. No patrols go hunting in Twolegplace."

"I saw them." Billystorm leaned closer toward her, his amber eyes full of concern. "Last night I was sitting on the wall around my housefolk's garden, in the shade of a thick bush. No cat could have seen me from below, and the flowers on the bush hid my scent. They walked right past me: Stick and Sharpclaw, Mintpaw and Rockshade."

Leafstar met his worried gaze. "You must have been mistaken," she meowed, trying to sound calm.

Billystorm shook his head, but he didn't seem inclined to argue. Inside, Leafstar felt puzzled and unsure. She could imagine some of the younger warriors setting off to explore Twolegplace, imagining it would be an adventure. *But Sharpclaw is Clan deputy! What was he doing there?* She didn't like the fact, either, that he had taken Mintpaw, whom he was mentoring while Waspwhisker recovered from his wound. *The Twolegplace is no place for an apprentice.*

As she watched Snookpaw practice his move, possibilities drifted through her mind like clouds. Had Sharpclaw and the others been chasing off a dog? If so, why hadn't he reported it?

"You can stop now, Snookpaw," she called as the apprentice leaped and rolled once again. "You've got the move down."

Snookpaw scrambled up and bounced over to his mentor at the edge of the training area. "Can we go and try it for real?" he puffed.

"Tomorrow," Billystorm promised. He added, "You would catch even more rabbits if you were a bit thinner." He gave his apprentice a gentle prod in the side.

"Aw, but I have to eat two lots of food every day!" Snookpaw protested. "My housefolk get really upset if I don't eat theirs. And they've made it extra tasty lately."

"You poor thing, I feel so sorry for you," Billystorm murmured. He caught Leafstar's eye, and they shared an amused purr at the way Snookpaw seemed genuinely downcast. Leafstar shoved the thought of Sharpclaw leading a patrol into Twolegplace to the back of her mind. SkyClan was strong and contented now, with the rats safely defeated. There was no need to go looking for trouble by challenging her deputy on something that might have a perfectly innocent explanation.

As the last scarlet traces of sunlight faded from the sky, Leafstar kept casting glances toward the top of the gorge. This was the time when Harveymoon and Macgyver were allowed to come back to the Clan.

But will they want to? Surely they should be here by now.

All the other daylight-warriors had stayed late in the gorge so they could attend the Gathering. Snookpaw and Frecklepaw were part of an excited huddle with their fellow apprentices, while Billystorm and Ebonyclaw waited with Patchfoot and Petalnose for the signal to climb the trail.

"I wonder if I was too harsh with Harveymoon and Mac-gyver," Leafstar murmured to herself. As Echosong padded past with a bunch of yarrow leaves, she meowed out loud, "Echosong, do you think I should have banished those two daylight-warriors?"

"'Course," the medicine cat mumbled around her mouthful of herbs. "They've got to learn." She headed for her den to store the leaves away.

Leafstar watched Echosong's fluffy tail whisk out of sight. *I'll feel a lot better when they arrive. But what will I do if they don't come back?*

Excited squeaking broke out behind her as Fallowfern brought her kits down from the nursery. "Nettlekit, sit still," she ordered. "Your neck fur is all rumpled, and I can't lick it straight when you're bouncing around like that."

Leafstar turned to watch the kits bundling around their mother.

"I'm going to sit on the Skyrock!" Plumkit announced. "I'm going to jump right over the gap and sit with the warriors!"

"You certainly are *not*," her mother scolded, pausing in her firm tongue strokes over Nettlekit's neck. Her sharp gaze traveled over her kits. "The Skyrock is for warriors. Besides, you're too young to leap across the gap, and if even *one* of you tries it, all four of you will go straight back to the nursery."

"But—" Rabbitkit protested.

"Not another word. You're only kits; you can't possibly jump that far."

"Can too," Plumkit muttered; her mother flicked her over the ear with the tip of her tail.

Leafstar was distracted from the antics of the kits as Wasp-whisker limped past. "How is your wound?" she called to him. "Do you think you can leap across to the Skyrock?"

The gray-and-white tom nodded determinedly. "I'll be fine, Leafstar."

She wasn't certain, but before she could protest she heard yowls of greeting coming from the top of the cliff. Relief rushed through her from nose to tail-tip as she recognized the outlines of Harveymoon and Macgyver.

"Hey, look who's here!" Patchfoot exclaimed as the two daylight-warriors raced down the trail.

Their Clanmates clustered around to welcome them back to the Clan, and Leafstar let out a sigh of relief. *Now maybe we can carry on and put their bad behavior behind us.*

As the initial excitement died down, Harveymoon spotted the Twolegplace cats, who were sitting together in the shadow of the Rockpile. His white neck fur started to fluff up. "Who are they?" he demanded, flicking his ears in their direction.

"They're cats from another Twolegplace," Rockshade explained, springing to his paws and padding over to the visitors. "Firestar met them on his way here. This is Stick," he began, touching each cat on the shoulder with his tail-tip as he spoke their name, "and this is Cora, Shorty, and Coal. These are Harveymoon and Macgyver," he told the visitors. "They . . . er . . . they haven't been here for a while. They're kitty . . . I mean, *daylight*-warriors like Billystorm and Ebonyclaw."

Stick dipped his head. "We're glad to meet you."

Harveymoon and Macgyver didn't look as if they wanted to return the compliment. "What are they doing here?" Macgyver asked.

"They're just staying here for a while," Patchfoot replied. "They've been helping us out."

"What, with hunting and everything?" Harveymoon sounded shocked.

Leafstar suppressed a sigh. The questions were natural enough, she supposed, but did he have to sound so unwelcoming?

"They've been great, actually," Sharpclaw meowed. "We would never have won the rat battle without them."

"Rat battle?" Macgyver spun around to face the Clan deputy. "What rat battle?"

"There was this huge heap of old stuff that the Twolegs left on our territory." Cherrytail's eyes stretched wide with excitement as she began to explain. "It was *full* of rats."

"We found it on patrol," Patchfoot added. "We had to get rid of the rats, and Stick and the others knew what to do. They have a lot of trouble with rats in their Twolegplace."

"They *eat* rats," Mintpaw chipped in.

"Stick built a practice heap here in the gorge," Petalnose went on, "and we all learned the right moves for fighting rats."

"Then we sneaked up to the heap one night. . . ." Bounce-fire began to describe the attack, how the Clan had blocked up all but two exits and driven the rats out into the claws of the waiting warriors.

"I was badly wounded," Waspwhisker told the kittypets, proudly turning sideways to display his scar. "I might have died if it wasn't for Echosong."

"But no cat died," Sharpclaw finished. "And we owe that to our visitors."

"I wish I'd been there," Macgyver meowed enviously as he gave Waspwhisker's scar a sniff. "I'd have killed loads of rats."

"Oh, you wouldn't have been there anyway," Rockshade told him. "It was too early in the morning for you."

"None of the daylight-warriors were there," Mintpaw mewed, as Harveymoon and Macgyver looked puzzled.

"But the Twolegplace cats were there?" Harveymoon checked, sounding offended.

"Yes, they organized the attack," Cherrytail replied.

Harveymoon and Macgyver exchanged a hurt glance. Leafstar could feel the rising tension. She was annoyed with Rockshade and Mintpaw for not being more sensitive—and with herself for doubting yet again that it had been the right decision to exclude the daylight-warriors.

As she caught Sharpclaw's eye, the deputy stepped forward. "That's all in the past," he mewed. "Tonight's the Gathering, and it's time we were off." He waved his tail and stood back for Leafstar to lead the way up the trail that led to the Skyrock.

I shouldn't worry so much, Leafstar told herself as she took her place at the head of her Clan. *Harveymoon and Macgyver probably just feel left out. And that might not be a bad thing, if it makes them better warriors.*

The moon cast soft silver light onto the cliffs, turning everything gray, as the cats of SkyClan reached the Skyrock. Leafstar felt her paws tingle when she jumped across the gap from the edge of the cliff to the ledge that jutted out over the gorge. This was the place where Firestar had shown StarClan to her, and where she had received her nine lives from the spirits of those long-ago cats.

Wind whispered over the surface of the rock as more cats joined her. Now that SkyClan had grown so big, there was only room for the senior warriors. The newly made warriors, Tinycloud, Rockshade, and Bouncefire, sat closest to the edge on top of the cliff, with Mintpaw and Sagepaw just behind them. The daylight-warriors sat a tail-length or so away, as did the visitors; Leafstar noticed with a pang of uneasiness that the three groups of cats were keeping themselves separate, even though there didn't seem to be any outward hostility among them.

Clovertail, Fallowfern, and her kits sat on a pile of curved stones at the end of the trail, a few tail-lengths from the gap. The two she-cats enclosed the wriggling kits with their tails, to make sure none of them tried to jump across. Lichenfur and Tangle joined them; the two elders had hauled themselves up the trail, complaining every paw step of the way, but

Leafstar knew that neither of them would dream of missing a Gathering.

When her Clanmates had settled down, Leafstar sat in silence for a heartbeat or two, gazing up at the full moon and the stars. It was easy to imagine that the cats she had met when she received her nine lives were looking down at her now.

What do they think about the way I'm leading their Clan?

She took a deep breath and let her gaze travel around the circle of warriors. "I, Leafstar, leader of SkyClan, call upon my ancestors to look down upon these cats," she began. These Gatherings were still unfamiliar, and she was sharply aware that she was forging traditions that her Clan would follow for season after season. *I need to get it right.* "Since last we Gathered on the Skyrock, we have defended our territory against a horde of rats. Every cat fought bravely and took wounds for the sake of our Clan. I commend especially Waspwhisker, who almost died in the fight, and Patchfoot and Sparrowpelt, who were particularly vigilant in keeping watch on the rats until we were ready to attack."

The three cats she named blinked proudly at her praise; Sparrowpelt gave his shoulder fur a couple of embarrassed licks.

"I also need to mention Frecklepaw," Leafstar went on. On the flat part of the cliff, the apprentice jumped and gazed wide-eyed at her leader, as if she was afraid she was going to be scolded for something in front of the whole Clan. "She worked hard to help Echosong care for the wounded warriors," Leafstar went on, "and she has learned a great deal about herbs and how to treat injuries."

Could she be a medicine cat? StarClan, please give me a sign!

But there was no response from the stars, glittering icily above her head. Leafstar spotted Echosong giving the young tabby an approving nod, and Frecklepaw ducked her head in response, her eyes shining.

"Visitors have arrived in the gorge, from a Twolegplace downriver." Leafstar went on with her report. "Stick, Shorty, Cora, and Coal have settled down well during their stay in the Clan, and we thank them for the help they gave in fighting against the rats."

Is this the time or the place to invite them to stay with us for good? Leafstar asked herself, aware of Sharpclaw's green gaze boring into her like a woodpecker attacking a tree. *No—and I'm not going to ask them what they are going to do next. I need to find a more private place for that.*

To her surprise, Stick rose to his paws and padded to the very edge of the cliff. "Thank you, Leafstar," he meowed, inclining his head formally to her. "We're all grateful for Sky-Clan's hospitality. We're glad that we were able to help you with the rats."

Leafstar dipped her head in reply, and the visiting cat withdrew again to sit beside his friends.

"Now," she went on, glancing once more around at her warriors, "does any cat have a question or a problem that they want to discuss?"

"I do." Clovertail rose to her paws and stretched her neck to look over the cats sitting in front of her. "I'd like to use one of the new dens as a birthing den. I know we drove off the rats, but if they come back, or if a fox or a badger finds its way into the gorge, one of those upper dens would be much safer for young kits."

"It would be easier for them to fall out, though," Petalnose warned.

Clovertail twitched her ears. "I know. We'd need to move the kits back into the nursery once they were strong enough to go outside."

Leafstar guessed that Clovertail was worried that her new litter would be overwhelmed by Fallowfern's rambunctious kits if they were born in the nursery. *She could have a point.*

"Very well," she replied to Clovertail. "Let's move you over there in the morning, and we'll see how it goes when your kits are born. Mintpaw and Sagepaw, please fetch bedding for Clovertail and make sure she's comfortable."

"We will, Leafstar," Mintpaw called out.

"Thank you. And if all goes well, we'll make the arrangement permanent."

Clovertail thanked her and sat down again.

Harveymoon and Macgyver got up and stepped up to the edge of the cliff, glancing at each other as if they weren't sure which one of them was going to speak first.

"We're glad to be back," Harveymoon meowed in a rush.

"We're looking forward to being part of SkyClan again," Macgyver added. "We've learned not to be so stupid."

"Good," Leafstar purred. "We're happy to welcome you back."

"I'd like to suggest something," Petalnose mewed as the two kittypets sat down again. "What about a special rat patrol, just to make sure that they don't return to that pile of stuff?"

"Good idea!" Shrewtooth agreed, flattening his ears.

A babble of comment broke out; Leafstar let it continue for a few moments before raising her tail for silence. "Sharpclaw, what do you think?"

The deputy paused for a moment, his green eyes narrowed. Finally he shook his head. "I don't think it's necessary. The border patrols and hunting patrols will spot any signs of rats in the territory."

Leafstar nodded. "I think you're right. But if there *are* any fresh signs of rats," she added to Petalnose, "then we'll set up a rat patrol right away."

"Thank you, Leafstar," Petalnose replied, seeming content with that decision.

"What about that loner my patrol scented near the rubbish heap?" Cherrytail asked. "Do we need to do anything?"

"Did the evening border patrol spot anything?" Leafstar meowed.

"We picked up the stale scent," Billystorm, who had led the patrol, replied, "but nothing new."

"Then I don't think there's anything we can do," Leafstar decided. "Except that all patrols should keep a good lookout in that area."

She was about to draw the Gathering to a close, when Lichenfur hauled herself to her paws, shaking her rumpled pelt. "What about the bedding in our den?" she demanded. "I don't think the moss has been changed for a moon."

Leafstar spotted Mintpaw open her jaws to protest, and Sagepaw quickly flicked his tail across her mouth. His sister glared at him, but kept quiet.

"Sorry, Lichenfur," Snookpaw called out. "I'll fetch some more as soon as I get here in the morning."

Muttering, the elder sat down again and leaned across to mew something into Tangle's ear.

When none of the other cats spoke, Leafstar rose to her paws. "We thank StarClan that our Clan is safe and thriving, and that prey is plentiful. The Gathering is at an end."

She watched as her senior warriors leaped back over the gap, with Sparrowpelt watching Waspwhisker carefully to make sure he didn't fall, and began to pad down the trail toward the camp. At last only she, Sharpclaw, and Echosong were left.

"I thought that went well," Leafstar commented. "There don't seem to be any serious problems."

"For now," Sharpclaw meowed, giving his chest fur a couple of thoughtful licks. "I heard what you said about Frecklepaw," he continued. "It sounds as if you're going to make her Echosong's apprentice."

"I'm thinking about it," Leafstar responded guardedly.

Sharpclaw's eyes stretched wide. "Have you got bees in your brain? You must know it's impossible."

"Why?" Echosong slid out her claws and her neck fur began to bristle; Leafstar hadn't often seen the gentle young tabby look this annoyed.

"Why do you need to ask?" Sharpclaw sounded exasperated. "She's a kittypet!"

"She's a SkyClan apprentice," Echosong retorted. "And she has an exceptional talent for healing. I wish I'd learned as quickly when I first came here."

Sharpclaw's tail-tip twitched. "But half the time she isn't here. I don't care how talented she is. What happens if a warrior is injured while their medicine cat is snoozing in a Twoleg nest?"

"And what happens if I'm killed before I've trained an apprentice?" Echosong hissed back. "The Clan wouldn't *have* a medicine cat."

"There are other possibilities," Sharpclaw argued.

"Name one!"

Leafstar stretched out her tail to separate the two angry cats. "Echosong is right that there's no full Clan cat with any interest in healing," she meowed carefully. "Being a medicine cat demands true dedication."

"But there are kits growing up all the time," Sharpclaw pointed out. "Fallowfern's four, and Clovertail's new litter. Maybe one of them—"

"And maybe not," Echosong snapped.

"We don't have to decide now." Leafstar realized she needed to bring this discussion to a close before either of the quarreling cats said something they would regret later. "Echosong, have you had any sign yet from StarClan about Frecklepaw?"

Echosong shook her head. "I've looked for one, Leafstar, but there's been nothing yet."

Sharpclaw let out a snort of contempt. "And there won't be!"

Leafstar glared at him. "We don't know that. It's in the paws of our ancestors. And maybe this can all be resolved easily," she went on. "Frecklepaw might decide to come and live permanently in the gorge. But Echosong, you're not to put any pressure on her."

"I wouldn't do that, Leafstar," the medicine cat promised.

"Then let's wait and see what happens. You'll let me know if you do have a sign—whatever it seems to say?"

Echosong nodded. "Of course."

Leafstar stood up and stretched each hind leg in turn. "Come on, let's get back to our dens."

The young medicine cat was the first to leave, dipping her head to Leafstar and shooting an icy glare at Sharpclaw before running lightly across the Skyrock and leaping across the gap.

"Sharpclaw, please don't ruffle her fur," Leafstar murmured.

"Then make sure she stays out of mine," Sharpclaw retorted.

CHAPTER 14

❧

Fluffy white clouds were building up above the gorge when Leafstar emerged from her den on the morning after the Gathering. The sun had not yet risen, and a stiff breeze buffeted her fur. She yawned and gave herself a quick grooming as she watched her Clanmates trot down the pathways to the Rockpile. Bounding down to join them, she found Sharpclaw setting the patrols.

"I'll lead the border patrol," he announced. "Stick, Billy-storm, and Tinycloud, you come with me. Sparrowpelt, I'd like you to lead a hunting patrol, with Shrewtooth, Cora, and Rockshade. Shorty, you lead the other hunting patrol, with—"

"Hey, Shorty's not a warrior," Patchfoot interrupted. "Should he be leading a patrol?"

Sharpclaw gave his tail an irritable twitch. "Sorry, you're right. You lead the patrol, then, Patchfoot. Shorty can go with you, with Bouncefire and Harveymoon."

Leafstar looked on with approval as the patrols started to move off. She liked to see her Clan like this, busy and well organized. *This is a new day; StarClan grant that all last night's tensions have vanished.*

"Are you coming, Snookpaw?" Billystorm called, glancing back at his apprentice as Sharpclaw led his patrol toward the bottom of the trail.

"Sorry, I can't," Snookpaw replied. "I promised to fetch fresh moss for Tangle and Lichenfur."

"Fine." Billystorm nodded. "We'll do some battle practice when you get back."

"Great!" Snookpaw's tail shot straight up into the air as he clambered over the Rockpile and bounded across to the other side of the river.

Leafstar was impressed with the young cat's loyalty to the promise he made last night to the elders. *He'll make a fine warrior. I hope he decides to stay with us full time.* She watched Snookpaw creep along the narrow ledge beside the stream until he disappeared into the tunnel from where the water flowed out beneath the Rockpile. Leafstar pictured him shuffling along the tiny stone path that led to the Whispering Cave where the moss grew.

With the patrols gone, the other cats settled down to rest, eat, or share tongues. Ebonyclaw took Frecklepaw up to the training area for some practice; Leafstar spotted the apprentice casting a longing look back at Echosong's den as she padded away.

Leafstar sat beside the river, intending to give herself a more thorough grooming, but she had barely licked one shoulder clean when Lichenfur shuffled up to her.

"I might have known that pesky apprentice didn't mean what he said," the elder grumbled. "There's no sign of him, and we're still stuck with our old moss."

Leafstar blinked in surprise. "I saw Snookpaw go into the cave myself," she mewed. "Hasn't he come back yet?" Lichenfur shook her head. "I'll go and see what's keeping him."

The ledge to the Whispering Cave was wet and slippery, and Leafstar had to set her paws down carefully. Black water rushed along beside her a couple of mouse-lengths below the ledge. Cold, damp air crept into her pelt, and she shivered. At last Leafstar saw a pale light up ahead, reflecting on the surface of the river. The ledge widened out into a flat path, and she quickened her pace as she padded into the Whispering Cave.

Leafstar paused at the cave entrance to admire the secret world underneath the gorge. The walls of the cave were broken into cracks and ledges; shaggy clumps of moss hung from every surface, giving off a pale, eerie light. Reflections of the water rippled across the cave roof; the sound of the river and unseen dripping water echoed in Leafstar's ears.

This was the place where Echosong came to share tongues with her warrior ancestors. Though she was no medicine cat, Leafstar felt very close to StarClan here, as if she might hear their voices if she listened hard enough.

At the far side of the cave, Snookpaw was stretching up on his hind paws to claw down a bundle of moss. A large heap of it already lay on the cave floor beside him.

"Well done," Leafstar meowed. "That should make a fine bed for Lichenfur and Tangle."

Snookpaw jumped with surprise and dropped to all four

paws. "Leafstar!" he exclaimed. "You nearly scared me out of my fur!"

"Sorry," Leafstar mewed. She decided not to tell him that Lichenfur had been complaining. "Do you want help carrying that lot out?"

"Please," Snookpaw puffed, beginning to roll the moss into two balls. "It *is* a lot, isn't it?" he added smugly.

Leafstar picked up one of the balls of moss and turned to head out of the cave, pausing to let Snookpaw go in front of her. The pale light from the cave slowly died away behind them; edging along the trail was even more difficult when their front paws were hidden by the clump of moss. Rounding the curve in the river, they drew closer to the ragged gap of daylight where the water swirled out.

Then Snookpaw's claws skidded on the slippery ledge. With a squeal of alarm he dropped his moss and toppled into the river, his paws flailing vainly for a grip on the stone. Dark water closed over his head.

"Snookpaw!" Dropping her own moss, Leafstar bounded to the spot where the apprentice had disappeared. She was in time to see him resurface a couple of tail-lengths farther downstream. His paws churned the water and his jaws opened in a terrified wail.

"Help! Help me!"

He was already sinking again as Leafstar flung herself into the water and gripped him by the scruff before he could disappear. The water was dark and shockingly icy. For a couple of heartbeats Leafstar was stunned into stillness and didn't know which way to swim. Then she caught sight of the light at the cave entrance. Striking out strongly with her hind legs, she reached the side of the cave, but the wall was smooth and slick with water; she couldn't pull herself up to the ledge again, especially with Snookpaw weighing her down.

StarClan help us!

All Leafstar could do was keep Snookpaw's head above water while the current bore them along. She felt a moment's panic as they were swept out into daylight and the sun dazzled her eyes, blinding her while the water swept them in a circle. Rolled over by a wave, Leafstar lost all sense of direction. Then her head bobbed to the surface. Still with her teeth fixed in Snookpaw's scruff, she let the current swirl them toward the side of the pool. At last she was able to crawl out and collapse on the stones, with Snookpaw a sodden mound of fur beside her.

"Leafstar! Leafstar!"

Still muzzy with exhaustion, Leafstar recognized Cherrytail's voice. She opened her eyes to see the young tortoiseshell gazing down at her anxiously.

"Check . . . Snookpaw," she rasped.

As Cherrytail bent over Snookpaw, he began struggling to sit up. Shivering with shock, he coughed up a stream of water and flopped back onto the stones again.

At least he's alive, Leafstar thought. *Thank StarClan!*

By now more cats were racing across the Rockpile, or leaping across the stepping-stones a little farther downstream. Echosong was among them, pushing her way through as they crowded around.

"Keep back and let me see him," she ordered, crouching

down beside the young black-and-white tom. "Leafstar, what happened?"

"He was fetching moss, and he slipped into the river," Leafstar croaked, managing to get to her paws and give her pelt a good shake.

Echosong nodded and gently pressed Snookpaw's belly with one paw. Another stream of water gushed out of the apprentice's mouth.

"You'll be fine," Echosong told him reassuringly. "Come with me to my den. I'll give you some thyme leaves for the shock, and you can have a good sleep."

Still coughing, Snookpaw tottered to his paws. "No," he rasped. "I want to go home. Don't make me stay here."

Startled, Leafstar took a pace back. She wanted to tell him that the medicine cat would look after him just as well as his Twolegs, but she couldn't bring herself to make him stay in the gorge when he looked so miserable.

"All right," she meowed. "If you're sure you can make it that far."

"I'll go with him," Cherrytail offered, letting Snookpaw lean against her shoulder. "I'll make sure he's okay."

"Thank you, Cherrytail." The young tortoiseshell warrior had been a kittypet once, and she would be familiar with the Twolegplace. "Make sure you get some rest, Snookpaw, and we'll see you again as soon as you're ready."

Snookpaw headed off with Cherrytail, then halted and glanced back. "Thank you, Leafstar. You saved my life."

"You're welcome," Leafstar mewed gently.

She watched Cherrytail helping Snookpaw across the Rockpile. Though she was thankful the accident had been no worse, she was still shaken. Gazing at the cats gathered around her, she announced, "From now on, no cat must go to the Whispering Cave alone—except for you, Echosong. And moss-gathering must always be supervised by a warrior."

"Good idea," Waspwhisker meowed.

Petalnose nodded. "When I think what could happen to our apprentices . . ." She shuddered.

Leaving her Clanmates to return to camp, Leafstar ventured back along the ledge until she found the remains of the moss that she and Snookpaw had dropped. Most of it had been washed away by the river, but Leafstar rolled up what was left and carried it across the Rockpile to the elders' den.

"What's that?" Lichenfur sniffed. "There's not enough moss there to make a bed for a tick!"

"Well, it's all you're getting for now," Leafstar retorted. "Snookpaw fell in the river fetching this. He could have died."

Lichenfur blinked. "Clumsy apprentice," she muttered. "He should watch where he's putting his paws."

Biting back an angry retort, Leafstar left her and went to find a sunny spot where she could sit and clean the river water from her pelt. She was drowsing in the sunlight when she heard excited squeaks behind her. Fallowfern's kits were scampering over to the bottom of the trail where Sharpclaw and the border patrol were climbing down.

"Billystorm! Billystorm!" Plumkit squealed. "Snookpaw

fell in the river and he nearly drowned!"

"What?" Billystorm leaped down the last couple of tail-lengths, his fur beginning to fluff up and his eyes wide with horror. "Where is he?"

"It's not as bad as that." Leafstar rose to her paws and padded over to the ginger-and-white tom. "He did fall in the river, fetching moss from the cave. But he was fine. He went home."

Billystorm let his neck fur lie flat again, though his eyes were still full of concern. "I'll check on him later," he promised. "My Twoleg nest isn't far from his."

"Thanks," Leafstar replied. "I'm worried about him. I wish he'd stayed and let Echosong take a look at him."

"You can come with me to see him if you like," Billystorm suggested.

"Me—come with you to the Twolegplace?" Leafstar felt every hair on her pelt start to prickle. "No thanks, Billystorm. I don't feel comfortable among Twoleg nests."

"Unlike your Clanmates," Billystorm murmured.

Leafstar didn't respond. She hadn't forgotten his report that he had seen—or *thought* he saw—Sharpclaw and Stick leading a patrol in the Twolegplace. But she didn't want to hear any more of the rumors. In the end she hadn't confronted Sharpclaw about it, because she knew her deputy would never do such a thing without telling her.

Billystorm must have mistaken some kittypets for our warriors.

"What's this I hear about Snookpaw?" Sharpclaw called, padding over to her with Fallowfern's kits tumbling around his paws. "Is he all right?"

"He will be," Leafstar assured him.

"At least we have enough warriors for the rest of today's patrols," Sharpclaw meowed. He hurried off, calling to Wasp-whisker and Petalnose as he went.

"I'd better go with him," Billystorm meowed. "I've nothing to do, seeing that my apprentice isn't here. I'd promised to show him some fighting moves."

"Show us instead!" Fallowfern's kits chorused, scrabbling at his fur until they nearly knocked him off his paws.

Billystorm cast an amused glance at Leafstar. "You're not apprenticed yet," he told the kits.

"But you could help me with them if you want," Leafstar mewed. "Fallowfern is worn out from looking after them. Besides, she wants to help Clovertail move into the new birth-ing den. We could take them off her paws for a bit."

"Yes, please!" Creekkit begged. "I can fight better than all the others."

"Can't!" Nettlekit squeaked, jumping on his littermate.

Leafstar let out a small *mrrow* of laughter as she watched the kits rolling around, battering at one another with tiny paws.

"Are they bothering you, Leafstar?" Fallowfern puffed, bounding up with a harassed look.

"Not a bit," Leafstar replied. "Should we take them for a while? It would leave you free to help Clovertail."

"Oh, would you?" Fallowfern's voice was full of gratitude. "Now listen," she went on sternly to her kits. "You do exactly what Leafstar and Billystorm tell you. I don't want to hear that you've put one whisker out of place. Do you understand?"

"Yes, Fallowfern." The kits sat up, their fur rumpled and their eyes wide and innocent. "We'll be good."

"And hedgehogs will fly," Billystorm whispered into Leafstar's ear.

As Fallowfern padded off to join Clovertail, Billystorm rounded up the kits. "Come on. We'll go to the training area."

"Yes!" Rabbitkit bounced up and down with his tail waving. "Last one there's a kittypet!"

All four kits took off in a flurry of sand. When Leafstar and Billystorm caught up to them at the training area, Creekkit was crouched in the middle of the open space. His lips were drawn back to display tiny sharp teeth. "I'm a fox and I'm attacking the camp!" he announced.

"Stay away or I'll rip your fur off!" Plumkit responded, sliding out her claws.

"That's enough." Billystorm strode out into the sandy space and raised his tail to block Plumkit as she hurled herself at her brother.

"Watch it, the fox will get you!" she squealed.

Billystorm sidestepped rapidly to stop Creekkit from sinking his teeth into his hind leg.

"This is *not* a training session," Leafstar reminded the excited kits. "That won't happen until you're apprentices."

"But that's *moons* away," Creekkit muttered, disappointed. "I want to show you my battle moves."

"We'll play some games instead," Billystorm meowed. "Let's

see how good you are at climbing."

The kits bounced around him as he led the way across to the thorn tree that Sharpclaw had used for his training exercises. Its lower branches were thick and strong, safe for the kits to improve their skills.

"When you climb," Billystorm began, holding the kits back with his tail so that they didn't hurl themselves into the tree, "you need to look for paw holds. Places you can dig your claws in. You must never move until you know where you're going to put your paws next. And *always* think about how you're going to get down. That way, climbing is safe."

The kits nodded seriously as the ginger tom finished speaking.

"Okay," Leafstar meowed. "Rabbitkit, let's see if you can climb up to that first branch."

The tiny brown tom scampered up to the tree and fixed his claws into a knot-hole, then scrabbled with his hind paws to boost himself up the trunk. Soon he sat panting on the branch. "I did it!" he exclaimed.

"Well done," Billystorm praised him. "Plumkit, you next."

The dark gray she-cat climbed quickly and neatly to sit beside her brother on the branch. Nettlekit followed. "I was faster than you," he boasted as he crouched on the branch next to the others.

"We're not trying to be fast; we're trying to be *safe*," Billystorm pointed out, waving his tail for Creekkit to climb.

The little gray tabby scrambled up the trunk, but when he reached the branch he slipped and dangled down with his hind paws waving. "Help!" he squealed.

"Go on, you can pull yourself up," Leafstar encouraged him.

With a massive effort Creekkit hauled himself up and managed to fasten his hind claws into the branch. "Made it!" he gasped.

"Very good, all of you," Billystorm meowed. "Now let's see you come down. One at a time, and *slowly*, Nettlekit."

Leafstar remembered her mother teaching her to climb, seasons ago in the woods. Coming down was always harder and more frightening than going up.

Billystorm guided Creekkit down, then Rabbitkit and Nettlekit. "Where's Plumkit?" he asked, looking around. "Did she get down already?"

A screech of terror interrupted him. Tipping her head back, Leafstar saw Plumkit perched almost at the top of the tree, all four paws clinging to the stump of a broken branch. "I'm stuck!" she wailed. "I can't get down!"

"You shouldn't be up there in the first place," Billystorm mewed exasperatedly.

"And we should have kept a better eye on her," Leafstar added. "Okay, Plumkit, I'm coming to get you."

Muscles pumping, Leafstar raced up the tree. Plumkit was trembling when she reached her. "I'm going to fall!" she whimpered.

"No, you're not," Leafstar reassured her, touching her on one shoulder with the tip of her tail. "Look, put your hind paw just here. . . ."

Slowly Leafstar guided the tiny she-cat down the tree. Plumkit's courage had returned by the time she reached the lowest branch, and she sprang off, landing on Billystorm, who had stretched out to rest underneath.

Billystorm jumped up, baring his teeth and growling with pretend fierceness. "I'll teach you to pounce on me!"

Plumkit let out a *mrrow* of laughter.

"Teach me, too!" Rabbitkit squealed, scrambling up the tree again and hurling himself down on Billystorm. "I'm not scared of you!"

Billystorm rolled his eyes at Leafstar as all four kits raced up the tree and jumped down, springing around with their tails high as he growled at them and swiped at them with his claws sheathed. Leafstar joined in, too, pretending to be asleep until some kit landed on top of her and cuffed her over the ears with tiny paws.

I haven't had so much fun in moons!

"We've got to fight these beasts!" Nettlekit announced. "Rabbitkit, Plumkit, you attack from that side."

His littermates scampered off; Billystorm and Leafstar found themselves surrounded with the kits creeping up on them in a kind of hunter's crouch.

"Are you scared?" Plumkit meowed.

"You should be!" Creekkit squeaked. "We're fiercer than you!"

"It's getting late," Billystorm mewed at last. "Time to go back to camp."

A chorus of protest came from the kits.

"We're not tired," Plumkit insisted. "We want to play some more."

"I know, but Fallowfern will be wondering where you are." Leafstar noticed that a blackbird had landed on one of the highest branches of the thorn tree. "You see that bird? Billystorm, do you think you could catch it?"

Billystorm looked up, his eyes narrowing. "I expect so."

"Off you go, then. Kits, this is how a SkyClan warrior hunts."

The kits watched, enthralled, as Billystorm leaped into the tree and crept up to the higher branches, trying not to shake the one where the bird was perching. Leafstar admired his perfect balance.

He's so good at jumping and climbing. He must be a SkyClan descendant.

Billystorm shuffled along a branch until he had enough space for a clear leap at the blackbird. At the last moment it tried to take off, but he grabbed it in his strong jaws and bounded down the tree again to drop the limp body in front of the kits.

"That was great!" Rabbitkit squeaked.

"I want to learn to do that," Nettlekit mewed. "Show us now!"

"Another time, little ones," Leafstar promised.

"You can share," Billystorm meowed, nudging his prey toward the kits. "Blackbird is very tasty."

The kits gathered around the fresh-kill, scrambling over one another in their eagerness.

"It's the best thing I've ever eaten!" Plumkit announced, looking up with a feather on her nose.

The sun was going down by the time the kits had finished eating.

"Come on," Leafstar meowed. "Now we really do have to go back to camp."

"Don't wanna . . ." Nettlekit protested, his words punctuated by a massive yawn. "Wanna climb some more . . ."

"The only place you're going to climb is into your nest," Billystorm told him, rounding up the littermates with a sweep of his tail. "Let's go."

The kits were stumbling from tiredness as they followed Leafstar back to the Rockpile, where Fallowfern was waiting.

"Thank you so much!" the pale brown she-cat exclaimed. "Have they behaved themselves?"

"They've been fine," Billystorm assured her.

"Good. We've made Clovertail really comfortable in the new birthing den. It won't be long before her kits come."

"Can we play with them?" Plumkit asked, her voice muzzy with sleep.

"Not at first," her mother warned. "They'll be too little. Now say 'thank you' to Leafstar and Billystorm for looking after you."

"Thank you!" the kits chorused.

"Can we do it again tomorrow?" Nettlekit pleaded.

"We'll see," Leafstar purred. "Go with your mother now. I don't know how Fallowfern manages all four of them," she added to Billystorm as she watched the she-cat herding her litter up the trail toward the nursery. "I'm worn out!"

"Me too," Billystorm agreed. "But they're great kits. I enjoyed playing with them."

"You'd better go home now and check on Snookpaw," Leafstar mewed. "Tell him to get well soon. We're all missing him."

"I'll do that." Billystorm whisked his tail lightly over Leafstar's flank, then headed up the trail that led to the top of the gorge.

Even though Leafstar had said she was worn out, the session with the kits had left her feeling playful. Her paws tingled with energy. Part of her wanted to race along the top of the cliff, feeling the wind in her fur, or roll in crackly leaves under the trees.

You're not a kit anymore! she scolded herself. *Better settle for a juicy piece of fresh-kill instead.*

Her heart lighter than it had been for many days, she padded off to join her Clanmates as they ate.

CHAPTER 15

❧

Leafstar brushed through the dew-laden grass, pausing to glance over her shoulder at the rest of the border patrol. "Shorty, try to keep up," she called. "I know the rats are gone, but it's not a good idea to get separated around here."

"Sorry." The Twolegplace cat plodded up to stand beside Petalnose. Trying to muffle a yawn, he added, "I can't get used to these early mornings."

"You will, sooner or later," Petalnose promised.

Leafstar gave him a nod and carried on. Above the trees the sky was pale and clear, promising hot sunshine later. The only sound was the swish of grass and the soft rustling of branches.

As they approached the clearing where they had fought the rats, Leafstar halted and stretched her jaws wide to taste the air, almost gagging on the rotting scents from the heap of Twoleg waste. But the traces of rat were faint and stale; they hadn't returned.

"I can smell another cat," she mewed after a moment. "Cherrytail, is that the loner you told us about?"

The fourth member of the patrol tasted the air. "That's

him," she confirmed. "Fresh, too. He's been here again."

Leafstar tracked the scent for a few paw steps. It led across the border in the direction of the Twolegplace, though she didn't think it had been left by any kittypet. The scent was too green and sharp for that, not muffled by Twoleg smells.

"Do you want us to follow it?" Cherrytail asked, her paws working in the grass.

Leafstar thought for a couple of heartbeats. "It doesn't seem worth it," she meowed. "It's the only scent here, so the loner hasn't been stealing prey. But I'll make sure all the Clan knows to keep a lookout."

Was that the right decision? she wondered as she led the patrol back through the trees. *What would Firestar have done?*

At the top of the gorge, Leafstar was pleased to spot Billystorm on the trail ahead of her, though her pleasure faded when she realized that his apprentice wasn't with him. She quickened her pace and caught up to the ginger-and-white tom as he reached the bottom of the ravine. "Hi. What happened to Snookpaw? Is he okay?"

Billystorm turned at the sound of her voice; his green eyes showed that he shared her concern. "I don't know. I went to his nest, but I couldn't find him, and he didn't answer when I called out to him. I think his Twolegs must have shut him inside."

Uneasiness stirred within Leafstar. Snookpaw had never found it hard to get out before. "Maybe he's still tired after yesterday," she began. "We'll have to—"

She broke off at the sound of excited squealing as

Fallowfern's kits swarmed around them.

"Billystorm!" Nettlekit squeaked. "We've been waiting for you. Play with us again!"

"Yes, be that giant beast," Plumkit urged. "Leafstar, you too. You were scary!"

"You'll have to wait," Billystorm told them. "You were very lucky to have your Clan leader all to yourselves yesterday."

Leafstar twitched her whiskers with amusement. "Maybe later, kits," she meowed. "I've got to check the patrols now."

As she was speaking, Fallowfern bounded up, looking flustered. "Are you bothering Leafstar and Billystorm again?" she asked her kits. "Come with me right away. You haven't even been groomed this morning!"

With an apologetic glance at Leafstar, she hustled the kits off to a flat stone near the water's edge and started to groom Rabbitkit with firm strokes of her tongue.

"Billystorm, are you ready for a hunting patrol?" Sharpclaw meowed, padding up with Stick and Sparrowpelt. When the ginger-and-white tom nodded, he waved his tail to where Waspwhisker was waiting with his apprentice, Mintpaw, and Tinycloud and Macgyver. "Over there."

Billystorm dipped his head to Leafstar and padded over to join the patrol, who headed downstream with Waspwhisker in the lead. Sharpclaw gathered his own patrol, beckoning with his tail to Coal, who was washing his paws near the fresh-kill pile.

"I thought we'd try the woods near the rat heap," he meowed to Leafstar.

"Good idea," Leafstar replied. "You can keep an eye open

for that loner. My border patrol scented him again today."

"Will do." Sharpclaw gave her a brisk nod and led his patrol up the trail.

With her Clanmates organized for the day, there was little for Leafstar to do, but she felt too energetic to sit and drowse in the sun. *I think I'll go and see how the prey is running,* she decided. *I haven't hunted alone for at least a moon.*

But as Leafstar climbed the trail, she found Cora outside the warriors' den with her paws tucked under her and her eyes fixed on the distance. She jumped when Leafstar's shadow fell across her.

"You startled me," she mewed. "I was . . . thinking of something else, I guess. Were you looking for one of the warriors? I think they're all out hunting."

"No, I'm just off for some hunting myself."

Cora hesitated for a moment, then asked, "Would you mind if I came with you?"

"Not at all." Leafstar tried to hide her surprise. Cora was the most reserved of the visitors, keeping her thoughts to herself, although she was always polite and joined in with Clan activities when she was asked to.

The black she-cat fell in behind Leafstar as they climbed to the top of the cliff, then padded beside her as they headed deeper into the woods.

"This must be different from hunting in the Twolegplace," Leafstar remarked. "Are there any trees there?"

"A few," Cora responded. "Trees and bushes, in Twoleg gardens."

"What kind of prey do you hunt?"

"Birds, mostly."

Leafstar pressed on, determined to make some sort of conversation. "Stick says you eat rats."

Cora nodded. "They don't taste that good, but they're food."

Leafstar gave up. The two she-cats padded on in silence until Leafstar heard the flutter of wings above her head and caught the scent of thrush. Looking up, she spotted the bird sitting on a low branch in a nearby tree.

If I try to climb the tree, it'll see me before I get close. . . .

Signaling with her tail for Cora to stay where she was, Leafstar crept through the long grass until she reached the next tree, a beech whose branches interlaced with the ash where the thrush was perching. Bunching her muscles, she jumped and clawed her way up the trunk until she reached a spot where she could look down on her prey. As lightly as she could, imagining she was stalking a mouse, she crept along a branch of the beech tree until she was a tail-length above the thrush.

Suddenly the bird realized it was being hunted. As it spread its wings, Leafstar let herself drop down with her front paws outstretched. The thrush tried to fly away, but Leafstar snagged her claws into one of its wings before it was fully spread. The bird fluttered in panic, its free wing beating frantically. Leafstar sprang on top of it and took its life with a bite to the throat.

"That was impressive!" Cora commented as Leafstar leaped down to the ground with her fresh-kill in her jaws.

"It's not that hard," Leafstar meowed. "I could teach you if you like, for when you're next on hunting patrol."

"Thanks, but I don't think it's worth it," Cora replied.

"What?" Shock prickled through Leafstar's pelt. "Are you thinking of leaving?"

Cora didn't meet her gaze, just lowered her head to give her chest fur a couple of embarrassed licks.

She said something she wasn't supposed to, Leafstar guessed.

"I . . . er . . . I'm not sure. It's not up to me," Cora mumbled.

"You're welcome to stay as long as you want, you know," Leafstar told her impulsively. A little startled at herself, she realized that was true. The newcomers fit well into Clan life, and the gorge seemed happier and busier now. "Was there . . . was there some trouble that made you leave your Twolegplace? Are you waiting for something to happen before you can go back?"

Cora blinked, looking almost panic-stricken. "Well, we—" she began awkwardly, then broke off. "Look! A mouse!"

Leafstar hadn't seen the prey, and wondered for a heartbeat whether Cora had invented it. Then she spotted the little brown creature nibbling on a seed underneath the roots of an oak tree.

Cora ran toward it without thinking about whether the mouse would sense her paw steps. The mouse heard the crack as she stepped on a dry twig, so it darted away, but Cora picked up speed and slammed one paw down on it before it could escape.

"Well done," Leafstar mewed as the visiting she-cat carried her prey back. *If I caught an apprentice hunting like that, I'd wonder what his mentor had been teaching him!* "You might want to watch where you're putting your paws," she added tactfully. "Then you won't tread on twigs or dead leaves. And keep your tail still so that you don't brush it against crackly undergrowth."

"Thanks, Leafstar," Cora panted, dropping the mouse beside Leafstar's thrush. "There's so much to remember!"

"Well, you might as well learn it, even if you're not here long enough to hunt in the trees," Leafstar meowed. "You never know, the skills might be useful in your Twolegplace."

"I'm sure they will," Cora answered, with a warmth in her voice that hadn't been there before.

I could be friends with this cat, Leafstar realized. *I hope she stays.*

As she was scratching earth over their prey to hide it until they were ready to collect it, she noticed a squirrel crossing a patch of open ground a few fox-lengths farther into the wood. It paused at the foot of an ivy-covered tree and scuffled around in the debris between the roots. Leafstar touched Cora lightly on the shoulder with her tail-tip and angled her ears toward the prey.

"Can we catch it?" Cora whispered. "It'll climb the tree."

"Let it," Leafstar murmured. "I'm going to climb the tree first, then you chase the squirrel so it runs straight up into my claws."

Cora's eyes shone. "Right!"

Leafstar approached the tree in a wide half circle so that she didn't alert the squirrel. She clawed her way up the trunk on the far side, and crouched on a fork in the trunk in the middle of a clump of ivy. The squirrel was still scuffling among the roots below. Leafstar waved her tail to show Cora she was in position. The black she-cat let out a fearsome screech and pelted toward the tree. The squirrel looked up, froze for a moment in terror, then raced up the trunk.

Leafstar scrambled out of the concealing ivy, her lips drawn back in a snarl. The squirrel let out a squeal of panic and made for the ground again. But Cora was ready for it. Leafstar watched as the she-cat sprang on the squirrel and raked her claws across its throat. It twitched once and then went limp.

Leafstar jumped down to the ground and padded up to Cora, who was standing proudly over her prey. "Great catch!"

"It was yours, really," Cora replied.

"No, it was both of us," Leafstar told her. "We worked well together."

Cora was even quieter as they returned to camp, laden with fresh-kill. Leafstar hoped she was reconsidering what she had said about leaving.

I need to find out what's going on. What is it that Stick and his friends want from us?

Dropping her prey on the fresh-kill pile, Leafstar heard voices raised in anger. She turned and spotted Ebonyclaw and her apprentice, Frecklepaw, standing at the edge of the pool, facing each other with their fur fluffed out and their eyes blazing. Both she-cats were normally so even tempered that

Leafstar padded over to find out what was going on.

"I don't come to the gorge to sit around grooming my tail while I wait for you!" Ebonyclaw hissed. "You missed a whole training session!"

"I was busy!" Frecklepaw retorted. "Echosong needed me to go fetch herbs because Rabbitkit had a pain in his belly."

"That's not your responsibility." Ebonyclaw lashed her tail. "Echosong isn't your mentor."

"I wish she was!" Frecklepaw flashed back.

Before Ebonyclaw could reply, Leafstar stepped forward. "Frecklepaw, you *never* speak to your mentor like that," she scolded. "You need to be respectful to Ebonyclaw. Apologize at once."

Frecklepaw's eyes widened with dismay as she realized that her Clan leader had heard the quarrel. "Sorry, Ebonyclaw," she muttered.

Ebonyclaw gave her a curt nod, her neck fur beginning to lie flat again.

"In the future," Leafstar went on, "you must check with Ebonyclaw before you do anything for Echosong."

"But—" Frecklepaw opened her jaws to protest, then clearly thought better of it. "All right, Leafstar, I will."

"Good. Ebonyclaw, there's still time for some training before you and Frecklepaw have to go home."

"Right." Ebonyclaw summoned her apprentice with a twitch of her tail, and stalked off toward the training area.

Frecklepaw followed, her head down and her paws dragging.

When the two she-cats had gone, Leafstar headed for Echosong's den, but the medicine cat emerged before she reached it, meeting her at the entrance.

"I heard that," Echosong meowed. "I'm sorry, Leafstar. I didn't know Ebonyclaw was waiting for Frecklepaw."

"That's not the point," Leafstar began, thinking Echosong didn't sound all that sorry. "You shouldn't give tasks to an apprentice unless you ask her mentor first."

"But I do think Ebonyclaw was too harsh on Frecklepaw," Echosong went on, as if Leafstar hadn't spoken. "Anyone would think she'd done something really wrong."

Leafstar bit back an irritated comment; Echosong clearly wasn't getting it. "You have to remember that Frecklepaw is here to be a warrior," she reminded the medicine cat.

"I thought she was here to be a member of SkyClan," Echosong retorted.

Leafstar's belly churned with tension. *I don't want to quarrel with Echosong!* To her relief, she spotted Sharpclaw returning down the trail with his patrol: Stick, Shorty, and Sparrowpelt. As he saw Leafstar he called her name and quickened his pace.

"We'll talk about this again later," Leafstar muttered to Echosong, and bounded off toward her deputy, meeting him at the bottom of the trail.

"Is everything okay?"

"Fine," Sharpclaw replied.

He didn't tell Leafstar where they had been, and they weren't carrying any prey. *But they went out to hunt,* Leafstar thought uneasily.

As Sharpclaw padded closer to her she caught a whiff of a Thunderpath, and her pelt prickled. *Have they been to the Twolegplace?*

She almost asked Sharpclaw straight out, then shook her head. There was no need to interrogate her deputy; if Sharpclaw had been there, he would tell her.

Almost as if he had picked up her thought, Sharpclaw murmured, "May I have a word in private? Maybe up there?"

Without waiting for a reply he turned back to the trail and started to climb. Leafstar followed, her belly lurching with apprehension. *Is he going to tell me about some sort of trouble in the Twolegplace?*

"What's all this about?" she prompted as they reached the cliff top.

Sharpclaw stood looking down into the gorge, his expression thoughtful. "It's about the visitors," he meowed. "I'd like them to be made full warriors of SkyClan."

Leafstar wasn't surprised by the request. Her deputy had obviously been thinking along those lines for some time now. "Is that what they want?" she asked.

"I haven't asked them," Sharpclaw admitted, "but they must. They carry out all the warrior duties, and they never talk about leaving."

Oh, no? Leafstar remembered her conversation with Cora earlier that day. The black she-cat obviously didn't believe that the visitors were going to stay permanently. But what she had said was so vague that Leafstar didn't feel she could tell Sharpclaw about it.

Standing beside Sharpclaw and looking down into the camp, Leafstar watched Stick and Coal settle down to eat near the fresh-kill pile with Sparrowpelt and Cherrytail. Shorty was playing some sort of game with the apprentices, trying to jump on one another's tail, while Cora sat outside Echosong's den talking to the medicine cat. No cat who looked at them would think they were any different from the rest of the Clan.

I didn't want Cora to tell me they were going to leave, Leafstar remembered. *This would be a good way of making them part of SkyClan for good.*

"You're right," she meowed to Sharpclaw. "It's time we honored them by making them warriors."

Sharpclaw's eyes glowed with approval. "I'm glad you agree. Would you like me to talk to Stick about it?"

"I don't think that's necessary, do you? It's a huge honor we're giving them, and I want the entire Clan there to witness it. It might not make them stay, but how else can we thank them?"

For a moment Sharpclaw didn't reply; then he gave a brisk nod. "Right. When do you want to do it?"

Leafstar stretched out her front paws and flattened her back, feeling the tension ease from the muscles in her shoulders. "I think now would be a good time."

With Sharpclaw following her, Leafstar padded down into the gorge. Glancing around, she saw Ebonyclaw and Frecklepaw returning from their battle training. She was glad to notice that even though their session had been short, they looked more at ease with each other. Petalnose and Sagepaw followed close behind them. Cherrytail, Macgyver, and Patchfoot were getting ready to go on the final border patrol of the day. Echosong and Cora still sat outside the medicine cat's den. Shorty had joined Stick and Coal near the fresh-kill pile. The two elders were sunning themselves beside the river in the last of the sunlight, while Fallowfern was rounding up her kits, ready to return to the nursery. There was no sign of Billystorm; Leafstar guessed that he had gone back to the Twolegplace to check on Snookpaw.

Bunching her muscles, Leafstar bounded up to the top of the Rockpile. "Let all cats old enough to catch their own prey join here beneath the Rockpile for a Clan meeting!"

The cats in the gorge looked up at her in surprise. Mintpaw shot out of the apprentices' den and scrambled down to join her fellow apprentices. Shrewtooth popped his head out of the warriors' den, staring wide-eyed as if he expected to see a horde of attacking badgers charging down the gorge. Waspwhisker followed him out, giving him a shove from behind to get him started down the trail.

Rockshade, Bouncefire, and Tinycloud all appeared at a run from somewhere downstream; Tinycloud had a vole in her jaws, which she tossed onto the fresh-kill pile before sitting down with her brothers. Clovertail poked her head out of the new birthing den, but stayed where she was.

"This is an important time in the life of a Clan, the naming of new warriors," Leafstar announced.

She saw Mintpaw and Sagepaw give each other a startled look; then Mintpaw shook her head and shrugged. The apprentices couldn't possibly think it was their turn yet, but clearly no cat expected Leafstar to name the visitors.

"Stick, Coal, Cora, and Shorty, come forward, please."

A murmur of surprise passed through the Clan as the four cats padded hesitantly forward to stand below the Rockpile. They looked puzzled—but only Cora looked wary, as if she was worried that Leafstar was going to say something about their plans to leave.

Leafstar steadied her paws on the warm stone. "Though these cats were not born and brought up in a Clan, they know the skills they need as warriors and they are ready to become full members of SkyClan." She gazed up at the sky, reddening with the streaks of sunset. "I, Leafstar, leader of SkyClan, call upon—"

"Hang on," Stick interrupted. "You're making us warriors?"

There was a gasp from more than one cat behind him. No cat interrupted a warrior ceremony, least of all one of the cats who was being named!

"Yes—yes, I am," Leafstar stammered, suddenly afraid that he was going to refuse. She gazed down at Stick, trying to read his reaction in his face, but he was completely closed to her. *I don't know this cat at all,* she realized with something like panic.

Catching Sharpclaw's gaze, Leafstar figured her deputy looked as alarmed and unsettled as she felt. *You were right. I should have let you talk to Stick first.*

The visiting cats had drawn together into a huddle, meow-ing quietly to one another. They kept casting swift glances at Leafstar. Finally they broke apart and faced her.

"That's okay," Stick mewed. "You can go ahead."

He and his companions looked interested, and mildly pleased, but they obviously had no idea what the ceremony represented. *They're not Clan cats,* Leafstar realized. *This isn't an honor for them.*

It was too late to back down. Taking a deep breath, Leaf-star continued. "I call upon my warrior ancestors to look down upon these four cats. In the time they have spent with us they have come to understand the ways of your noble code, and I commend them to you as warriors."

Jumping down to stand in front of them, she meowed, "Stick, Cora, Coal, and Shorty, do you promise to uphold the warrior code and to protect and defend this Clan, even at the cost of your own lives?"

"I do," all four cats replied.

Was Cora a bit hesitant there? Leafstar wondered. *Or am I imagin-ing things?*

"Then by the powers of StarClan, I give you your warrior names," she continued. "Stick, from this moment—"

Stick raised his tail. "Wait."

"Yes?" Leafstar asked, trying not to sound impatient. *That's the second time he's interrupted. They really don't understand what this cer-emony means.*

"We'll keep our own names," Stick meowed.

Leafstar stared at him. Was this something StarClan would

allow? Even the kittypet warriors had taken warrior names, more or less.

"We don't feel the need to change who we are by name," Coal explained. "We haven't acted differently by becoming part of the Clan."

Leafstar could see the point of that, and she spotted Sharpclaw nodding as if he agreed. "Very well," she mewed, rapidly revising the words with which she would conclude the warrior ceremony. "StarClan honors your courage and skill, and we welcome you as—"

"What's going on?" The outraged yowl came from behind Leafstar. She turned to see Harveymoon pelting down the gorge from the direction of the training area. He skidded to a halt beside her.

"Why are you making them warriors?" he demanded.

CHAPTER 16

❧

Every cat turned to gaze at the kittypet. Harveymoon's eyes were glaring and his fur was fluffed up in anger so that he looked twice his size. "Well, why are you?" he repeated.

"I don't know," Sparrowpelt replied with biting sarcasm. "Could it be because they're brave and loyal and good at hunting, or is that just crazy?"

"But they haven't had any proper training," Ebonyclaw pointed out.

"They didn't need any," Patchfoot retorted.

Frecklepaw eased herself closer to her mentor, backing her up. "I bet they don't even know the warrior code!"

"And what about apprentice tasks?" Sagepaw chipped in with a mutinous look on his face. "*We* all have to do them!"

Leafstar raised her tail for silence. She was furious with Harveymoon for breaking into the ceremony, and disturbed that other cats were backing him up, when they had kept their opinions to themselves until now. But with a pang of guilt she had to admit that there was some truth in what they said.

"There's no need for fur to be ruffled over this," she meowed. "Sharpclaw and I believe that this is the best way to acknowledge all that the visitors have done for SkyClan. They have learned our skills, and taught us skills we never knew before. How could we treat them as apprentices? However," she added, forestalling another protest from Harveymoon, "I'm sure they won't mind helping with the apprentice tasks so that they experience every part of Clan life."

The visitors glanced at one another, as if they weren't so sure about that.

"If it's all too much trouble . . ." Cora murmured.

"This is my decision!" Leafstar raised her head and stared out across her Clan. No cat was going to bully her out of finishing the ceremony. She felt Sharpclaw's green gaze fixed on her, and saw him give her a tiny nod of approval.

"Stick, StarClan honors your courage and skill," she went on, "and we welcome you as a full member of SkyClan." She rested her muzzle on Stick's head, and after a moment's hesitation Stick licked her shoulder and moved back to stand beside Sparrowpelt.

In the same way Leafstar made the other three Twolegplace cats full members of SkyClan. She felt flustered; the ceremony didn't seem right without giving the cats warrior names.

"Stick! Cora! Coal! Shorty!"

At the end of the ceremony some of the SkyClan cats called out the names of the new warriors, but others, Leafstar noticed, kept silent. Harveymoon, of course, who had turned his back and refused to watch the ceremony. Ebonyclaw and Frecklepaw, Macgyver and Sagepaw . . . *I'll need to keep an eye on them, and make sure they don't create trouble.* Tinycloud was quiet, too, Leafstar noticed with a sinking feeling in her belly. *And Lichenfur, Waspwhisker, and Clovertail. Great StarClan! Please don't let this split the Clan.*

When the voices had died away, Stick stepped forward again and inclined his head formally to Leafstar. "I thank you on behalf of all four of us," he meowed. "I'm sure we have much to learn from one another."

"Yes, I'm sure we do," Leafstar responded.

But she still felt uneasy. It hadn't been a proper ceremony, and she was sure there were things about the Clan's four newest warriors that were being hidden from her.

And I have to say something to Harveymoon about the way he disrupted the ceremony, she thought, anger still tingling through her pelt. *But what?*

The kittypet was already on his way out of the gorge, followed by Macgyver, Ebonyclaw, and Frecklepaw. They hadn't even waited to say good-bye.

The rest of the Clan gathered around the fresh-kill pile to feast and celebrate the newest warriors.

"Don't forget you have to keep vigil tonight and guard the camp," Sharpclaw reminded them.

"Don't worry," Shorty replied. "If any rats come, they won't get a whisker past us!"

Leafstar didn't feel comfortable joining in. She chose a sparrow from the pile, picked at it moodily for a few heartbeats, then headed for her den.

"Are you okay?" Echosong asked as Leafstar padded past her.

"Fine," Leafstar replied shortly, unable to forget the frost that had formed between them over Frecklepaw's apprenticeship. As she stalked on toward her den she was aware of the medicine cat's gaze still following her.

Leafstar was troubled as she lay down in her den. Was it really the destiny of these cats to join SkyClan? *Surely we need as many members as possible, to grow strong?*

She remembered the prophecy from the brown tabby tom she had seen in her dream. "Greenleaf will come, but it will bring even greater storms than these. SkyClan will need deeper roots if it is to survive." And she remembered her other dream, of the terrifying flood that had uprooted the trees in the gorge and swept her cats away to drown helplessly in the torrent.

Have I created roots? she asked herself. *Or is this just another storm?*

Worn out with worrying, she closed her eyes, and instantly found herself in the flat, grassy area on top of the gorge. The stars of Silverpelt blazed down on her, but barely a twinkle came from the Twolegplace; it seemed to be much farther away than usual. Everything was still; there wasn't even a breeze to stir the grass.

Movement at the edge of the forest caught Leafstar's eye as a cat emerged from the trees: a pale gray tom with patches of white. Stars twinkled like frost in his fur and around his paws as he paced toward Leafstar.

"Cloudstar!" she whispered.

The former SkyClan leader gazed at her from pale blue eyes that shone like tiny moons. "Leafstar," he acknowledged her, dipping his head. "It's good to see you here."

"I'm glad to be here, Cloudstar," Leafstar replied. "Do you have a message for me?"

The starry cat did not reply. Leafstar caught her breath as she saw more cats approaching from every side. She recognized Spottedleaf and padded up to meet her, drinking in her sweet scent.

"Greetings, Spottedleaf," she meowed. The she-cat blinked at her.

Leafstar felt strangely calm as the star-furred warriors thronged around her. Except for Spottedleaf and Cloudstar, none of them seemed to realize that she was there; instead they wove among themselves, greeting one another—sometimes warily, sometimes with friendly warmth—and occasionally paused to dole out a lick on another cat's ear, or to trail their tail-tip along a sleek flank. Leafstar watched Cloudstar's mate, Birdflight, touching noses with her two children, and her heart jumped when she spotted Rainfur, the gray tom who had died in the first battle against the rats, on the far side of the crowd.

Spottedleaf stood beside her, so close that their pelts were brushing, and waved her tail toward three cats just padding up to join their Clanmates in StarClan. In the lead was a dignified she-cat, her dense blue-gray fur shimmering with starlight. Her eyes were the brilliant blue of a clear greenleaf sky. Behind her came a graceful white she-cat with gray tips to her ears, and a powerful white tom.

"This is Bluestar," Spottedleaf meowed, angling her ears toward the first cat. "She was the leader of ThunderClan when Firestar first came to the forest."

Leafstar bowed her head in respect. *So this is the cat who made Firestar a warrior!* "Firestar told me she was a great leader," she murmured.

"And this is Bluestar's sister, Snowfur," Spottedleaf continued, "and Snowfur's son, Whitestorm. He was once Firestar's deputy."

Leafstar blinked, humbled that these warriors would make their way to see her from such distant skies. "You are all welcome here," she meowed.

A stir in the air behind her made her look around. She felt a shiver run through her pelt, light as a mouse's paws, when she spotted the brown tom who had spoken the prophecy in her dream. The bigger cat, the dark brown tabby tom who had been with him, was beside him, the two cats standing a little way apart as they watched the others assembling.

Leafstar wondered if she dared go across and speak to them, when she heard a voice behind her.

"Greetings, Leafstar."

She turned to see a handsome gray tom with piercing blue eyes standing in front of her, and recognized Skywatcher. Leafstar felt warmed from ears to tail-tip to see him looking tall, strong, thick-pelted once more.

"It's good to see you, Skywatcher," she purred. "Why are you all here? I've seen StarClan warriors in dreams before, but never so many of you."

"It's been a long time since StarClan came together like this," Skywatcher replied. "And it's because of you. You and your Clanmates, who have forged a new Clan with the courage and the honor that would make any warrior proud to be a part of it. All five Clans have gathered to celebrate SkyClan's survival."

Amazement and disbelief flooded through Leafstar as she gazed at the starlit warriors. *We did this? My Clan?*

"We won't always be in the same place like this," Skywatcher warned, as if he guessed she was about to question what was happening. "Our Clans are in different places, and the skies are not always open to us. So let us enjoy the moment while we can."

"Yes—oh, yes!" Leafstar breathed out, feeling that happiness was about to well up inside her and spill over like rain from an upturned leaf. She felt as if she could stand there forever, basking in the whispering, starlit warmth.

"Let's hunt!" one cat yowled.

Immediately the cats of StarClan gathered and shifted like a shoal of glittering fish before flowing smoothly toward the forest, their belly fur brushing the grass and their tails streaming out behind them. Leafstar was swept along with them. Energy crackled through her like a bolt of lightning.

There's nothing better than this! Being among warriors, running through the trees, searching for prey . . .

She basked in the strength and speed and skill she could feel sparking in her legs. She had lost sight of the cat who had made the prophecy, and his Clanmate, but Spottedleaf raced briefly at her side. "Seize the moment!" she urged. The glow in her eyes told Leafstar that the words had special meaning for her. "Destiny will arrive, whether we seek for it or not."

Leafstar felt comforted, the worries of her waking life melting away like icicles in the sun. These cats seemed to be telling her to celebrate being part of the Clan as it was now, that the future was hidden and they must live in the present.

But she wished she had been able to talk to the cat she had dreamed of at the bottom of the gorge.

Skywatcher and Spottedleaf said nothing about storms lying ahead. Does that mean the storm will never come?

Leafstar wasn't ready to discount the prophecy, yet the visit tonight had reassured her. She knew that her Clan had to be prepared, with training and battle practice, but that was all they could do. As her paws flew over the shining grass of the dream forest, Leafstar knew she must not try to see the future that was hidden from her.

CHAPTER 17

❧

Paw steps on the rock outside her den woke Leafstar. Blinking in the sunlight, she made out Billystorm's head and shoulders as he looked in. Anxiety flooded through her as she realized how late she had slept.

"I'm sorry, Leafstar!" Billystorm exclaimed, his forepaws scrabbling at the floor of the den in embarrassment. "I didn't realize you were still asleep."

"It's okay," Leafstar mumbled around a huge yawn. She sat up, wincing at the ache in her muscles. *Any cat would think I had been racing through the forest all last night!* "Come in."

She felt as embarrassed as Billystorm as she shook moss out of her pelt and tried to give herself a quick grooming. "What can I do for you?" she asked.

"I'm worried about Snookpaw," Billystorm meowed, sitting in the entrance to the den. "He's still shut up in his housefolk's nest. I'd like to make sure that he's okay, and that they're not keeping him there against his will."

Every hair on Leafstar's pelt prickled, and she stopped washing to face the daylight-warrior. "That's not good," she commented. "You're right, you should do everything you can to find out what's going on."

Billystorm looked down, examining his paws. "Actually, I was hoping you would come with me."

Leafstar's heart began to beat faster with a mixture of excitement and apprehension. "I don't belong in the Twolegplace!"

"I'd look after you," Billystorm assured her. "And I know exactly where we're going."

Leafstar, you're being a fox-heart! Leafstar told herself, remembering her dream of the night before. The joy she had felt then in being a cat, the energy that had flowed through her body as she hunted with the warriors of StarClan, gave courage to her heart and paws.

"All right," she mewed. "I'll come. I'll just let Sharpclaw know."

Down in the gorge, Sharpclaw was organizing the hunting patrols. "Shorty, you lead this one, with Patchfoot, Petalnose, and Sagepaw," he ordered. "Stick, you can lead the other; take Ebonyclaw, Frecklepaw, and Cherrytail."

Leafstar couldn't help noticing that Ebonyclaw flicked her tail with annoyance as she fell in behind Stick, while Sagepaw padded up to his mother and muttered into her ear, "I don't want to take orders from *him*!" with a glare at Shorty.

StarClan, please let them get used to it in a few days.

Sharpclaw blinked in surprise when Leafstar told him she was going to the Twolegplace with Billystorm. "You'll need to take care," he meowed. "And listen, about Billystorm—"

"What?" Leafstar interrupted sharply.

Sharpclaw hesitated, then gave his fur a shake. "Nothing. Don't worry, Leafstar. I'll look after everything here."

Leafstar watched him closely to see if he gave any flicker of knowing more about Twolegplace than he should—she hadn't forgotten about Billystorm's accusation of Sharpclaw's secret night patrols—but her deputy's gaze showed nothing but concern for her, and confidence that he could take care of the Clan while she was gone. With a sigh, Leafstar pushed Billystorm's report to the back of her mind. He was the very last cat she could imagine lying to her, but she couldn't believe that Sharpclaw would keep anything from her that threatened the safety of their Clan.

A stiff breeze was blowing, flattening the grass, as Leafstar rejoined Billystorm and they climbed to the top of the gorge. The sun shone brightly from a clear blue sky with only a few wisps of cloud. Leafstar was cast back into her dream, and the starlit cats who had surrounded her the night before seemed to be there once more, scenting the air with the history of countless moons; the memory was so vivid that she was surprised to realize that only Billystorm was running beside her.

He slowed down as they crossed the border and drew closer to Twolegplace. "We'll have to cross a Thunderpath soon," he told her. "They can be pretty scary, but it should be quiet at this time of day. And just beyond that there's a Twoleg nest with a dog that barks its stupid head off every time I go past. But you don't need to worry; it can't get at us. Then there's another Thunderpath, and after that we have to crawl underneath some really thick shrubs—"

"I'm sure we'll be fine, Billystorm," Leafstar interrupted.

But her confidence began to ebb away as they crossed the Thunderpath, with anxious glances at a sleeping monster a few fox-lengths away. *What if it wakes up?* she wondered, ready to flee if it let out a roar and leaped toward her.

Billystorm led her along a fence; she could smell the dog on the other side and her heart thumped at the sound of its high-pitched yapping, but Billystorm was right; the dog scrabbled frantically against the fence, but it couldn't get through to attack them. They crossed the second Thunderpath; the black surface felt sticky under Leafstar's paws, and she wrinkled her nose at the acrid scent. Then she followed Billystorm through a gap in a fence and emerged in a tangle of thick bushes. They squirmed underneath the lowest branches, their belly fur brushing the soft, moist earth.

Billystorm raised a paw to halt Leafstar as they emerged from the shrubs. A stretch of smooth Twoleg grass separated them from the nest. On the far side a couple of Twoleg kits were tossing something round and brightly colored between them, squealing happily as they jumped up to catch it.

"What are they doing?" Leafstar whispered.

Billystorm shrugged. "They call that thing a ball. I think it's for some sort of apprentice training exercise. Sometimes my housefolk throw one for me to chase."

"And do you chase it?" Leafstar asked.

Billystorm gave his chest fur a couple of embarrassed licks. "It's good fun, actually. And it's practice for hunting."

Leafstar purred, amused.

Billystorm led her across the grass at a swift trot, in the shade of the bushes so that the Twoleg kits didn't spot them. "We have to be careful now," he warned Leafstar as they approached the next fence. "There's a dog through here, and the Twolegs let it roam loose."

Leafstar felt her pelt prickle and her neck fur begin to rise. She wanted to ask, *Do we have to go this way?* But she was afraid that Billystorm would think she was a coward. *I'm his Clan leader! He has to respect me.*

"Right, lead on," she mewed tensely.

Billystorm crept along the fence until he came to a spot where the wooden boards had rotted away at the bottom. He squeezed underneath, then poked his head back through the hole. "It's okay," he whispered. "But keep quiet."

Leafstar pushed herself through the gap, feeling the bottom of the rotting wood scrape her back. She rose to her paws among more shrubs with dark leaves and huge, sweet-smelling flowers.

"The scent should hide us from the dog," Billystorm explained.

As she followed him through the bushes Leafstar caught glimpses of the dog between the branches: a huge creature with shaggy black-and-brown hair and floppy ears. It was lying on a stretch of stone near the door of the Twoleg nest, separated from the cats by a stretch of grass; its nose lay on its paws and it looked as if it was asleep.

As she and Billystorm started along the second side of the enclosure, Leafstar began to relax, though she kept casting cautious glances at the dog. But the heavy scent of the flowers was tickling her nostrils, and before she and her Clanmate could reach the safety of the far fence, she let out an enormous sneeze.

Instantly the dog sprang to its paws and hurled itself across the grass with a series of deep-throated barks.

"Run!" Billystorm yowled, shoving Leafstar in front of him.

Leafstar raced through the bushes, imagining she could hear the dog panting behind her, and feel its hot breath on her fur. Its rank smell swamped everything, even the heavy scent of the flowers.

With Billystorm hard on her paws she crashed between two shrubs at the foot of the fence and clawed her way to the top. Billystorm sprang up beside her as she crouched there, shivering. Below them, the dog was standing on its hind paws with its forepaws halfway up the fence, and its tongue lolled as it barked.

"Shove off, flea-pelt," Billystorm hissed. "Go and chase beetles." He didn't seem frightened, just annoyed. Turning his back on the dog, he led the way along the top of the fence. Leafstar began to follow him, only to freeze again as another flurry of barking broke out from the next Twoleg den.

"It's okay," Billystorm meowed, glancing back. "This dog is usually shut in the house."

"'Usually' isn't 'always,'" Leafstar muttered as she forced her paws to move again.

They had crept several fox-lengths along the fence when

Leafstar heard a rattling noise. Her belly fluttered as a small door in the big Twoleg door swung open. But no dog appeared; instead a dark tabby tom slid through the opening. He brought with him a waft of familiar scent, and there was a distinctive shape to his pricked ears.

"Shortwhisker!" Leafstar gasped. "No—sorry—I mean Hutch." She leaped down from the fence and bounded across the garden to touch noses with the dark tabby.

Billystorm followed more slowly. "You two know each other?" he asked, looking stunned.

"Oh, yes," Leafstar replied. "Hutch used to belong to Sky-Clan, back in the early days when Firestar was with us. But he decided that being a kittypet suited him better."

"The life of a warrior wasn't for me," Hutch declared quite cheerfully. "It's good to see you again, Leafstar. The Clan must be doing well—you look almost as well fed as me." He paused, looking Billystorm over from ears to tail-tip. "What do you want, trespassing on my territory?"

"He's with me," Leafstar meowed. "He's my Clanmate."

Hutch looked puzzled. "But I've seen him around here before. Isn't he a kittypet?"

"Er . . . I'm sort of both," Billystorm admitted, giving his shoulder a couple of embarrassed licks.

"*Both?* Can't you make up your mind?" Hutch asked with a disdainful sniff.

"There are several cats like that in SkyClan now," Leafstar put in. "They come to the gorge for training and hunting, and then go back to their housefolk at night." She hesitated and then added, "You could do that if you want to, Hutch. You could be Shortwhisker again."

For a heartbeat she thought that Hutch might agree. Then he shook his head. "I'm sorry, Leafstar. I like my life as it is. But it's still great to see you," he added warmly. "I'm glad Sky-Clan is still there."

"Always," Leafstar promised, hoping that it was true.

Hutch turned his head at the sound of a Twoleg voice calling from the nest. "I'd better go," he went on with a touch of wistfulness. "Good-bye, Leafstar. Say hi to all my old Clan-mates for me."

"I will." Leafstar touched noses with Hutch again before he bounded back across the garden and into the Twoleg den.

I wonder if I should have tried harder to persuade him to be a daylight-warrior, she wondered as she followed Billystorm back onto the fence. *He has skills we could use, learned from Firestar and Sandstorm. Maybe Sagepaw and Ebonyclaw would be more willing to take orders from him than the other Twolegplace cats.*

Billystorm led her down from the fence, across an alley, and through a half-open gate into yet another enclosed square of grass. "This is where Snookpaw lives," he announced.

To Leafstar, the Twoleg nest looked exactly like all the others they had passed. "How do you know?" she asked.

"The blue pots over there," Billystorm replied, pointing with his tail to some round shiny things near the nest door. "The scent of the herbs by the fence. And the little birch tree in the middle of the grass."

"Okay, if you're sure." Leafstar narrowed her eyes. The tree was a spindly thing trapped in a circle of earth in the middle of a patch of grass. *It's not a proper forest tree.*

She tasted the air for Snookpaw's scent, but there was such a mingled smell of Twolegs and monsters that she couldn't pick up any trace of it. *He must still be shut in. He certainly hasn't been out here recently.*

She and Billystorm crept closer to the nest until they could hide behind a big green object with round paws. Leafstar wrinkled her nose at the rotting scent of Twoleg rubbish that came from it.

"Snookpaw!" Billystorm let out a low wail. "Snookpaw, we're here! Come out!"

Leafstar joined her voice to his, but there was no sign of the apprentice. Every hair on her pelt prickled with fear. *Have the Twolegs taken him away?*

She was almost ready to give up, when she spotted a small black-and-white head pop up inside one of the windows.

"There he is!" Billystorm yowled.

Their pelts brushing, the two cats raced up to the window and jumped onto the narrow ledge outside it. Snookpaw pressed his nose against the shiny stuff that filled the window space. Leafstar thought he looked thin and sorry for himself.

"Snookpaw, are you okay?" she meowed.

"I'll be fine," Snookpaw replied, his voice faint because of the shiny stuff in the way. "Leafstar, I can't believe you came here!"

I can't believe it, either.

"We can't talk to him like this," Billystorm muttered with

an annoyed flick of his tail. "Leafstar, do you think you could get in through there?" He angled his ears toward a tiny open window at the top of the big closed one.

Go inside a Twoleg nest? I didn't plan on that. "What about the Twolegs?" she asked. "They won't want strange cats inside their den."

"They've gone out," Snookpaw told her, stretching up to press his forepaws against the window. "Why don't you come in? I'm lonely all on my own here."

Leafstar was still reluctant, but she wouldn't let her nervousness show in front of her Clanmates. "It'll be a tight squeeze," she replied, eyeing the gap doubtfully, "but I'll give it a try."

A vine was growing up the side of the window; Leafstar used the tough stem to claw her way up. Scrabbling with her hind paws she forced her way through the narrow gap and plopped down onto the floor of the Twoleg nest. Billystorm dropped down beside her a couple of heartbeats later.

The floor felt cold and unwelcoming underpaw, and the air was filled with unfamiliar scents. There was a faint buzzing noise in the air. Huge shiny objects lined the walls of the den; Leafstar thought they were gazing at her in the dim light, waiting for the right moment to pounce.

Every hair on Leafstar's pelt began to rise. There was too much to take in at once, and all her muscles were shrieking at her to flee. Taking a few deep breaths, she made herself stand her ground.

"What's going on, Snookpaw?" she hissed.

Snookpaw didn't reply right away. "Come this way," he mewed, waving his tail. "It's better through here."

Keeping low, Billystorm and Leafstar crept through an open door into a different part of the den. Here the floor was covered with something like grass, but it was short and much softer, and made up of different bright colors.

"Weird . . ." Leafstar muttered, flexing her claws in it.

This area was filled with what looked like squashy boulders, in the same bright colors; remembering the pile of Twoleg waste, Leafstar recognized what Snookpaw had called a *sofa*. She watched as the apprentice sprang up onto it and settled down; it looked comfortable, but Leafstar decided not to join him, preferring to stay on her paws with one eye on her escape route.

"We've missed you, Snookpaw," she meowed. Her voice sounded strange in the enclosed space, muffled by the fuzzy floor and the sofas. "Why haven't you been back to the gorge?"

Snookpaw looked at his paws, and gave one of them a lick. "I had a pain in my chest. My housefolk took me to the medicine Twoleg, and he gave me some sort of weird food to eat—things like white seeds, and they taste foul."

"You would be better off with herbs from Echosong," Leafstar told him. "I'll bring you some, if you like."

"No, thanks, Leafstar." Snookpaw shook his head. "I'm feeling better now. Besides, my housefolk hardly ever leave me alone. This is the first time I've been on my own since I came back from the gorge, so you probably won't be able to get in here again." He heaved a deep sigh. "I really miss being in the Clan."

Gloomily he stared out of the window. Following his gaze, Leafstar could see nothing but a small patch of sky and a Twoleg fence. *He can't see any real trees,* she realized, sharing his pain. She felt trapped and hot, and couldn't figure how any cat could stand being inside here all day and all night, without even the chance to feel earth beneath their paws.

While Leafstar had been talking to Snookpaw, Billystorm had been padding around the den, poking his nose into corners and giving everything a good sniff. Leafstar wondered how he had the confidence; she had a hard time not freezing into a crouch with her eyes closed, trying to shut out the stifling sights and smells.

"This nest isn't too bad," Billystorm meowed, returning from his explorations. "I hope your housefolk gave you a comfortable place to sleep."

"I'll show you," Snookpaw invited, jumping down from the sofa.

Waving his tail, he led them back into the first area and pointed to a small squashy boulder in one corner. Its bright surface was covered in Snookpaw's fur, and heavy with his scent.

"That looks . . . nice," Leafstar murmured politely, though privately she thought the moss and bracken of the dens in the gorge was much better for sleeping.

"And there's my food bowl," Snookpaw added, twitching his whiskers toward a brightly colored Twoleg thing half full of small brown pellets.

"They feed you rabbit droppings?" Leafstar gasped. "Do

they want you to get sick?"

"No, that's a special sort of Twoleg food for kittypets," Billystorm explained. His eyes glimmered with amusement and he gave Leafstar an affectionate nudge with his shoulder. "Try one."

Leafstar shot him a doubtful look. The last thing she wanted was to put one of the shriveled brown things into her mouth, but it would be cowardly to refuse. She padded up to the bowl and sniffed. *Yuck!* Delicately she picked up a single pellet and rolled it around on her tongue; the den was so full of harsh smells that she couldn't really taste anything. *Just as well,* she thought, *if it tastes anything like it looks!*

Just then Leafstar heard the sound of a monster, growing rapidly louder and then cutting off abruptly. Alarm sprang into Snookpaw's eyes and his fur bristled.

"My Twolegs! They're back!"

Leafstar gulped down the pellet, almost choking. "We've got to get out of here!" she rasped.

Even while she was speaking she heard a harsh clicking sound, and footsteps just beyond the den wall. For a few heartbeats her terror paralyzed her.

"I'll delay them! You climb out, quick," Snookpaw mewed. With a whisk of his tail he vanished through another door.

Billystorm was already streaking across to the window and leaped up to the opening in one massive bound. "Come on," he urged Leafstar, balancing precariously. "I'll pull you up."

Leafstar bunched her muscles and put all her strength into her jump. She felt her front paws land on the edge of the window, and slid out her claws to grip. Billystorm's teeth met in her scruff.

At the same moment she heard Snookpaw, somewhere out of sight, his voice raised in loud mewing. "Oh, I've missed you! Where did you go? Stroke my ears! I'm feeling better now."

Billystorm dragged Leafstar through the open window and both cats tumbled onto the stony path outside the nest in a tangle of legs and tails.

A last yowl came from Snookpaw. "Run!"

Leafstar didn't need telling twice. With Billystorm beside her, she raced across the garden and out through the half-open gate.

"Just get us back to the gorge!" she panted to Billystorm, and added silently to herself, *I'll chew my own tail off before I come here again!*

CHAPTER 18

❧

"Leafstar, I'm so sorry!" Billystorm wailed. "I should never have let you get into danger like that. I wasn't thinking."

The two cats had crossed the border of SkyClan territory and were heading across the open grassy stretch toward the edge of the gorge. Leafstar paused, thanking StarClan for the clean air and yielding earth of her home.

"It wasn't your fault, Billystorm," she meowed.

The ginger-and-white tom refused to be reassured. "It was my fault," he insisted. "I should have been more careful. But I promise you, the Twolegplace isn't always as dangerous as that."

"I'm sure it's not," Leafstar responded as they went on. "It's just that I'm not used to it." Inwardly her heart was still pounding, and she didn't ever want to go back to the Twolegplace. She watched Billystorm moving confidently through the long grass at the top of the cliff, his ears pricked and his nostrils flared.

He's a warrior! How can he stand living somewhere like that?

"Don't you miss being outside, under all this sky, with the wind and the scent of trees in your fur?" she blurted out.

Billystorm turned to face her, a puzzled look in his eyes. For a couple of heartbeats he didn't reply. "Yes," he mewed at last, "but I get to feel it every day when I come here." He blinked. "It's not a hardship for me to be in my Twolegs' nest. I love my housefolk, and they love me."

Leafstar still found it impossible to understand. How could any cat want to live in that world of harsh scents, loud noises, and hard surfaces underpaw? She couldn't imagine what Billystorm's housefolk offered that tempted him back every night.

When they reached the gorge, Sharpclaw was just returning at the head of a hunting patrol, with Cora, Shorty, Ebonyclaw, and Frecklepaw.

"Where's Snookpaw?" he asked, dropping a squirrel onto the fresh-kill pile. "I thought you were going to rescue him."

"He doesn't need rescuing," Billystorm replied. "He's been ill, and his housefolk are keeping him inside until he's better."

"What do Twolegs know?" Sharpclaw gave a scornful sniff. "Snookpaw would be better off here in the fresh air, with Echosong to give him the herbs he needs."

Leafstar agreed with him, but she saw Billystorm start to bristle at the deputy's contemptuous tone, and thought it wasn't a good idea to say so.

"Has any cat checked the elders' bedding?" she meowed, to distract the two toms before a quarrel developed. "I don't want Lichenfur complaining again."

"Good thought," Sharpclaw mewed with a brisk nod. "Frecklepaw, will you get onto that?"

Frecklepaw blinked, and it was Ebonyclaw who replied, "All by herself?" Her tone was sharp. "Mintpaw and Sagepaw are out on patrol."

"I don't mind—" Frecklepaw began, only to be interrupted by Cora, who padded up from the fresh-kill pile.

"We'll help, won't we, Shorty? We said we'd do apprentice tasks."

The brown tom nodded. "We're happy to. Especially when Snookpaw isn't here. It's a shame his Twolegs won't let him out."

"I hope he'll be okay," Cora added.

"I'm sure he will. He'll be back soon," Leafstar assured them.

Mollified, Ebonyclaw stepped back, and Frecklepaw went off happily with the two warriors toward the elders' den. Leafstar watched them go, impressed by how willingly Cora and Shorty had offered their help, and their concern for Snookpaw.

They're really starting to fit into the Clan.

"Leafstar! Leafstar, hurry!"

Startled by Cherrytail's voice raised in an excited yowl, Leafstar turned to see the young tortoiseshell warrior bounding down the trail.

"Come quick," she puffed as she leaped down the last couple of tail-lengths to land in front of Leafstar. "There's something you have to see." Without waiting for a response, she whipped around and bounded back up the trail.

Leafstar exchanged a baffled glance with Sharpclaw, then

followed, catching up to Cherrytail at the top of the cliff. "What's all this about?"

"I was on a border patrol with Sparrowpelt, Petalnose, and Sagepaw," Cherrytail explained breathlessly, leading Leafstar into the woods. "We picked up that loner's scent again, beside the rubbish heap. This time we followed it over the border—"

"You did what?" Leafstar interrupted. "Without telling me or Sharpclaw? You know you shouldn't do that."

"Sorry," Cherrytail meowed, not sounding repentant in the least. "We didn't go far. And we found him, though he doesn't know it yet!"

Leafstar felt even more puzzled as she followed the young cat through the woodland and past the clearing with the heap of Twoleg waste. She smelled fresh scent markers as they crossed the border; a few fox-lengths farther on Cherrytail dropped to a crouch and crept forward through a belt of thick undergrowth.

Petalnose, Sagepaw, and Sparrowpelt were waiting in the shelter of a bramble thicket.

"He's still here!" Sparrowpelt whispered excitedly, waving his tail toward a nearby clump of fern.

Peering through the fronds, Leafstar spotted a skinny, cream-colored tom as he leaped into a beech tree, easily gaining the lowest branch. As she watched he climbed higher, jumping from branch to branch and crossing from one tree to the next, where he leaped down to the ground again. As far as she could see, he wasn't stalking anything. *He's just having fun!*

"He's like us!" Cherrytail hissed, pressing up to Leafstar's side. "He must be descended from Old SkyClan."

Leafstar could see what Cherrytail meant. The loner had powerful hind legs for jumping and climbing, and now he was walking comfortably on a stretch of pebbles underneath the trees as if his pads were naturally tough enough to cope with the rough surface.

"Let's go and talk to him," Sparrowpelt urged.

"Wait a moment." Leafstar raised her tail. "Look, he's just spotted a bird."

The cream-colored tom had focused his gaze on a thrush perched on a branch of the beech tree he had climbed at first. He clawed his way up the trunk of the tree next to it, keeping to the side away from the bird. Leafstar watched as he crept out onto a branch some way above the thrush and slid cautiously back into the beech tree. She remembered her hunt with Cora, when she had executed almost the identical move.

"He's got it!" Sagepaw whispered, his eyes gleaming as the loner dropped down and landed with perfect balance onto the narrow branch where the thrush was perching. With one swipe of his paw the tom sank his claws into the bird's shoulder as it tried to fly away, and killed it with a bite to the back of its neck.

"Very neat catch!" Sparrowpelt declared.

As the cream-colored loner climbed down the tree with his prey clamped in his jaws, Leafstar led the way out from the clump of ferns, with the patrol behind her. As soon as he spotted them, the loner spun around, ready to flee.

"No, wait!" Leafstar mewed. "We're not trying to steal your prey. We just want to talk to you. I'm—"

The tom interrupted her before she could introduce herself or the others. "I've seen you before," he told her, setting down his fresh-kill. "You're those cats who live in the gorge."

"You know about us?" Sparrowpelt asked curiously.

"Not much. I know that you hunt together."

Sparrowpelt let out a puff of indignation. "It's a bit more than that!"

Leafstar touched Sparrowpelt's cheek gently with her tail to silence him. "I am Leafstar, leader of SkyClan," she announced, dipping her head. "Many seasons ago, other cats lived in the gorge. They were the original SkyClan, and some of these cats are descended from that ancient Clan."

The loner's whiskers twitched; Leafstar could see that he didn't understand what this had to do with him.

"Let me show him!" Cherrytail volunteered eagerly.

Leafstar nodded assent. Instantly Cherrytail swarmed up the beech tree, balanced along the branches until she crossed into the tree beside it, and dropped neatly onto a lower branch, just as the loner had done. "See?" she called, curling her tail up.

The cream-colored tom didn't look impressed. "She's just copying me."

"I am not!" Cherrytail retorted, her fur fluffing up. "I've always been able to do that. Now I teach apprentices to do it, too."

The loner shrugged. "Okay, but I don't know why you're telling me."

Is he mouse-brained or what? Leafstar wondered. *Can't he see that he must be descended from Ancient SkyClan, too?* "Would you like to visit the gorge and find out more about us?" she offered.

The tom stared at her. "Why would I do that?"

"Because you might want to join us!" Sagepaw blurted out, bouncing on all four paws with excitement.

Leafstar bit back a rebuke. *I was trying to take it slowly, and now he'll think we're trying to force him into something.*

The loner was gazing at Sagepaw as if he thought the apprentice had gone mad. "No, thanks, I can hunt for myself," he replied.

"But it's really great in the gorge," Cherrytail insisted, jumping down to join the others. "We all look out for one another—"

"And we meet on the Skyrock to talk to StarClan," Sparrowpelt added.

Leafstar winced. *Now he'll think we've got bees in our brain!*

"Do come," Petalnose persuaded. "You'll learn all sorts of stuff, and meet new friends."

The loner took a step back; Leafstar realized that the others were overwhelming him. "That's enough," she told the patrol. "He doesn't have to come if he doesn't want to. Take care," she added to the tom.

"And stay out of our territory, too!" Sparrowpelt chipped in. "Don't try any of your fancy hunting skills on the other side of those border marks!"

The cream-colored loner snatched up his prey and raced off into the trees without looking back.

"I wish he'd stayed," Sagepaw murmured, his whiskers drooping with disappointment.

"Yes, he's already as good as a trained warrior," Cherrytail agreed, with a lash of her tail. "And he has no idea what his hunting skills mean!"

"I wish I was descended from SkyClan," Petalnose murmured.

"You might be," Cherrytail meowed loyally.

"Well, I can't climb trees like you can."

"I don't care." Sagepaw affectionately nuzzled his mother's shoulder fur. "You're perfect just as you are!"

The sun was going down; the trees cast long, black shadows and a chilly breeze whispered over the grass. It was time to return to the gorge. Leafstar collected her patrol with a sweep of her tail; as they headed back through the trees, Sparrowpelt came to pad beside her.

"If I see the loner again, I'll have another go at trying to persuade him," he promised.

"Don't try too hard," Leafstar warned him, brushing his shoulder with her tail-tip. "And don't be too tough about chasing him off. SkyClan is open to those who want to join, but there's room in the woods for loners, too, as long as they respect our borders."

We don't need to force any cat to swell the ranks of SkyClan. Let's wait and see what happens.

CHAPTER 19

Stick padded across the grass of a Twoleg garden. Ahead of him, the nest was outlined against a harsh scarlet sky. There was a metallic tang in the air, and when Stick looked down he saw that his paws were clogged with blood. A Twoleg rabbit lay dead in front of him, and scraps of black-and-white fur littered the ground.

I didn't kill it! Stick thought, bewildered.

He turned to flee as the door of the Twoleg nest was flung open and a huge male Twoleg charged out. It opened its jaws to yowl, but what came out was the terrified screech of a cat.

Stick jumped; his eyes blinked open and he found himself curled up in a huddle with Red, Cora, and Shorty in the shelter of a sloping sheet of wood that rested against the wall of a Twoleg den. Wind swirled along the alley and rain spattered down, pushing cold claws into Stick's fur.

The terrified screech came again. Raising his head, Stick spotted Percy a few fox-lengths away, his fur bristling as he gazed around wildly with his one good eye. "They're here!" he yowled. "Dodge and Misha are coming!"

Stick stiffened and Cora started awake, but at that moment

Snowy appeared from behind a garbage can and rested her white tail over Percy's shoulders.

"No cat is coming," she mewed soothingly. "You had a bad dream, that's all. Come back here with me and Coal."

Percy stood still for a moment longer, his fur gradually beginning to lie flat, then followed the white she-cat back into shelter.

Cora stretched her jaws in a yawn. "Percy and his nightmares. He's afraid he's going to lose the other eye."

Anger churned in Stick's belly. *We have to do something about Dodge.*

Cora had already lowered her head and curled up again. Stick checked on Red and Shorty, who were still asleep; Shorty was snoring softly, blowing out his breath through his whiskers, while Red's ear twitched as if she was dreaming.

Stick settled down and closed his eyes. *We need all the sleep we can get if we're going to catch enough prey at night.*

The cold weather meant that prey was scarce, especially when they had to compete with Dodge and his followers for every mouse, bird, and scrawny squirrel. Stick unsheathed his claws and let them sink into the damp soil, remembering how Dodge was claiming more and more time for his cats to hunt, even though the days grew dark early.

I don't want to give into him. But how can we hunt if we have to get into a fight every time?

Red's scent and the feeling of her pelt pressed up against his soothed Stick's anger. The young she-cat had been away so much lately; it was good to have her back. She was looking sleek and well fed, too, suggesting to Stick that she had been hunting farther afield.

That's fine with me. Just as long as she doesn't put herself at risk of getting attacked by Dodge and his flea-ridden friends while she's on her own.

Not for the first time, Stick wondered if they should all leave and find somewhere else to live, maybe the place where Red was hunting.

But we were here first. This is our home, and I don't want to give it up.

A faint sound from the corner of the alley disturbed him as he was slipping into sleep again. As he lifted his head, unsure what had roused him, Red rose to her paws.

"I'll go and investigate," she meowed, trotting off with her tail raised high.

Stick sprang up. "Wait, I'll come with you."

Red turned on him, her lips drawn back in the beginnings of a snarl. "Don't you trust me?" she snapped. "I'm not a kit anymore! Don't you think I can look after myself?"

Stick struggled out from the narrow gap behind the sheet of wood and ran after the young she-cat as she stalked away down the alley. "Wait!" he called. "I didn't mean . . ."

"I know exactly what you meant," Red hissed, refusing to look at him.

"No, you don't!" Stick picked up his pace. "I'm trying to help you."

This time Red whirled around to face him. Her green eyes blazed with anger and she gave a single lash of her tail. "I don't *need* help. I'm not stupid; I know how to stay away from Dodge. And if I do run into him or his cats, I can fight as well as the rest of you. Why won't you see that?"

"I *do* see it, but . . ." Stick ran out of words. With a growl of frustration, he finished, "Everything would be easier if Velvet was still here."

As soon as the words were out, he knew he had said the wrong thing.

"Don't you dare blame my mother!" Red spat. "I know what's wrong. You wish I'd never been born! I'm obviously too much of a burden for you."

Spinning around again, she raced off, her tail flowing out behind her.

"Red, come back and—"

Stick broke off as he spotted a flash of gray-brown fur at the corner where Red was heading. *One of Dodge's cats is lying in wait for her!*

"Red!" he yowled.

Red whisked around the corner as if she hadn't heard. The other cat slipped closer, though he kept to the shadows and Stick couldn't get a good look at him.

Stick was about to follow, when a terrible noise exploded behind him: yowling and crashing and rattling coming from the other end of the alley. Stick spun around, every hair on his pelt standing on end.

Twolegs were pouring into the mouth of the alley. They carried sticks, banging and clattering them against shiny silver circles and sheets of wood. Their voices were raised in shouts and screams that made a flock of sparrows rush up from a nearby wall, chattering in alarm.

Stick raced back down the alley to where Cora and Shorty were huddled behind a garbage can, their eyes wide with terror.

"Out!" he snapped, shoving them both into the open. "Run!"

Closer to the Twolegs, Coal and Snowy were trying to urge Percy along, but the dark gray tabby could hardly stagger between them, his legs stiff and his gaze fixed as if he had seen his worst nightmares come true.

There was no sign of Red or the other cat Stick had spotted in the shadows. For a moment he was torn between staying to help his friends, or going after his daughter. With a quick glance up and down the alley he realized that his companions could look after themselves and help one another.

Red is all alone, with that strange cat after her!

He turned tail on the Twolegs and bolted around the corner after Red and the other cat. Almost at once he picked up his daughter's scent and the scent of the cat he had glimpsed in the shadows. Red was definitely being followed. The banging and crashing carried on behind him, but he was too worried about Red to turn back. He opened his mouth to distinguish the cat scents among all the other smells that thronged the air and kept his ears pricked to pick up the tiniest sound beneath the din from the attacking Twolegs.

The trail led him down the alley and through a series of backyards until it reached a crumbling wooden Twoleg nest. The door hung off its fastenings, and there were gaping holes in the walls and roof. Brambles had wound their tendrils around the walls as if they were trying to pull it into the earth.

Stick's belly churned. *That cat has Red trapped in there!*

There was no sound when he paused to listen, so he followed the scent trail through a gap in the brambles that led to a jagged hole in the shed wall. In the darkness he could just make out two shadows close together, the larger figure bending over the smaller one.

Has that cat killed her?

Stick leaped into the shed with a screech and thrust the other cat away from his daughter. They rolled together on the hard earth floor in a tangle of legs and tail.

"What are you *doing*?" Red hissed.

Stick scrambled to his paws and let his opponent roll away from him. It was a powerful gray-and-brown tabby tom. Green fire blazed in his eyes, and he bared his teeth in a snarl as he slid out his claws and crouched, ready to spring on Stick again.

"Harley, don't!" Red cried.

Stick whirled to face his daughter.

"I *knew* you didn't trust me," Red spat, glaring at her father. "You followed me to spy on me!"

"I didn't!" Stick growled. "I thought you were in danger."

"She's not." The gray-brown tom, Harley, padded over to Red and stood so close to her that their pelts brushed. "I'd never let anything happen to her."

"I don't believe you!" Stick was still braced for an attack, even though the tom had sheathed his claws. "You're leading her into a trap."

"Are you completely mouse-brained?" Red thrust her face close to her father's, her whiskers quivering in fury. "Harley came to take me away from the alley today because he knew the Twolegs were going to attack."

Stick stared at her. If the wooden nest had fallen around his ears at the moment, he wouldn't have been able to move. "You *knew*? And you never thought to warn the rest of us? You just went off and left us?"

"What else could I do?" Red stood her ground, unrepentant. "None of you would have believed a warning from one of Dodge's friends, would you?"

Stick wasn't going to admit she was right. "If you left us to die, you're no daughter of mine," he snarled.

"Fine!" Red flashed back at him.

A red haze swept across Stick's eyes. He slid out his claws and raised a paw to lash his claws across his daughter's face. Harley leaped in front of her, knocking Stick's paw to the side. As Stick struggled to stay on his feet, the haze of anger died away, and he saw the fear in Red's eyes. Every muscle in his body turned to ice as he realized what he had almost done.

Stick wanted to tell her how sorry he was. But the words wouldn't come. He couldn't meet her eyes or talk to her at all. "She's all yours," he growled to Harley, and turned away.

Thrusting his way through the gap in the shed wall, Stick crawled out through the bramble tunnel and across the yards into the alley. He picked up the pace until he was racing along, as if he could leave his horror and disgust behind with Red and the gray-brown tom.

The Twoleg noise had died away as Stick approached the corner of the alley. The air was filled with a silence that made his ears ring. As he turned the corner, Snowy and Cora came to meet him; their eyes were wide and their fur fluffed up.

"Stick, where were you?" Cora wailed. "The Twolegs took Percy!"

CHAPTER 20

❧

"*With so many new warriors in* the Clan," Sharpclaw meowed, "maybe we ought to think about expanding the territory."

The sun was up, pouring golden light into the gorge, but Leafstar's den still lay in shadow when her deputy arrived, dipping his head politely as he padded in.

"That's a good point," Leafstar mused, waving her tail to invite Sharpclaw to sit beside her.

"I suggest sending out two patrols, one on either side of the gorge," the ginger tom went on. "They can investigate the area just outside our borders, and see if there are any good hunting grounds or moss places that we should include."

"That could work," she agreed. "And they ought to look for possible dangers as well. We don't want to enclose territory that we can't defend."

Sharpclaw gave her a brisk nod. "I'll go and set up the patrols, then. I'll get Stick and Shorty to lead them."

"Just a moment." Leafstar stopped her deputy as he was rising to his paws. "There were problems the other day when you assigned Stick and Shorty to lead hunting patrols. The other cats aren't used to them yet."

"Then they'll have to *get* used to them," Sharpclaw snapped. "Stick and the others are full warriors of SkyClan now."

Leafstar sighed. "True, but it's not as easy as that. You can't control how cats feel. Besides, is it a good idea to let newcomers lead these patrols, instead of cats who are more familiar with the territory?"

"They've all taken part in border patrols often enough," Sharpclaw pointed out with a flick of his tail.

"All the same," Leafstar mewed firmly, "I don't think it's a good idea to single out the newcomers for special duties instead of cats who have grown up in the Clan. Not all the time. It's going to cause problems."

Sharpclaw flexed his claws in annoyance, while Leafstar tried to ignore the rising tension between herself and her deputy. *What's happening to us? Why is Sharpclaw always trying to challenge me?*

"The way I see it is—" Sharpclaw began, his voice rising irritably.

He broke off as a shadow fell across the mouth of the den and Ebonyclaw poked her head inside. "Leafstar, may I have a word with you?"

"We're busy," Sharpclaw meowed. "Come back later."

Already ruffled by their argument, Leafstar was furious that her deputy was answering for her. "No, Ebonyclaw, it's fine," she replied, keeping her voice steady. "Sharpclaw and I were just finishing. Stick and Patchfoot will lead the patrols," she added to her deputy, with a wave of her tail to dismiss him.

"Fine." Sharpclaw gave his leader an icy glare and stalked out of the den.

Ebonyclaw watched him go. "I'm sorry if I interrupted something. . . ."

"Don't worry about it," Leafstar mewed. *And now I suppose Ebonyclaw is going to complain about Frecklepaw helping Echosong again. If it's not one thing it's another.* "I'll have another word with Echosong—"

"No, it's not that," Ebonyclaw responded. "I wanted to talk to you about something else. Have you noticed that Shrewtooth hasn't been himself recently?"

Leafstar blinked in surprise. She hadn't thought much at all about the young black tom. Apart from his excessive nervousness, he was quiet and he didn't cause trouble, which made him easy to overlook when other cats were making more noise.

"I'm worried that he's feeling left out," Ebonyclaw went on. "He's always been shy, but lately he hardly says anything. He never said a word at the last Gathering, and he never volunteers for patrols anymore. It's as if he thinks that no cat will want to hunt with him."

Leafstar's neck fur had begun to stand up. It sounded as if Ebonyclaw was deliberately hunting for trouble. "If Shrewtooth has a problem," she mewed, "then he ought to know he can come to me about it."

"But what if he *doesn't* know?" Ebonyclaw suggested. "You've been very busy with the visitors lately."

Leafstar bristled even more at hearing the new warriors referred to as "visitors." She didn't like Ebonyclaw's implication that she had neglected the existing members of her Clan in favor of Stick and his friends. *Is it true? Have I really been unfair to Shrewtooth?*

Leafstar had to admit that she hadn't talked to Shrewtooth for a while, and she struggled to remember putting him on any patrols. *He must have been fulfilling his warrior duties, or I would have heard about it from Sharpclaw.*

"I have time for all my Clanmates," she meowed to Ebonyclaw, keen to show that she was in control. "I'll go hunting with Shrewtooth today, and give him the chance to speak to me in private."

Ebonyclaw dipped her head. "Thank you."

Once again Leafstar felt her fur rising. *I shouldn't need to be thanked for doing my duty as Clan leader!* Forcing her fur to lie flat again, she tried to convince herself that she was being oversensitive, but she still felt unsettled when Ebonyclaw had gone and she went to look for Shrewtooth.

The black tom was crouched by himself at the edge of the stream, staring into the water. He jumped up as Leafstar approached, his claws skittering on the stones. "Uh . . . Leafstar . . ." he stammered.

"Hi, Shrewtooth," Leafstar mewed, trying to sound casual. "I'm going hunting. Do you feel like coming with me?"

The black tom's eyes widened. "Yes . . . yes, that would be great," he choked.

"Good." Leafstar couldn't help thinking he looked as if he'd just been given a punishment. "It'll give us a chance to catch up away from all the noise and bustle around here."

Shrewtooth gave her a scared nod, as if she'd suggested they should go and fight foxes.

Leafstar's paws felt clumsy and oversized as she led the way across the Rockpile and up one of the trails on the other side of the gorge. She was acutely aware of the young tom following her, and a thorn of guilt stabbed her as she wondered if he was actually afraid of her.

I'm his Clan leader! He should trust me, not act as if I'm going to claw his ears off!

At the top of the cliff, she headed for the deeper woodland on the border of their territory. Shrewtooth padded behind her, starting at every rustle in the undergrowth. When a blackbird shot out of the ferns just ahead, he jumped, then arched his back and dug his claws into the ground as if he was facing an enemy.

"It's only a blackbird," Leafstar mewed mildly.

"Sorry! I'm really sorry!" Shrewtooth looked so miserable that Leafstar wished she hadn't spoken.

I just wanted to reassure him, not tell him off!

"It's okay," she muttered. "Let's hunt."

Shouldering her way through the bracken, she tasted the air and picked up the scent of a thrush. She glanced back at Shrewtooth and angled her ears toward the bird, which was pulling a worm out of the ground at the foot of an oak tree a couple of fox-lengths ahead.

At once Shrewtooth dropped into the hunter's crouch and began to creep forward. Leafstar watched his action approvingly. *He would be a good hunter if he weren't so nervous.*

But Shrewtooth had hardly moved when the thrush tugged the worm free and flew up with it onto a low branch of the oak tree. Shrewtooth turned to Leafstar, his eyes wide with distress, as if he expected a scolding for letting the prey escape.

"Not your fault," Leafstar whispered. "We'll catch it anyway. Work your way around the tree and climb up from the other side. Find yourself a branch just above the thrush."

Shrewtooth nodded and slipped off. When he had gone, Leafstar slid through the bracken in the other direction until she could climb an ash tree whose branches mingled with the oak's.

The thrush had swallowed the worm and was shifting from foot to foot on the branch. Leafstar spotted Shrewtooth's face peering out from a clump of leaves just above. Cautiously she crept out along a branch until she could cross into the oak, this time below the thrush. When she was a tail-length away she rose to her paws and let out an earsplitting screech.

Now, Shrewtooth!

The black warrior was ready. As the thrush fluttered upward with a raucous alarm call, Shrewtooth swiped out a paw and snagged his claws in its feathers. He grabbed it by the neck in his jaws and scrambled out of the leaves, his eyes glowing with triumph.

"Well done!" Leafstar meowed.

She leaped down to the ground; a heartbeat later Shrewtooth landed beside her with a soft thud, his prey in his teeth.

"That was great!" he puffed, dropping the thrush at

Leafstar's paws. "Can we do it again?"

He was quivering with excitement now, not fear. *He's a different cat,* Leafstar thought. "I certainly hope we can," she replied. "Let's just bury this, and we'll see what else we can find."

When she had scratched earth over the thrush, Leafstar padded on, relieved that Shrewtooth had boosted his confidence with a good catch. She tasted the scent markers as they crossed the border, but there was no scent of prey close by.

Where has everything gone? she wondered, flicking her tail in frustration as she headed deeper into the woods. Instead of the prey-scents she was hoping for, she picked up the taint of rotting crow-food and the smell of dog. Rounding a bramble thicket, she found herself in a clearing. At the opposite side was a broken-down Twoleg fence, with an untidy red-stone nest beyond.

I know this place! she realized, halting in shock. *It's where we rescued Petalnose and the kits from the Twoleg who kept her a prisoner.*

The fur along her spine stood up as she remembered being part of the patrol led by Firestar: how Sharpclaw and Patchfoot had made such a racket fighting in the garden that the Twoleg had come out, leaving the door open for Leafdapple, Firestar, and Rainfur, Petalnose's mate, to slip inside the den and bring out Petalnose with her kits.

Leafstar had never meant to come back here. It was a dark place, heavy with the memory of Twoleg cruelty. "Come on, Shrewtooth," she meowed. "Let's—"

She broke off when she turned and saw the young black tom crouched on the ground, his claws digging into the earth and his eyes tight shut. "Oh, no, no . . ." he whispered.

Puzzled, Leafstar touched her tail to the black warrior's shoulder. "Shrewtooth? What's the matter?"

The young tom stared up at her, his eyes stretched so wide with horror that she thought they might burst out of his head. "It's a trap . . . a trap," he moaned. "You brought me here. . . . I knew you never wanted me in the Clan! But I'll never go back!" he added fiercely. "Never!"

"Shrewtooth, I don't know what you mean." Leafstar spoke gently. She had never seen any cat as frightened as this, not even when Firestar had led them against the rats in the barn. "Of course I want you in SkyClan. I made you a warrior, didn't I?"

Shrewtooth blinked, but he was still shaking with terror. "Yes . . . you did . . . but this place . . . It's evil. . . . Evil . . ."

Leafstar guessed that for whatever reason the Twoleg den had driven Shrewtooth into a daze of fear. She decided that pointing out there was no sign of danger right now wouldn't help at all. "Yes, it's a foul place, so we won't stay here," she meowed. "We'll find somewhere else to hunt. Come on."

She nudged Shrewtooth to his paws and guided him with her tail across his shoulders, back around the bramble thicket and through the woods until they crossed the border into SkyClan territory.

But Shrewtooth was still in no state to hunt. His eyes were unfocused as if inwardly they were still fixed on the dark den. He kept on shaking, and stumbled over every pebble and twig in his path. Leafstar realized that all she could do was lead him back to camp.

* * *

"Leafstar, what happened?" Echosong popped her head out of her den as Leafstar guided Shrewtooth into the medicine cat's outer cave.

The young black tom sank to the ground, shivering, and covered his nose with his tail. Leafstar sat beside him, exhausted by the long journey back, nudging Shrewtooth every paw step of the way.

"Is he hurt?" Echosong queried, padding up to Shrewtooth and giving him a sniff.

"No, I don't know what the matter is," Leafstar replied. "We were out hunting, and we ended up beside that Twoleg den—the one where Petalnose was shut up. And suddenly Shrewtooth was like this. He won't explain why."

"Shrewtooth?" Echosong bent closer to the quivering black tom and touched his ear lightly with her nose. "You're safe here. Tell us what we can do to help."

But Shrewtooth's only reply was a low moaning sound.

Echosong sighed and shook her head. "I think the best I can do is give him some poppy seeds to help him sleep. Maybe when he wakes he'll be able to talk about it."

Leafstar nodded. "If you think that's best."

While Echosong went to fetch poppy seeds from the niche in the rock where she kept her supplies, Leafstar slipped out of the den. Glancing around, she spotted Mintpaw padding past with a mouse dangling from her jaws.

"Mintpaw, I need you to fetch Petalnose," she meowed. "Tell her it's urgent."

The apprentice sped off, tossing her prey onto the fresh-kill pile as she went. *Maybe Petalnose can get some sense out of Shrewtooth,* Leafstar thought as she returned to the den.

She found that Echosong had moved Shrewtooth into one of the scrapes in the floor of the outer cave, where sick cats lay to be treated. She was shaking out a poppy head so that the black seeds fell out near Shrewtooth's nose.

"Lick those up," she ordered.

The black warrior shuddered, but raised his head to do as he was told, then sank back into the nest with a sigh. Gradually his breathing steadied and his shivering died away. Leafstar thought that he might be drifting into sleep, when Petalnose appeared at the mouth of the den.

"Mintpaw said you wanted me," the gray she-cat meowed, with a polite nod to Echosong.

As quickly as she could, Leafstar told her about their visit to the old Twoleg den, and how it had affected Shrewtooth.

Understanding flooded into Petalnose's blue eyes. "Can't you see?" she asked when Leafstar had finished. "That Twoleg must have shut Shrewtooth up there, too."

Without waiting for Leafstar to reply, she padded across the outer cave to Shrewtooth and crouched down beside him, stroking his shoulder with her tail. "You were there, weren't you, in that horrible den?" she mewed softly. "Do you want to tell us about it?"

"I was born on a farm," Shrewtooth began, his voice a drowsy whisper. "My mother died when I was still a kit, and I strayed off into the woods. I was managing all right, hunting mice and shrews, and then this filthy old Twoleg came and grabbed me."

A shudder ran through him. Petalnose went on stroking him and murmured, "But it's over now. You're safe."

"He shut me in his den with a nest of dirty old pelts," Shrewtooth went on. His voice had sunk even lower, so that Leafstar and Echosong had to creep closer to hear. "He fed me on crow-food . . . when he fed me at all. Even the smell made me sick. His dog was always barking and snuffling around the den where I was shut in, and I was terrified that it would get at me."

"A dog?" Petalnose sounded shocked. "That's awful. There was no dog when I was there."

"It's a huge brute, with such big teeth. . . ." Another shudder rippled through Shrewtooth.

"It's not here now. You'll never have to see it again," Petalnose promised.

"But what if it gets loose in the woods?"

Leafstar wondered if that was the reason for Shrewtooth's nervousness. *Is he always expecting the Twoleg's dog to leap out at him?* "The dog won't come after you here," she meowed. "And even if it does, we have warriors who can deal with it."

"How did you escape?" Echosong prompted him.

"I climbed up and up." Sleep, brought on by the poppy seeds, was blurring Shrewtooth's words. "Up through a long, dark tunnel that led into the sky. And then I fell down and down until I landed in a bramble thicket."

"You were very brave." Petalnose gave the black tom's ear a lick.

"The dog knew I was there," Shrewtooth went on. "But I was in the middle of the thicket, and it couldn't get at me. At last it went away, and I got out. I'd wrenched one of my legs, but I managed to make it as far as the cliffs."

"And Waspwhisker found you there," Leafstar finished for him. "I'm glad he did, Shrewtooth. I'm proud to have you as a warrior of SkyClan."

Shrewtooth shook his head, rustling the bracken underneath him. "I was ashamed because the Twoleg kept me a prisoner," he confessed. "That's why I never told any cat where I came from."

"There's nothing to be ashamed of," Petalnose assured him gently. "I was a prisoner there, too, with Mintpaw and Sagepaw, when they were kits."

Shrewtooth blinked and struggled to focus on the pale gray she-cat. "You were?"

"I don't like to talk about it either," Petalnose continued. "And I had to be rescued. You escaped all by yourself. You should be proud, not ashamed."

Shrewtooth's only reply was a long sigh; he seemed to relax.

"He's sleeping now," Echosong murmured, giving him another sniff. "You'd better leave him to rest."

Leafstar padded out of the den with Petalnose close behind. Her belly churned with a mixture of fury and helplessness. "Twolegs!" she spat, scraping her claws on the path. "They think they can do anything they want!"

"How *dare* he do that to Shrewtooth!" Petalnose was just as angry, flexing her claws and lashing her tail. "I hate thinking that more cats have suffered like I did. Leafstar, we need to teach that Twoleg a lesson!"

Leafstar stared at her. "We're just cats. What can we do against Twolegs?"

"Plenty." A threatening meow came from behind Leafstar; she glanced over her shoulder to see Sharpclaw padding up, his green eyes flashing fury. Obviously he had overheard enough to work out what was going on. "That Twoleg is an enemy of SkyClan," he announced, swiping one forepaw through the air to emphasize his words. "And he'll be treated as such!"

Leafstar wasn't sure what Sharpclaw intended to do, but she told him everything that Shrewtooth had said.

"So there's a dog there now," Sharpclaw mused when she had finished. "That makes it more complicated. We'd have to deal with it. . . ." His voice died away thoughtfully.

"Just a moment," Leafstar meowed. "I haven't said that we're going to *deal with* anything."

"You can't ignore this." There was a flame burning in Petalnose's blue eyes that Leafstar had never seen there before. "How many more cats does this Twoleg get to torture?"

"I think you should call a Clan meeting," Sharpclaw suggested. "See what other cats think."

Leafstar considered her deputy's idea for a moment. She wasn't happy about it; she felt as if she was putting a paw into a fast-flowing river that might well sweep her away, and her Clanmates with her. But Sharpclaw and Petalnose had a point: The Clan was at risk with this cruel Twoleg living so close to their borders.

"Very well," she decided, and jumped up to the top of the Rockpile.

The clouds had built up while Leafstar and Shrewtooth

were returning from the woods, and a cold wind buffeted her fur as she stood on the smooth gray boulders. She shivered as she let out a yowl. "Let all cats old enough to catch their own prey join here beneath the Rockpile for a Clan meeting!"

Cherrytail, Rockshade, and Waspwhisker appeared from the warriors' den and padded down the trail. Lichenfur and Tangle emerged to sit in the entrance to their den, while Clovertail listened from the ledge outside the new birthing den. Sagepaw joined his littermate, Mintpaw, near Echosong's den. The medicine cat sat in the entrance, where she could keep an eye on Shrewtooth as he slept.

Fallowfern guided her kits down the trail from the nursery and tried hard to make them sit quietly while they bounced around with excitement. Billystorm, Ebonyclaw, and Frecklepaw appeared from the direction of the training area, and sat side by side, grooming sand out of their pelts.

Leafstar looked around. None of the newcomers had arrived for the meeting, nor had Harveymoon and Macgyver. *They must still be out on patrol.* She was about to start speaking, when she spotted Patchfoot heading up the gorge with Cora, Shorty, and Sparrowpelt. They looked surprised to see a Clan meeting in progress, and bounded up to listen.

Leafstar began by explaining what had happened that morning, adding the story of Petalnose's imprisonment for the benefit of those cats who hadn't been Clan members at the time. While she was still speaking Stick's patrol returned, with Coal, Bouncefire, and Tinycloud, who were quickly brought up to date by their Clanmates.

As Leafstar finished, she saw pelts beginning to fluff up, claws sliding out, tails lashing, as her warriors learned what had happened to Petalnose and Shrewtooth. Her misgivings increased.

Sharpclaw will easily convince them we have to fight back. And I'm not sure that's the right thing. It's not the same as fighting against the rats.

"So why are you telling us this?" Cherrytail called. "What are we going to do about it?"

"Claw the Twolegs' ears off!" Sparrowpelt yowled from the back of the crowd.

"Yes, and his dog!" Tinycloud added.

Murmurs of agreement rose from the rest of the Clan, though Leafstar noticed that the new warriors didn't join in. They sat close together, glancing uneasily at one another and saying nothing.

Sharpclaw rose to his paws from where he was sitting at the foot of the Rockpile, and raised his tail for silence. "You're right, something must be done," he began, "but—"

He broke off as Harveymoon and Macgyver raced over the rim of the gorge and skittered down the trail, only just managing to come to a halt at the edge of the crowd of cats.

"Sorry!" Harveymoon panted. "I know we're late, but Macgyver's Twolegs didn't let him out."

"What's going on here?" Macgyver wheezed.

Tinycloud bounced over to them and repeated the story in an excited whisper while Sharpclaw continued.

"This Twoleg is a danger to any cat who goes near him. He could be a danger to us, especially if we decide to expand our territory on that side of the gorge. Something has to be done."

"I know!" Sparrowpelt jumped up. "Let's dig a big pit and lure the Twoleg into it."

"Great idea!" his littermate Cherrytail agreed. "We could throw things at him."

Sharpclaw rolled his eyes. "Right, let me know when you've dug a pit big enough. Like, by next leaf-bare."

Mrrows of amusement broke out among the Clan. Sparrowpelt sat down again, twisting his head to give his back a couple of licks, trying to seem unconcerned.

"I've got a better idea," Harveymoon announced, bouncing gently on his paws. "Let me go and make friends with the Twoleg. I could purr and stuff to make him like me, and he'd take me inside his den—"

"And then we'd have to rescue *you*, mouse-brain!" Tinycloud interrupted.

"No, listen!" Harveymoon kinked his tail over his broad white back. "Then I let the rest of you in. And we trap the Twoleg in his own den!"

There was silence as the Clan thought about this. "What would we do with the Twoleg once we trapped him?" Leafstar asked. "And what about the dog?"

Harveymoon tipped his head to one side, looking puzzled.

"Any more brilliant ideas?" Sharpclaw meowed scathingly.

Before Harveymoon could say anything, a loud wail came from Echosong's den. The medicine cat vanished rapidly inside, and returned a heartbeat later with Shrewtooth. She padded close beside him as they came to join the meeting.

"Nightmares," she mewed briefly in explanation. "I think he'll feel better if he's with the rest of us."

"Sorry," Shrewtooth muttered, his head hanging.

"You've got nothing to be sorry for," Leafstar told him. "And you're welcome to join us. You might come up with some useful ideas."

"*We* have an idea." Bouncefire and Rockshade had been murmuring to each other with their heads close together; now Bouncefire rose to his paws. "We're SkyClan cats, right? So we should use SkyClan skills to deal with the Twoleg."

Rockshade stood beside his littermate. "Some of us should climb trees near the Twoleg nest. Then some others lure the Twoleg out and underneath the trees."

"And then we jump on him!" Bouncefire finished. "That's using skills from how we hunt prey. Why should we treat the Twoleg like a different kind of enemy?"

"Because he *is* a different kind of enemy!" Coal leaped to his paws. "Are you all flea-brained? You've no idea what you're getting yourselves into."

Several cats flinched with surprise as the black tom spoke. Leafstar scanned the group of newcomers. It was as clear as the sun in greenleaf that none of them wanted to take part in a raid on the Twoleg.

What do they know about Twolegs that we don't?

"Go on, Coal," she prompted.

But it was Cora who spoke. "Why are you talking about

hurting this Twoleg?" she demanded. "That's not the kind of thing that cats do. You should stay well clear, and be thankful you can live separately, here in the gorge. If you take on Twolegs, you are risking too much. They can hurt you worse than dogs or foxes, you know. This is not a battle that can be won—or should be fought," she finished, sitting down again with a swish of her tail.

Yowls of protest broke out from among the Clan.

"How do you know we can't win?" Waspwhisker growled.

"Yes," Billystorm agreed. "We're strong, and we can fight."

"I think you're scared!" Ebonyclaw meowed, glaring at the newcomers.

"I'm sure that's not true." Leafstar raised her tail to end the protests. "No cat is scared of the Twoleg. We just need to find a way to teach him to stop hurting cats."

A short silence followed her words; it was broken by Stick, who stood up and let his gaze travel solemnly around the Clan until every cat was waiting for him to speak.

"Fear is your best weapon," he announced quietly. "Fear leaves you hollow, paralyzed, unable to think." He dipped his head toward Shrewtooth, who was quaking miserably at the back of the crowd. "You can't hurt the Twoleg," Stick went on, "but you can frighten him."

Staring at the ragged brown tom, Leafstar wondered if he was speaking from his own experiences. Her pelt itched all over with curiosity, but she knew this wasn't the right time or place to question him. *Besides, he would never give me a straight answer.*

"I think Stick is right," Sharpclaw meowed. "We need to give the Twoleg a taste of his own medicine, and make him as scared of cats as Shrewtooth is scared of him."

"So we won't actually attack the Twoleg?" Leafstar checked.

Sharpclaw looked grim. "Oh, we attack him all right—we'll make him think his worst fears are coming true, that the cats he once tortured have come back to seek revenge. But we won't get close enough for him to touch us, and that way we'll keep ourselves safe. Stick is right, cats don't fight Twolegs, and never will." He shot a glance at Shrewtooth, who seemed to have shrunk even further into his pelt. "But there are ways to hurt that don't leave scars."

Leafstar narrowed her eyes. Was it possible to scare the Twoleg into leaving cats alone without risking their own pelts? "Tell us what you think we could do," she invited Sharpclaw.

Leaping down from the Rockpile, she joined her deputy on the flattened sand. The rest of the Clan gathered around, huddling in the shelter of the boulders as the wind rose, sending clouds scudding across the sky.

Sharpclaw stretched out one claw and drew lines in the dust in front of him. "Here's the clearing, and this is the Twoleg nest," he began as he sketched the shapes. "And this is where we'll start. . . ."

CHAPTER 21

❧

Leafstar woke as a paw prodded her in the side. "Leafstar! Leafstar, wake up!"

It was Sharpclaw's voice. Leafstar opened her eyes and blinked at him as he stood over her, one paw raised to prod her again.

"What's the matter?" she muttered, scrambling out of her nest. "Are we being attacked?"

"No, but we have to go now," Sharpclaw hissed. When Leafstar stared at him, puzzled, he added, "To the Twoleg's nest, to give him a fright he won't forget."

"No." Leafstar shook her head. "We agreed to attack tomorrow night, as long as the weather was better."

"But the clouds have cleared. Look!" Sharpclaw backed away to the entrance to the den, and stood on the trail outside, his shape outlined against an almost full moon. He waved his tail at a sky glittering with the warriors of Silverpelt. "You couldn't hope for a better night than this."

"But the kittypets have gone home," Leafstar argued. "They promised to stay tomorrow night and help with the attack. We can't leave them out again, not when they were so upset about the fight against the rats."

Sharpclaw twitched his tail impatiently. "That's their problem. This is the best night for attacking. We need as much light as possible."

Leafstar twitched her nose. "I suppose you're right," she admitted reluctantly.

But as she shook moss out of her fur and headed down the trail into the gorge, she couldn't shake off a nagging sense of guilt. She could imagine the shock and disappointment on the faces of the daylight-warriors when they heard that the attack had taken place without them. *What am I going to say to them? And will Billystorm think that I lied to him?*

Sharpclaw ran nimbly across the face of the cliff to rouse the warriors in their den, then led the way down to the river. Leafstar joined them near the foot of the Rockpile. The moon cast black shadows across the cliffs and turned the surface of the river to bubbling silver; every rock and tree stood out sharply against the wash of pale light. *Sharpclaw was right. This is a good night to attack.* But deep inside, she still knew that this wasn't right.

Though no cat had called them, Sagepaw and Mintpaw burst out of their den and raced down to join the warriors.

"Are you going now?" Mintpaw panted, her eyes gleaming. "I want to come, too!"

"And me," Sagepaw added. "I want to teach that Twoleg a lesson, after what he did to our mother."

"Mintpaw, you can certainly come," Leafstar replied. "But I'm not sure about you, Sagepaw. It's a long way. Will your leg hold out?"

"My leg is fine now!" the apprentice insisted.

"Echosong, what do you think?" Leafstar asked the medicine cat, who had padded up in time to hear the discussion.

Echosong twitched her ears. "I know how much this means to Sagepaw . . ." she began hesitantly. "I suppose he can go," she mewed at last. "But keep an eye on him, Leafstar, and if he starts limping, then take him out of the action."

Leafstar nodded. "I'll do that. And Sagepaw," she added sternly, "if I tell you to back off, you do it. No arguments, okay?"

"I'll keep an eye on him, too," Petalnose promised, shouldering her way through the throng of cats to stand beside her kits.

"You're sure you want to come?" Leafstar meowed, faintly surprised that the she-cat would be willing to return to the den where she had been a prisoner for so long.

"You need me," Petalnose replied steadily. "I know that Twoleg and his nest better than any cat."

"True." Leafstar dipped her head in approval.

"I'll come, too," a shaky voice meowed.

Leafstar spun around to see Shrewtooth, who had crept up behind Echosong, a black shadow in the night. He was trembling, but there was determination in his gaze.

"Thanks, Shrewtooth, but there's no need," Leafstar responded. *Great StarClan! What if he panics like he did this morning?*

"But I want to. I don't want to be a coward anymore."

"No cat will call you a coward," Leafstar promised. "But we don't need every cat to come. Patchfoot is going to stay behind to guard the camp, but he can't do it alone. What if the rats attacked Clovertail and Fallowfern and the kits?"

"Leafstar's right," Sharpclaw added, with more sympathy for the young black tom than Leafstar had expected. "Guarding the camp is the most important job there is. We trust you, Shrewtooth."

The young warrior blinked and stood a little straighter. "Okay, Sharpclaw. I won't let you down."

"I know you won't," Sharpclaw told him.

With a grateful glance at her deputy, Leafstar gathered the rest of her Clan together and led them over the Rockpile and up to the top of the cliff on the far side of the gorge. She noticed that all four newcomers had joined the patrol without any more protest, though they padded along in a tight group at the rear, their tension clear in the swift glances they cast from side to side, and the bristling of their fur.

What secrets are they hiding?

The wind had dropped and the night was warm and still. The only sounds were the soft paw steps of her Clanmates and the swish of ferns and grass as they brushed against well-groomed fur. *It would be a good night for a hunt,* Leafstar thought, not looking forward to what was coming.

As the SkyClan warriors crept across the border, Leafstar noticed that Petalnose was trembling. Slipping through the ferns to her side, she touched her nose briefly to the gray cat's ear. "If it gets too bad, you can go back," she murmured.

Petalnose shook her head. "I can do this, Leafstar," she vowed.

Leafstar padded alongside her to bolster her courage as they headed for the Twoleg den. *Did ThunderClan ever fight Twolegs?* she asked herself, wondering whether their starry ancestors were watching from the sky. *I should have asked Echosong if she had a sign from StarClan about this attack,* she thought with a stab of concern. But wouldn't Echosong have told her? If StarClan was silent, perhaps it meant that they were happy for SkyClan to make their own decision. Leafstar flicked her tail in frustration. Why did it always feel as if she was leading her Clan in the dark? All the stars in the sky didn't seem to give enough light to see where the future lay.

There was a soft hiss from Sharpclaw as the patrol reached the edge of the clearing and halted under the trees opposite the Twoleg nest. It was dark and silent; Leafstar could almost believe the nest had been abandoned. *That would make everything much easier.*

"Right, this is it," Sharpclaw whispered. "You all know what you have to do. Waspwhisker, Shorty, and Cherrytail, go collect dead branches and brambles, and drag them outside the nest door as quietly as you can. We don't want to wake the dog and warn the Twoleg."

The three warriors, already primed from the earlier planning, twitched their ears in acknowledgment and melted into the shadows.

"Cora, Bouncefire, Rockshade." Sharpclaw beckoned the next group of cats with his tail. "You're the fastest runners, so you're going to lead the dog away. Get into position now."

"And make sure you have a good escape route," Leafstar added before the three cats could move. "Climb a tree if you need to. I don't want any cat getting hurt tonight."

"We *know* all this," Bouncefire muttered as he led the others away.

"We'll be careful, Leafstar," Cora mewed; her eyes were full of sympathy, as if she shared her Clan leader's misgivings.

"The rest of you, spread out around the clearing," Sharpclaw went on. "And don't so much as twitch a whisker until you hear Leafstar's signal."

Leafstar crouched beneath the bushes at the edge of the Twoleg garden, her nose quivering at the rank smells that came from the den; scents of dog and rotting Twoleg waste drowned out the sweet night scents of grass and herbs. Moonhigh was close, and the silver light cast sharp-clawed shadows on the walls of the den.

There was a thick whispering sound. Cherrytail, Waspwhisker, and Shorty crept across the open space, dragging branches and tendrils of bramble behind them. Her paws tingling with tension, Leafstar watched them make several trips back and forth from the edge of the wood until they had built a dense, bristling mound outside the door of the nest. Then they melted silently into the bushes. Now the only sounds Leafstar could hear were the faint rustling of leaves and the distant bark of a fox. Her warriors were in position. For a heartbeat her belly cramped as if she had eaten crowfood.

This is it.

"Attack!" she yowled, bunching her hindquarters underneath her and springing forward.

All around her the warriors of SkyClan burst out of the undergrowth and raced toward the Twoleg den. Their yowls split the still night air and sent birds crashing out of the trees with shrieks of alarm. Sharpclaw was the first to reach the den. He leaped up onto the narrow ledge outside the gap in the wall; his paws rattled the hard, transparent barrier as he battered at it. Leafstar, a pace behind him, jumped up to the gap on the other side of the door and hurled herself against it, feeling the transparent stuff shift in its crumbling wooden frame.

Sparrowpelt sprang up beside her, while Tinycloud and Petalnose bounded over the thorn barrier and raked their claws down the door in long, whistling scratches. Leafstar saw the light of battle in Petalnose's eyes; the gray she-cat's nerves had vanished now that the attack had begun. The rest of the Clan gathered close to the nest, wailing as they lashed their tails and dug their claws into the ground. Leafstar's misgivings returned; these looked like cats just waiting for a chance to slash at their enemy with claws and teeth. Would they be able to resist getting dangerously close to the Twoleg or his dog?

Her gaze met Sharpclaw's; the deputy gave her a swift nod, and jumped down to join the warriors on the ground. "Remember we're only trying to scare the Twoleg," he yowled. "We don't want any injuries."

Suddenly light appeared in one of the gaps high up in the den wall, throwing a hard-edged yellow square onto the grass that trapped Mintpaw and Sagepaw in the glare. The two apprentices crouched, frozen in shock.

"Get back!" Sharpclaw screeched, waving his tail to urge his Clanmates away from the nest.

Leafstar repeated the signal. "Keep back! Hide!" she ordered.

The cats dashed for cover on either side of the nest, leaving a clear space in front of the door. Leafstar found herself crouching in a clump of ferns with Shorty beside her. The brown tom was shivering, his eyes wide and his gaze fixed on the light in the wall of the Twoleg den. Leafstar could hear crashing inside the nest and shouts from the Twoleg. The door flew open and the dog stood on the step, its tongue lolling. Leafstar shuddered. The dog's legs were long and bony, its muscles hard and stringy under its smooth pelt. Its small eyes glittered with moonlight as it stared around.

The cats beside the Twoleg nest fell silent, leaving a single eerie wail that came from the far end of the garden. Every hair on Leafstar's pelt prickled. *It even scares me, and I know what it is!* Poking her head out of the ferns she spotted Bouncefire, Cora, and Rockshade, blurry black shapes at the edge of the garden. There was a glint of pointed white teeth as Bouncefire stopped wailing and snapped shut his jaws.

"Come on, flea-pelt!" Rockshade dared the dog. "See if you can catch us!"

The Twoleg—still invisible inside the den—barked out what sounded like a command. The dog leaped over the thorn barrier and hurtled across the garden toward the three warriors.

Run! Now! Leafstar willed them silently.

To her horror, all three cats stayed still, hissing a challenge, until the dog was almost on them. Then they whipped around and raced through the broken-down fence toward the edge of the forest, with the dog hard on their paws.

StarClan, keep them safe! Leafstar prayed, losing sight of them as they led the dog deeper into the brambles.

When the dog had vanished, the remaining SkyClan warriors started yowling again. A heavy, shuffling movement in the doorway caught Leafstar's attention and she narrowed her eyes with cold anger as the old Twoleg who had tormented Petalnose and her kits loomed into view. Gathering his ragged pelts around him, the Twoleg let out an irritable snarl and stepped forward, right into the barrier of thorns. With a screech he toppled over as the branches snagged on his hind feet and sprawled forward onto his face. His hind paws got more and more tangled in the brambles while he flailed around with his forepaws, trying to get up.

When he managed to struggle upright, he held a branch clutched in one forepaw. Leafstar flinched from his anger and fear-scent as he glared around the clearing. Sparrowpelt slipped out from the shelter of a bush; the Twoleg staggered forward, swiping at him with the branch. Sparrowpelt dodged easily to one side. Then more cats began to appear from their hiding places, racing over the grass with their ears flattened and their lips curled to show pointed teeth.

Not too close! Careful!

Petalnose, Mintpaw, and Sagepaw stood directly in front

of the Twoleg with their backs arched, hissing. Leafstar doubted the Twoleg would recognize them as the half-starved she-cat and her terrified kits who'd escaped from him two seasons ago. Petalnose spat vengeance and fury, and the apprentices beside her looked ready to tear the throats from a whole pack of foxes. Behind them, Wasp-whisker ripped at the grass with his claws, his lips drawn back in a snarl. Stick and Coal stood close together; Leafstar could see the uncertainty in their eyes, and guessed that it wouldn't take much for them to turn tail and flee back to the safety of the trees. Cherrytail and Tinycloud advanced side by side, hissing out their hatred as the Twoleg swung the branch at them.

With a growl from deep in her throat, Petalnose took one step forward. The Twoleg paused with the branch held high in the air and looked at her. Petalnose didn't blink. Instead, she took another step forward, this time lowering her front paws slowly so that the Twoleg could clearly see her long claws. A strange noise came from the Twoleg, a bit like a cough. He let the branch fall onto the ground beside him.

Leafstar sought out Sharpclaw, and spotted him in the shadow of the nest, close to the wall. She curled her tail as a signal. *We must end this now, before some cat gets hurt.*

Sharpclaw stalked out into the open and Leafstar joined him at the center of the ragged semicircle of cats. They had all fallen silent, their gaze fixed on the Twoleg, challenging him to raise the branch again.

"Leave us alone!" Leafstar yowled. She knew that the

Twoleg wouldn't understand, but she spoke the words so that her own Clan could hear them, and hoped that her tone would be enough to warn the Twoleg. "Lay one paw on another cat and we'll do more than show you our claws."

The old Twoleg was letting out high-pitched whimpering sounds now. His hind legs had started to shake and one of his back paws twitched, knocking the branch into the heap of brambles. His fear-scent was rank as a fox. For a couple of heartbeats Leafstar felt sorry for him. Then she looked at Petalnose and her kits and remembered how weak and ill they had been, how close to death, when Firestar had led the patrol that released them from the Twoleg's prison. And she remembered Shrewtooth's horror when he found himself back in the Twoleg's clearing.

The Twoleg deserves to feel as scared as these cats have been.

Leafstar waved her tail to tell her Clanmates that the attack was over. Moving as one, they spun around and raced off into the trees. A glance over her shoulder showed the old Twoleg stumbling back inside his den. The slam of the door echoed into the night.

Pride surged through Leafstar as she led her Clan back through the forest. They had just crossed the border when she heard panting and yelping coming from just ahead, and froze as the dog burst out from a clump of hazel saplings. Sharpclaw shouldered his way to her side, his claws extended.

But the dog paid no attention to any cat, not even pausing to give them a sniff. With its tail between its legs, it fled back toward the Twoleg nest. Dark spots of blood dripped from its nose and spattered over the ground.

Yes! Leafstar thought as she started walking again, through moonlight that was sliced by the shadows of trees.

SkyClan has won!

CHAPTER 22

❦

Leafstar and the rest of the cats caught up to Cora, Bouncefire, and Rockshade near the top of the cliff, so the whole patrol raced across the Rockpile hard on her paws and poured down into the camp.

"You're back!" Patchfoot appeared out of the shadows near the fresh-kill pile, the white patches on his pelt shining pale in the half-light. "What happened?"

"Is any cat hurt?" Echosong called, bounding up from the direction of her den.

It was Sharpclaw who replied. "No, we're all fine. And we gave that crow-food-eating Twoleg a fright he won't forget in a hurry."

"That's great!" Patchfoot exclaimed, his eyes gleaming. "You're all heroes!"

"What about the dog?" Shrewtooth mewed, peering out from behind Patchfoot.

"I doubt the dog will bother us again," Leafstar told him. "We taught it a lesson, too."

"I clawed its nose," Bouncefire announced, pressing forward to give Shrewtooth a friendly nudge. "I wish you'd been there to see it."

Shrewtooth blinked. "I do, too."

"You shouldn't have been near enough to claw it!" Clovertail scolded as she padded up with Fallowfern and the kits. But her eyes glowed with pride as she gazed at her son, and she touched his shoulder approvingly with her tail.

"I can't believe we did it!" Cherrytail panted. "We took on a Twoleg and we beat him!"

"If we can do that, we can do anything!" Sparrowpelt purred.

The cats crowded around the fresh-kill pile to choose a piece of prey while their Clanmates who had stayed behind hailed them with questions. Fallowfern's kits bounced around gleefully, even though it was the middle of the night, getting under every cat's paws as they tried to act out what they imagined had gone on. As she waited to choose her own prey, Leafstar noticed that the four newest warriors had withdrawn a few tail-lengths, and were murmuring to one another with their heads close together. Her paws pricked with uneasiness. *Why don't they want to celebrate with us? It's their victory as much as any cat's.*

Trying to shrug off her nagging anxiety, Leafstar picked out a plump vole for herself. Seeing that her Clanmates were settling down while Sharpclaw began to tell the full story of the attack, she carried her fresh-kill up the trail and sprang over the gap to reach the Skyrock.

The moon was close to setting but the stars of Silverpelt still shone brightly in an indigo sky. A soft breeze, laden with the scents of newleaf, whispered over the surface of the rock. Down below, the river was a silver snake winding among the rocks; Leafstar could just make out the dark huddle of cats at the foot of the Rockpile. She wondered if the spirits of her ancestors were looking down on them. *I hope they are.* She was proud of her warriors, the way they had carried out the plan to scare the Twoleg without putting themselves in danger, the courage they had shown in seeking vengeance on behalf of Shrewtooth and Petalnose. For once, Leafstar hadn't been in doubt that SkyClan was following the right path. But now the attack was over; the Twoleg had been given a fright that would hopefully keep him from torturing more cats in the future; and Leafstar felt herself staring into darkness once more.

She stopped eating with the vole half finished and padded to the very edge of the rock to lay it down. "An offering for the cats who walk the skies," she whispered. *Perhaps I should do this more often,* she thought. *Maybe our ancestors won't come down to share our fresh-kill, but at least they'll be able to see that they are not forgotten. We still hunt in their memory, surviving by their skills.*

Almost as if she had summoned it, she caught a whiff of cat scent and heard the soft pad of paws approaching her from behind. She turned to see Skywatcher stepping lightly through the air toward her, his pelt pure silver and his eyes shining like pools of starlight.

"Welcome," Leafstar murmured, dipping her head.

Skywatcher padded past her to sniff at the prey she had left at the edge of the rock. "A fine, plump creature," he commented, though he didn't eat.

"Skywatcher," Leafstar began hesitantly, "did you and . . . and the other warriors of StarClan see our attack on the Twoleg?"

Skywatcher's reply was a brief nod; Leafstar was disappointed when he didn't tell her what his Clanmates had thought of it. "We planned what we needed to do, and we did it," she meowed, feeling that she had to justify herself to the starry warrior. "Every cat was so brave! And the Twoleg deserved to be frightened. You know what he did to Petalnose and her kits, and to Shrewtooth."

"You certainly won that battle," Skywatcher grunted. "The Twoleg is good and scared, I'll give you that."

Leafstar flicked her tail, frustrated. "Did we do the right thing?" she blurted out.

Skywatcher gave her a long look from fathomless green eyes. "Only time will tell," he mewed at last. "Twolegs aren't the usual sort of enemies for a Clan. They don't steal prey or threaten borders like other cats, and they don't kill kits like foxes or badgers."

"Then have I broken the warrior code?" Leafstar whispered in dismay. "Was I wrong to take a battle to a Twoleg nest?"

To her relief, Skywatcher shook his head, scattering starlight around them. "You are the leader of SkyClan," he pointed out. "You must have confidence in what you do. If the Twoleg was a threat to your Clan, then you were right to attack."

He certainly was a threat, but still . . . "I just want to know what the other Clans would have done," she confessed.

"But you are not the other Clans." The silver glow in Skywatcher's fur blazed out strongly and then began to fade. "You must find your own path."

His outline grew fainter, until it was no more than a glitter of stardust against the rock, and then was gone.

Leafstar remained staring at the place where he had stood. She still felt troubled. How could she find a path for SkyClan when there were no obvious choices to take? *I hope I made the right decisions tonight. I wish I could be sure....*

When Leafstar returned to the gorge, the Clan was still feasting and sharing tongues around the bottom of the Rockpile. She was relieved to see that the four newcomers had joined the others and were sharing prey.

Sharpclaw padded over to meet her at the foot of the trail. "We did well tonight," he remarked, twitching his whiskers in satisfaction. "The Clan feels strong and united."

"That's true," Leafstar murmured.

"The attack on the Twoleg has brought us all together," her deputy went on. "You see, we don't really need the kitty-warriors at all."

Leafstar gazed at him, her mouth open in shock. *Does he resent the daylight-warriors so much?* She and Sharpclaw had worked well together during the attack, reinforcing each other's leadership, reading silent signals to keep their Clanmates safe and focused. But now the old divisions were reappearing. Unable to find a reply, Leafstar turned her back on her deputy and stalked off to her den.

The sound of cheerful yowling outside woke Leafstar the next morning. Yawning, she scrambled out of her nest, wincing at the stiffness in her muscles from the trek through the forest and the attack. She felt as though she hadn't slept for more than a couple of heartbeats, but when she padded to the entrance of her den she saw that the sun had risen above the gorge; warm light slanted over the rocks and glittered on the surface of the river.

Five cats were tumbling over the rim of the gorge and racing down the trail, calling out greetings as they came. Seeing Leafstar, Billystorm halted and waved his tail. "We're here! We're ready for the attack!"

Leafstar felt her heart drop down into her paws. *What am I going to tell them?* She began to make her way across the cliff face toward Billystorm and the others, setting her paws down carefully on the narrow trail. But before she reached them, Cherrytail popped her head out of the warriors' den, a few tail-lengths below where the daylight-warriors had halted.

"You're too late!" the tortoiseshell she-cat announced. "We attacked last night, and it went really well!"

Leafstar flinched. *If I'd had the chance, I would have been a bit more tactful than that!*

"What?" Ebonyclaw arched her back and let out a hiss of annoyance. "You went without us?"

The usually gentle Frecklepaw flicked her tail, looking as angry as her mentor.

Harveymoon and Macgyver glanced at each other with indignation in their eyes. "Hey, I was looking forward to that!" Harveymoon exclaimed.

"Yeah, I made my Twolegs give me more food, just so I'd be ready," Macgyver agreed.

"I'm sorry," Leafstar meowed as she reached Billystorm's side. "Come down by the river, where I can explain properly."

More cats were emerging from their dens as Leafstar led the way down into the gorge and found a sun-warmed stone near the water's edge where she could sit and talk to the daylight-warriors. She was aware of their hostile looks and bristling fur as they gathered around her. She was grateful to see Sharpclaw padding up to join her, though less so when Cherrytail, Sparrowpelt, and Waspwhisker bounded after him and sat down on the edge of the group.

We've got the makings of a serious split in the Clan here, unless I'm careful.

"I can't believe you didn't wait for us!" Ebonyclaw burst out, before Leafstar had the chance to speak. "We planned it all so carefully."

"Yeah, why did you leave us out?" Harveymoon demanded.

"I'm sorry," Leafstar began. She sympathized too much with the kittypets to be able to justify herself convincingly. "We needed a clear night for the attack, and after the clouds disappeared—"

"That's right," Sharpclaw chipped in. "We couldn't be sure when we would get another chance."

Billystorm glanced up at the cloudless blue sky and flicked his ears, though he said nothing. Embarrassment flooded through Leafstar, making her pelt itch. She could see that tonight promised to be just as clear as the night before; they could easily have waited for the kittypets. *But we didn't know that.*

"You know, you kittypets want to have it both ways," Sparrowpelt meowed, stepping forward with his head thrust out aggressively. "You spend time here in the Clan, but then you shove off to your Twoleg nests for strokes and soft beds."

"It shouldn't be like that," Cherrytail agreed. "When Firestar was here, he told us we had to choose, and that's what we did."

"But Firestar isn't here anymore," Harveymoon pointed out, swinging his head around to glare at Sparrowpelt and his sister.

"The warrior code hasn't changed," Sparrowpelt countered. "You have to be proper Clan cats if you want to be included in everything."

Ebonyclaw jumped to her paws. "Are you saying that we're *not* proper Clan cats?" she demanded, her tail lashing.

"You tell me," Sparrowpelt growled. "Do proper Clan cats eat Twoleg food? Do they purr around Twolegs and beg to be stroked?"

Leafstar's belly churned as the quarrel she had dreaded erupted; more of the Clan cats were clustering around now, and there were more glares aimed at the daylight-warriors.

"This isn't right," Billystorm meowed. He was calmer than the rest, but there was a bitter edge in his voice. "We train and hunt with you, but when there's anything important going on, you don't want us. You left us out of the rat attack, and now this."

"And we managed fine without you, thanks," Cherrytail flashed back at him.

Before Leafstar could say anything, Sharpclaw shouldered his way between the hostile cats.

"That's enough," he growled. "The attack happened, it's over, and that's the end of it. Next time we plan something," he added, "you kittypets might make more effort to be here."

Sparrowpelt blinked in satisfaction, but Leafstar was appalled by the unfairness of Sharpclaw's comment. He almost seemed to be deliberately setting the gorge-based cats against the daylight-warriors.

He wouldn't try to make the full Clan cats drive them out, would he? That would split the Clan forever!

"We're sorry it happened like this," Leafstar repeated, rising to her paws. "We made what we thought was the right decision at the time. Now let's put it behind us."

As she spoke, she spotted Sharpclaw glaring at her, as if by apologizing she was showing signs of weakness. *My Clan, my decisions,* she told herself.

"It's past time to set the patrols," she reminded Sharpclaw tartly. "Or are we going to sit around in the gorge all day?"

The cats were still grumbling as the deputy sorted them into patrols, and Leafstar guessed it would be a long time before their ruffled feelings were forgotten. At least Sharpclaw had the sense to include all the kittypets in the first set of patrols, though he didn't ask any of them to lead.

"Petalnose, you and Waspwhisker can take your apprentices and give them some hunting training," he ordered. "Ebonyclaw and Frecklepaw, go with them. Billystorm, you too. No sign yet of Snookpaw?" he asked after a moment's pause.

Billystorm shook his head. "I went by his nest on my way here this morning," he replied. "But everything was shut up and quiet."

"He's missing a lot of training," Sharpclaw commented.

Leafstar wondered if Billystorm would take offense at the veiled criticism, but the ginger-and-white tom just dipped his head in agreement. "I'll make sure he catches up when he comes back."

"See that you do," Sharpclaw mewed.

Petalnose took her patrol toward the trail that led up the cliff. After hesitating for a moment, Leafstar decided to follow. It was a while since she had observed the apprentices in training, but what she really wanted to see was how the full Clan cats and the daylight-warriors worked together after the earlier tension.

When Leafstar reached the top of the cliff, she spotted Petalnose leading the patrol toward the nearest thicket, the apprentices barely visible in the long grass. As Leafstar bounded up to join them, she heard Mintpaw's voice raised boastfully.

"We really scared that old Twoleg! You should have seen us."

"And heard us," Sagepaw added. "We yowled so loud, I'm surprised we didn't wake you up in your Twoleg nests!"

Leafstar stiffened. Had the apprentices no sense at all, to taunt the daylight-warriors by bragging about the attack? Ebonyclaw's tail-tip was flicking irritably from side to side; Frecklepaw was looking sulky, and Billystorm opened his jaws to speak, then obviously thought better of it.

"You kittypets missed an awesome patrol!" Mintpaw continued.

Leafstar's paws itched to intervene, but it was up to the mentors to discipline their apprentices. She was surprised that neither Petalnose nor Waspwhisker said a word. *They probably feel the same,* she thought, biting back an angry comment.

"This patrol is too big for a successful hunt," she meowed, padding up to join the others. "Billystorm, why don't you come with me? Ebonyclaw and Frecklepaw, too."

"Good idea," Billystorm responded instantly, with a flash of understanding in his amber eyes.

As he spoke, Leafstar spotted Mintpaw and Sagepaw exchanging a glance, their eyes gleaming. *Now what's their problem?* she wondered, but neither apprentice said anything.

Petalnose nodded in reply to Leafstar's suggestion, and led her remaining patrol farther into the thicket. Leafstar turned the other way, along the top of the cliff in the direction of the Twolegplace. She could feel the relief among the daylight-warriors as they followed her, and she wondered bleakly if her Clanmates would ever learn to work together.

"Right," she began as they approached a stretch of bushes and thick undergrowth. "What I'd like to try today is working out ways of hunting as a group. We all do better if we cooperate. We—"

She broke off as Echosong emerged from some close-growing stems of fern with a bundle of herbs in her mouth. The medicine cat blinked with barely concealed surprise as she saw Leafstar's patrol, and padded up to her Clan leader.

"Can I have a word with you?" she meowed, laying her bundle down.

"Of course." Leafstar glanced at Billystorm. "Take the others into the bushes and see what you can find."

Billystorm flicked his ears in acknowledgment, and vanished among the undergrowth with Ebonyclaw and Frecklepaw hard on his paws. Leafstar noticed that Frecklepaw glanced regretfully over her shoulder at Echosong as the ferns closed behind her.

"Well?" Leafstar prompted, fully prepared for Echosong to raise the question of an apprentice again.

"Are you sure you're doing the right thing?" Echosong queried. Leafstar blinked at her in surprise. "I know there was trouble this morning," the medicine cat went on, "but you won't solve it by keeping the daylight-warriors separate from the others."

Leafstar hadn't noticed Echosong among the cats beside the river that morning, but she obviously knew all about the quarrel. "What else can I do?" she protested. "Wait until they start clawing one another's ears off?"

"I don't know," Echosong admitted. "But splitting the cats up won't help the tensions in the Clan. In the end, it'll make them worse."

Leafstar had a grudging feeling that her Clanmate was right. "Then what's the answer? I don't want to turn any cat away, but allowing daylight-warriors—okay, *kittypets*—into the Clan obviously isn't working." She lowered her head, feeling as if dark storm clouds had rolled across the sky to blot out the sun. "I sometimes wonder if Firestar was right to give me the leadership of SkyClan."

"That's mouse-brained," Echosong mewed briskly. "*Star-Clan* chose you as our leader, not Firestar. And I know that there's no cat in the Clan who could do it better. But Leafstar, you—" She broke off.

Leafstar wondered what the young she-cat wasn't telling her. "Go on," she prompted. "Say what you want to say."

Echosong shook her head. "Nothing . . . nothing, really. Just—Leafstar, be careful of your own feelings, that's all."

She picked up her bundle of herbs and padded off toward the top of the trail, leaving her Clan leader staring blankly after her.

Be careful of my own feelings? What did she mean by that?

CHAPTER 23

❧

"What do you mean, the Twolegs took Percy?" Stick spat, scraping his claws on the hard stone of the Twoleg alley.

Snowy's ears were laid flat to her head with horror and distress. "He couldn't run fast enough. They just grabbed him!" she wailed.

"I'm sorry!" Shorty panted, bounding up with Coal to join Cora and Snowy. "There wasn't anything we could do to stop them."

Coal's neck fur was bristling and he drew his lips back in a snarl. "This means war!" he declared.

Cora nodded. "It's mouse-brained to think that we can live alongside Twolegs. They're our enemies!"

Stick narrowed his eyes. "It's not the Twolegs," he growled. "This is all Dodge's fault."

"What do you mean?" Shorty meowed.

Stick told them about the time he had come upon Skipper and Misha torturing the rabbit in the Twoleg garden. A shudder ran through him as he remembered his dream, his paws clogged with blood and fur. "The Twolegs won't let cats attack their rabbits. I think Dodge arranged this so the Twolegs would drive us out."

"But aren't we going to fight for our home?" Coal hissed, his claws rasping against the smooth gray stones that lined the alley.

"Of course we are," Stick retorted. "But not against the Twolegs. Dodge and his cats are the ones we have to fight."

"I'll rip their fur off," Coal snarled. "I'll—hey!" he mewed, breaking off. "Where's Red? Did the Twolegs take her as well?"

"Red's fine," Stick growled. "She got away." Before his friends could ask any more questions, he went on, "So how can we attack Dodge and his cats? Any ideas?"

The others looked at one another.

"It would be easier if we knew where they sleep," Shorty commented.

"But we don't," Cora meowed.

Stick realized how clever Dodge had been. He had taken over the hunting grounds that Stick and his friends had thought of as their own, but he had given nothing away. *The crow-food-eating mangebag has always stayed one step ahead.* "Then find them!" he snapped.

"Do you want to wait until Red comes back?" Cora asked.

"No!" Stick wasn't sure that she was coming back. "We don't need her."

His friends exchanged uneasy looks before heading off in different directions.

"No, *I'll* go that way," Stick ordered Snowy, shouldering the white she-cat away from the direction Red had taken. "You climb the wall and search behind the Twoleg nests."

"Okay." Snowy was obviously surprised, but she leaped the

wall without arguing and disappeared down the other side.

Shame flooded over Stick as he retraced his steps toward the place where he had confronted Red. He couldn't tell the others that his daughter had betrayed them all. *She must have told Harley where we slept, and helped Dodge plan the Twoleg raid.*

Reaching the shed where he had confronted Red and Harley, he picked up his daughter's scent and followed it around the next corner. Her scent mingled closely with Harley's, he noticed with disgust. Scrambling over a low, sloping roof, Stick dropped down into the next alley. He had barely begun following the scent-trail again when he heard paw steps thundering up behind him.

Stick froze, then spun around to see Shorty bounding along the alley.

"I can't let you go off on your own," the brown tom panted as he halted in front of Stick. "It's madness!"

"I'm fine," Stick growled. "And you make so much noise, you couldn't creep up on a fox with no ears."

Whipping around, he carried on up the alley, only to realize that Shorty was keeping pace with him. "I told you, I'm fine!"

Shorty halted again, his amber eyes fixed on Stick. "I've known you too long, old friend," he meowed. "What's wrong?"

Stick couldn't hold his gaze. "It's Red," he muttered, turning his head away. "I . . . I think she betrayed us to Dodge."

Though he wasn't looking at Shorty, he heard his friend's gasp of horror. "I don't believe it!" Shorty protested. "Red would never do that."

"Well, maybe she would. Her mother didn't show much loyalty, did she?"

There was a furious hiss from Shorty. "You know exactly why Velvet did what she did. Red may have her mother's pride and stubbornness, but she gets that from her father as well!" More gently, he added, "You've always been proud that your daughter knows her own mind."

"I'm not sure if she does know her own mind anymore," Stick muttered. "She always—"

He broke off as he spotted a whisk of movement underneath a straggling bush a few fox-lengths away, its roots sinking down into the gap left by a broken paving stone. Bounding up to the bush, Stick paused for a heartbeat to check the scent. *Enemy!* He plunged through the twisted branches and sank his teeth into the scruff of a black-and-silver she-cat who was crouching in a gap between the branches and the wall.

"One of Dodge's lot," he mumbled through a mouthful of fur as he dragged her into the open.

He let the she-cat go, but kept her pinned down with a paw slammed onto her neck. "What's your name?" he snarled.

The she-cat looked too shocked to struggle. "I—I'm called Onion," she stammered.

"Hey, don't be too harsh," Shorty protested, padding up to join them.

Stick ignored him. He slid out his claws until he felt their tips pricking into Onion's skin through her pelt. "Tell me where Dodge is!"

Onion opened her jaws to speak, but only choking sounds

came out. Stick realized that he was squashing her neck. He raised his paw a fraction, but as soon as the pressure eased, Onion reared up, trying to throw him off. Stick flung himself on top of her and crushed her under his weight. He pushed his face close to hers; fierce satisfaction rushed through him when he saw the fear in her green eyes. He raised one paw, ready to slice his claws through her neck.

"Stick, no!" Shorty pushed Stick's raised paw aside. "What are you doing? You can't kill her!"

"Yes, I can!" Stick spat. "But I won't. You, mange-pelt, tell me where Dodge is."

The she-cat's breath came fast and shallow with terror; underneath his paw, Stick could feel the frantic beating of her heart.

"He's by the stream," she gabbled out. "Behind the Twoleg nests. He sleeps in some old boxes. . . . Let me go, please!"

A red mist of fury swirled through Stick's mind. He flexed his claws, yearning to slice them through Onion's flesh.

"Stick!" Shorty's voice cut through his anger. "She's told us what we need to know. Now let her go."

There was a grim note in his friend's voice that Stick couldn't ignore. Gradually the mist faded. He sheathed his claws and rose to his paws, releasing Onion, who fled down the alley with her tail streaming behind her. Once she had disappeared, Stick turned and headed in the direction of the stream.

"Stick, wait!" Shorty planted himself in front of his friend. "What are you going to do? You can't attack on your own."

Stick breathed deeply. He knew that he was a whisker away from hurling himself on his friend with his claws outstretched if the brown tom didn't get out of his way.

"Has this become personal?" Shorty pressed, his gaze steady. "Is it about Red?" When Stick didn't reply, he went on, "Dodge can't steal Red away, you know. She's not helpless, and she wouldn't stand for it."

"I know that," Stick growled. *If she's joined Dodge, it's because she wants to.*

"Then this might be a battle you can't win," Shorty warned. "Focus on what's really at stake here: our safety and our right to hunt."

"You're right. We'll collect the others, and come back to fight."

Shorty blinked. "What, even if that means fighting Red?"

"So be it," Stick responded grimly.

Shorty gaped at him. "You don't mean that." Stick didn't reply, and after a few heartbeats, Shorty went on, "I think you should go talk to Velvet. She might know what Red's doing, and she might be able to change her mind before it's too late."

Stick stared at his friend. "Velvet is dead to me."

"No, she's not." Shorty faced up to his friend with more courage than Stick had expected. "She never has been, and she never will be. You think of her every time you look at Red." He took a pace forward so that he and Stick were nose to nose. "She's your daughter's mother, Stick. Go to her; ask her for help. She might be your only chance to save Red."

CHAPTER 24

❧

"Snookpaw!" Leafstar rose to her paws to greet the apprentice as he padded down the trail behind Billystorm. "It's good to see you again."

A few sunrises had passed since the raid on the Twoleg nest, but Leafstar was still sharply aware of tension within the Clan. The cats were milling around her now, where she stood at the foot of the Rockpile while Sharpclaw set the patrols. Morning mist still lay over the river, and the air was damp, promising rain later.

"Ebonyclaw, I want you to lead a hunting patrol," Sharpclaw meowed. "Take Frecklepaw, of course, and . . . let's see . . . Bouncefire and Sparrowpelt."

Leafstar was agreeably surprised to hear Sharpclaw putting a daylight-warrior at the head of a patrol. Then she wondered whether her deputy had a hidden motive. Sparrowpelt was one of the best hunters in the Clan, and he had been loud in his criticisms of the kittypets. *Does Sharpclaw hope Ebonyclaw will fail, and Sparrowpelt will have to take over?* Leafstar let her gaze rest on her deputy, his gleaming ginger pelt and sharp green eyes. *I know he's a strong deputy—but I can't help wondering whether he's trying to stir things up!*

"It's great to be back," Snookpaw meowed as he reached the bottom of the trail and padded over to Leafstar. "I've really missed the Clan."

Leafstar dipped her head. "We've missed you, too. Are you all right now?"

"I'm fine. I—" Snookpaw broke off to cough, and Leafstar looked at him in alarm. "No, I'm really fine," he assured her when he had got his breath back. "I can't wait to start training again. But I can't stay all day," he added, stifling another cough. "My housefolk would be really worried."

His love and respect for his Twolegs shone in his eyes. Leafstar felt a sudden pang, wondering what it would be like to live with housefolk. The Clan cats who accused the daylight-warriors of choosing a life of comfort were wrong. There could be real affection between a kittypet and their Twolegs. *Are we wrong to expect them to give that up?*

Snookpaw trotted away to join Billystorm, who was waiting for Sharpclaw to give him an assignment. As she watched the patrols beginning to move off, Leafstar's ears twitched at the sound of excited squeaking. She turned to see Fallowfern's kits stalking up to Clovertail, who lay dozing on a rock near the stream with one paw lying protectively over her swollen belly.

"That's a *huge* Twoleg!" Nettlekit squealed. "We have to scare him off, or he'll attack the camp."

"I'm going to be Sharpclaw!" Plumkit announced. "I'll lead the attack!"

"But *I* want to be Sharpclaw!" Rabbitkit charged into his

sister, pushing her over in a flurry of paws and tail. "Anyway, you're a she-cat, mouse-brain. You can't be Sharpclaw."

"Can too," Plumkit muttered, then changed her mind with a whisk of her tail. "Okay, I'll be Cora."

"And I'll be Stick!" Creekkit announced. "He's a great warrior. What about you, Nettlekit?"

"I'm going to be Billystorm," Nettlekit mewed. "He knows *everything* about fighting."

"You can't be Billystorm." Plumkit stared scornfully at her brother. "He's not a real warrior."

"Yeah, he's a kittypet," Rabbitkit agreed with a contemptuous flick of his tail.

"He wasn't even at the raid," Creekkit pointed out. "So you can't be him."

Leafstar listened in growing alarm. *Have the kits forgotten the way Billystorm taught them? Have even the kits picked up this tension between the daylight-warriors and the full Clan cats?*

"I don't care!" Nettlekit defended himself stoutly. "I still want to be Billystorm."

"Then you can go and be him by yourself," Plumkit meowed, giving her littermate a push. "You're not playing with us if you want to be a *kittypet*."

She turned her back on Nettlekit and pattered over the rocks toward Rabbitkit and Creekkit, who had crouched down and were starting to creep up on Clovertail once more.

Nettlekit watched for a heartbeat, then flicked his ears. "Okay, I'll be Sparrowpelt." He ran to join his littermates and dropped into a crouch beside Creekkit.

As Leafstar watched, she became aware of a cat standing beside her, and turned to see Billystorm. Embarrassment flooded over her when she realized that he must have heard every word of the kits' game. "I—I'm so sorry . . ." she stammered.

Billystorm shrugged. "What they say is true," he murmured. "I wasn't part of the raid."

Leafstar winced at the edge beneath his calm voice. She didn't want to quarrel with Billystorm.

To her relief, the ginger-and-white tom said nothing else about the raid. "I'm leading a hunting patrol," he told her. "Sharpclaw thought you might like to join us. Snookpaw and Cherrytail are coming, too."

"That would be great." Leafstar felt a tingle in her paws at the thought of hunting with Billystorm and the others. *I spend too much time in camp,* she thought. *It makes me see too many problems.*

There was a startled screech from Clovertail as the tiny raiding party pounced. Leaving Fallowfern to rescue her denmate from the kits, Leafstar followed Billystorm up the trail that led into the woods. Snookpaw and Cherrytail brought up the rear.

"You can't hunt birds in the same way as squirrels, mousebrain," Cherrytail was telling the apprentice. "They have wings!"

"Well, they both hide in trees," Snookpaw argued. "So leaping up and stalking them along the branches will work for both."

"Maybe . . ." Cherrytail admitted reluctantly. Leafstar was pleased to hear that while she sounded as bossy as usual when she was talking to an apprentice, she wasn't being unfair on her daylight-Clanmate. "You have to be really careful when you jump on them, though."

Leafstar left them to their debate and picked up her pace until she was padding beside Billystorm. "I'm truly sorry about the raid," she mewed quietly. "We should have waited for you. I promise you, it won't happen again. In the future we—"

"I understand why you did it," Billystorm interrupted. "I don't bear you any ill will." He paused for a heartbeat to taste the air for prey, then added, "I know we're in an odd position, living with a paw in both worlds. Maybe the time is coming for us all to make a choice."

Leafstar found that her heart was suddenly beating faster. *What if he decides to go back to his housefolk?* "Which would you choose?" she whispered.

"It's so hard," Billystorm responded with a sigh. His amber gaze was fixed on a tiny beetle as it climbed up a grass stem a mouse-length from his nose. "I love my housefolk, and they're kind to me. I know they make my life much easier than it would be if I lived in the Clan all the time." He took a deep breath, swinging his head around so that his warm gaze fell on Leafstar. "But I could never leave you," he murmured.

Leafstar's heart beat faster still, and the forest blurred around her into a chaos of green and gold. "I would never want you to," she breathed.

Her muzzle touched Billystorm's, and she felt her tail twining with his.

"Stop!"

At Cherrytail's yowl, Leafstar leaped back. Billystorm sprang away from her, his eyes startled and his fur beginning to fluff up defensively. But when Leafstar spotted Cherrytail among the long grasses, the tortoiseshell she-cat had her back to them. She was talking to a cream-colored tom who looked vaguely familiar. It was the cat they had watched hunting near the border! He was crouched in the shade of a straggly bush, much closer to the camp than when Leafstar had seen him before.

"Why are you in our territory?" Snookpaw demanded, shouldering his way through the ferns to confront the loner. "Didn't you smell our border scent marks?"

The tom flattened his ears to his head and showed the whites of his eyes.

"Back off a bit, Snookpaw," Leafstar ordered. "But he's right," she added to the tom. "You were given the chance to join SkyClan and you turned it down. So now you have to stay out of our territory."

The loner ducked his head awkwardly. "I know," he meowed. "But I've changed my mind. I'd like to join your Clan, if you'll still have me. My name's Egg."

"What made you change your mind?" Billystorm padded up beside Leafstar, suspicion glinting in his amber eyes. "It's a bit sudden, isn't it?"

Egg blinked rapidly, as if he wasn't sure how to answer

Billystorm's question. Leafstar's paws tingled; she didn't want to put off a possible new warrior by interrogating him. After all, she'd seen this cat move through the trees, and he clearly had natural hunting skills.

"The offer still stands if you can prove your loyalty to Sky-Clan," she told him.

"Sure. Of course I can." Egg's blue eyes lit up with eagerness. "Can I start now?"

Leafstar turned to Billystorm. "Can you take the hunting patrol from here, while I take Egg back to the camp?"

Billystorm looked undecided, with another uneasy glance toward Egg. "I'll come with you if you want."

Warmth spread through Leafstar at the thought that Billystorm wanted to protect her, even while her paws prickled in protest. *I'm Clan leader; I don't need protecting!*

"I'll be fine," she mewed briskly, then added more gently, "I'll see you later. Maybe we could go hunting together another time?"

As she spoke, she spotted Cherrytail and Snookpaw staring at her in wide-eyed amazement. Her embarrassment flooding back, she didn't wait for Billystorm to reply. "Come on," she ordered Egg, with a whisk of her tail. "It's this way."

As they headed back to the gorge, Leafstar noticed how jumpy he was, leaping into the air at every rustle from the undergrowth. He was almost as spooked as Shrewtooth. *Maybe he's been hurt by a Twoleg, too?*

"Why did you change your mind about joining us?" she asked, trying to make her tone unthreatening.

"Well . . . er . . . it just made sense," Egg stammered, still sounding as if the question bothered him.

At that moment they arrived at the top of the trail, and there was no chance for Leafstar to question him any more. Egg followed her down the trail; glancing back over her shoulder from time to time, Leafstar saw his eyes stretch with interest as he saw the activity in the camp: Lichenfur and Tangle washing themselves on a rock; Tinycloud and Rockshade dropping prey on the fresh-kill pile; other cats crowding around Sharpclaw as he sorted out more patrols.

By the time Leafstar and Egg reached the bottom of the gorge, Sharpclaw was heading toward the training area with Petalnose, Waspwhisker, and their apprentices. He paused, his ears pricked, as Leafstar padded up to him.

"This is Egg," Leafstar announced. "He's decided that he wants to join SkyClan. Egg, this is Sharpclaw, the Clan deputy."

Egg dipped his head politely.

"We're glad to have you!" Sharpclaw's green eyes glowed. "We're just going for some battle training. Do you want to come with us?"

Egg's tail shot right up in the air. "Great!"

"Come on, then." Sharpclaw led the way up the gorge.

Leafstar was about to follow when her deputy looked back and gave his whiskers a dismissive twitch. "We'll be fine, thanks."

At first Leafstar began to bristle, her claws flexing in annoyance. *Am I Clan leader, or has Sharpclaw taken over?* Then she figured that her deputy probably didn't want her breathing down his neck the whole time. He was perfectly capable of handling a training session.

I think I'll ask Sharpclaw to mentor Egg, she thought as she turned back toward her den. *I know Egg is more than six moons old, but he'll need to go through an apprenticeship to learn all the ways of the Clan.*

In spite of a spatter of rain in the air, she felt warm as she padded back to her den. She was happy to have such a promising new addition to the Clan, especially when he had inherited the powerful legs and jumping skills of the old SkyClan. Letting her gaze travel around the camp, Leafstar watched Lichenfur and Tangle fluff up their fur against the rain and snatch a piece of fresh-kill before plodding back to their den; Echosong was returning with a mouthful of herbs; Fallowfern's kits protested loudly as their mother tried to herd them back to the nursery.

And Billystorm will be back soon. . . . Everything would be perfect if he decided to live here all the time.

CHAPTER 25

♣

Leafstar dozed in her den until sunhigh. By then the shower was over and the sky had cleared; the rocks steamed as the hot sunlight sucked up the rain. Looking down into the gorge, Leafstar saw that most of the cats had returned from patrol. Sharpclaw and Egg were sitting together near the fresh-kill pile, talking with their heads close together as they ate. Stick and Cora were with them, too.

Egg seems to be settling in well, Leafstar thought.

She ran lightly down the trail into the gorge and jumped onto the Rockpile. "Let all cats old enough to catch their own prey join here beneath the Rockpile for a Clan meeting," she yowled.

Most of the Clan were already there, glancing up curiously at Leafstar poised on top of the rocks. Tangle and Lichenfur emerged from their nests, their fur rumpled with sleep. Echosong appeared from her den and padded up to listen.

"We have a new Clanmate," Leafstar announced, angling her ears to where Egg sat beside Sharpclaw. "Egg has decided to join us, and will become an apprentice today." With her tail she beckoned Egg forward until he stood alone at the foot of the Rockpile. "From this day forward," she went on, "this apprentice will be known as Eggpaw. Sharpclaw, you are a brave and skillful warrior, and I know you will pass on these qualities to your apprentice."

Sharpclaw showed no surprise in being named Egg's mentor. He dipped his head to Leafstar, then padded over to Egg and touched noses with him.

"Eggpaw! Eggpaw!" the Clan cats yowled, crowding around the new apprentice to congratulate him. Sparrowpelt and Rockshade looked particularly pleased, pressing up close to him and burying their muzzles in his shoulder fur.

Leafstar spotted Billystorm on the edge of the crowd; he had called out Egg's name to welcome him, but he still looked slightly doubtful. Leafstar reminded herself to ask what was worrying him when she had the chance.

As the yowls of welcome died down, Egg looked up at Leafstar where she still stood on the Rockpile. "Er . . . Leafstar, Eggpaw's an okay name, but if you don't mind I'd like to stay as Egg. Stick said that's what he and his friends did."

Leafstar's tail-tip twitched. She didn't like the way that Stick and the other newcomers didn't think that warrior names were important, and she was even more annoyed that they were spreading their opinion throughout the Clan. *Names matter. They're part of who we are as warriors.*

The Clan waited in tense silence for their leader to make her decision, while Egg gazed up at her, blinking cheerfully as if he had no idea that he had said anything wrong. With an effort Leafstar hid her irritation. There was no point in putting Egg off right at the beginning of his apprenticeship. *Maybe when he's been with us for a while he'll be ready for a warrior name.*

"If that's what you want," she replied evenly. She was relieved when none of the Clan cats argued, though she saw Snookpaw lean over to say something to Billystorm, and she caught the young cat's murmur. "I think Egg should be *proud* to have his apprentice name!"

Leafstar's paws were itching; she jumped down from the Rockpile and made her way over to Sharpclaw and Egg as the crowd around them broke up. "I missed out on hunting this morning," she meowed. "Do you want to come out with me now? Ebonyclaw, you and Frecklepaw can join us."

"Good idea," Sharpclaw replied, while Egg kneaded the ground in front of him in excitement. "Egg will get an idea of how SkyClan cats hunt."

Leafstar headed for the bottom of the trail, weaving a path through Fallowfern's kits, who were wrestling together near the foot of the Rockpile. But before she had gone more than a few paw steps, she heard Echosong calling her name, and waited for the medicine cat to catch up to her.

"Can Frecklepaw help me find herbs this afternoon?" Echosong puffed. "There's no cat in the medicine den right now, and I want to build up my supplies for when Clovertail has her kits."

Trying to ignore the eager light in Frecklepaw's eyes, Leafstar shook her head. "Echosong, we've already discussed this," she meowed. "Frecklepaw is Ebonyclaw's apprentice, and she needs to keep up with her patrol duties."

"But I *need* an apprentice," Echosong protested, her ears flicking back in frustration.

"Well, then, wait until Fallowfern's kits are old enough," Leafstar suggested. "It won't be long."

"What?" Plumkit sat up suddenly, twitching her tail away from Rabbitkit. "I don't want to be a medicine cat!"

"Neither do I," Nettlekit agreed, scrambling to his paws from where he had been rolling Creekkit in the dust. "It's stinky and yucky!"

"And *boring!*" Rabbitkit added.

"We're going to be warriors," Creekkit announced, scrambling to his paws and drawing his lips back in an attempt at a fierce snarl. "I'm going to be Clan leader."

"No you're not, I am!" Plumkit hurled herself at her brother.

Creekkit dodged and ran off; his littermates followed him, squealing at the tops of their voices. Leafstar sighed. *None of them will ever make a medicine cat,* she admitted to herself.

Echosong dug her claws into the ground while her gaze traveled around the listening Clan. Leafstar realized she was angry that most of the Clan had heard the argument, and found herself struggling hard not to show it.

"We'll discuss this later," the medicine cat hissed. "I don't want to hold up your hunting patrol."

Leafstar felt close to despair as she watched Echosong stalk away. *We were so close once.*

As the patrol headed up the trail and into the woods,

Frecklepaw lagged behind. "I wanted to stay and help Echosong," she complained.

"Well, you can't." Ebonyclaw sounded cross and frustrated, and Leafstar couldn't blame her. "You're my apprentice, and you need to train."

"I don't want to have a stupid training session."

Leafstar guessed that Frecklepaw hadn't meant her mentor to hear her last muttered comment, but the black she-cat's ears were sharp.

"I'm not too keen, either!" she snapped, giving her apprentice a sharp flick over the ear with her tail. "Now stop moaning and concentrate!"

Leafstar spotted Sharpclaw rolling his eyes. "Both of you need to concentrate," he meowed. "Carry on like that, and you'll scare away all the prey between here and the Twolegplace."

Ebonyclaw lashed her tail but said nothing. Relieved that she didn't have to step in to end the quarrel, Leafstar led the way deeper into the woodland, picking up the strong scent of squirrel.

It was Sharpclaw who spotted it first. "Over there," he whispered, angling his ears to where the squirrel was crossing a clearing just ahead of them in a series of short bounces. "Aren't we lucky?" He glanced sideways at Ebonyclaw. "There's still some prey left. Maybe it's deaf. Egg, do you think you can catch it?"

Egg's eyes gleamed. "I'll try."

Frecklepaw gave her fur a bad-tempered shake. "He's only

just been made an apprentice!" she grumbled.

Egg dropped into a crouch and began to creep forward, using tufts of long grass as cover. But he had forgotten to check the wind direction; the breeze was blowing directly from him to the squirrel. Suddenly the creature sat upright, then raced for the nearest tree, its bushy tail waving in the air.

Letting out a screech of frustration, Egg erupted out of the grass. He hurtled across the clearing, cutting down the squirrel's lead, but he was still several paw steps behind when it reached the tree and began to climb. With a massive SkyClan leap, Egg hurled himself up the tree behind it, and fastened his jaws in its tail before it could reach the safety of the branches. Egg and the squirrel fell to the ground together; the squirrel struggled frantically for a couple of heartbeats, then went limp.

Egg rose to his paws with his prey dangling in front of him. "Was that okay?" he panted through a mouthful of fur.

"Great catch!" Sharpclaw declared, padding over to him and giving the squirrel a sniff.

Leafstar noticed that Ebonyclaw was nodding in agreement, and Frecklepaw's eyes were wide with awe, her ill temper forgotten.

"Well done," Leafstar meowed as they padded over to join Egg at the foot of the tree. "But next time, remember to check the wind. If you'd worked your way around so your scent wasn't carried to your prey, you wouldn't have had to chase it like that."

Egg's eyes were still shining with triumph. "I'll remember," he promised, dropping the squirrel at Leafstar's paws.

"When we've caught some prey we bury it," Sharpclaw explained, scratching busily at the soft ground beneath the tree with his hind paws. "Then we come back and fetch it later, when we've caught enough to take back to camp."

"I can see a pigeon!" Frecklepaw hissed in an excited whisper as Sharpclaw dropped the squirrel into the hole and began scraping earth back over it. "Can I try to catch it?"

Ebonyclaw nodded, and her apprentice slipped away into the undergrowth. Leafstar spotted the pigeon: a fine plump bird pecking among the roots of a nearby oak tree. Frecklepaw was carefully skirting the clearing to approach from the right direction; Leafstar guessed she was extra eager to make a catch of her own to prove she was just as good as Egg.

As Sharpclaw finished burying the squirrel and dropped a beech husk on the spot to mark it, Leafstar caught sight of Frecklepaw peering out of a clump of fern next to the oak tree. But something alerted the pigeon; it fluttered upward to land on a branch.

"Bad luck!" Ebonyclaw muttered.

But Frecklepaw hadn't given up. She emerged from the ferns and bunched her muscles to take a leap into the tree, on the side away from the pigeon. Though Leafstar didn't think she could possibly have startled the bird, it flew off into another tree before she could get close enough to pounce. Frecklepaw followed with a neat jump from the end of a branch onto a fork in the next tree.

"Come on." Leafstar waved her tail to beckon her patrol.

"Let's see what happens."

Frecklepaw was gradually drawing closer to the pigeon. Leafstar's pelt prickled with excitement as she watched the apprentice's agile progress through the branches. Ebonyclaw had taught her well. Even so, Leafstar wasn't sure that Frecklepaw would be able to manage the kill on her own. The pigeon was large, and becoming more and more flustered as Frecklepaw drew closer. With every heartbeat Leafstar expected it to fly off.

"Spread out," she whispered to the rest of the patrol. "Climb trees so that we're surrounding the pigeon."

Sharpclaw, Egg, and Ebonyclaw headed off in different directions. Leafstar chose the tree next to the one where the pigeon had finally settled on a branch. Frecklepaw was edging closer, prowling along another branch a tail-length higher.

Leafstar had just started to climb when a terrified yowl split the silence of the woods. "Watch out! Get away from there!"

The pigeon flew off, vanishing into a more distant clump of trees. "Mouse dung!" Frecklepaw exclaimed, staring after it indignantly.

Leafstar dropped to the ground again to see Egg hurtling across the forest floor, his voice still raised in a loud wail. He charged into Ebonyclaw as she braced herself to jump onto the trunk of a fallen tree, bundling her away from it. "There's a fox! A fox!" he screeched.

"Get off me!" Ebonyclaw pushed Egg away and scrambled to her paws, spitting in fury.

Leafstar paused for a heartbeat to taste the air. She picked up the SkyClan border markings a few tail-lengths ahead, and sure enough, a strong scent of young fox.

"How did you know about that?" she asked Egg, padding over to where the new apprentice had crouched in the grass and was staring around fearfully.

Egg staggered to his paws, trying to force his bristling fur to lie flat. "My den is on the other side of that tree," he explained. "At least, it was until the fox came."

Leafstar nodded worriedly. "Thanks for warning us," she meowed. "We don't want a fox in our territory. We'll have to organize a patrol to hunt it down, and chase it away if we have to."

"No need," Sharpclaw assured her, strolling over to her side. "The fox has gone now."

"You knew about it?" Leafstar asked, baffled. "Why didn't you say anything?"

Sharpclaw shrugged. "There was no point. I knew the trail led away from our territory."

"That's not what you told me!" To Leafstar's amazement, Egg pushed himself between her and her deputy, gazing at his mentor with troubled blue eyes. "You said that the fox had come to live here permanently, and I wouldn't be safe if I stayed here on my own."

A thorn of suspicion stabbed Leafstar. "When did he say this?" she asked Egg.

"A few days ago, when he came to find me to warn me about the fox," Egg replied, looking confused. "He was right, wasn't he? I mean, foxes won't hurt me, now that I live with the Clan."

Leafstar's suspicions hardened into certainty. *Sharpclaw lied to me! And he lied to Egg about the danger from the fox, just to get him to join the Clan.*

With an effort, she fought back her shock and anger. She didn't want to let the others know what Sharpclaw had done.

"Foxes are very unlikely to attack the gorge," she assured Egg. "And even if they do, we have plans in place to defend ourselves. There's nothing for you to worry about."

"That's great!" Egg puffed with relief.

Leafstar glanced at Ebonyclaw and Frecklepaw. The apprentice had clambered down from the branches and was sniffing around the fallen tree. "The fox scent is quite stale," she reported to Ebonyclaw with a bewildered look.

Her mentor looked just as puzzled, while Sharpclaw was standing by with defiance in his green eyes, as if he was challenging Leafstar to say something about his plot.

"Ebonyclaw," Leafstar meowed, "take Frecklepaw and Egg and see if you can find another pigeon. No, Sharpclaw," she added, as her deputy was about to move off with the rest of the patrol, "you stay here. I want a word with you."

She kept silent until the other three cats had disappeared among the trees. Sharpclaw gave his shoulder fur a couple of nonchalant licks as he waited for her to speak. Once she was sure they couldn't be overheard, Leafstar turned on him angrily. "You can't recruit Clan members with lies!"

Sharpclaw met her gaze steadily. "It wasn't a lie. There was a fox here, and Egg will be much safer with the Clan. Look at him," he added, waving his tail in the direction the cream-colored tom had taken. "Long legs, powerful haunches. He's obviously one of us."

"True." Leafstar twitched her ears. She wondered what other secrets her deputy was keeping from her; suddenly she remembered what Billystorm had told her about Sharpclaw and Stick roaming through the Twolegplace at night. *Can that possibly be true?*

With a shock like a plunge into icy water, Leafstar realized that she no longer trusted her deputy.

"Is that all?" Sharpclaw interrupted her thoughts. He looked quite cheerful now, as if he was satisfied that he had explained himself successfully. "If so, I'll go catch up with the others."

He bounded off. Leafstar watched him, shaking her head sadly. *He doesn't even see that he's done anything wrong.* She resented his secrecy and the way he had manipulated Egg, yet she had to admit that the new apprentice would be a valuable addition to the Clan. He had natural talent, and seemed like a quick learner. *Maybe it doesn't matter how Egg was persuaded to join us. Sky-Clan is obviously where he's meant to be.*

The sun was starting to go down, filling the forest with red-gold light as the patrol made its way back to camp. Frecklepaw was delighted that she'd managed to catch another pigeon, and staggered along with it proudly. Ebonyclaw was carrying two mice, while Egg had caught a sparrow and Sharpclaw a blackbird.

When they were almost at the gorge, Leafstar set down her own prey, a couple of shrews. "Sharpclaw, can you manage to carry these back?" she asked. "I'll go dig up Egg's squirrel and follow you down."

Sharpclaw gave her a brisk nod, and managed to get his jaws around the extra prey. Leafstar padded through the trees until she reached the spot where Sharpclaw had buried the squirrel, spotted the beech husk marker, and began to dig. As she was shaking damp earth off the fresh-kill she heard a rustle in the undergrowth, and Echosong came into view, with a bundle of herbs in her mouth. She looked tired; her pelt was ungroomed and its white patches were grubby.

A pang of sympathy shook Leafstar. "I'll get you some help," she promised when she had greeted Echosong. "Maybe Shrewtooth would like to take a break from his warrior duties."

Echosong dropped her burden and stalked forward, tension in every line of her body. "Shrewtooth has never shown any interest in being a medicine cat," she mewed bitterly. "But Frecklepaw obviously wants to change her apprenticeship!"

Leafstar sighed. "We've discussed this. We can't have a daylight-warrior as our medicine cat."

"We could find a way to make it work," Echosong argued. "It's not as if my bones are creaking with age. I plan on being around for a long time yet!"

Warmth flooded through Leafstar as she felt her old friendship with the medicine cat beginning to revive. "Good. I'm very glad," she murmured, touching Echosong's ear lightly with her nose.

Carrying the squirrel, she headed for the camp again. Echosong retrieved her bundle of herbs and padded by her side. Near the edge of the wood they came upon a sunlit tree trunk overgrown with grass and fern.

"Let's rest for a bit," Leafstar suggested, letting the squirrel fall.

Echosong put down her herbs next to the fresh-kill and joined Leafstar as she stretched out in the patch of warmth, enjoying the fresh green scent of the undergrowth.

"How's Billystorm?" the medicine cat asked.

Leafstar felt her pads prickle at the cautious note in her friend's voice. "He's fine. Why do you ask?"

Echosong didn't meet her gaze. "I think you ought to know," she began, patting at a grass stem with outstretched paw. "Cats are beginning to talk."

"What about?" Leafstar meowed.

"You and Billystorm. You're obviously very . . . close."

"He's a good warrior!" Leafstar pointed out. She felt a burst of excitement. It felt so good to be able to talk about Billystorm to a friend. "We . . . we have a real connection," she confessed. "He seems to think the same way I do, and when he's not here, I feel . . . empty."

"Yes, he's a great Clanmate," Echosong agreed, still with her gaze fixed on the waving stem. "We're lucky to have him. But . . . Leafstar, you need to be careful not to show favoritism toward the kitty . . . daylight-warriors."

"This isn't favoritism!" Leafstar protested. "I . . . I want Billystorm and me to become mates."

Her heart beat faster as she spoke her most secret hope aloud; but it was the truth.

Echosong turned to her, her eyes wide with shock. "But you can't! Not now, with things so tense between the full warriors and the daylight-warriors. At the very least, you and Billystorm ought to wait until things are easier."

If they ever are, Leafstar thought. *I don't* want *to wait,* she added to herself, aware that she sounded like a mutinous apprentice or an impatient kit.

"I can cope," she replied shortly to the medicine cat. "That shouldn't make any difference to me and Billystorm."

"Besides," Echosong went on as if Leafstar hadn't spoken, "it could be difficult if you had kits. I know that you have a deputy and a medicine cat to help you look after the Clan, but what if there was a battle?"

"Who said anything about kits?" Leafstar asked. "You're being mouse-brained. It's far too early to be thinking about that."

"No, it's not." Echosong rose to her paws so that she was standing over Leafstar. "You have to stop thinking about Billystorm in that way, right now! You have a different destiny, one that involves the future of the whole Clan." Her voice softened and her deep green gaze glowed with sympathy. "And it is a path that you must walk alone."

CHAPTER 26

The sun had dipped below the level of the gorge, casting long shadows over the rocks. Leafstar padded across to the fresh-kill pile and dropped her squirrel on top of the rest of the prey. Her belly was still churning after her conversation with Echosong; she felt as if every hair on her pelt were a pricking claw, reminding her of her duty as Clan leader.

As she turned away, Petalnose looked up from the vole she was gulping down. "Hi, Leafstar. Do you want to come and eat with me?"

"No, thanks," Leafstar meowed. "I'm not hungry."

She noticed a flicker of surprise in Petalnose's eyes. "Is everything okay?" the gray she-cat asked.

Leafstar was in no mood for her Clanmate's concern. "Everything's fine," she snapped. "Why wouldn't it be?"

Stalking toward the trail that led up to her den, Leafstar was relieved that there was no sign of Billystorm in camp. *I hope he's gone back to his housefolk with Snookpaw.*

But as she began to climb the trail, she heard the ginger-and-white tom's voice. "If you twist like this as you leap, Snookpaw, you'll throw your enemy off balance."

Looking down, Leafstar spotted Billystorm a few fox-lengths farther up the gorge, demonstrating a battle move to Snookpaw and Tinycloud.

"That's a great move," the white she-cat meowed. "Can I give it a try?"

Leafstar didn't stop to watch any more. Instead, she leaped up the last few paw steps to her den and bounded inside, letting out a breath of relief to be on her own at last. Her mind whirled with unwelcome thoughts. Part of her was angry with Echosong, but mostly she was afraid that the medicine cat was right. *Would it really be wrong of me to become Billystorm's mate?*

Gazing out at the darkening sky, where the first warriors of StarClan glimmered over the trees, Leafstar remembered Firestar explaining how her ancestors had marked her out as the leader of the new Clan.

"You told me plenty about StarClan," she growled softly. "But you never told me this." Fury tore through her like a stab of lightning, and she scraped her claws across the floor of her den; if Firestar had been there, she might have raked them across his flame-colored pelt. "*Why* didn't you tell me that I'd have to put the Clan first, before having a mate or kits? You have Sandstorm. Is it so different for she-cats? Why did you make me leader?"

But even as she spoke, she knew she was being unfair. It was StarClan who had chosen her to be leader, after they sent the sign of dappled leaf shadows to Echosong. *They trusted me to be the best leader,* she thought, sighing as her rage ebbed away. *I can't let them down.*

Curling up in her mossy nest, Leafstar fell into an uneasy sleep. Mist surged around her, and she found herself stumbling over rocks, with looming cliffs of black stone on either side. She struggled against panic, knowing that this was a dream, but unable to shake off the feeling that she was trapped in an unfamiliar place.

"Is any cat there?" she called out.

There was no reply, nothing but the echoing sound of water dripping from the rocks.

"Leafstar! Are you okay?"

The voice cut through Leafstar's dream. She struggled back to wakefulness to see Billystorm at the entrance to her den, outlined against the twilit sky.

I must have only slept for a few heartbeats, but it felt like seasons.

"I'm fine," Leafstar replied, rising groggily to her paws and padding over to him.

"I wanted to ask you if you'd like to come with me to the Twolegplace tonight," Billystorm went on. "We could look out for Sharpclaw and Stick leading one of their patrols." When Leafstar didn't reply right away, he added, "Besides, it would be nice to spend some time away from the Clan for a while."

Oh, yes, it would. . . . Leafstar yearned to agree, to run beside Billystorm along the mysterious paths of the Twolegplace. And it would be useful to discover whether Sharpclaw really was up to something.

But I can't. I'm Clan leader. I can't.

"No," Leafstar replied, sounding harsher than she had

intended. "I can't go chasing around the Twolegplace. My Clanmates need me here."

Even in the dim light, she could see the hurt in Billystorm's eyes. "I'm your Clanmate, too," he pointed out.

"But you have housefolk." Every word felt like a thorn in her throat. "I'm sorry, Billystorm. Go home."

Confusion tightened Billystorm's expression. "But Leafstar—" he began, then broke off. "What about Sharpclaw and Stick?" he asked.

"Why are you so eager to accuse them?" Leafstar challenged. "You're not showing much loyalty to your Clan deputy, are you? No other cats have mentioned Sharpclaw and Stick leaving the gorge at night. And I don't believe that Sharpclaw would order a patrol without discussing it with me first."

As she finished speaking, Billystorm backed away, his eyes cold. "I thought I meant something to you, more than just another Clanmate," he meowed. "But you won't let yourself get close to me, because you think I'm just a kittypet, don't you?"

The accusation took Leafstar's breath away, and she had no words to respond.

"You're no better than Sharpclaw and Sparrowpelt," Billystorm went on, the fur along his spine fluffing up with indignation. "They look down their noses at us because we stay loyal to our housefolk as well as to our Clan. I thought you were different, Leafstar, but I was wrong."

Leafstar stared at him in dismay. That wasn't what she thought at all! *But if Billystorm is so quick to think badly of me, then maybe I'm better off without him.*

Abruptly she turned away. "You don't know everything, Billystorm," she mewed.

For a heartbeat there was silence; then she heard Billystorm padding away, the sound of his paw steps fading as he climbed the trail. Part of her wanted to run after him and call him back; instead, she plodded across her den to her nest and settled herself back among the moss.

She had barely closed her eyes when she found the mist swirling around her once again, scudding across glistening black cliffs that trapped her on either side. But this time she could hear the sound of many cats in the gorge ahead of her. Padding forward, she rounded a spur of rock and found herself on the edge of a crowd.

Her heart beating faster, Leafstar tensed her muscles and slid out her claws in case the strange cats attacked her, but none of them even looked at her or seemed to scent her.

In the middle of the throng, a gray tom with white patches on his fur stood on top of a rock. Leafstar's paws tingled as she recognized Cloudstar, who had been the leader of SkyClan when they were driven out of the forest and came to live in the gorge. But this was not the warrior of StarClan with starlight in his fur; this was a scrawny, exhausted cat who gazed at his Clanmates with desperation in his eyes.

"We'll never find a home here," a cat called to him. "We should have stayed in the forest and *made* the other Clans give us some of their territory."

"You know they would never have done that," Cloudstar

retorted. "They wanted us *gone*. They don't care if we starve out here."

"We have to do something," a gray she-cat rasped; she was sitting close to Leafstar, who could see that her belly was swollen even though every one of her ribs was visible through her pelt. "My kits will be born any day now. They need a nursery. And I need fresh-kill, or I'll have no milk to give them." Her voice rose to a wail. "My kits will die!"

"Don't be afraid." A light brown tabby she-cat leaped up onto the rock beside Cloudstar; it was Fawnstep, the Clan's medicine cat. "Our warrior ancestors are watching over us, even here."

Her voice faded as she spoke, and Leafstar opened her eyes, blinking as the pale light of a new day crept into her den. She had glimpsed the cats of that long-ago SkyClan as they struggled to find themselves a new home after they had been forced to leave the forest.

"They came here," she whispered. "But in the end, they were driven away."

She remembered the pale brown tom she had seen in her dream, and the words he had spoken as he left the gorge forever. "This is the leaf-bare of my Clan. Greenleaf will come, but it will bring even greater storms than these. SkyClan will need deeper roots if it is to survive."

I must be one of those roots, Leafstar decided. *I must tether SkyClan to its home for all the moons to come.*

Yawning and stretching, she remembered her other dream, when she had raced through the forest with Spottedleaf and other cats of StarClan. "Seize the moment!" Spottedleaf had told her.

This is one of those moments, Leafstar decided. *I can't be with Billystorm. I have to stay apart from him, for the good of my Clan.*

For the next few days, Leafstar managed to avoid Billystorm. She spotted him once heading to the training area with Snookpaw, and later joining a hunting patrol with Sharpclaw, Stick, and Egg. When the Clan settled down to eat beside the fresh-kill pile, Leafstar carried her prey back to her den so she didn't have to talk to him.

On the third sunrise after their quarrel, Leafstar padded down from her den to find Sharpclaw organizing the morning's patrols. Billystorm shouldered his way through the cats toward the deputy, who was standing beside Stick at the foot of the Rockpile.

"Can I join your patrol today, Sharpclaw?" Leafstar heard him ask. "It might be a good idea to go into the Twolegplace and see if we can persuade any more cats to join the Clan."

Is that really what he wants to do? Leafstar wondered. *Or is he trying to spy on Sharpclaw, to find out what he's doing in the Twolegplace?*

But Sharpclaw shook his head. "We're hunting today. I doubt we'd find many squirrels in the Twolegplace. Besides, we don't need any more cats. The Clan is full enough."

You didn't say that when you persuaded Egg to join, Leafstar thought. Her suspicions of her deputy were reviving, and she wished she could discuss the problem with Billystorm. She realized that she had lost not only a potential mate but also a wise friend whom she could rely on for advice.

"I'm putting you in charge of a training patrol," Sharpclaw went on to Billystorm. "Take Ebonyclaw and Frecklepaw, and you can have Patchfoot, too. See if you can find any prey near the rat pile; no cat has hunted there for a while."

Billystorm dipped his head in agreement, though he looked dissatisfied.

Unexpectedly, Sharpclaw turned to Leafstar. "Do you want to join Billystorm's patrol?"

Leafstar couldn't meet Billystorm's eyes. "Uh . . . I don't think so," she stammered. "Cherrytail brought back a really fat squirrel from the far border yesterday, so I thought I'd take a patrol up there and see if there are any more."

There was a spark of surprise in Sharpclaw's eyes. Leafstar felt uncomfortably hot, wondering if he realized she was making an excuse.

"Fine," he mewed at last. "Which cats do you want to take with you?"

Leafstar remembered with a pang how Billystorm had accused her of being biased against the daylight-warriors. *That wasn't fair, and I'll prove it to you!*

"I'll take Harveymoon and Macgyver," she replied. "And may I have Egg? I'd like to see how he's getting on."

"Sure," her deputy replied, turning away to call to Sparrowpelt and Bouncefire.

Billystorm collected his patrol and headed for the trail up the cliff, while Leafstar looked around for Harveymoon and Macgyver. They seemed surprised and pleased to be chosen for a patrol by their Clan leader.

Maybe if I paid them a bit more attention, they wouldn't be such pains in the tail.

With the daylight-warriors hard on her paws and Egg bounding along excitedly in the rear, Leafstar led the way toward the Rockpile, ready to cross to the other side of the gorge. Before she reached it, she saw Echosong urgently waving her tail, and halted for the medicine cat to catch up.

"You're going into the woods on the other side?" Echosong called, setting down some wilted leaves she was carrying. When Leafstar nodded, she mewed, "Can you look for borage while you're there? I need some to help Clovertail's milk come when she has her kits."

"Of course," Leafstar replied.

Echosong patted the leaves. "This is borage. It's the last I have, and you can see it's past its best."

Leafstar studied the herbs and gave them a good sniff, then ordered her patrol to do the same. "Remember the shape of the leaves and the scent," she instructed them, and added to Echosong, "We'll bring you back a good supply, don't worry."

Echosong slid closer to her Clan leader as the rest of the patrol sniffed the leaves. "You've made the right decision about Billystorm," she whispered. "I know it wasn't easy, but StarClan will thank you for putting the Clan first."

Leafstar felt her fur start to bristle, and struggled to hide her reaction from the medicine cat. *She has no idea how hard it is to have Billystorm as an enemy!* "Are you ready?" she asked her patrol, waving her tail to move them on again.

"Thank you for looking out for the borage," Echosong meowed, and added in a lower voice, "and good luck with Harveymoon and Macgyver. Maybe they'll even catch something this time."

This time Leafstar didn't try to conceal her indignation. "I'm sure they'll be fine!" she snapped.

Echosong blinked in surprise, and Leafstar felt slightly guilty, though she said nothing more as she led the patrol away.

On the way back to camp, Leafstar had to admit that Echosong had been right about the daylight-warriors. Harveymoon and Macgyver had managed to catch only one small sparrow between them, and let a perfectly good rabbit escape because they were messing around. Egg, however, had hunted brilliantly, catching two squirrels and a young pigeon.

"You've picked up the SkyClan hunting techniques really quickly," Leafstar told him, managing to speak around her own prey, a blackbird. "Are you glad you joined the Clan?"

Egg nodded eagerly. "It's great, bringing prey for the fresh-kill pile," he mumbled around the feathers that filled his jaws. "And Sharpclaw's a really good teacher. I've learned so many battle moves! If that fox comes back, it'd better watch out!"

"That's good to hear," Leafstar replied. "But don't even think of tackling a fox on your own."

It was sunhigh when the patrol returned to camp. As she

crossed the Rockpile, Leafstar realized that almost all the Clan were out in the open, circling anxiously at the foot of the boulders.

"What's going on?" she asked after she dropped her fresh-kill on the pile.

Fallowfern pressed up close to her, with her kits around her paws; for once they weren't jumping about and getting in every cat's way. "Nettlekit and Plumkit heard a strange noise," she explained, "and we've all heard it now."

"It's really weird!" Plumkit squeaked, her eyes wide with curiosity.

Leafstar's pads began to tingle. "Where's Sharpclaw?"

"His patrol isn't back yet," Cherrytail replied.

"What do you think the noise could be?" Clovertail fretted. "Do you think it's a fox?"

Tangle flicked his ears dismissively. "I've never heard a fox that sounded like that."

"It might be some sort of bird," Waspwhisker suggested.

"Or maybe it's the Twoleg's dog?" Shrewtooth's black pelt was fluffed up and his eyes were wide with fear.

"I don't think so." Billystorm let his tail rest on the young cat's shoulders.

"Then it's rats!" Tinycloud's tail lashed. "Why are we standing here? Let's go fight them!"

"Please, everyone be quiet!" Leafstar waved her tail to quiet the excited suggestions. "Let me hear this noise for myself."

Gradually the chatter died away. As silence fell, Leafstar heard a drawn-out, eerie wail coming from farther up the gorge, on the far side of the spur of rock that sheltered the training area.

The whole Clan stood frozen as the sound went on and on. Just as it died away there was a flurry of paw steps, and Sharpclaw arrived with Stick and Sparrowpelt.

"What's that?" he demanded, his gaze raking the Clan.

"That's what we're trying to find out," Leafstar explained. "We don't know what can be making that noise."

Sharpclaw tipped his head to one side. "It sounds like a Twoleg to me."

"It's that horrible old Twoleg!" Rabbitkit squealed.

"Yes, he's come to punish us!" Plumkit bounced up and down in a mixture of fear and excitement.

Shrewtooth gazed in horror at the kits and his fur bristled even more until he looked twice his size.

"That's nonsense," Clovertail mewed sternly to the kits. "Stop trying to frighten every cat. If that is a Twoleg, it sounds like a young one, and it's in trouble."

"We need to investigate," Leafstar decided. "Clovertail, Fallowfern, stay here and look after the kits. Cora, Shrewtooth, and Ebonyclaw, guard the camp. The rest of you, follow me, but quietly."

With Leafstar in the lead, the SkyClan cats crept up the gorge, past the training area, and around the next corner. The wailing sound started up again, louder now as they came closer.

Peeking around a boulder, Leafstar saw the source of the noise. A young Twoleg kit—a female—was lying among the rocks. She was small, about half the size of a full-grown Twoleg, with brown head-fur and brightly colored pelts covering everything except her smooth, pink front paws and face. As Leafstar padded closer she saw that the kit's face was streaked with mud and moisture, and there was earth smeared on her pelts; up above were raw gashes on the rock face. Even worse, one of her hind legs was splayed at an awkward angle beside her, and from the way the kit's muscles were tensed, it was clear she was in agony.

"She fell over the cliff," Leafstar murmured, raising her tail to halt her Clanmates who were following her. "Poor kit, she's badly hurt."

She had halted a few tail-lengths away, but even at this distance the kit's pain and fear-scents were almost overwhelming. "Keep back," Leafstar warned her Clan. "She's so scared, she might lash out at us. Echosong, come with me."

"Hang on a moment." Sparrowpelt pushed his way to the front of the crowd. "I don't think we should have anything to do with this. It might be a trap."

"That's right," Shorty mewed. "There could be bigger Twolegs hiding, ready to trap us."

"They do that sort of thing," Coal agreed.

Petalnose was nodding, too, and some of the other cats looked uncertain. *And they might be right,* Leafstar thought. She pricked her ears and tasted the air, but the scents of the young Twoleg, and the noise she was making, drowned out everything else.

"That's nonsense." Echosong padded forward with a flick

of her tail. "This is an injured kit, for StarClan's sake. Look at her leg! No Twoleg would put one of their own in that much pain just to trap us."

Without waiting for Leafstar's order, she padded past and approached the little Twoleg. Leafstar heard her purring loudly; her tail was straight up in the air and her fur fluffed up in a way that made her look soft and pretty. *She must have been such a popular kittypet!* Leafstar thought suddenly.

The Twoleg kit stopped wailing as Echosong trotted up to her and reached out feebly with one paw to stroke her. Echosong purred even louder, and pushed her head up against the kit. "I don't want to frighten her," she mewed apologetically, with a glance back at Leafstar.

Leafstar gestured with her tail for the rest of the Clan to back off and hide among the rocks. She was conscious of their gleaming eyes peering out as she padded cautiously forward. *Now I have to behave like a kittypet, with all the Clan watching me,* she thought, wincing. *I'll never hear the last of it!*

She wasn't sure exactly how kittypets behaved, but she tried to copy Echosong, who was brushing her pelt against the Twoleg kit and making affectionate trilling sounds. Leafstar flinched as the kit stretched out to touch her, but she felt a purr rising in her throat at the feeling of the Twoleg paw stroking along her back. *It's kind of . . . nice.*

She let the kit stroke her while Echosong gave the injured leg a good sniff. "It's broken," the medicine cat reported. "But it's too big for me to treat with a splint. And I'm not sure that Clan medicines would be any good for Twolegs."

"If we can't help her, we shouldn't waste any more time with her." Leafstar jumped at the sound of Sparrowpelt's voice, and glanced over her shoulder to see that the brown tabby tom had approached without her noticing. "There are patrols to get on with," he reminded them.

Leafstar was uneasy about leaving the kit, yet she didn't see what else they could do. But as she stepped back out of reach, the little Twoleg started wailing again and her pink paws scrabbled on the stones.

"We have to do something!" Echosong protested.

"Like what?" Sharpclaw growled, emerging from behind a rock and padding up to stand beside Sparrowpelt. His voice was harsh and unsympathetic.

"We have to find her family," Echosong insisted, her neck fur bristling at the deputy's tone. "We can't help her, so we must find Twolegs who can."

Cocking his head to one side, Sharpclaw fixed Leafstar with his brilliant green gaze; he was waiting for her order, but it was clear what he wanted her to say.

Leafstar felt uneasy. She wanted to help the Twoleg kit, but she wasn't sure if that was the sort of thing that Clan cats were supposed to do. *Should we work alongside Twolegs to help them?* She couldn't imagine that Firestar would get involved in something like this. Not that the ThunderClan leader wouldn't care that a Twoleg was hurt, but his life seemed so completely separate from the affairs of Twolegs.

But I'm not Firestar, and this isn't his Clan.

Suddenly Leafstar was aware of the presence of Spottedleaf

close beside her. She seemed to hear the tortoiseshell she-cat's voice: *Seize the moment!* Leafstar felt as though Spottedleaf was telling her that this could be very important for the future of SkyClan.

"Echosong is right," she announced. "SkyClan will help the injured Twoleg."

CHAPTER 27

"Okay, but how are we going to find out where the Twoleg kit comes from?" Sharpclaw queried.

Leafstar was relieved that her deputy seemed to be accepting her decision, even if he didn't agree with it. "Snookpaw, Billystorm, come here," she ordered, beckoning with her tail. "You know the Twolegplace. Have you ever seen this kit before?"

She tensed as Billystorm approached, but the ginger-and-white tom padded past without even looking at her. He and his apprentice stood gazing down at the little Twoleg's face for a couple of heartbeats.

"Sorry," Billystorm meowed. "I don't recognize her."

I'd better send back to the camp for Ebonyclaw, Leafstar thought. *I'm not sure about asking Harveymoon and Macgyver. They live quite close to Billystorm. Maybe this kit comes from a different part of the Twolegplace.*

But before she could give the order, Snookpaw, who had turned away from the kit, suddenly turned back and gave her a deep sniff. "I know that scent!" he chirped. "There's a Twoleg nest with really strong-smelling flowers outside, and that same scent is on her pelts." Examining the Twoleg again, he added, "I think I've seen these pelts hanging on the Twolegs' spiky silver tree, too."

"That's great, Snookpaw," Leafstar mewed, while Billystorm blinked proudly at his apprentice. "Can you take us there?"

"I think so." Snookpaw straightened up, looking very serious. "I'll try."

"Then let's get back to camp and sort out a patrol."

As Leafstar was gathering her cats together, ready to head back down the gorge, Echosong padded over to her. "I'll stay behind," she meowed. "I might be able to do something. And the Twoleg seems calmer when we're here."

Leafstar nodded. "Good idea. I'll send some cat to help you."

Cherrytail and Sparrowpelt raced back to camp ahead of the others, so that by the time Leafstar arrived the cats who had stayed behind had been brought up to date with the news.

"We want to come!" Nettlekit squealed, hurling himself at Leafstar.

"Yes, we want to see Twolegplace," Plumkit added, bouncing up behind her brother.

"Certainly not." Fallowfern followed them, gathering all four kits together with her tail. "You're not even apprentices. You can't expect to be chosen for patrols yet."

"It's not fair," Rabbitkit grumbled, lashing his tiny tail. "We never get to do the fun stuff."

The rest of the Clan was clustering eagerly around Leaf-star; for a few heartbeats she felt bewildered about whom she should choose.

"You should take all the kittypets!" Macgyver suggested. "We know Twolegplace really well."

Sharpclaw fixed the black-and-white tom with a hard gaze. "It's *Leafstar's* decision who she takes."

Leafstar flicked her ears at her deputy in acknowledgment. "I want you to come, Sharpclaw," she mewed. "Snookpaw, of course, because you know where we're going. And Billy-storm."

It was hard not to let her voice shake as she named the ginger-and-white tom. This would be the first time they had patrolled together since their quarrel. *It'll be so hard to have him with us, but I can't leave him out; he's Snookpaw's mentor.*

"Cora and Cherrytail," she finished quickly. "Patchfoot, you're in charge of the camp while we're away. Have a few cats keep watch in case of trouble. Clovertail, I have a job for you."

The light brown she-cat twitched her ears in surprise and padded over to Leafstar clumsily, because of the weight of the kits in her belly.

"Go up the gorge and join Echosong," Leafstar instructed, waving her tail in the direction of the injured Twoleg. "She might need a bit of help."

"From me?" Clovertail sounded even more surprised. "I don't know anything about being a medicine cat."

"You won't need to. Echosong wants some cat to help her

comfort the little Twoleg. Pretend she's one of your kits. Cuddle up to her. Purr."

"Cuddle? Purr?" Clovertail gave Leafstar a doubtful look. "Okay, Leafstar, if you say so." She plodded off up the gorge, shaking her head.

Leafstar watched her go, feeling faintly amused in spite of everything. Then she gathered her patrol with a wave of her tail. "Let's go."

Leafstar stared up at the Twoleg nests as she and her patrol halted on the outskirts of Twolegplace. The red stone walls loomed over the cats and blocked out part of the sky. Already her senses were attacked by a chaos of scents and noises: monsters, dogs, strange cats, and the weird aromas of Twoleg food.

How can the kittypets put up with this every day?

"Okay, Snookpaw," she meowed. "You're in charge now. Which way do we go?"

Snookpaw gave her a scared look, as if he was overwhelmed now that he was actually faced with the task of finding the little Twoleg's nest.

"Take your time," Billystorm murmured. "You'll be fine."

Snookpaw flashed a grateful glance at his mentor. "I think it's this way."

He padded down an alley, pausing every few paw steps to taste the air. Leafstar followed, with the rest of the patrol bunched close behind her. After a few heartbeats, Sharpclaw brushed past her and bounded up beside Snookpaw. His paw steps were firm and his tail was erect, as if he was completely confident in these strange surroundings.

Leafstar watched him through narrowed eyes, her pelt quivering with concern. Had Billystorm been right after all, about the secret night patrols in the Twolegplace? She tried to catch the ginger-and-white tom's eye, but Billystorm was resolutely not looking at her.

Sadness stabbed at Leafstar's heart like a thorn. More than anything she wanted to forget her duty to her Clan, just for once, and ask Billystorm's forgiveness. *But I can't do that,* she thought with a sigh, trying to push the sadness away. *And right now we have to concentrate on helping the little Twoleg.*

Snookpaw led the patrol around a corner and to the edge of a small Thunderpath. "I think we have to cross here," he mewed.

"Right." Sharpclaw took over at once. "Every cat get ready. Run when I say 'Now!'"

Leafstar stood at the edge of the Thunderpath beside her Clanmates, wrinkling her nose at the acrid scent that rose from the hard black surface. Her ears flicked up at the sound of a monster, and she exchanged a warning glance with Sharpclaw. The noise grew louder; the cats crouched down as the monster growled past, rushing on round black paws. A gust of wind buffeted their fur as it raced by, a couple of tail-lengths in front of their noses.

"It didn't see us," Cherrytail whispered as the noise died away.

Leafstar glanced up and down the Thunderpath. The monster had left a foul stink behind it; she passed her tongue over her lips a few times, trying get rid of its taste.

"Now!" Sharpclaw yowled.

All six cats launched themselves forward. Leafstar felt her flying paws beating on the hard surface; then she was safely across, looking around to make sure the rest of the patrol had made it, too.

"Nothing to it, really," Sharpclaw mewed nonchalantly.

Oh, yes? Leafstar thought. *And how come you're so experienced with Thunderpaths?*

Snookpaw took the lead again, over a fence and across a garden where a strange kittypet peered out at them from under a bush, but didn't try to approach the patrol.

"I think the next nest is the one we want," he told Leafstar.

Bounding up to the fence, he clawed his way up it and balanced, swaying, at the top, his fur spiked in shock. In the same heartbeat, a dog started yapping loudly on the other side of the fence.

"Now what?" Sharpclaw muttered. "He never said there was a dog."

The wooden fence shook as something thumped into it from the other side, and the yapping grew louder still. Snookpaw half jumped, half fell down and staggered across the grass to where the patrol was waiting.

"S-sorry," he stammered. "That's the wrong garden."

"Thank StarClan for that!" Cherrytail exclaimed, with a glance across to where the dog was still hurling itself at the fence.

"So what do we do now?" Sharpclaw asked with an irritable

flick of his tail-tip. "Are we lost?"

"I'm really sorry . . ." Snookpaw repeated.

"Take it easy." Billystorm rested his tail across his apprentice's shoulders. "Just think. When was the last time you were really certain of where we were?"

"When we crossed the Thunderpath," Snookpaw replied with a look of relief.

"Then let's go back there," Leafstar meowed.

She took the lead, all her senses alert for more dogs or monsters, until the patrol stood once more by the side of the Thunderpath. "Do we need to cross again?" she asked Snookpaw.

The apprentice shook his head. "I think it's this way," he meowed, pricking his ears as he led the patrol farther along the Thunderpath, slipping along in the shade of bushes that hung over the walls. He whisked around the next corner, picking up the pace as if he felt he was getting close, only to come to a halt when the path ended in a high wall built of the same Twoleg red stone.

"I don't remember that at all," he murmured unhappily.

Leafstar heard Cora's claws scraping impatiently on the ground and cast a swift glance at the black she-cat. Cora's eyes were snapping with annoyance, but she didn't say anything.

Sharpclaw's tail-tip was twitching back and forth. "Snookpaw—"

"Are you sure we turned the right corner?" Billystorm interrupted, padding up to his apprentice. "Try to remember what it looked like the last time you were here."

Snookpaw closed his eyes, wrinkling his nose up as if he was thinking hard. "There was a holly tree," he began. "I know that's right. . . ." He hesitated a heartbeat longer, then exclaimed, "But the tree was much bigger! Now I know where we are!"

Confident now, he raced back to the corner with the patrol hurrying after him. He ran along the edge of the Thunder-path they had crossed, until he reached the next corner, where a huge holly tree loomed over the top of a pale wooden fence. Around the corner was a narrow alley with Twoleg nests on either side, separated from the path by low stone walls.

"This is it!" Snookpaw trilled. "I can smell the flowers already."

As she followed him down the alley, Leafstar could hear Twolegs yowling; the sound grew louder until they reached a nest about halfway down the alley. Snookpaw leaped up onto the wall, and Leafstar followed him.

A large square of grass stretched in front of them, with the Twoleg nest at the far side. A male Twoleg was in the garden looking under bushes and inside a small wooden den. He kept on yowling as he searched; a few moments later a female Twoleg appeared from the nest and added her yowls to her mate's. Even though she had no idea what they were saying, Leafstar could pick up their fear-scent and realized how distressed they were. There was something familiar about their actions, too. It reminded her of the time Sagekit had gone missing among the boulders near the training area, and Clovertail had hunted for him as if he was the most precious piece of prey.

"I think they're looking for the kit," she meowed. "Well done, Snookpaw. You brought us to the right place."

"Yes, you did well," Billystorm agreed, leaping up onto the wall on the opposite side of Snookpaw from Leafstar.

Snookpaw blinked at his mentor and let out a purr. "I never thought I'd do it," he confessed.

"So now what do we do?" Sharpclaw demanded, jumping up and gazing out into the garden. "How do we tell the Twolegs where their kit is?"

"I'll get them to follow me," Snookpaw mewed, leaping down onto the grass before Leafstar could stop him.

Sharpclaw shrugged. "He's a kittypet. Maybe he knows how to talk to Twolegs."

Snookpaw raced across the garden and up to the female Twoleg, who let out a sharp exclamation as he wound himself around her ankles. The Twoleg male spun around and let out a growl as his gaze fell on Snookpaw. He lumbered toward the apprentice, waving his arms and making hissing noises.

Snookpaw stepped back, bewildered. "I know where your kit is!" he meowed loudly. "You have to come with me!"

The Twolegs obviously didn't understand. The female flapped her hands and screeched at Snookpaw, who backed farther away.

"Come back here, mouse-brain!" Sharpclaw yowled.

At the sound, the male Twoleg turned toward the wall and spotted the cats perched on top of it. He let out a sharp exclamation, and dived to pick up a rounded Twoleg thing that looked as if it was made out of the same reddish stone as the nest.

"Uh-oh . . ." Sharpclaw muttered. He whipped around and leaped down into the alley.

At the same moment the Twoleg flung the red thing. Snookpaw fled across the grass and launched himself at the top of the wall; Billystorm bundled him down into the alley and Leafstar jumped down after them. The red thing hit the wall just below the spot where they had been standing and shattered into pieces.

"That was close," Sharpclaw muttered.

Cora and Cherrytail, who had been keeping watch in the alley, were kneading the stony ground with claws extended.

"We've got to go," Cora hissed. "The Twolegs don't want us here."

"I don't understand!" Snookpaw's fur was ruffled and his eyes wide with disbelief. "Why did they do that? We're only trying to help."

"Twolegs are stupid," Sharpclaw stated, shrugging. "We've done all we can here," he added with a glance at Leafstar. "We'd better get back to camp before there's any more trouble."

With every paw step back to the gorge, Leafstar's uneasiness increased. She couldn't accept their failure as easily as Cora and Sharpclaw. *There must be something we can do!* She wished she could ask Billystorm's advice, but every word she might have spoken stuck in her throat.

When she led her patrol down the trail into the gorge, the

rest of the Clan was waiting to hear what had happened.

"Did you manage to find her kin?" Lichenfur rasped, raising one hind leg to scratch behind her ear. "It gives me the creeps, having a Twoleg in the gorge."

"At least the wailing has stopped," Tangle muttered.

"We found them," Sharpclaw reported before Leafstar could reply. "They were searching in their garden for the kit. But they wouldn't listen when Snookpaw tried to tell them where she was."

"They threw a flowerpot at us!" Snookpaw exclaimed, his eyes stretched wide with distress and indignation. "I never thought Twolegs would behave like that."

"Then you've learned something, *kittypet*," Sparrowpelt murmured under his breath.

"Snookpaw, I don't think you should let it worry you," Billystorm told his apprentice, giving him a friendly flick over the ear with his tail. "You know that some Twolegs don't like strange cats in their gardens."

"That's true," Ebonyclaw agreed. "And if they were searching, they might have thought you were getting in the way."

Snookpaw's tail drooped unhappily. "They didn't have to get so angry."

"I'm sure this means we shouldn't get involved," Petalnose meowed, dipping her head to give her neck fur a few brisk licks. "The Twolegs don't deserve our help if they're going to throw things at us."

Waspwhisker nodded. "There's nothing more we can do, anyway."

Leafstar didn't agree; her paws tingled with the conviction

that the Clan was meant to help. And she felt more worried still at the news that the wailing had stopped. The ordinary sounds of the gorge—the rushing water that poured out of the rocks, the rustle of trees, the pad of paws on stone—seemed muted and ominous.

"I'm going to go and see how Echosong is getting along," she announced.

Several of her Clanmates padded after her as she headed up the gorge. As she rounded the spur of rock to reach the place where the little Twoleg was lying, Echosong came to meet her. Leafstar's nose twitched at the strong scent of comfrey that wreathed around the medicine cat.

"Did you find her parents?" Echosong asked, her deep green eyes wide with anxiety. "Are they coming?"

"We found them, but they're not coming." Quickly Leafstar told Echosong what had happened in the Twolegplace. "How is the Twoleg kit?"

"Not good." Echosong shook her head, and led the way back to the kit's side. "She closed her eyes and stopped moving soon after you left. Unless we can get help for her, I don't think she's going to wake up."

The Twoleg lay motionless, her leg still bent at the awkward angle. Her face looked paler than before and her eyes were closed; Leafstar might have thought she was dead, except for the faint rise and fall of her chest. Clovertail was curled up asleep in the crook of her arm, with one of the Twoleg's forepaws lying lightly across her back.

"I tried putting a poultice of comfrey on her broken leg," Echosong explained, pointing to the patches of chewed-up herb plastered to the kit's skin. "But it's hard to get a poultice to stick when there isn't any fur for it to stick to."

Leafstar looked down at the little Twoleg for a few heartbeats without speaking. *What if I had kits and one of them was lost, or hurt?* she asked herself, pushing away the bleak knowledge that her duties wouldn't allow her to have kits of her own. *I'd be frantic!*

"We're not going to give up," she announced. "We have to try again."

"But what else can we do?" Sharpclaw asked, with a frustrated lash of his tail. "We didn't manage to get through to the Twolegs, and I don't see how we'll ever be able to."

"That's right," Sparrowpelt agreed. "It's impossible to know the way that Twolegs think. They don't seem to have any reason."

Leafstar's pelt tingled as the beginnings of a plan slid into her mind. "If we don't know the way Twolegs think," she began thoughtfully, "we'll have to use the way cats think instead. The Twolegs were hunting for their kit; we'll just have to help them."

CHAPTER 28

❧

"When we're tracking prey, we follow a scent trail," Leafstar mused, tasting the kit's strong Twoleg scent. "Is there any way to lay one for the Twolegs?"

"There's no point," Harveymoon pointed out. "Twolegs have enormous noses, but their sense of smell isn't worth a mouse-tail. Otherwise they'd know we were here!"

Leafstar admitted that the daylight-warrior had a point. "Then how can we let them know where their lost kit is?"

She wasn't expecting an answer, but just then an excited cry came from Frecklepaw, who had been scrambling among the rocks at the foot of the cliff. "Look what I've found!"

Her voice woke Clovertail, who blinked and stretched her jaws in an enormous yawn. "That was the best sleep I've had in moons," she meowed. "Leafstar, what's going on? Are the kit's parents coming?"

Leafstar explained what had happened in the Twolegplace while she padded over to Frecklepaw to see what the apprentice had discovered.

Clovertail stepped carefully out of the Twoleg's grasp and followed, her whiskers twitching in disappointment. "Poor little kit," she murmured. "We have to do something."

"Look," Frecklepaw repeated as the two she-cats approached. She pointed with her tail at a bright blue object lying between two rocks.

"What is it?" Leafstar asked, stretching out a paw to give the object a tentative prod. "It looks as if it's made of Twoleg pelt-stuff."

"It's the kit's backpack," Frecklepaw told her. Her eyes shone with pride at being able to help. "Twolegs use them to carry stuff."

Leafstar nodded. "I see. Like a very big leaf wrap."

She gripped the edge of the backpack between her teeth and tugged it up onto the surface of the nearest rock. Several smaller objects fell out of it, scattering around the cats' paws.

More of the Clan cats were starting to gather around, murmuring among themselves as they saw what Frecklepaw had found. The apprentices wriggled to the front, their faces alive with curiosity.

"Twolegs are weird," Mintpaw mewed, dipping her head to sniff at a scrap of white pelt. "Why do they want to drag all this stuff around with them? What's it all for, anyway?"

"That's a hanky," Frecklepaw told her importantly. "Twolegs wipe their noses with them."

"Wipe their . . . ?" Mintpaw's eyes widened and she took a pace back. "You mean they don't just lick it off? Yuck!"

"And what's this?" Sagepaw asked, nosing at a round green thing that looked a bit like the backpack, but much smaller.

Something inside it jingled when he moved it.

"Sorry, I don't know," Frecklepaw replied, her sense of importance suddenly deflating. "But this is a hair band," she added, snagging her claws into a long pink thing and holding it up. "Twoleg females tie up their head fur with them."

Egg gave the hair band a nervous sniff, while Mintpaw exchanged a glance with her brother.

"Hey, you should try that," Sagepaw suggested, giving her a friendly shove. "Tie some bindweed around your head fur."

"My head fur is fine as it is, thanks," Mintpaw snapped.

Meanwhile Snookpaw had approached, carrying something long and glittery in his jaws. "Here's her necklace," he mumbled around it. "I guess it came off when she fell."

"And what's *that* for?" Mintpaw squeaked.

Snookpaw shrugged. "Dunno. My Twoleg female puts them around her neck. I thought maybe it was to stop her head from falling off."

"That can't be right," Sagepaw murmured, puzzled. "This one's head hasn't fallen off—"

"That's all very well," Clovertail interrupted, rolling her eyes at Leafstar, who suppressed a *mrrow* of amusement. *The apprentices could go on like this all day!* "But what are we going to do with all of this? Does it help us at all?"

"I think it does, actually," Leafstar replied slowly. "The Twolegs can't follow a scent trail, but they can see all right, can't they? We can use this stuff to lead them from Twoleg-place to here, so that they find their kit."

"Let's hope they have some tracking skills," Sharpclaw commented.

"Well, I can't believe you're going to so much trouble," Petalnose meowed, gazing disdainfully at the scattering of Twoleg objects.

"Nor can I," Sparrowpelt agreed. "It's nothing to do with us. Why should we care whether the Twolegs find their kit or not?"

Clovertail's eyes stretched wide. "I can't believe you said that!"

Sparrowpelt shrugged. "I just think it's too much trouble. We're putting ourselves in danger, and for what?"

"Well, I think it's a great idea!" Cherrytail glared at her brother. "Are we going now?"

Leafstar glanced up at the sky; the sun was starting to go down, and not much time was left if they were to lead the Twolegs to the gorge before dark. "Yes, right now," she decided. "I'll take the same patrol as before. We all know the way now. Each of you pick up something and follow me."

"I'll stay here, if that's okay," Sharpclaw meowed. "I've got a few ideas that might help when the Twolegs come to the gorge."

Leafstar wondered for a moment what her deputy was planning, then told herself firmly that she couldn't keep suspecting his motives, or nothing would get done. "Fine," she mewed briskly. "We'll see you later."

Wincing at the strong Twoleg scent, Leafstar gripped the green jingly thing in her jaws, while the rest of the patrol gathered up the other objects. Billystorm picked up the back-pack, dangling it between his forelegs like some weird piece of fresh-kill.

Leafstar led the way up the cliff face, scrambling over the rocks, for there was no clearly defined trail just here. Halfway up she came upon a round object made of Twoleg pelt-stuff, with a hard crescent shape sticking out at one side. It was about the size of a Twoleg's head.

That must be to cover their head fur, she thought, pleased with herself for guessing as she grabbed it up and carried it with her.

Near the spot where they reached the top of the cliff, a straggling thornbush grew, thrusting its roots between the rocks. "Hang the backpack there," Leafstar instructed Bil-lystorm, gesturing with her tail at a jutting branch. "It's big and bright. The Twolegs will be able to see it from a long way off."

Billystorm nodded and did as she told him, though he didn't speak to her. Leafstar's heart ached all over again. *This mission would feel much more exciting if we were still friends!*

Working their way across the open ground between the gorge and Twolegplace, Leafstar and her patrol positioned the objects where they thought the Twolegs would easily spot them: on a tree stump, a flat rock, the top of a steep bank. Leafstar checked carefully that each object could be clearly seen behind them before she placed the next one.

Finally, Cherrytail scrambled up and left the hair band on an overhanging branch of a chestnut tree beside the

Thunderpath, on the edge of the open ground. "Now what?" she panted when she jumped down again.

The only thing left was the head fur cover that Leafstar was carrying. By now she was sick of it; it was heavy and awkward and kept tripping her up. She set it down for a moment to take a breather from the all-pervading scent.

"I'll take this to the Twoleg nest," she meowed. "With any luck, someone there should recognize it."

"Be careful," Cora warned her. "They might throw things again."

Leafstar nodded. *That's a risk I'll just have to take.*

She picked up the cover again and headed for the nest with her patrol padding cautiously behind her. The sun was sliding below the roofs of the Twoleg nests, and the shadows in the alley seemed to reach out for her. She suppressed a shiver as she jumped up onto the wall and looked out across the bright green grass.

At first she thought the space was empty, though the door to the nest was still open. Then she noticed the male Twoleg pacing up and down in the shadow of the bushes on the opposite side. A moment later the female came out and called something to him. Worried that they would both go back inside, Leafstar sprang down and carried the head fur cover across the grass toward the female, letting out a hiss of annoyance as her paws got tangled up again in the pelt-stuff.

As soon as the female Twoleg spotted her, she let out a screech and started flapping her arms again, trying to chase her off.

Yes, we've done all this, Leafstar thought irritably. *Just look at what I'm carrying, will you?*

She dodged to one side as the female swiped at her, fighting the urge to flee back into the alley. Glancing over her shoulder, she spotted Cora and Cherrytail side by side on the top of the wall, looking on with horrified expressions.

Then the male Twoleg let out a yowl. He ran across the garden and grabbed the female's foreleg, stopping her from swiping again at Leafstar. He was pointing urgently at the head fur cover.

At last!

The male Twoleg crouched down, talking in quiet tones with one pink paw stretched out to Leafstar. The female had stopped screeching, and was staring at her with her eyes wide. Leafstar wanted to drop the cover and run, but she knew that wouldn't do any good. She backed away slowly, trying to keep her fur flat in case the Twolegs thought she was trying to threaten them. The head fur cover dragged on the grass in front of her, luring the Twolegs forward as if it were a tasty piece of fresh-kill. When she reached the wall Leafstar spun around and leaped onto it, noticing with relief that the rest of the patrol had vanished. They didn't want to scare the Twolegs with a horde of unfamiliar cats.

Jumping down into the alley, she looked back at the male Twoleg, who stared over the wall at her for a couple of heartbeats, then opened a gate and followed her out.

That's right. Just keep following. . . .

Reaching the Thunderpath, Leafstar dropped the head fur

cover and ran toward the chestnut tree where Cherrytail had left the hair band. When she stopped and looked back, she saw that the male Twoleg had picked up the cover and was turning it over in his paws; then he raised his head and gazed after Leafstar. It was hard for her to read Twoleg expressions, but she thought he looked puzzled.

A moment later the female Twoleg joined her mate. He gave her the cover and she examined it in her turn. Leafstar twitched her tail impatiently. *Come on! How hard can it be?*

Then her jaws dropped open in dismay as the male turned away and headed back into the mouth of the alley.

"No!" Leafstar let out a despairing wail. "This way!"

The female paused, then headed alongside the Thunderpath, toward Leafstar. Her mate followed her, yowling something, but the female didn't reply. Leafstar's instincts were telling her to race across the Thunderpath and back toward the gorge, but she made herself retreat slowly so that she didn't lose the Twolegs.

She was close to the chestnut tree when the female suddenly let out a screech. She started to run, passing Leafstar, who sprang out of the way, and grabbed the hair band from the low branch where Cherrytail had left it.

"Thank StarClan!" Leafstar purred. "They've found the trail."

The male Twoleg caught up with his mate and pointed across the open ground, to where Snookpaw had spread the hanky over a rock just beyond the line of Twoleg nests. Sure now that the Twolegs could find their own way to the gorge,

Leafstar waved her tail to summon her patrol. They emerged from hiding places in the shadows and underneath bushes and crowded around her.

"We did it!" Cherrytail exclaimed, with an excited bounce.

"Then let's head back to camp," Leafstar meowed. "I want to get there before the Twolegs."

They raced back to the cliffs, staying well clear of the trail of Twoleg objects. Through the dusk, Leafstar could hear the Twolegs shouting as they found each new thing. Her heart soared as she realized that the plan had worked. When the patrol scrambled down the trail that led to the camp, Leafstar skidded to a halt and stared around in surprise. The gorge had never looked so busy. Petalnose, Waspwhisker, and Shrewtooth were dragging branches and fronds of fern across the den entrances. Ebonyclaw was supervising the three remaining apprentices in moving the fresh-kill pile across the Rockpile and into a hollow among the rocks on the other side of the river. Tangle and Lichenfur were down by the river, using their tails to wipe out paw prints.

They're hiding the camp!

"Are they coming?" Sharpclaw demanded, bounding up to Leafstar.

"They're on their way," Leafstar told him. "You're doing a good job," she continued, grateful for her deputy's quick thinking. "It's hard to tell there have ever been cats here."

Sharpclaw replied with a terse nod. "I'd rather the Twolegs didn't come anywhere near the gorge," he meowed. "But you're right that the injured kit can't stay here. It's better to control the invasion than have the Twolegs swarming all over us when we're not ready for them."

Leaving her patrol to help with the concealment of the camp, Leafstar headed up the gorge to find Echosong. The medicine cat and Clovertail were sitting beside the injured kit, who still wasn't moving. Her tiny pink paws lay on the stones beside her, all scratched and smeared with dried blood. Leafstar blinked. *Oh, you poor little kit.*

"Did it work?" Echosong sprang to her paws and rushed over to Leafstar as soon as the Clan leader rounded the spur of rock.

Before Leafstar could reply, they heard the sound of huge paws trampling around on the cliff above their heads, and Twoleg voices yowling.

"Thank StarClan!" Clovertail whispered. "They're calling for their kit."

"But the kit can't answer," Echosong mewed anxiously.

"Then we'll have to answer for her." Leafstar jumped onto a nearby rock and let out an earsplitting screech.

At first she thought that the Twolegs were ignoring her. She took a deep breath and yowled on a long, throbbing note that echoed off the rocks. A couple of heartbeats later she spotted first the male Twoleg, then his mate, peering over the top of the cliff. Suddenly they let out answering cries and pointed at the motionless kit.

Echosong leaped up beside Leafstar and waved her tail triumphantly. "They've seen her!"

"And now they'll come to get her," Leafstar mewed, letting her yowl die away. "By then I want no sign of SkyClan anywhere in this gorge. Let's get back to camp right away."

Sharpclaw was waiting at the foot of the Rockpile when Leafstar and the other she-cats returned to the camp. The rest of the Clan were already in their dens; Leafstar spotted them peering out between the ferns and branches that had been piled against the entrances.

"Well?" Sharpclaw asked tensely.

"The Twolegs are here," Leafstar reported. "They—"

She broke off as yowls of triumph erupted from the cliff.

"I knew we could do it!" Harveymoon exclaimed, pushing his shoulders through the barrier across the warriors' den.

"Quiet!" Sharpclaw snarled. "And get back in there. Do you want the Twolegs to come looking for us?"

Harveymoon vanished abruptly, though Leafstar could still hear squeals and meows of excitement coming from the dens. Fallowfern's kits were scrambling among the branches outside the nursery; Clovertail hauled herself up the trail and helped Fallowfern to round them up and take them back inside.

"I want to know what the Twolegs are doing," Sharpclaw commented to Leafstar. "But I don't think we can leave the camp. The whole Clan sounds as if it has bees in its brain."

Leafstar could understand her cats' need to celebrate their success, but she was relieved when the noise died down after a few moments. Choosing a small patrol—Sharpclaw, Cherrytail, Echosong, Billystorm, and Snookpaw—she crept back up the gorge and peered out from behind the rocks to watch the rescue of the Twoleg kit.

By the time they returned to the spot, the adult Twolegs had been joined by many, many more. They wore bright yellow pelts, and lowered themselves down into the gorge on long tendrils suspended from the top of the cliff.

"See, Twolegs aren't bad all the time!" Snookpaw whispered, bouncing lightly on his paws. "They've all come to help the kit."

"Maybe." Sharpclaw's green eyes were wary. "But I'm not happy about all these Twolegs in our territory. What if they decide to come back?"

Leafstar watched the Twolegs lower a flat, bulky object down the cliff face and lift the little Twoleg gently onto it. "I can't see why they would do that," she murmured.

"But they must know we're here," Cherrytail murmured, sounding uncharacteristically troubled. "We brought them here, after all."

"And they've got what they came for," Leafstar reassured her.

All the same, as the Twolegs fastened the kit onto the bulky object and started to haul her up the cliff on the tendrils, Leafstar admitted to herself that she shared her Clanmates' concern. *Clan cats and Twolegs lead separate lives,* she thought. *Have I brought them too close together by what I did today?*

Echosong brushed against her shoulder. "You did the

right thing," she insisted, as if she had read her Clan leader's thoughts.

But Leafstar could see a shadow behind the medicine cat's gaze, telling her that Echosong was worried, too.

What have I done? she wondered. *And what's going to happen now?*

CHAPTER 29

❧

First thing next morning, Leafstar padded up the gorge to check out the spot where the Twoleg kit had been lying. Rain had fallen during the night; her paws splashed through puddles and she narrowed her eyes as the rising sun glittered on water dripping from the rocks. A stiff breeze sent small white clouds scudding across the sky.

Leafstar peered cautiously from behind the spur of rock, then padded forward, her jaws parted to taste the air. She could still pick up the mingled scents of many Twolegs, but they were faint and fading; the night's rain had helped to wash them away. There were still many marks of the Twolegs' heavy paws, but Leafstar guessed that they too would fade with time.

Maybe it's all over, and we are safe.

When Leafstar returned to the camp, she found Sharpclaw arranging the morning's patrols. At once she picked up the feelings of restlessness among her warriors; they roamed distractedly around the Rockpile, not really listening to Sharpclaw as he called their names.

"What are we going to do if the Twolegs come back?"

Petalnose fretted. "Maybe we should leave and find ourselves somewhere else to live."

"I'm not moving anywhere," Clovertail retorted. "Not until my kits are born and fit to travel."

"I'm sure we won't have to." Patchfoot brushed his pelt reassuringly against Clovertail's side. "What can the Twolegs do, after all?"

Shrewtooth shuddered, but didn't try to reply.

Looking around, Leafstar spotted Stick and the other cats from the Twolegplace huddled together, and she wondered what they were talking about. *What if they decide to leave?* Maybe they didn't feel comfortable in a Clan that had too much to do with Twolegs.

A high-pitched squealing drew Leafstar's attention to the edge of the river. Plumkit was lying on her back with her paws in the air.

"I'm an injured Twoleg!" she wailed. "Help meeeeeee!"

Her brothers frisked around her, darting forward now and then to give her a prod.

"We have to find her Twolegs!" Rabbitkit announced.

Leafstar suppressed a *mrrow* of laughter. At least Fallowfern's kits weren't worried about the possible threat from Twolegs. She wished she could say the same about the rest of the Clan. Even the apprentices were looking subdued, and she spotted Tinycloud and Bouncefire facing each other with bristling fur, as if the tensions had to break out somehow.

"This is no good," Leafstar muttered. "I have to do something."

A yowl of greeting rang out from the top of the cliff; Leafstar looked up to see all the daylight-warriors arriving together: Harveymoon and Macgyver in the lead, followed by Billystorm and Ebonyclaw with their apprentices.

That's it! Leafstar thought. *I know what will pull the Clan together and make them feel better.*

Leaping up to the top of the Rockpile, she yowled, "Let all cats old enough to catch their own prey join here beneath the Rockpile for a Clan meeting."

The gaze of every cat was turned on her. Leafstar waited for the daylight-warriors to reach the bottom of the gorge, and for Echosong to emerge from her den. Tangle and Lichenfur appeared too, stretching out in a sunny spot near the edge of the river.

"Cats of SkyClan, one of the most important ceremonies for any Clan is the making of a new warrior," Leafstar began when every cat was listening. "And that is why I have called you together today."

The apprentices brightened up, gazing at one another with excitement sparkling in their eyes, as they wondered which of them their Clan leader meant.

"Yesterday Snookpaw helped his Clan by finding the injured Twoleg's nest," Leafstar went on. "Without him, the little Twoleg would still be lying in the gorge. She might even have died. Snookpaw, you acted as a warrior and you deserve your warrior name."

The apprentice's jaws gaped open. "But . . . but Leafstar," he protested, "I didn't do anything!"

"You did what no other Clan cat could have done," Leaf-star assured him. "Billystorm, has your apprentice, Snookpaw, learned the skills of a warrior?"

Billystorm's amber eyes were glowing with pride. "He has."

Leafstar's heart wrenched at the thought that his warm look wasn't for her. "And does he understand the meaning of the warrior code?"

"He does."

Leafstar leaped down from the Rockpile and stood in front of Snookpaw, who still looked as if some cat had hit him over the head with a dead pigeon.

"I, Leafstar, call upon my warrior ancestors to look down on this apprentice," she declared. "He has trained hard to understand the ways of your noble code, and I commend him to you as a warrior in his turn. Snookpaw, do you promise to uphold the warrior code and to protect and defend this Clan, even at the cost of your life?"

Snookpaw was shivering as he replied, "I do."

"Then by the powers of StarClan I give you your warrior name. Snookpaw, from this moment you will be known as Snookthorn. StarClan honors your courage and your intelligence, and we welcome you as a full member of SkyClan."

She rested her muzzle on the top of Snookthorn's head; the young tom licked her shoulder and took a pace back to stand beside Billystorm.

"Snookthorn! Snookthorn!"

The SkyClan cats clustered around to welcome the newest

warrior. Leafstar watched them with a deep sense of relief, thankful for their shining eyes and enthusiastic voices. *It worked! Now they're not so worried about the Twolegs. And Snookthorn will be a valuable member of the Clan.*

But as the yowls died away and his Clanmates moved back from Snookthorn, the young cat turned to her with trouble in his eyes.

"I'm really sorry, Leafstar," he mewed, "but I can't stay here."

Shocked murmuring broke out among his Clanmates; Tinycloud let out a yowl of protest, echoed by Sparrowpelt and Rockshade.

"What?" Leafstar stared at the new warrior, baffled, as she raised her tail for silence. "Why not?"

Snookthorn shook his head in confusion. "I—I hated it yesterday, when the Twolegs yowled at us and chased us away. We were trying to help them, but they treated us like enemies."

"They didn't understand—" Leafstar began.

"I know. But that doesn't make it any better," Snookthorn went on miserably. "I've enjoyed being a Clan cat, but I don't want to be an enemy of Twolegs. I can't stay."

"Now hang on a moment." Sharpclaw shouldered his way to the front of the crowd. "You just made a promise to protect and defend your Clan. Were you lying when you said that?"

"No . . ." Snookthorn protested. "I didn't mean . . ." His voice trailed into silence and his tail drooped to the ground.

"I think you'd better decide what you did mean," Sharpclaw snapped, his eyes glittering with anger.

Snookthorn hung his head without speaking. Leafstar listened with mounting anger to the whispering among her Clan; she heard Bouncefire hiss, "Traitor!" and glared at him until he looked away.

Before Leafstar could speak, Billystorm stepped forward, touching Snookthorn's ear with his nose. "I know it's hard, to have a paw in two lives."

Snookthorn lifted his head and nodded. His eyes were bleak with pain. "I thought I could do it, but I can't," he confessed. "Living as a Clan cat is making me something I don't want to be—fierce and wild and unwelcome among Twolegs. I'm honored that you think I'm good enough to be a warrior, but it's not something I want. Not anymore."

Billystorm tipped his head to one side. "It was just one misunderstanding with Twolegs," he meowed. "Your housefolk would never treat you like that."

"Really?" Snookthorn retorted, and now he looked taller and stronger, more like the warrior Leafstar knew he could be. "How do you know that? They were so worried when I got sick after falling in the river. Will they have to keep mending me, after battles and hunting accidents and scraping my paws on these rocks all day? It's not fair to them, to keep putting myself in danger."

Sparrowpelt let out a snort. "Well, if you're not *brave* enough . . ." he hissed.

Snookthorn spun around and faced him. "I have the courage to know what I truly am," he replied quietly. "I am a *kittypet*. Twolegs are not my enemies, and I never want to see that look in their eyes again." He turned back to his former mentor. "Billystorm, you have taught me so much, and I'll always be grateful for that. But I cannot walk with my paws in two worlds. Not anymore."

Leafstar let out a long sigh. She admired the warrior's conviction; it was a shame his loyalty wasn't to SkyClan, because he would have been a Clanmate she'd be proud of. "We can't keep you here, Snookthorn. But I'm sorry you've made this decision. We'll miss you."

She glared at Sharpclaw as her deputy opened his jaws to speak again. *If he tells Snookthorn we're better off without him, I'll claw his ears off!* Sharpclaw obviously got the message, because he closed his mouth without speaking.

"I'll miss you, too," Snookthorn replied, letting his gaze travel over his former Clanmates. "I'll never forget the friends I've made in SkyClan." Dipping his head, he added, "Thank you for everything, Leafstar."

He turned away and walked toward the bottom of the trail with his head high. Leafstar felt her heart wrench with sorrow as she watched him. *We've lost a fine warrior.*

"Good-bye, Snookthorn," she called after him; some of her Clanmates called their good-byes too, but the chorus was thin and ragged, and others just turned away. Snookthorn never looked back.

Twilight was filling the gorge as Leafstar returned from a patrol with a fat squirrel in her jaws. Cherrytail, Tinycloud, and Rockshade followed her, carrying their own prey.

The hunting had been good.

As she crossed the Rockpile, Leafstar spotted Sharpclaw sitting on the edge of the pool. The dark blue water swirled close to his paws before veering away downstream. He glanced up at her; Leafstar's paws prickled when she thought she could make out a spark of triumph in his eyes.

As soon as she had dropped her squirrel on the fresh-kill pile, Leafstar padded over to talk to her deputy. "I'm sorry we won't be seeing Snookthorn again," she remarked, trying to sound casual.

Sharpclaw rose to his paws and dipped his head politely at her approach. "I'm sorry, too," he agreed.

At least he hasn't said, "I told you so."

"It makes me think that we need to be absolutely certain about the daylight-warriors' loyalty," Sharpclaw continued. "Including Billystorm," he added, with a meaningful look.

Anger surged through Leafstar, fierce as a flood in leaf-fall. It took every scrap of self-control she possessed not to fall on her deputy and rake her claws across his pelt. "Do you doubt Billystorm's loyalty?" she demanded, hardly able to believe the strength of her own feelings as she strove to keep her voice steady.

Sharpclaw took a step back, surprise flickering in his eyes. "No." His voice was mild as he replied. "No more than I doubt the loyalty of any of the kittypets. It must be very hard for them, split between two lives." He licked one paw and drew it thoughtfully over his ear. "Maybe when the seasons turn colder, more of them will want to stay with their housefolk."

Leafstar had listened to him belittle the daylight-warriors for long enough. "It sounds as though you doubt the warrior code," she meowed icily, "if you think it would be so easy for our Clanmates to reject it."

Not waiting for a response, she spun around and stalked away. She was furious with Sharpclaw for his constant questioning of cats she had come to value, and even more furious with herself for letting the discussion end in a quarrel.

Why did Snookthorn have to leave us? Have we really so little to offer compared with housefolk?

She was heading for her den when she spotted Billystorm beginning to climb the trail that led to the cliff top. *He's on his way back to the Twolegplace.* Sudden fear clawed at her heart and she ran after him, scrambling up the trail until she caught up to him.

"Are you leaving?" she blurted out.

Billystorm turned to look at her, his eyes wide with surprise. "Only until tomorrow," he meowed. As Leafstar struggled to hide her relief, he added, "I'll go and visit Snookthorn, but I don't think I'll be able to change his mind."

That wasn't what I wanted to talk about at all, Leafstar thought, confused. *I wanted to tell you how much I want you to stay in SkyClan.*

"That's fine," she mewed evenly. "I just wanted to make sure that Snookthorn is okay. He can come back any time, you know."

Billystorm's ears twitched skeptically. "Really? And will all his Clanmates welcome him back?"

Leafstar remembered the protests when Snookthorn

announced his intention to leave. She couldn't deny that some of the Clan would be hostile to the young cat who had made a promise and then broken it. "*I* will welcome him back, and that's what counts."

Billystorm dipped his head and turned to go, glancing back after he had taken a couple of paw steps. "Be careful, Leaf-star," he murmured. "You cannot force cats to be loyal—not to you and not to the warrior code."

Leafstar stood on the trail, watching the ginger-and-white tom climb to the top of the cliff and vanish into the gathering darkness. Her fur prickled with loneliness. Then she reminded herself that all Clan leaders were alone in making decisions on behalf of their Clan. *We have to trust our own instincts, more than any other cat's.*

As she headed for her den again, she spotted tiny figures jumping around on top of the Rockpile, and she recognized Fallowfern's kits. *What are they doing there at this time? They should be tucked up in the nursery.* Between curiosity and concern, she headed down into the gorge again.

"Then by the powers of StarClan I give you your warrior name," she heard in Plumkit's squeaky voice. "Nettlepaw, from this moment you will be known as Nettlewhiskers. StarClan honors your . . . your battle skills and your courage, and we welcome you as a full member of SkyClan."

A warrior ceremony! Leafstar thought, amusement pushing aside her gloomy thoughts. She waited to see Nettlekit dip his head so that his littermate could rest her muzzle on it.

Instead, Nettlekit swiped one forepaw at Plumkit, his

claws extended. "No!" he squealed. "I don't want to be a warrior! Nettlewhiskers is a dumb name!"

"What?" Plumkit's eyes stretched wide with astonishment, though Leafstar could tell that she wasn't really surprised. This was all part of their game. "What do you want, then?" she asked.

"I want to live with Twolegs," Nettlekit declared. "Then I won't have to hunt for food anymore, or sleep on moldy moss—with *your* paws in my mouth!" he added to his sister, drawing back his lips in a tiny snarl. "You take up far too much room!"

Paws pattered up behind Leafstar, and Fallowfern appeared, to stand at the foot of the Rockpile with her neck fur bristling angrily. "Come down from there *at once*!" she ordered. "Sorry," she added, with an embarrassed glance at Leafstar.

"Don't worry about it," Leafstar responded as the kits came tumbling down from the pile of boulders. She knew she couldn't make an issue out of what she had just seen. *They were just playing, nothing more.* "If you don't want to be apprentices, that's fine," she told them, shrugging as if she didn't care. "If you don't want to learn how to hunt and climb trees and patrol the borders . . ."

"No! No!" Rabbitkit squeaked, jumping up and down. "We want to do all that."

"Please!" Nettlekit begged. "It was only a game."

Plumkit and Creekkit just stood watching Leafstar, their eyes wide with dismay.

"Don't worry, kits," Leafstar mewed, brushing their heads

gently with her tail. "I'm sure you'll all learn well when the time comes. Go with your mother now."

Trying to ignore the churning in her belly, Leafstar made for her den. But before she reached the bottom of the trail, she spotted Sharpclaw again, crouched in the shadow of a boulder with Stick, Sparrowpelt, and Coal. The soft murmur of their voices was cut off as she padded past, and they all turned their heads to watch her.

What have they been discussing that they don't want me to hear?

Her pelt prickling, she wanted to stop and confront them. But she suspected she wouldn't get a straight answer, so she simply nodded and went on.

"I'm going to be the best at training!" she heard Rabbitkit boast behind her as Fallowfern herded her rambunctious litter up to the nursery.

"No, I am!" Plumkit argued. "And I'll be so brave and loyal. . . ."

It's true, they will. Their game today would be forgotten when the next adventure cropped up. Feeling more optimistic, Leafstar bounded up the trail to her den. Curling deep into the moss and bracken of her nest, she closed her eyes, but for the moment she didn't try to sleep. She tried to picture where Billystorm might be now, and what his Twoleg den was like. *Is it like Snookthorn's nest, all hard-edged and shut away from the sky?*

Gradually sleep crept up on her and she imagined herself prowling around a Twoleg nest, wailing as she tried to get into Billystorm's den. Her ears picked up the sound of cats padding softly with hushed whispers, and she imagined that kittypets were surrounding her, closing in, angry because she was invading their territory. . . .

Leafstar's eyes flew open and she breathed a sigh of relief as she saw the familiar curved walls of her den, silvered by the moonlight seeping through the entrance. There were no hostile kittypets, but she could still hear the soft sounds of her dream. She rose to her paws, shaking moss from her pelt, and crept to the entrance of her den. Poking her head out, she stared across the cliff face to the trail that led to the cliff top.

Sharpclaw was padding up the narrow path, his dark ginger fur almost black in the icy light. Behind him were Stick, Cora, and Shorty, and behind them several more of her warriors. They paused briefly to talk to Coal, who was on watch halfway up the cliff, then continued silently up the trail.

So many! Leafstar thought, staring at them in dismay. *Where is Sharpclaw taking them?*

CHAPTER 30

❧

For a few heartbeats Leafstar crouched frozen in the mouth of her den. Then, setting down her paws as lightly as if she was stalking a squirrel, she crept out and headed for the top of the cliff. She made a wide detour around Coal, who was gazing down into the gorge, unaware that his leader was sneaking past him. The moon was a claw-scratch, low in the sky, giving just enough light for Leafstar to make out which of her warriors were following Sharpclaw and the cats from the Twolegplace.

Rockshade, his black pelt no more than a moving shadow. Cherrytail, her excited bounce as she reached the cliff top giving her away. Sparrowpelt, his tabby fur a flicker of light and shade.

Pulling herself up onto level ground, Leafstar paused, watching the patrol as it headed across the open ground to the Twolegplace. Their confident strides told her that they had done this many times before.

Billystorm was right!

Creeping along with her belly fur brushing the grass, Leafstar followed, thankful that the breeze was blowing toward her; her scent wouldn't alert Sharpclaw that she was tracking his paw steps. At the edge of the Twolegplace she hid behind a boulder and watched as Stick lined up the patrol along the edge of the Thunderpath.

"There's not as much chance of monsters after dark," the Twolegplace cat meowed. "But you still need to be careful. Don't look into their eyes. They can freeze you like a scared rabbit."

Who put you in charge? Leafstar wondered, thinking that Stick sounded like a mentor teaching a group of apprentices.

The growl of an approaching monster drowned out Stick's next words. It swept past, its glaring eyes angling over the row of cats; Leafstar blinked as they were outlined as dark shapes against the dazzle.

When the noise had died away, Stick glanced both ways along the Thunderpath, then raised his tail. "Now!"

The patrol pounded over the black stone and vanished into the shadows on the opposite side. Leafstar followed more cautiously, forcing her legs not to shake as she crossed the hard surface of the Thunderpath. She had lost sight of the patrol, but their scent trail was fresh and strong; she followed it over a fence into an enclosed space behind a Twoleg nest, where she spotted them again, slinking alongside the stretch of flat, green grass under cover of the overhanging branches of bushes.

On the opposite side of the grass, Stick beckoned with his tail and hissed, "This way!" He slithered under a gate into an alley, and the rest of the patrol followed him, with Shorty at the rear. The brown tom seemed to be keeping a lookout; Leafstar shrank into the shadow of a holly bush until he too had vanished under the gate.

Bounding across the garden, she pressed herself close to the gate and peered between the wooden strips. The patrol was standing in a huddle a couple of fox-lengths away.

"Remember your paw steps sound louder when you're walking on stone," Stick warned. "You need to practice being completely silent."

"And use the shadows," Cora added.

Stick nodded. "Cora's right. Don't forget that your eyes reflect the light more here. Cats will spot you even in the shadows if your eyes are gleaming."

"Look sideways to check what's ahead," Shorty advised.

Leafstar felt her pelt start to prickle as she listened. *Is Stick leading an attack on cats in the Twolegplace?* Horror rooted her paws to the ground. *They can't be targeting our daylight-warriors! Sharpclaw would never do that.* Then she remembered all the times Sharpclaw had criticized the kittypets or left them out of Clan duties, and she couldn't be sure.

As soon as the patrol moved off again, Leafstar slipped under the gate and followed, remembering what the Twolegplace cats had said about the best ways to hide. She kept to the shadows and turned her head to look sideways along the alley so that her eyes didn't catch the light full on. Her muscles were shrieking at her to leap forward and confront them, but she forced herself to watch and wait.

Stick led the patrol around a corner and halted in front of a high wall built of red stone. Orange light flooded over it from a glowing stone tree.

"If you can't reach the top of the wall in one leap, you have to learn how to grip it," Shorty explained, his voice a low murmur. "It's not like a tree; you can't dig your claws in. But look at the lines where the stones are put together." He pointed with his tail. "There are tiny gaps in there. The trick is to drive your foreclaws into one set of gaps, and find another set to drive in your hind claws. Then you can push off and get to the top. Cora, show them."

The black she-cat nodded and took a few paces back to get a good run at the wall. Leafstar had to admire her graceful leap and the way she hung poised for a heartbeat on the smooth surface before she propelled herself higher and landed lightly on the flat top.

"Any cat want to try?" Stick asked.

Sparrowpelt nodded agreement, then took a run up to the wall as Cora had done. His jump was strong and focused, but his claws slipped on the stone and it took an undignified scramble before he could haul himself up to stand beside Cora. Cherrytail followed him; her strong SkyClan haunches sent her flying upward, and she managed to push off again and reach the top of the wall on her second leap.

"You're lighter; it's easier for you," Sparrowpelt grumbled.

Leafstar watched as Rockshade tried the leap in his turn; the black tom's claws scraped vainly at the stone and he slid back to the ground again, hissing in annoyance.

"Never mind," Stick consoled him. "You'll get it in the end."

"I hope so," Rockshade muttered. "It's all so different from what I'm used to."

Leafstar could understand why the young warrior would be embarrassed by failing at something that Twolegplace cats and even former kittypets could do. *But it doesn't seem as if Cherrytail and Sparrowpelt remember much about being kittypets,* Leafstar thought. *They're nearly as nervous here as gorge-born cats.*

"Meanwhile, we'll go this way," Stick meowed, leading the rest of the patrol along the bottom of the wall. A few fox-lengths farther on, he pushed his way between the wooden strips of a gate into the enclosed space beyond. The cats balancing on the wall jumped down to join their Clanmates.

Leafstar tracked their paw steps as Stick padded along a path of bare earth between leafy plants on either side, then headed through a gap in the fence opposite into the next space. Her pelt rose as she heard the loud barking of a dog inside the Twoleg nest.

"Dogs!" Rockshade's fur bristled and he turned to flee.

Leafstar crouched under a bush, afraid that the black warrior would run straight into her, but Stick slipped in front of him and blocked him.

"Don't worry," the brown tom mewed. "The dog won't come out."

Rockshade cast uneasy glances at the nest as the patrol padded across the garden. Once again Leafstar followed, clinging to the shadows, trying not to shiver as the terrifying barking went on. Suddenly the door at the back of the nest was flung open. The barking grew louder as the dog raced into the open: a lean, long-bodied animal, its gray pelt turned to silver in the moonlight.

Rockshade let out a panic-stricken yowl. "You said it wouldn't come out!"

"Sometimes they do!" Stick yowled in reply.

"Scatter!" Shorty ordered. "It's easier here for one cat to hide on its own."

The patrol shot apart as the dog bounded among them; its teeth came within a whisker of grabbing Sparrowpelt's tail. Leafstar fled back the way she had come, clawing her way up the wooden side of a small den at the end of the garden and hauling herself up onto its flat roof. She crouched on the edge, watching the dog as it ranged around the grass, its jaws wide and its tongue lolling.

A voice growled behind her. "What are you doing here?"

Leafstar spun around. "Billystorm!"

The ginger-and-white tom's gaze traveled over her; his expression was wary.

"I—I didn't know you come out at night," she stammered.

Billystorm shrugged. "Sometimes. My housefolk's den isn't far away. But you still haven't answered my question," he went on, with an edge of hostility to his tone. "I thought you didn't believe me about Sharpclaw's night visits here. And now you're taking part in one!"

"Of course I'm not taking part!" Leafstar retorted. "I saw them leaving the gorge, and I followed."

"So you believe me now?"

Leafstar twitched her whiskers. *I'm his Clan leader; he doesn't have the right to interrogate me!* "I didn't disbelieve you, okay? The important thing is, what are they doing?"

"I'm not sure," Billystorm replied with another shrug. "I haven't seen them for a while. And it's not always the same cats that Sharpclaw brings. Last time, it was Patchfoot, Tinycloud, and Bouncefire."

Leafstar's anxiety rose. *How many cats are involved in this?*

"I've seen them crossing Thunderpaths," Billystorm went on. "Back and forth, like they weren't going anywhere. And learning how to climb walls. But always in different places, as if they weren't targeting any cat in particular."

I've seen some of that myself, Leafstar realized, staring at Billystorm. "They're *training*, aren't they?" she whispered. "But why? They would never launch an attack on the Twolegplace."

"You might not," Billystorm meowed with a flick of his ears. "But maybe they would."

Leafstar wondered if he was right. She and Sharpclaw had differences of opinion, but she could still trust him, couldn't she? The sharp fangs of her anxiety bit deeper. "I'm going to find Sharpclaw and the others and ask him what's going on," she decided.

Billystorm padded to her side as she crouched at the edge of the roof and gazed down, trying to work out where the patrol had gone. At least there was no sign of the dog anymore, and the door to the den was closed.

"I'm coming with you," Billystorm told her.

"No—stay here," Leafstar responded.

She could see the hurt in Billystorm's green eyes. "I'm supposed to be your Clanmate," he protested. "Or doesn't that count when I'm not actually in the gorge?"

I don't have time for this right now, Leafstar thought. "This is an issue between me and Sharpclaw," she told Billystorm, trying to keep her voice crisp and impersonal. "No other cat."

Deep down, she wasn't sure that was entirely true. She was doubtful about turning up to challenge the others with a Twolegplace cat by her side. It would draw too much attention to the split in SkyClan, in spite of all her efforts to heal it.

"I see," Billystorm murmured, in a tone that suggested he understood Leafstar's concerns only too well. He lifted his head, his ears erect and his jaws parted to taste the air. "They went that way," he meowed after a moment, pointing with his tail.

"Thank you." Leafstar was grateful for her Clanmate's familiarity with the sounds and scents of the Twolegplace. She wished she could tell him how much she wanted him to go with her. But it would cause only more trouble. "I'll see you in camp tomorrow."

Billystorm didn't respond, but watched Leafstar as she leaped down from the roof. Before she headed across the grass in the direction he had shown her, she glanced over her shoulder to see him looking down at her. His eyes glowed with the harsh orange light that filled the Twolegplace. It was impossible to tell what he was thinking. *Does he really think I don't need him?*

Trying to push Billystorm out of her mind, Leafstar raced through the next fence, scrambling through dense shrubbery until she popped out at the edge of a path covered with sharp white stones. A moment later she slid back into hiding as a gray-and-white kittypet padded slowly along the edge of the path and disappeared through a small flap at the bottom of the door to the den.

The next enclosed space was filled with a strong scent of dog. With nowhere to hide, Leafstar slunk along the bottom of the fence on the tips of her paws in case she alerted the animal. Thankfully she spotted a gate, and squeezed through into another alley. Her heart was pounding and she halted for a moment to catch her breath in the shelter of a big green Twoleg thing with round black paws.

Snookthorn's housefolk had one of these, she remembered, wrinkling her nose with disgust. *That stank of crow-food, too.*

"Water won't do you any harm." Leafstar stiffened as she heard Stick's voice coming from somewhere up ahead. "Just roll in it. It will hide your scent."

"I don't *want* to hide my scent!" Rockshade's voice was horrified. "In the forest, SkyClan scent is something to be proud of. It's part of defending our territory."

"But you're not in your territory now, are you?" Shorty pointed out quietly.

Peering out from behind the Twoleg thing, Leafstar spotted the patrol at the corner of the alley where it joined a small Thunderpath. Harsh orange light spilled down from another of the stone trees, gleaming on the surface of a puddle. The acrid stench reached Leafstar, even drowning the scent of crow-food.

"Just roll," Sharpclaw growled. "You're keeping us all waiting."

Leafstar heard the sounds of splashing as Rockshade lowered himself into the puddle and rolled over. Anger surged up inside her. She leaped out from her hiding place and stalked up to the patrol.

"What in StarClan's name is going on?"

Concentrating on Rockshade, none of the patrol had heard or scented her approach. They spun around to face her; behind them, Rockshade scrambled up out of the puddle, shaking himself to try to get rid of the water. His black pelt was clumped and messy. His eyes were clouded with guilt; Sparrowpelt and Cherrytail looked uncomfortable, too, but the Twolegplace cats were quite calm.

Sharpclaw was the first to speak. "What does it look like?" he meowed. "We're exploring Twoleg territory in case we ever need to fight here."

His confident reply took Leafstar by surprise. "Why didn't you tell me?"

"You've been too busy," Sharpclaw replied.

Meeting his calm green gaze, Leafstar barely managed to stop herself from raking her claws over his ears. Words exploded from her, fierce as a greenleaf storm. "Not too busy to know that my warriors are leaving the gorge at night! And why do we need to know how to fight in the Twolegplace? What are you planning?"

The cool look Sharpclaw gave her made Leafstar feel as if she were some crazy elder with burrs in her pelt. "We're planning nothing," he meowed, as if that should have been obvious. "We're *preparing* for the future, which cannot be seen.

Stick brought knowledge that we don't have, and I thought it would make us even stronger."

Leafstar took a deep breath; with a massive effort she made herself calm down. Sharpclaw was undermining her in front of her Clanmates, and widening the rift between these cats and the daylight-warriors, but screeching and fighting was not the answer.

"Don't you think you're endangering our regular hunting and border patrols, if our cats are tired after being out all night?" she queried evenly.

"That's why we bring only two or three cats at a time," Sharpclaw explained, his voice as patient as if he was telling a new apprentice how to stalk a mouse.

Leafstar could tell he thought she was making an antheap out of a single grain of dirt. Desperately she held on to her resolve to be calm, but it was growing harder with every breath she took. "You mean you do this regularly? I can't believe you'd go behind my back like this!" She heard her voice growing shrill, and forced herself to lower it. "I am the leader of SkyClan. Does the warrior code mean nothing to you?"

Sharpclaw blinked. "It means everything. Which is why I want to learn how I can fight wherever I need to, so that I can protect my Clanmates."

Tension burning through her pelt, Leafstar took a paw step forward, so that she stood nose to nose with her deputy. "You should have told me what you were doing," she hissed. "You can't give one half of the Clan extra training and ignore the others."

"You mean the kitty-warriors? It's not my problem if they aren't here for night training."

"That's not the issue, and you know it!" Leafstar crouched, lashing her tail; a red mist was filling her vision. *I can't believe Sharpclaw brings everything back to this!*

She was about to spring, when Cora's quiet voice broke through her fury. "Leafstar, wait." The black she-cat turned to Stick and addressed him. "Stick, please. It's time to tell them the truth."

The long-legged brown tom glared at her, bristling. "*I'll* decide when it's time," he snapped.

Shorty padded up to him and gave him a nudge on the shoulder. "Cora's right," he mewed. "The SkyClan cats deserve to know."

Stick hesitated a heartbeat longer, glancing at Sharpclaw, then nodded. "It was my idea to train your cats to fight in a Twolegplace," he told Leafstar. "We didn't come here to join your Clan. We came because we need your help."

CHAPTER 31

❧

Stick jumped onto the top of the wall and looked down into the Twoleg yard. His pelt prickled with uneasiness. The place should have been familiar, but it had been a long time since he had come this way, and he was unsettled by how much had changed.

That bush has grown much bigger, he thought, jumping at the unexpected throaty bark of a dog from the next garden. *And that dog was a yapping little puppy.*

Stick parted his jaws to taste the air and realized regretfully that the clump of catmint that once grew beside the door of the Twoleg nest had vanished. *It was the catmint that brought me here in the first place.* He had followed the scent and jumped down from the rough stone wall to bury his nose in the leaves. And a voice, quiet and wary, had spoken behind him. . . .

"Why have you come here?" It was the same voice, but harsher than Stick remembered. A sleek, gray-furred she-cat had emerged from the nest and stood looking up at him, every hair on her pelt oozing hostility, her lips drawn back in a snarl.

Stick leaped down from the wall and faced her. "It's Red."

The gray she-cat gave him a cautious look. "Is she all right?"

"She's fine, I think."

"What do you mean, you *think*?" The she-cat's claws slid out. "You promised you would look after her."

"Velvet, I didn't come here to fight," Stick mewed wearily. "I know you made your choice, but our daughter needs our help."

Velvet paused for a heartbeat, then waved her tail toward the low-growing branches of a bush. "Okay, come under here. I don't want my housefolk seeing you."

Stick pressed his belly to the ground and slid underneath the bush behind Velvet. Memories pressed around him, clutched in the thick leafy scents. "Do you remember catching your first mouse here? You said you'd never tasted anything so good."

Velvet flicked her ears. "That was a long time ago."

"I know. And then you made me go into your nest and try your Twoleg food, and you thought it was so funny when I spat it out." Stick let out a faint sigh. "How did we grow so far apart?"

"We share our daughter, nothing else," Velvet replied coldly. "I thought you came to talk about her?"

"I did. There's a problem." As briefly as he could, Stick told his former mate about Dodge and his followers, how they had moved into his part of the Twolegplace and were terrorizing the other cats, not allowing them to hunt. While he was talking, he looked in vain for any spark of sympathy in Velvet's eyes.

"You chose to live like that, fighting for your food like

foxes," she meowed when Stick had finished. "You can't stop other cats from moving in."

"That's not the point!" Stick snapped. "I'd be willing to share prey in a fair fight, but these cats seem intent on taking everything. Including Red."

Velvet's eyes stretched wide. "Have they stolen her?"

"Not exactly. But I think that Red has become . . . attached . . . to one of Dodge's cats."

"You mean she's fallen in love with a cat who lives by a different set of rules?" Mockery glinted in Velvet's blue eyes. "You wouldn't dream of doing anything like that, would you?"

Stick felt his fur prick along his spine. "It's more than that. I think Red helped those cats to plan a Twoleg attack on the alley where we sleep."

"Red would never do that!" Velvet hissed. Stick wasn't sure; he knew his doubt must have shown in his eyes, because the gray she-cat went on, "Being in love doesn't change who you are! Do you distrust your own daughter, just because she has feelings?" More gently, she added, "Stick, you and I stayed true to ourselves, didn't we? I never told you I would give up my home for you, but that didn't mean I didn't love you. I gave you our daughter, remember?"

Stick looked down at the earth beneath his front paws. "And I've lost her!"

"No, you haven't," Velvet meowed, stretching out her tail-tip to touch him on the shoulder. "You know exactly where she is. Go talk to her; maybe she doesn't even know about the attack in the alley."

"Oh, she knows." Stick slid his claws into the soil. "She was there—and she escaped just in time."

Velvet's blue eyes clouded. "You're assuming too much." She hesitated, then added, "You're planning to attack these cats, aren't you? Turn your daughter into a scrap of food to be fought over? Red won't thank you for that. She knows her own mind."

And you know me—too well, Stick thought ruefully. "These cats know only about fighting."

"No. *You* know only about fighting." Velvet started to crawl backward, retreating out of the shelter of the bush.

"Wait!" Stick called. "I . . . I thought you could talk to Red."

"Me?" Velvet's blue eyes chilled. "Oh, no. My life is here, with my housefolk. Red knows where I am if she wants to see me."

"You can't hide here with your kittypet slop while our daughter is in danger!"

"Why can't I? Are you going to force me to come with you? I've told you, Stick, what we did was a mistake. I will never understand the way you live."

"But—but you let me take Red!" Stick hissed.

"I like my life the way it is," Velvet replied. "A kit would have changed that. You told me that Red would be safe, and I believe that she is. It's only your stubbornness and pride that put her in danger." Stick opened his jaws to protest, but Velvet swept on. "You're just angry that she could do something that you don't want her to. Leave her be, or she'll end up hating you."

Not waiting for a reply, she slid out from under the bush and headed for her nest. By the time Stick scrambled out after her, she had vanished.

Shaking leaf-mold from his pelt, Stick climbed the wall again and leaped down into the alley. As he landed, he spotted Shorty sitting a few tail-lengths away, his stumpy tail wrapped over his paws.

"You followed me!" Stick snarled.

Shorty cocked his head to one side. "We're in this together, Stick, whether you like it or not. What did Velvet say?"

Stick padded along the alley to sit beside his friend. "She thinks I should leave Red to make up her own mind."

"But it's more than that!" Shorty meowed, shocked. "Our cats are being hurt, and we've lost Percy, all thanks to Dodge."

Stick gave him a long look. "I'm not going to let Velvet think we're weak, okay?"

Shorty let out an impatient huff, but made no comment. After a moment he went on, "Let's go. I've found a place where we can spy on Dodge's camp."

Stick narrowed his eyes in surprise. "Where?"

"Follow me."

The two cats trekked across the Twolegplace until they reached the edge, where spindly trees grew up to the bank of a dirty shallow stream. Stick gazed out across the sluggish yellow water, wrinkling his nose at the scent of the Twoleg waste that choked the current. There was a scent of cat, too, coming most strongly from a heap of Twoleg boxes tumbled at the water's edge; some of them leaned over the stream, their flimsy material growing soggy as the waves lapped against them.

"That's where Dodge lives?" Stick murmured. "It's just about right for a mange-pelt like him!"

"Come up here," Shorty urged him, waving his tail at a small wooden den a few fox-lengths from the river. "We don't want Dodge to catch us."

He scrambled up the wall to the flat roof of the den, and Stick followed, hissing with annoyance as splinters of wood stuck in his belly fur. He flattened himself to the roof beside Shorty and peered over the edge.

At first there were no cats to be seen. Then the side of one of the boxes flapped and Misha and Skipper emerged into the open. Stick let out a low growl as he remembered Misha's claws slashing across Percy's face, ripping out his eye. The two cats padded a little farther up the bank to where another of the boxes cast a heavy patch of shade. Stick stiffened as he made out movement and the glint of eyes in the shadow.

"Dodge is there!" he hissed.

Misha and Skipper stood in front of Dodge for a few heartbeats. Stick could hear the murmur of their voices, but he was too far away to hear what they were saying. Then he glimpsed movement among the trees on the other side of the stream. His claws slid out, digging into the wooden roof, and he bunched his muscles as Red and the gray-brown tom Harley came into sight. Red was carrying the limp body of a squirrel.

"Steady," Shorty whispered, laying his tail across Stick's shoulders.

Though Stick burned to jump down into Dodge's camp, yowling a challenge, he watched in silence as Red and Harley crossed the stream by a set of stepping-stones. Red was hanging back as if she was nervous—*and so she should be, going into Dodge's camp!*—but Harley seemed to be encouraging her.

Misha and Skipper dipped their heads coolly as Red and Harley approached: not welcoming Red, but making no attempt to chase her away, either. Stick's ears strained to hear what they were saying. He managed to catch a few words; Harley was introducing Red to them.

"How do we know we can trust her?" Skipper asked.

"You know who her father is!" Misha put in spitefully.

Skipper said something else that Stick couldn't catch; then Red stepped forward and laid her squirrel down at the two cats' paws.

"Look, she caught us a squirrel!" Harley announced.

Memories flooded over Stick, of how he had taught his daughter to catch squirrels near their alley, and he sank his claws even farther into the roof. *Why is she doing this to me?*

Red stood watching while Misha and Skipper crouched down to eat the squirrel. Meanwhile, Dodge rose to his paws and emerged from the shadows, his gaze scorching Red's ginger pelt. After a couple of heartbeats he mewed something to her; Red nodded.

"He's asking her for information about us!" Stick snarled. "We have to stop them! Let's get the others." Spinning around, he jumped down from the den roof and headed back toward his own territory.

Shorty caught up to him in a swift patter of paws. "We can't stop them," he warned. "Not on our own."

"We *are* on our own," Stick snapped. "If Velvet is anything to go by, the kittypets around here aren't going to be any help."

"No, not kittypets," Shorty replied. "But there are other cats we could ask, cats who are trained to fight and wouldn't flinch at killing to protect their home."

Stick halted.

"Do you remember those cats who came here just after the flood?" Shorty continued. "From a forest downriver? They were on their way to find other cats, weren't they? Just like them." His voice grew hopeful. "If we could find them, maybe they would help us to sort out Dodge."

Stick stared at his friend. He remembered the tom with the flame-colored pelt, who had lost his mate in the flood and was looking for her, full of strength and determination, even though he was exhausted from battling the water. His muscles had been strong and lean under his fur, and there was a glint in his eyes that Stick had never seen in a kittypet.

"You're right, Shorty," he growled. "We must find those cats."

CHAPTER 32

❧

Leafstar sat in the shadow of the Rockpile; Sharpclaw, Stick, and his friends crouched around her as she listened to Stick describing battles and betrayals in his Twolegplace. She had sent Rockshade, Cherrytail, and Sparrowpelt back to the warriors' den; the rest of the cats were asleep, except for Coal, still keeping watch from a ledge halfway up the cliff.

A chill night breeze whispered down the gorge, though at the top of the rocks Leafstar could make out the first pale streaks of dawn. The moon had set, and the warriors of Star-Clan were fading.

"Please, will you help us?" Stick asked, bringing his story to a close. "You're the only hope we have."

Leafstar felt like a twig whirled around and around in the pool where the river poured out from the cave. Her pelt prickled with annoyance at the way she had been distracted from her discovery that Sharpclaw was training her cats secretly at night.

There's no way I'm letting that go unchallenged!

"I need to think," she meowed. "Go to your den now, and I'll let you know what I decide."

Stick looked as if he was about to argue, but Cora touched him on the shoulder with her tail and jerked her head toward the path that led up to their den. Stick gave in and moved off, with Cora beside him; Shorty dipped his head to Leafstar and murmured, "Thank you for listening," before he followed.

Leafstar was left with Sharpclaw; the ginger tom was flexing his claws impatiently.

"I can't see that there's much to think about," he told her, once the Twolegplace cats were out of earshot. "We're going to help them, aren't we? We have the strength and the skills, and what Dodge has done is wrong."

Leafstar fixed him with a hard gaze. "Where in the warrior code does it say that we have to use our skills to help other cats? I'm sorry for what has happened to Stick and the others, but I don't see how it's SkyClan's responsibility."

"What?" Sharpclaw gave a single lash of his tail. "Look at the way Stick and the others helped us with the rats! And they've hunted for us and carried out all the other warrior duties. Are you saying that SkyClan shouldn't be loyal to them?"

"It's not a matter of loyalty," Leafstar pointed out, determined to keep her temper. "Stick and his friends never intended to stay with us for good. Surely that means they're not warriors like us."

Sharpclaw twitched his whiskers. "They're not the only cats to have a life outside the gorge."

"Why does it always have to come back to the daylight-warriors?" Leafstar snapped. She took a couple of breaths and continued, "I said I'd think about it, and I will. But it will be *my* decision, Sharpclaw."

Her deputy met her gaze, then nodded and headed off toward the warriors' den.

Leafstar watched him go, then climbed the trail to her own den and settled into her nest. But although she was tired, she couldn't seem to get comfortable in the moss and fern. Her paws prickled with restlessness; leaving the den again, she wandered up the gorge in the growing light of dawn. As she rounded the spur of rock before the training area, she spotted Skywatcher sitting on the edge of the sandy circle; the warrior of StarClan looked up as if he had been waiting for her.

"Greetings, Leafstar," he meowed. "You are troubled."

Leafstar dipped her head. "Greetings, Skywatcher. Do you know what's happening? What the Twolegplace cats want us to do?"

"I do." Skywatcher swept his starry tail around, beckoning Leafstar to sit beside him. "You must feel as though these visitors have been using SkyClan for their own ends."

"Yes!" Leafstar exclaimed, warmed by the spirit cat's sympathy. "That's exactly how it feels."

"But they have been loyal to their adopted Clan," Skywatcher went on. "They have hunted and fought for you. Remember the rats, and the cruel Twoleg, and the wounded Twoleg kit? Other Clans would help one another in times of great need."

"You mean the forest Clans?" Leafstar checked. "They didn't exactly help SkyClan in the end, did they?"

Skywatcher shrugged. "Maybe this is your chance to show

forgiveness, to prove that SkyClan has recovered and grown stronger from that time, and can show mercy of its own."

Leafstar didn't have a chance to reply before she glimpsed a movement among the rocks above the training area, and a black tom bounded into the open. The fur on her neck started to rise, thinking that a rogue was invading the gorge, until she spotted the glitter of stars around his paws.

The newcomer stormed up to Skywatcher, his ears flat with fury, his eyes blazing. "No mercy!" he snarled. "SkyClan has to survive alone! These intruders do not deserve to be warriors if all they ever wanted was our strength and experience to fight their battle." He spun around and fixed his burning gaze on Leafstar. "SkyClan cannot leave the gorge!"

Skywatcher reached out with his tail in a calming gesture. "Swallowflight," he meowed, "you are blinded by the wounds that were given to you long ago."

"It was a wound from which we never recovered," Swallowflight hissed.

"But the Clan did recover." Skywatcher nodded to Leafstar. "Look, it's back where it belongs, in the gorge that you found."

"This is not a true Clan!" Swallowflight spat. "How many of them are kittypets, refusing to leave their pampered nests of slop and Twolegs fawning over them? Their leader doesn't even know where half of them are when she's asleep."

Anger and horror flooded through Leafstar. "That's not true!" she whispered, rising to her paws and backing away. *Or is there a truth there that I dare not admit?*

She looked at Skywatcher for support, but the gray tom did not speak. Instead, he leaped at Swallowflight, knocking him over and rolling him in the sand. Swallowflight fought back viciously, his hind paws scrabbling at Skywatcher as he tried to sink his teeth into the gray cat's neck.

Skywatcher let out a screech. Leafstar jumped at the noise, and found herself back in her own nest, scrabbling among the moss and bracken.

"It was a dream!" she gasped, struggling for deep breaths to steady the pounding of her heart.

Sunlight poured into her den, and from outside she could hear the movement and voices of cats going about the tasks of the new day. She sat up and started to groom her pelt, feeling as if every hair of it was tangled and filthy.

A few heartbeats later a shadow fell across the sunlight as Echosong popped her head into the den. "Are you okay?" she meowed. "It's late; I thought you might be sick."

"No, I'm fine," Leafstar replied, her voice still shaky.

She was lying. Her dream clung to the corners of her mind and Swallowflight's challenge echoed off the walls around her. How many StarClan warriors felt the same scorn for her Clan of daylight-warriors? *Have I really gone so far wrong?*

Then she reminded herself that Skywatcher had been ready to fight on her behalf. And Spottedleaf, Cloudstar, Birdflight, and Fawnstep had all encouraged her. *Maybe Swallowflight, whoever he is, has his own problems.*

Even so, she was unsettled by the knowledge that StarClan cats would fight among themselves. Leafstar had been taught by Firestar to rely on the wisdom of her warrior ancestors, and she had never seen such rage unleashed among their own ranks before now. Two sides to an argument meant that one side had to be wrong, didn't it? So which cats was she supposed to listen to?

Great StarClan, what am I going to do if I can't even trust you?

Leafstar followed Echosong down toward the river. The sun was climbing into a clear sky, filling the gorge with warmth. Even the rocks were hot under Leafstar's pads as she made her way down the trail.

Fallowfern's kits were sprawled in a patch of shade at the foot of the cliff, with their mother standing over them.

"But we don't want to clean out the nursery," Nettlekit was complaining. "It's too hot."

"I just want to sleep," Rabbitkit murmured drowsily.

"That's too bad," Fallowfern meowed, giving the nearest kit a prod with one paw. "The nursery won't clean itself."

"Why can't the apprentices do it?" Plumkit argued.

Fallowfern's eyes widened and she let out a shocked hiss. "Don't be so lazy!" she scolded her daughter. "You're old enough to do it yourselves now. Come along right away, and don't let me hear another word from any of you!"

Groaning and muttering under their breath, the four kits hauled themselves to their paws and trudged up the path, with Fallowfern right behind.

That must be the first time I've seen those kits when they weren't bouncing around, Leafstar thought, amusement driving away some part of her worries. She spotted Clovertail stumbling awkwardly down from the new birthing den and padding over to Echosong. Her pale brown fur was clumped and untidy.

"I feel as if my belly's going to burst!" she complained to the medicine cat. "And this heat isn't helping at all."

"I know, it's hard for you when it's time for your kits to come," Echosong soothed her. "Come and sleep outside my den—there's a cool and shady patch there. And I'll give you some borage; that should help."

"Thank you, Echosong," Clovertail mewed, limping off behind the medicine cat. "I don't know what we'd do without you."

Blinking approvingly, Leafstar turned toward the Rockpile, where Sharpclaw was sorting out the patrols. Her deputy didn't speak to her, but gave her a cautiously cordial nod. Leafstar returned the gesture, though she was still unhappy that they hadn't yet discussed the way he had kept secrets from her. All four Twolegplace cats were standing in a cluster at one side. They seemed more subdued than usual; Leafstar wondered if they had given up all hope of finding help. A pang of guilt stabbed through her. *I wish I knew what was the right thing to do.*

She was still pondering when the daylight-warriors appeared at the top of the gorge. No cheerful yowling announced their arrival this morning; the heat seemed to be affecting them, too, as they padded down the trail with Billystorm in the lead.

As the ginger-and-white tom approached Leafstar he gave

her an inquiring look and cocked his head toward Sharpclaw. Even in the hot sunlight, a chill ran through Leafstar. Billystorm obviously wanted to know what had happened after she left him the night before. She felt like a coward for turning away from him. *But what can I say to him? I'm not even sure myself what this all means.*

"It's so hot!" Macgyver complained, his paws dragging as he headed toward Sharpclaw. "Do we have to hunt in this weather?"

"Yeah, I feel as if my pelt is burning," Harveymoon added.

Sharpclaw opened his jaws for a scathing retort, but Leafstar forestalled him. She was grateful to Harveymoon and Macgyver for distracting her from Billystorm, and she noticed that their pelts were especially thick. They were probably feeling the heat more than their Clanmates.

"Fallowfern is cleaning out the nursery," she meowed. "Why don't you fetch her some fresh moss from the cave? It must be nice and cool in there."

"Great! Thanks, Leafstar," Macgyver responded, waving his tail to beckon Harveymoon. "Let's go!"

"Be careful of the path—it's slippery!" Leafstar reminded them as they climbed the Rockpile. She turned back to Sharpclaw, expecting some complaint that she was favoring the kittypets, but her deputy said nothing.

The last patrols were leaving; Leafstar slipped alongside Shrewtooth as he led Ebonyclaw and Frecklepaw toward the Rockpile. "Mind if I join you?" she asked.

Shrewtooth blinked in pleased surprise. "We'd be glad to

have you, Leafstar," he meowed, dipping his head and falling back to let her take the lead.

"No, *you* lead, Shrewtooth," Leafstar instructed.

She noticed Ebonyclaw giving her a pleased look, and remembered how concerned the black she-cat had been that Shrewtooth wasn't getting on well in the Clan. He was doing better now, Leafstar reflected, as the young black tom led the way across the heap of boulders and up the opposite side of the gorge. He was carefully checking each marker, tasting the air for any unfamiliar scents, and sending Ebonyclaw to check on a hole that had opened up among the roots of an oak tree.

"I think it's just fallen earth," the black she-cat reported. "There's no scent of anything but leaves and beetles."

Leafstar began to relax as the patrol continued along the border. The thick green leaves overhead sheltered them from the worst of the heat; the forest floor was dim and cool, and the long grass brushed refreshingly against her pelt.

This is how Clan life should be.

Suddenly Shrewtooth halted, his ears pricked. "I hear something!" he announced.

Gazing around for the source of the sound, Leafstar spotted a hollow tree just across the border. Bees were flying in and out of a hole high up in the trunk. Their low-pitched humming was what had alerted Shrewtooth.

"Bees!" Frecklepaw exclaimed, her whiskers quivering. "Honey is so good for soothing sore throats. And for binding poultices together."

Leafstar couldn't resist a glance at Ebonyclaw, expecting to see the black she-cat looking annoyed. Instead, she caught a resigned eye-roll from Frecklepaw's mentor. *Maybe Frecklepaw is meant to be a medicine cat after all.*

"No, Frecklepaw! Get back!"

Shrewtooth's urgent yowl made Leafstar jump. She spun around to see that Frecklepaw had started to climb the tree, her gaze fixed on the hole in the trunk. Shrewtooth's warning startled the apprentice; she lost her balance and grabbed at the nearest branch.

There was a loud crack. The branch Frecklepaw was holding gave way, and she half fell, half leaped to the ground in a tumble of mottled brown fur. The low humming of the bees grew to a high-pitched, angry buzzing. More and more of them poured out of the hole in a swelling cloud, reaching out toward the cats like a dark paw.

"Run!" Leafstar screeched.

She pushed the dazed Frecklepaw in front of her as the patrol fled back to the gorge. Her heart pounded as the striped black-and-yellow bodies whirled around her head, and she braced herself for the stab of their vicious stings. The swarm pursued them all the way, a threatening storm that hovered over them, occasionally darting down in a noisy frond to strike. Ebonyclaw let out a yowl as a bee stung her ear, flailing her tail wildly to try to keep them off.

As the patrol bounded over the Rockpile, the cats who still remained in the gorge sprang up in alarm. Clovertail, roused from a doze outside Echosong's den, let out a terrified wail. Tangle and Lichenfur slid out their claws as if this was an enemy they could attack. Echosong shot out of her den and gazed upward, her fur bristling.

"Into the water!" Leafstar yowled. "Quick!"

As her paws hit the ground at the foot of the Rockpile she launched herself at Tangle and Lichenfur, pushing them into the river. Tangle let out an outraged screech that ended in a splutter as Lichenfur shoved his head under. Echosong was helping Clovertail. Shrewtooth, Ebonyclaw, and Frecklepaw ran into the water without breaking stride and ducked their heads under the surface.

Leafstar followed them, crouching at the edge of the river with just her nose and eyes out of the water. She shivered at the cold touch of the current that threatened to carry her off her paws. *Thank StarClan that most of the Clan are out on patrol! And that Fallowfern and her kits are safely in the nursery!*

The bees buzzed furiously overhead; Leafstar thought she could hear their frustration that their prey had escaped. They circled around the pool, hovering low over the surface, but there was nothing for them to attack. After what felt like several moons, the swarm bunched together again and flew away.

Leafstar hauled herself out of the pool; her fur felt heavy and water streamed from it, pooling around her paws. The rest of her Clanmates dragged themselves onto the bank; they looked thin and bedraggled with their pelts plastered to their sides.

"What were you trying to drown me for?" Tangle snapped at Lichenfur.

"Next time I'll let you get stung," the old she-cat muttered.

Echosong was staring around at the drenched cats, speechless with shock. Leafstar couldn't understand what was bothering her; she was usually far quicker than this to react to an emergency.

"Hey, what happened?"

The voice came from the other side of the river; Leafstar looked up to see Harveymoon and Macgyver, carrying bundles of moss from the cave and staring down in amazement at their sodden Clanmates.

"Bee attack," Tangle grunted.

"Bee attack?" Harveymoon echoed, his eyes bulging from his head. "How did that happen?"

"It was an accident, but it's over now. Take the moss to Fallowfern," Leafstar told the daylight-warriors. "Tell her to keep her kits in the nursery in case there are any bees hanging around. I'll come up and see them in a moment."

As Harveymoon and Macgyver raced off, Leafstar realized that almost all the cats were hurt. Clovertail had a sting dangerously close to her eye; it was swelling fast as she pawed at it with whimpers of pain. Ebonyclaw was circling, trying to reach a bite on her rump, while Shrewtooth was biting at his forepaw in a vain attempt to get the sting out.

Leafstar padded over to Echosong. "Don't these cats need help?" she prompted, giving the medicine cat a gentle prod on her shoulder.

Echosong jumped. "Yes, of course. Sorry, Leafstar." She padded forward, beckoning her Clanmates with her tail. "Line up here so I can take your stings out," she instructed. "Don't scratch them; you'll only make it worse. Frecklepaw, are you hurt?"

"No, I'm fine," the apprentice replied, pattering up.

"Then you can help me. Go into my den and fetch some blackberry leaves."

Frecklepaw gave herself a good shake, scattering water droplets everywhere, before plunging into Echosong's den.

Seeing that everything was under control, Leafstar padded away to check on the nursery. "Come and see me later!" Echosong called after her.

Leafstar waved her tail in acknowledgment and headed up the trail. To her relief, none of the swarm had found their way into the nursery.

"It's not fair!" Plumkit complained. "We never got to see the bees."

"Trust me, you don't want to," Fallowfern assured her. "We're very lucky that we were safe in here."

When Leafstar returned to the bottom of the gorge, she discovered that Sharpclaw had returned with his hunting patrol; Shrewtooth was reporting on how Frecklepaw had disturbed the bees.

"It's a good thing it was no worse," Sharpclaw commented, glancing over to where Echosong was treating the cats who had been stung. "Do you think we should do something?" he asked Leafstar as she padded up.

"I don't think there's anything we can do," Leafstar replied, "unless you want to try moving a whole swarm of bees. No, we'll just have to stay well clear, and reset the border markers to keep all the cats away from the tree."

Sharpclaw let out an annoyed hiss. "You're right—but I hate losing territory."

"Leafstar! Leafstar!" Frecklepaw came bounding over, her eyes wide and troubled, the sharp scent of blackberry leaves clinging to her fur. "I'm so sorry. It was all my fault. It was stupid to climb that tree."

Leafstar touched the apprentice's shoulder with the tip of her tail. "It wasn't the best idea you've ever had, but you were right that honey is very useful for Echosong. It's a pity we can't get any from there."

"Next time think before you act, or ask your mentor," Sharpclaw added, though he didn't sound as scathing as Leafstar had expected, seeing that he was speaking to a daylight-warrior.

Frecklepaw nodded. "I will, I promise."

Leafstar glanced toward the medicine cat's den to see that she had finished treating the injured cats: Shrewtooth was just limping away from her, to flop down beside the river and begin to groom his damp fur.

At least the sun will soon dry us off, Leafstar thought.

She bounded over to the medicine cat's den as Echosong was heading inside with the remains of the blackberry leaves. "You wanted to talk to me?" she asked.

"Yes, I—" Echosong broke off, staring at Leafstar's shoulder. "You've got a sting in there," she murmured. "Hold still while I get it out."

"I never even realized," Leafstar meowed, while Echosong

parted her fur and delicately removed the sting with her teeth.

The medicine cat chewed up some of the blackberry leaves and patted the poultice onto Leafstar's shoulder. "The bee attack meant something else," she told Leafstar while her head was still bent over the wound. "It was a sign."

Leafstar blinked. "What sort of sign? Does it mean that Frecklepaw shouldn't be a medicine cat?"

Echosong shook her head. "No, it's more serious than that." Hesitating, she stared out across the gorge, as if she was seeing something more distant than the cliffs opposite. "It was definitely a sign," she went on at last, "but I don't know exactly what it means. Maybe you do."

She cast a glance at Leafstar as if she was acknowledging that they hadn't been so close lately, that Leafstar might well know something that she hadn't shared with her medicine cat. Leafstar couldn't think of anything to say. She hadn't been keeping secrets from Echosong, had she? *She doesn't know you saw Billystorm in the Twolegplace last night.*

"There is trouble somewhere, far off now. A great battle between cats who believe they are right and cats who believe they have been wronged beyond all measure." Echosong spoke unexpectedly, in a voice that sounded as if it was coming from far away. "If we don't act, it will come to us. A force of pain and violence, seething with rage, will come right into the gorge, and there will be no escape, not even the river. Our Clan will be devastated, and the quarrel will become ours."

Leafstar felt a chill run through her from ears to tail-tip, as if a storm cloud had covered the sun. *Echosong, no. Don't tell me this.* . . .

Echosong looked at her leader, her beautiful green eyes troubled. "Does that make any sense to you?" she asked, her voice sounding normal again. "Is there a battle we can fight somewhere else, before it comes to our camp?"

CHAPTER 33

❧

Leafstar fluffed up her fur against the dawn chill. The sky was pale
gold where the sun would come up, but shadows still lay thick
in the gorge. From where she sat on the Rockpile, she could
watch her warriors as they slipped silently out of their dens
and gathered beside the pool.

She and Sharpclaw had arrived first, followed almost
at once by the four Twolegplace cats. They stood huddled
together; Leafstar remembered the hope that flared in their
eyes when she gave them her decision the night before; now
they just looked anxious, murmuring quietly to one another.

Sparrowpelt and Cherrytail stood side by side, their pelts
brushing, while Shrewtooth paced nervously up and down the
riverbank. Leafstar hoped she was right to include the young
black tom on this mission. *But he's started to show such promise. I
want to give him a chance to prove himself.*

Rockshade was saying farewell to his littermates, Bouncefire and Tinycloud. "I guess we'll be back in a few days," he
meowed, trying and failing to sound cheerful.

"It's not fair!" Tinycloud exclaimed enviously. "Why do
you get to go and we don't?"

There was a sudden patter of paws as Fallowfern's kits scampered down the trail and hurled themselves at Waspwhisker while he was padding toward the meeting place.

"No! You can't go!" Plumkit squealed.

"We'll miss you." Nettlekit pushed his head into his father's shoulder. "What if you never come back?"

All four of the kits set up a loud wail.

"That's enough," Waspwhisker told them, nuzzling each kit in turn. "Of course I'm coming back. And you have to look after your mother while I'm away. Make sure you do everything she tells you."

"We will!" Creekkit promised.

Waspwhisker's gaze met his mate's as Fallowfern padded up to him. "Take care," she whispered.

"Of course I will." The two cats stood with their tails twining for a moment before Waspwhisker turned away and went to join Sharpclaw and the others.

Leafstar's whiskers twitched as she spotted a pale shape slipping into the midst of the cats. *What's Egg doing? I said that no apprentices were to come.* She thought that the cream tom was trying to stay unnoticed, but Sharpclaw's eyes were sharper than that.

"Egg? What are you doing here? Didn't you hear Leafstar say no apprentices?"

Egg shouldered through the cluster of cats until he could face his mentor. "But Sharpclaw—"

"I don't have time for this," the deputy interrupted, waving him away with a swift lash of his tail.

"I've been in Twolegplaces before," Egg went on, his voice growing louder until Leafstar could hear him clearly from where she stood on the Rockpile. "And I'm just as old and strong as some of the warriors, even though I haven't finished my training. You *know* this, Sharpclaw. You said as much when I did my assessment the other day."

Sharpclaw paused, unusually hesitant, while his gaze traveled over the young tom. "That's true. . . ."

"I really want to come." Egg kneaded the ground with his forepaws. "I want to prove my loyalty to SkyClan."

Sharpclaw hesitated for a heartbeat longer, then turned to look up at Leafstar. "What do you think?"

Leafstar gazed down at the eager apprentice. It was true that he was strong; his thin frame had filled out since he had lived with the Clan, and his muscles swelled beneath his sleek pelt. And she had watched him in training; he was swift and agile in battle, easily outmatching the other apprentices.

"Very well," she meowed. "You can come, Egg. But remember, Sharpclaw is your mentor. You must do as he tells you."

"I will!" Egg promised, his eyes shining. "Thanks, Leafstar, Sharpclaw. You won't be sorry." He dipped his head to Leafstar and went to stand beside Rockshade.

The cats who were to leave the gorge were all gathered beside the pool, their Clanmates standing a little way off to bid them farewell. Sharpclaw padded over to Patchfoot, who would be in charge while the Clan leader and the deputy were away. Leafstar could see that Sharpclaw was giving the black-and-white tom some final instructions, but they were too far away for her to hear what they said.

Tension hung over the gorge like mist. Leafstar could read it in the bristling fur and jerky movements of the cats who were leaving, and in the somber gazes of those who were left behind. Letting out a long sigh, she lifted her head to the fading stars. "Please let this be the right thing to do," she murmured. "Bring all my cats safe home again."

"For what it's worth, *I* think you're doing the right thing."

For a heartbeat, Leafstar thought that a warrior of StarClan had answered her. Then she recognized the voice; opening her eyes, she spun around to see Billystorm standing on the Rockpile a little way below her. Her heart swelled with joy as she realized that he was looking at her warmly, if with a wariness that she hadn't seen before.

"It means a lot, actually," she managed to reply, giving him a nod of welcome. "Thank you."

Billystorm stepped up onto the rock beside her. "I—I want to apologize," he meowed.

Surprise rippled through Leafstar. "What for?"

"I wasn't fair to you," the ginger-and-white tom replied. "Above everything else, you are leader of SkyClan. Which means you are my leader, and you have my loyalty, always."

Leafstar caught her breath. Did this mean he had forgiven her for being bound by her duty to their Clan? She longed to brush her pelt against Billystorm and twine her tail with his, but this was not the time. Lowering her head, she murmured, "Thank you."

"I want to come with you," Billystorm announced.

Leafstar blinked in surprise. "You don't have to."

"Why?" Billystorm's voice was challenging. "Because I'm half kittypet? But I'm half warrior, too. And when I'm here, I'm *all* warrior. As one of your warriors, I wish to help these cats."

Leafstar gazed at him. Suddenly she felt more confident at the idea that she could set out on this mission with Billystorm beside her. She had never considered including the daylight-warriors. This wasn't like leaving them out of Clan activities; this was a dangerous expedition into unknown territory, and that made it harder for the kittypets than for any other cat.

"What about your housefolk?"

"You mean if I don't come back?" Billystorm's green gaze burned into Leafstar. "I have no more to lose than any of my Clanmates. We all have something precious that we risk losing every time we fight."

Leafstar could not meet that intense stare. She turned her head away, and Billystorm let out a small trill of satisfaction, as if he recognized that she had agreed.

Down below, Sharpclaw was gathering the patrol together, ready to head downstream. Echosong had emerged from her den and was distributing traveling herbs to give the warriors strength for their journey.

"It's time to go," Leafstar mewed.

She leaped down from the Rockpile; as Billystorm was about to follow he checked and pointed with his tail at a dead mouse that she had left lying at the very summit of the rocks. "You forgot your fresh-kill."

Leafstar glanced back. "Some other cat will eat it." *StarClan, please take this food and watch over us.*

Sharpclaw flicked his ears in surprise at Billystorm's presence as he and Leafstar joined the patrol. Leafstar nodded, braced to argue with her deputy, but he made no comment.

"Stick, you lead the way," he ordered, waving his tail at the Twolegplace cat.

Stick padded downriver until he could cross by the stepping-stones. As the patrol lined up to follow, Cora paused in front of Leafstar.

"Thank you for doing this," she meowed.

"Thank us all later," Leafstar responded.

She was waiting for her turn to cross when Echosong came over to her with a mouthful of traveling herbs. She looked even more troubled than when she had told Leafstar about the sign on the previous day. Leafstar knew that she felt entirely responsible for SkyClan's getting involved in the problems of the Twolegplace cats.

"I know this is what StarClan wants us to do," Leafstar reassured her, wishing that she felt as certain as she sounded. "They will watch over us."

Echosong nodded, though her troubled gaze did not clear. "May StarClan light your path," she whispered as she stretched forward to touch noses with her Clan leader. "I will await your return."

Leafstar dipped her head and joined the long line of cats who were crossing the river and climbing the trail that led out of the gorge.

The sun rose before the cats had gone far along the edge of the cliffs. The pale blue of the sky deepened; fluffy white clouds floated across it on a gentle breeze. Leafstar silently thanked StarClan that they had good weather for traveling.

As sunhigh approached they left the forest behind and the cliffs sank away until the cats were walking along a pebbly path beside the river. There was a roaring in the air that gradually grew louder.

"What's that?" Leafstar asked.

"A waterfall," Cora replied.

Leafstar's paws tingled. "Do we have to climb down it?"

The black she-cat shook her head. "No, there's another way, but it took us ages to find it when we were on our way here."

She had hardly finished speaking when the patrol came to the top of the waterfall. The river fell over it in a smooth curve and plunged into a pool far below that churned and foamed, filling the air with fine mist. Jagged rocks poked out of the water on either side. Beside the river the ground fell away in a sheer cliff; Leafstar scanned it, but she could see hardly any paw holds that would help a cat trying to climb down, nothing but a few scrubby bushes too far apart to be of any use.

"This way," Stick called, waving his tail. He led the patrol along the top of the cliff until it gradually began to slope down, and the ground sprouted gorse and thick clumps of heather rather than bare rock, slick with moss.

"We can get down here," the brown tom announced. "Follow me and watch where you're putting your paws."

The cats straggled out into a long line as they followed

Stick down the slope. The ground underpaw was treacherous; there were unexpected dips and hollows, and places where the ground crumbled away under the weight of a single paw. Leafstar found it tough to force her way through the tightly woven heather stems, and the thorns of the gorse bushes raked her pelt. Every cat was exhausted by the time they reached the bottom and headed back to the river.

"Let's rest," Sharpclaw suggested. "And we might take some time to hunt."

Leafstar nodded, though the Twolegplace cats didn't look happy; she guessed that they wanted to force the pace as much as they could, to get back to their home all the sooner.

But that's not going to happen. What use will it be, if we're all worn out when we get there?

When they went on, the path beside the river became smooth and sandy, easier on their paws. They passed a clump of elder bushes, and followed a curve to see several Twoleg nests standing beside a round, shallow pool.

"Is that your Twolegplace?" Sparrowpelt asked Shorty.

"No, ours is much bigger than that," Shorty told him, adding discouragingly, "and we've got a long way to go yet."

Stick led them away from the river, skirting the Twoleg nests in a wide circle. Twilight was gathering by the time they came to a small Thunderpath and halted at the edge.

"At least when it's getting dark you can see the monsters' eyes," Waspwhisker murmured.

But everything was dark and quiet, and they crossed the Thunderpath without any problems.

"It's time we made camp for the night," Leafstar announced when they reached the other side. "Stick, do you know any good places?"

"Yes, but we'll have to get away from these Twoleg nests first."

Stick brought them to a spot where the riverbank sloped down steeply and there were hollows among the roots of trees that shaded the water. Leafstar fell asleep with the gentle gurgle of the current in her ears.

The cats rose at dawn; there was plenty of prey among the trees, and they hunted successfully before carrying on. Not long after sunhigh they came to open fields, with Twoleg nests here and there at a safe distance. Leafstar relaxed and enjoyed the warmth as they padded through lush grass at the edge of the river.

"What are those?" Shrewtooth whispered, waving his tail at a group of huge short-haired animals who stood in the grass several fox-lengths away; their pelts were black and white, and they chewed placidly as their gaze followed the cats.

"Cows," Shorty replied. "Don't worry; they're not dangerous."

But even Leafstar felt doubtful when a couple of the beasts padded over and snuffled curiously at her and her Clanmates. *Their feet are so big and hard, like yellow rocks!* Sharpclaw snapped out an order to pick up the pace, and to Leafstar's relief the cows didn't follow them as they bounded away.

Sliding under a fence made of shiny tendrils strung between wooden uprights, the patrol came to a field that at first glance seemed to be empty. The ground sloped upward to the horizon; the rough clumps of grass were shorter, with the occasional outcrop of rock.

"I don't like this," Rockshade muttered to Egg. "It's too quiet."

Almost before he had finished speaking, the silence was broken by the barking of a dog. The cats froze; the sound grew rapidly louder, and the dog bounded over the brow of the hill: a massive creature with a rough, gingery pelt. Its tail flapped and its barking rose to a high-pitched yapping as it made for the cats.

"Run!" Shrewtooth yowled.

But there was nowhere to run to. The field stretched away, empty in all directions. There were no fences or walls in sight, not even a tree to climb.

"No!" Leafstar ordered, aware that at any moment the patrol would panic and scatter. "Hide—here, under the bank."

Sharpclaw went first, launching himself over the grassy edge before any cat had a clear idea of what they might find there. "It's all right!" he yowled when he was out of sight. "Come on!"

Leafstar stood guard, her claws extended and her lips drawn back in a snarl as the dog hurtled toward her. "Stay back, flea-pelt!" she spat.

The dog hesitated just long enough for the rest of the patrol to bundle themselves over the edge of the bank. Leaf-star leaped after them and found herself on a narrow pebbly stretch of ground, washed by the river. Grass and foliage hung over the water, making it harder to see them from above.

The patrol huddled together, staring upward, while the dog ran up and down above their heads, whining and snuffling. Leafstar knew it would be only a moment before it tracked them by their scent and launched itself down on top of them.

Then what do we do? Swim?

To her relief she heard the sound of a Twoleg voice, raised in a loud yowl. It sounded angry. The dog went on whining and searching for a moment more; then Leafstar heard its receding paw steps. Its scent began to fade.

"That was close!" Sparrowpelt panted.

Leafstar warned her cats to wait a few heartbeats more to make sure that the dog had gone before they climbed back onto the bank. Egg hung back, gazing into the water; then he darted a paw into the stream and hooked out a fish that flopped and wriggled on the stretch of pebbles until he killed it with a bite to the neck.

"Egg, that was brilliant!" Billystorm exclaimed. "Where did you learn to fish like that?"

The young tom ducked his head modestly. "I used to stay beside the river sometimes."

He lugged his catch up into the field and the whole patrol crowded around to share it. The fish was big enough for every cat to have a few bites.

"That was good," Sharpclaw meowed, swiping his tongue around his jaws. "It looks as if we were right to bring you, Egg."

The cream-colored tom's eyes shone with pride. *Sharpclaw*

was right all along, Leafstar mused. *SkyClan is stronger for having Egg with us.*

By the time the patrol had finished eating, the sun was sliding down the sky and there was a chill in the air.

"We'd better look for somewhere to spend the night," Sharpclaw meowed. "Stick, do you know of anywhere safe, where that dog won't bother us?"

Stick looked doubtful. "We've only been this way once before," he reminded the deputy. "We'll just have to hope the Twoleg keeps the dog shut up at night."

The patrol plodded on beside the river until they came to a thick hedge. Beyond it was another field; Leafstar peered through the thorny branches and spotted more of the gigantic black-and-white cows.

"I think we should stop here," she decided. "We probably won't find anywhere better. If we sleep under the hedge the branches should keep us safe from the dog."

"All the same, we should set a watch." Sharpclaw stretched his jaws in a vast yawn. "I'll go first, and wake one of you later on."

He sat just outside the hedge, his gaze scanning the field and the river; Leafstar stood beside him while the rest of the patrol crawled into shelter underneath the branches.

"Ow!" Cherrytail gave a hiss of annoyance. "I've just put my paw on a thorn."

"Then watch where you're putting it, mouse-brain," Sparrowpelt muttered. "And take your tail out of my ear."

Once her warriors were settled, Leafstar crept under the

hedge and managed to make a nest for herself among the dead leaves. *It's not going to be a comfortable night,* she realized with an inward sigh. *My pelt feels as if it's full of thorns.*

She jumped at a low-pitched, sorrowful noise coming from the other side of the hedge. Shrewtooth, curled up close by, raised his head with his eyes stretched wide. "What was that?"

As the noise came again, Billystorm stuck his head out of the branches on the other side. "Don't worry," he reported. "It's only one of those cows."

"Well, I hope they're not going to keep it up all night," Rockshade snapped from farther down the hedge. "I want to get some sleep."

Leafstar closed her eyes and wrapped her tail over her nose. For a few heartbeats the noise of the cows disturbed her, but gradually she slipped into sleep.

Mist surged around her; she couldn't see more than a tail-length beyond her muzzle. Damp grass brushed her pelt and the gurgle of the river over stones sounded unnaturally loud. *Where am I?* she wondered, knowing that she was dreaming. *StarClan, have you something to show me?*

As if in answer, a company of cats burst out of the mist in front of her and streamed past her, all heading upriver. She could see the closest ones clearly, make out the color of their pelts, and pick up their wild, distant scent, but others were no more than blurred shapes in the cloud.

"Come on!" Voices began to echo around her. "We're bound to find somewhere soon."

"My paws are dropping off." The voice of a cranky elder. "And my bones have never been so damp."

"Beechpaw! This isn't the time to be chasing leaves. Get back here right now!"

"We must keep going." The words were low and urgent, and Leafstar thought she recognized the voice of Cloudstar. "Sooner or later we'll find a new home."

The cats pressed on around Leafstar; they all seemed to know that the new home they had never seen must lie upriver. It was a struggle for Leafstar to walk through them against the flow; she tangled with their legs and tails as they pushed her from both sides, almost carrying her off her paws.

Are they trying to tell me I'm going the wrong way?

At last Leafstar managed to thrust her way to the back of the group. An old cat with a scruffy ginger pelt and rheumy eyes was bringing up the rear. As his gaze fell on Leafstar he halted and stared straight at her: the only cat who had noticed that she was there.

Leafstar shivered as he spoke the words of the prophecy to her: "This is the leaf-bare of my Clan. Greenleaf will come, but it will bring even greater storms than these. SkyClan will need deeper roots if it is to survive."

With a gasp, Leafstar jumped awake, scrambling to her paws. Next to her, Shrewtooth started up, his fur bristling as he tried to look in every direction at once.

"It's okay," Leafstar soothed him, resting the tip of her tail on his shoulder. "It was just a dream."

The young black tom sank back into his nest. "Are you all

right?" he whispered. "Did you have a message from Star-Clan?"

Leafstar realized that other cats had roused and were watching her; Sharpclaw had come off watch and had his intent green gaze fixed on her.

She shook her head. "No, it was nothing but a bad dream."

I can't share this sign with them. Is StarClan telling me that I'm doing the wrong thing?

More than anything, the repetition of the prophecy disturbed her. Surely she wasn't putting down deeper roots for her Clan by taking off like this to help other cats far away? Desperately she wished that SkyClan's destiny wasn't so obscured by shadows and doubts and so many possibilities. *Nothing seems clear, and I'm frightened that it's weakening my Clan.*

Sharpclaw held Leafstar's gaze for a moment longer, then stretched out his forepaws and raised his rump in a long stretch. "We're all awake," he meowed. "Why don't we carry on? It should be dawn soon."

"Good idea," Waspwhisker agreed. "I think every thorn in this hedge is pricking me."

Leafstar nodded agreement; the Clan deputy called to Cherrytail, who was keeping watch, and the patrol crawled out into the field beyond. Clouds had risen to cover the sky and there was little light, but the sound of the river guided their paw steps. Dew-laden grass brushed their pelts as they padded through it; Leafstar shivered as the moisture soaked through her fur.

She realized as they continued that Stick and the other

Twolegplace cats were clearly growing more tense. They seemed always on the alert, starting at every unexpected noise.

"Are we near your Twolegplace?" she asked Stick.

The brown tom shook his head. "Not yet. But we should get there today if we make good time."

As the sun came up the clouds cleared away and the dew dried from the grass. The day grew hotter, and it was harder to keep putting one paw in front of another with the sun beating down on their backs. With Stick urging them on, the cats kept going until sunhigh, then stopped to hunt and take a brief rest. When they went on, the ground began to slope away from them; the river tumbled over rocks in a series of shallow waterfalls, gurgling into pools where foam spun on the surface.

"The water looks so cool," Cherrytail murmured. "I'm going to rest my paws in it." She padded down the bank and waded into the water, letting out an appreciative little trill. "It's lovely! Come and try it!"

The Twolegplace cats looked doubtful, but all the Clan cats followed Cherrytail into the water. Leafstar enjoyed the cool touch on her paws. *We've come so far, even SkyClan pads get sore!*

"I'm getting out," Rockshade announced after a few moments. "I'm being splashed, and my fur's cold."

"Yes, come *on*," Stick called from the bank. "We'll never get there at this rate."

The river grew wider, with trees shading it on either side. The flow seemed almost sluggish here, after the bubble and chatter of the waterfalls.

"This is where we had the flood two seasons ago," Coal told Leafstar. "Firestar and Sandstorm were caught in it. That's how we met them: Firestar came looking for Sandstorm in our Twolegplace."

Leafstar nodded; Firestar had told them the story while he was with SkyClan. She shuddered at the thought of a wall of water thundering down this quiet river. *If Firestar had drowned, SkyClan would never have been reborn.*

The sun was starting to go down again when the river curved in a wide loop and Leafstar spotted the walls and rooftops of a Twolegplace in the distance. "Is that where we're going?" she asked Cora, who was padding next to her.

The black she-cat nodded. At the same moment, Stick veered away from the river and led the patrol across a stretch of open ground and into a patch of sparse woodland, made up mostly of spindly hazel saplings. Leafstar could detect faint scents of cat among the trees, and tried to decide if any of them belonged to Stick and his friends, from when they lived and hunted here. She picked up one scent that seemed familiar, but it was a she-cat scent, and not Cora's.

I wonder if that could be Red?

Stick led the way through the wood to a narrow, shallow stream at the other side. A fallen tree lay across it; Stick ran nimbly over to the other bank, and the rest of the patrol followed him. The walls of the Twolegplace lay in front of them on the other side.

"Dodge lives up there," Coal told the patrol, angling his ears upstream. Leafstar glanced in the direction he pointed, but there were no cats in sight, and no scents; Dodge's camp must be a good way away.

She and her warriors followed Stick down an alley and into the depths of the Twolegplace. Leafstar's pelt prickled as the walls closed around her. This wasn't like the Twolegplace near the gorge. There was crumbling stone everywhere she looked; debris lay in the alleys, and with each breath she took in the faint stench of crow-food.

The SkyClan cats bunched closer together as Stick led them onward. Leafstar felt comfort in Billystorm's pelt brushing hers on one side, and Cherrytail's on the other. Their route led around corners, over walls, and through tunnels that led underneath Thunderpaths, until Leafstar had lost all sense of direction.

I hope we can follow our scent trail back if we need to get out quickly.

Stick increased the pace as they headed farther into the Twolegplace, until he was bounding along. Cora, Shorty, and Coal ran faster too, their eyes shining. *They're really glad to be back,* Leafstar thought, amazed that any cat could actually enjoy living in this dirty, Twoleg-scented place.

Shorty and Cora raced past Stick as the cats emerged into a stretch of open ground where a few straggling bushes grew, with the occasional twisted tree. They pelted across the rough grass and into the mouth of an alley on the opposite side.

"Snowy! Are you here?" Shorty yowled.

There was a pause, then Cora let out a gasp. "Percy! You're back!"

Stick and Coal raced after their friends into the alley.

Leafstar and the Clan cats followed. As they entered the narrow passageway, Leafstar saw the Twolegplace cats crowding around a dark gray tabby tom, with a white she-cat beside him; Leafstar flinched when she saw the raw pink scars around the tom's eye. *Dodge did that to him.*

"He just appeared!" the she-cat, Snowy, was explaining. "The Twolegs brought him back."

Shorty was giving his friend a thorough inspection. "You smell different," he pronounced.

Percy nodded. "I feel kind of different, too."

Sparrowpelt shouldered his way into the crowd around the gray tom and sniffed at him curiously. "You've been to the Cutter, haven't you?" Glancing around, he realized that every cat was staring at him, and gave his chest fur a couple of embarrassed licks. "It happened to some of the cats back when I lived in my Twolegplace."

Billystorm nodded. "You can tell when a tom has been, because when they come back they're really different."

"Yeah," Sparrowpelt added. "Fatter and lazier!"

Faintly amused, Leafstar wondered when Sparrowpelt would stop sticking his paw in his mouth. A look of horror spread across his face as he realized what he had said.

"Sorry . . . er . . . Percy," he stammered. "I didn't mean . . ."

"That's okay," mewed Cora, giving Sparrowpelt a friendly nudge. "He was lazy to start with!"

Leafstar felt herself begin to relax. She had imagined that they would be walking into a place tense with the threat of war but this could be the reunion of any Clanmates separated by a longer than usual patrol.

"It's great to have you back," Snowy purred. "We thought we'd never see you again."

"And you found the fighting cats," Percy added. "That's even better!"

"We're not just fighting cats." Leafstar felt that she had to explain what it was like to be part of a Clan. "We live by the warrior code, and train apprentices to hunt for the whole Clan as well as to protect our borders."

Snowy and Percy exchanged a look. "That's nice," Snowy mewed politely, though Leafstar could tell that neither of the Twolegplace cats understood what she was trying to tell them.

"Anyway, you're here now," Percy went on. "We'll soon show Dodge and his friends what's what."

"Has Dodge been causing any more trouble?" Stick asked.

Snowy's cheerful look died away and her tail drooped. "A couple of kittypets got badly hurt trying to protect their housefolk's guinea pig."

While Stick and the other Twolegplace cats shot one another dismayed glances, Leafstar leaned closer to Billystorm. "What's a guinea pig?" she whispered.

"It's like a rabbit, but smaller and with tiny ears," Billystorm explained. "They squeak a lot. And they don't have legs, just spiky feet."

Leafstar found it hard to imagine such a weird creature. "That sounds like prey," she murmured. "Why would the kittypets want to protect it?"

Before Billystorm could reply, Shorty broke in, his voice outraged. "The Twolegs will drive us all out if Dodge keeps attacking the animals that live by their nests!"

Leafstar began to understand. For these cats, living on the fringes of Twoleg dens, it was essential not to make the Twolegs angry.

Thinking about that, she missed the rest of the Twoleg-place cats' comments, only paying attention again when Shorty asked quietly, "Have you seen Red?"

Snowy studied her paws. "Sometimes," she admitted. "Always with the brown-and-gray tom."

"Harley." Stick spat the name out through gritted teeth. "His name is Harley. And he must have tricked Red, or threatened her, if she's still with him. He needs to be taught a lesson!"

Leafstar exchanged a glance with Sharpclaw; she could see her deputy shared her thoughts. *Stick has a personal grudge against this cat. But still, it sounds as if Dodge and his friends are treating the others unfairly. There must be something we can do.*

"How far does your territory extend?" she asked the Twolegplace cats. "And how often does Dodge trespass?"

Percy looked puzzled. "Territory? Trespass?"

"We don't have borders here like you do in SkyClan," Coal explained. "Cats can go anywhere."

"What about prey?" Sharpclaw prompted with a twitch of his tail.

"We eat what we catch." Cora shrugged. "If every cat can hunt for themselves, then we should all have enough to eat."

"Then how are we going to stop Dodge threatening you if you don't have a border to keep him out?" Leafstar meowed.

"We have to get rid of him once and for all," Stick growled.

Cherrytail shot Leafstar an anxious glance. "That's not part of the warrior code," she pointed out. "We chase cats out of our territory, and patrol the border to make sure that they stay out. How far would we have to chase Dodge before he agreed not to come back?"

Good question, Leafstar thought. She was feeling worse about the battle with every heartbeat that passed. *Just what does Stick want us to achieve?*

"You have to fight him," Sharpclaw meowed to Stick. "And we'll help you. Do you have a plan?"

"We'll wait until nightfall," Stick replied. "Then I'll show you Dodge's camp. Meanwhile, you can hunt here. There's usually some prey in the waste ground we just passed."

He led the way back to the mouth of the alley. Leafstar glanced around the stretch of rough ground; it felt odd to be hunting for herself, not in a patrol. She watched Cherrytail and Sparrowpelt dive into the bushes nearby, while Sharpclaw, Egg, and Waspwhisker set out for the long grass at the foot of the opposite wall.

From the corner of her eye Leafstar glimpsed movement in one of the scrubby trees; her ears pricked as she made out a squirrel, half-hidden among the leaves. Pressing herself to the ground, she crept up to the tree and clawed her way up the trunk on the far side from the squirrel. She was fairly confident of making her catch; there was no other tree close enough for the squirrel to leap into.

But the squirrel was alerted by her progress through the rustling leaves. It sat straight up on the branch, then took a flying leap to the ground.

"Mouse dung!" Leafstar spat.

Then she spotted Billystorm near the foot of the tree. Panicking, the squirrel launched itself almost into his paws, and he killed it with a neat bite to its throat.

"Well done!" Leafstar exclaimed, dropping to the ground beside her Clanmate. "That was a great catch."

"You set it up," Billystorm meowed. "Let's share."

Even in this strange and disturbing place, joy washed through Leafstar from ears to tail-tip as she settled down beside Billystorm to eat the squirrel.

"Thank you, StarClan, for giving us this prey," she murmured, adding to herself, *Are you still watching over us, even here?*

She took a mouthful of the prey, her whiskers brushing the side of Billystorm's face. "I'm glad you're here," she purred.

Billystorm blinked at her, his green eyes warm. "So am I," he mewed.

CHAPTER 34

A *paw prodding in her side* woke Leafstar; she opened her eyes on glaring orange light that cast thick shadows across her sleeping Clanmates. For a few heartbeats she wasn't sure where she was. Then Cora's face came into focus as the black she-cat bent over her.

"Wake up!" she hissed. "Stick says it's time."

Memory flooded back into Leafstar, of the long journey to the Twolegplace and Stick's promise to show them Dodge's camp. She stumbled to her paws, realizing that she had been sleeping with her back pressed against Billystorm. Her movement woke him, and their eyes met for a moment in embarrassment.

Then Billystorm leaped up. "I'm ready," he announced.

Urgency swept through Leafstar, overpowering her doubts and pumping energy into her paws. She woke her other Clanmates and led them to where Stick was waiting with Shorty and Cora.

"Let's go," Stick meowed.

Whipping around, he led the way across the waste ground and down another alley. Leafstar and the other SkyClan cats bounded after him, along alleys and tiny paths that led through piles of split wood and past sleeping monsters, with scarcely a glance to make sure that they wouldn't wake. They passed so close to Twoleg nests that Leafstar's fur brushed against the rough red stone.

Eventually Stick led them up onto the top of a small wooden nest. As Leafstar leaped up, she saw him crouching at the far side of the roof, staring down at what lay beyond. She padded across the roof and crouched down beside him. The orange light showed her a pile of square Twoleg things, tumbled together on the bank of the shallow stream that they had crossed on their way into the Twolegplace. Its banks were muddy, with only a sluggish trickle of water at the bottom.

"Those boxes are where Dodge lives," Stick told her.

As Leafstar looked more closely, she could make out the shadows of cats slinking between the boxes, and caught the occasional gleam from their eyes. Then a sturdy-looking cat emerged into the open and called out, looking back over his shoulder.

A cheerful chirrup answered him, and a slender she-cat pushed her way out of the nearest box to join him. Although the harsh light drained all the color from their pelts, Leafstar guessed that they were Stick's daughter, Red, and her mate, Harley; she could feel Stick stiffening, and heard a faint snarl coming from the depths of his throat.

It was clear that Red wasn't a prisoner in Dodge's camp; she looked relaxed and happy to be there. With their tails twined together, the two cats strolled across the ditch and vanished into the woods.

Stick had sunk his claws so deeply into the wooden roof that he had to yank them out before he could sit up. His gaze swept over the cats who were crowding up behind him. "We'll attack now," he growled.

"Wait." Shorty stepped forward, his ears flicking anxiously. "What about Coal, Snowy, and Percy?"

"Go fetch them," Stick directed. "If we wait until tomorrow night, Dodge will know there are strangers here, and he might be on his guard."

Waspwhisker leaned over to murmur into Leafstar's ear. "He wants to attack while his daughter is out of the camp."

Leafstar nodded. She could understand why Stick had made his decision, but she was reluctant to go into battle unprepared. They didn't know anything about the layout of the camp beyond what they could see from the roof of the little den, nor how many cats were inside the boxes.

"Don't worry," Stick mewed, as if he could read her mind. "We'll outnumber them."

His eyes burned with a cold fire; Leafstar shivered, reminding herself that these cats did not live by the warrior code. *They'll kill, if that's the only way to win.*

"I want to take a closer look at the camp," Sharpclaw announced, beckoning Egg and Sparrowpelt with his tail. "We can't go into battle blind," he added as Stick seemed about to object, "and there'll be plenty of time before Shorty and the others get here."

Stick nodded; Leafstar felt her fur start to bristle at the way he was taking charge, just as he had done when Sharpclaw took the patrol into the Twolegplace.

"Good idea, Sharpclaw," she meowed. *Just so he's sure who is Clan leader here.*

Sharpclaw flicked his ears in acknowledgment; he and the two cats he had chosen slunk down the side of the nest and melted into the shadows.

"Don't worry, Stick." Cherrytail's voice was warm with pride in her Clanmates. "They won't get spotted."

While they waited for the others to join them, Leafstar scanned the camp below, but there was little movement to suggest how many cats might be there, or what they were doing. Behind her she could hear Shrewtooth's teeth chattering, but when she turned to give him a word of encouragement, she saw grim resolution in his eyes.

"Don't underestimate Shrewtooth's courage," Billystorm whispered to her. "I've seen him chase off a fox on border patrol, when the rest of us were stuck in brambles."

"Really?" Leafstar's pads tingled. *Shrewtooth had a bad start, but I think he may turn out to be one of our best warriors.*

Scrabbling sounds on the wall of the nest announced the return of Sharpclaw with Egg and Sparrowpelt. "There are cats in almost all of the dens," he reported to Leafstar, "but it's impossible to tell how many. We—"

"I told you, they won't outnumber us," Stick interrupted. "Not when the others get here."

Leafstar exchanged a concerned glance with Sharpclaw. Nothing was going to stop Stick from attacking. He was telling them what he wanted to hear.

"We need to attack from three sides," Sharpclaw went on. "From both ends of the ditch, and from this point here."

Stick and Cora were listening closely to what the deputy said. With a shock like a gust of icy leaf-bare wind, Leafstar realized that she had given them exactly what they wanted: the expertise of highly skilled warriors in a battle that might be nothing more than personal revenge.

With a flick of her tail she beckoned her Clanmates closer. "Remember, we fight according to the code!" she whispered. "No cat is to be killed for the sake of victory, and we fight as one, or not at all."

Stick's ears pricked up as she spoke, and he swung around to face her. "What is the point of fighting if you don't mean it? We fight to *win*!"

Leafstar did not respond, just let her gaze travel over her warriors to make sure they were certain whose orders they were following. To her relief, Stick fell silent and listened to Sharpclaw describing the terrain along the line of the ditch. Before he had finished, Shorty returned with Snowy, Coal, and Percy.

"Right," Stick growled. "The time has come for Dodge to leave this place. He has stolen too much from us!" Without hesitating, he launched himself off the top of the nest and raced across the open ground toward the boxes. Leafstar raised her tail to stop the others following him like a swarm of bees.

"Waspwhisker, Cherrytail, and Egg, you attack from that end of the ditch," she mewed rapidly, waving her tail.

"Billystorm, Sparrowpelt, and Shrewtooth, from the other end. Wait for my signal."

The Clan cats moved briskly off. Before he climbed down from the roof, Billystorm glanced back. "Be careful," he told Leafstar.

Leafstar replied with a nod.

Rockshade and Sharpclaw remained with her on the roof, along with the Twolegplace cats. Snowy was crouched on the edge, staring down at the boxes.

"I—I don't think I can do this," she whispered, looking up at Leafstar. Her voice was hoarse. "I saw what they did to Percy. . . ."

Leafstar touched her shoulder with the tip of her tail. "Okay, go back to your den."

But as the white she-cat rose to her paws and turned to go, Coal stepped forward to block her way. "We're in this together," he snarled.

"Not with reluctance, and not with fear." Leafstar took a pace forward and faced Coal, her head raised challengingly. "Let her go."

Coal hesitated for a couple of heartbeats, then stepped aside, his fur bristling and his tail-tip twitching. Snowy flashed a grateful glance at Leafstar, then vanished over the other side of the roof.

Staring down again at the camp, Leafstar spotted Stick poised on the edge of the jumble of boxes. His tail flicked impatiently as he glanced back over his shoulders at the others, beckoning them to join him.

"Line up," Leafstar hissed. "Do *not* lose sight of the cat beside you."

Her mind felt like leaves falling, whirled by the wind. *This is my first battle against other cats as leader, and I've had no chance to plan the fight. I'm going in blind. . . .*

"Sharpclaw, I need you with me," she meowed to her deputy. "You're the only cat who has any idea of the layout."

Sharpclaw nodded. "Don't worry. I'll be on your tail," he promised. "If we—"

"*Go!*" Coal yowled.

Furious that the black tom had given the signal before she was ready, Leafstar had no choice but to obey. The Twolegplace cats were already leaping down from the roof. Leafstar waved her tail to gather her Clanmates, and they streamed over the side of the nest. The SkyClan cats handled the drop best, landing neatly and pelting toward Dodge's camp without breaking stride. Leafstar spotted Cora stumble, but the black she-cat recovered herself quickly. Shorty had fallen awkwardly on his side; Leafstar paused to drag him to his feet and shoved him ahead of her as they raced on.

As she drew closer to the camp, Leafstar waited for the sensation of cats running alongside her: StarClan cats sharing her battle, just as Firestar had told her they accompanied him when he fought against BloodClan. But there was no starry glimmer, no insubstantial brushing of pelts against hers, no scent of the icy stretches of the night sky. Just real, live cats, smelling of fear and fury.

A cold stone seemed to settle in the pit of Leafstar's belly.

Have our ancestors deserted us because this is not our battle?

Yowls erupted from the other side of the camp, and a small flame of confidence rekindled inside Leafstar. The cats sent down to the ditch must have arrived.

Then a ginger-and-white tom hurtled out of the camp, heading straight for the attackers. Stick leaped on top of him, knocked him over, and held him down, gazing around him with the flame of battle in his eyes. "Cora!" he yowled.

When the black she-cat bounded up to him he left the tom to her and ran on, screeching, "I want Dodge!"

No, Leafstar thought, *you want your daughter.*

Shorty had joined Cora to wrestle with the ginger-and-white tom. Leafstar pelted past them and plunged into the tangle of nests. The strong scent of cats caught her by the throat; the flimsy walls closed in on her, dark and stifling.

Suddenly one of the nests was ripped open and a huge tom with ragged gray fur leaped out, his teeth bared. Leafstar stumbled onto her flank; before she could regain her paws Sharpclaw charged between her and her attacker, driving the gray tom back in a whirl of teeth and claws. They vanished into the darkness of the den, the walls heaving with the force of their fight.

One flap of the Twoleg-stuff collapsed on top of Leafstar; tearing with teeth and claws, fighting back panic, she managed to struggle free of it. As she shook the last scraps off her pelt, she found herself staring into a den where three kits mewled and scuffled in a nest of grass and leaves. Their mother, a young tortoiseshell-and-white queen, arched her back and hissed at Leafstar, her claws extended.

Turning away—she had no quarrel with kits—Leafstar spotted another den with eyes gleaming from its depths; ahead of it yet another den collapsed, revealing Cherrytail and a silver-and-black she-cat rolling on top of the battered walls in a screeching tangle of legs and tails. Just beyond them, Egg leaped onto the back of a tabby tom, clawing him around the ears.

As Leafstar pressed forward, Waspwhisker and Sparrowpelt appeared; they broke down the nests underneath their paws as they drove two of Dodge's cats in front of them until their opponents turned tail and fled. Leafstar felt a swift claw-stab of satisfaction that her warriors were working so well together.

"I'm with you, Leafstar," Rockshade panted from behind her. "What—?"

He broke off with a shriek as the cat leaped out and fastened his claws in his rump. Leafstar spun around and flung herself on the enemy cat, raking her claws down his side. The cat let Rockshade go as he turned to face Leafstar, but before the black tom could scramble to his paws a cream-colored she-cat hurled herself on him. Her lips were drawn back in a snarl as she buried her teeth in Rockshade's neck. The young black warrior let out a shriek of pain.

Chasing the first cat off with a pawful of claws slashed across his ears, Leafstar turned to battle the cream-colored she-cat. She flung her away from Rockshade and tried to pin her down, but the she-cat wriggled out from under her, slippery as a fish.

"Mange-pelt!" she snarled, baring her teeth at Leafstar.

Leafstar sprang at her, but the she-cat darted to one side, cuffing Leafstar over her head as she did so. Leafstar managed to trip her, and rolled over with her in the ruins of a nest; the she-cat's hind paws pummeled at her belly. A half-admiring thought slid through Leafstar's mind: *She's a vicious fighter, just as skilled as a warrior.*

Then Rockshade threw himself against the she-cat's shoulder, knocking her off balance and giving Leafstar the chance to scramble to her paws. She and Rockshade faced the enemy cat side by side. Undaunted, she let out a hiss and leaped right over their heads, to sprint off among the nests.

Leafstar bunched her muscles to spring after her. But before she could move, a nest nearby exploded into fragments and a dark brown tabby tom stalked out. His tail lashed and his fur was bristling as he let out a roar of rage. At the same moment Stick appeared from a gap between two nests and faced him.

"Coward!" the tabby tom spat. "You came skulking into my camp like rats—"

"At least I came myself," Stick retorted, stalking stiff-legged up to his enemy. "Not like you, Dodge, getting Twolegs to do my dirty work."

So that's Dodge, Leafstar thought.

Dodge and Stick leaped at each other, meeting in midair and crashing to the ground in a flailing knot of fur. They almost squashed Egg, who was wrestling with a black-and-white she-cat; he rolled out of the way and leaped up onto one of the sturdier dens. Shrewtooth jumped up beside him and the two warriors balanced there precariously for a couple of heartbeats. Then Shrewtooth spotted a ginger tom sneaking up on Cherrytail, who had emerged from a nearby den and had paused to lick a wound on her side. The young warrior let out a screech; then he and Egg jumped down on top of the ginger tom.

We work together, Leafstar thought, a tiny trickle of warmth penetrating the haze of battle.

Shrieks and growls rose around her; the cat scent was shot through with the reek of blood. Stick and Dodge were still locked together in a vicious, clawing bundle. Dragging her gaze away from them, Leafstar spotted Sharpclaw battling two toms at once, easily holding them off with SkyClan battle moves. Then a gap opened up between two dens, and Leafstar gasped in horror as she spotted the cream-colored she-cat grappling with Billystorm. She had him pinned down; as Leafstar watched she clawed out a pawful of his belly fur.

Leafstar sprang forward to help her Clanmate, but before she reached him a shriek went up from the nursery den. "Please don't hurt my kits!"

Leafstar spun around to see Coal and Shorty stalking toward the nest. The tortoiseshell-and-white queen was backing away to stand over her kits. Her hackles were raised and her eyes wide with fear. She stretched out one forepaw, its claws extended, as her gaze flickered from one attacker to the other.

Rushing over to the den, Leafstar thrust herself between the queen and the Twolegplace cats. "No!" she yowled. "You can't attack these kits. This is not their battle."

Shorty and Coal exchanged a baffled look. Then their eyes narrowed suspiciously as they stared at Leafstar. "Are you betraying us?" Coal growled.

Desperation surged through Leafstar. *I can't fight Coal and Shorty! But I have to protect these kits!*

Suddenly Rockshade appeared at her side. His black pelt was ruffled, and blood trickled from a scratch on his forehead, but his eyes were clear and filled with courage.

"We have to get these kits to safety," Leafstar told him.

"No!" the tortoiseshell queen exclaimed. "You're not going to touch my kits!"

Leafstar turned to her, making her voice quiet and soothing. "You have to trust us. If they stay here, they'll be hurt—maybe killed."

The young queen's eyes stretched wide with amazement. "But you're on the other side!"

Rockshade stepped forward. "Kits take no sides," he meowed. "They are the responsibility of all of us."

Leafstar felt a stab of pride in her young Clanmate. Flashing him a grateful look, she stepped into the den and dipped her head to the kits' mother before picking up a tiny black kit by its scruff; it let out a shrill squeak and waved its paws in the air. Rockshade followed her and picked up another kit, and their mother took the third. Coal and Shorty stepped aside as they left the den.

"This is not what we asked you to do!" Coal hissed as Leafstar passed him.

"We're not here to take orders from you," Leafstar replied, making her words sound clear through the mouthful of fur. She felt confidence grow inside her as she led the way to the ditch, weaving a path through knots of fighting cats with Rockshade and the tortoiseshell queen just behind her.

This is how Clan cats fight. We do not try to kill, and we do not make enemies of the weak or the young.

The ditch gaped ahead of her; beyond it, the woods were quiet. Leafstar was about to jump over when she spotted the cream-colored she-cat break free from Billystorm and streak toward her. Billystorm raced behind, his ginger-and-white fur dabbled with blood.

The SkyClan leader had no time to protect herself or the kit she carried. The cream-colored she-cat pounced on her and sank her teeth deep into Leafstar's neck.

A shriek of horror from Billystorm echoed around Leafstar. Then pain engulfed her, and the whole world went black.

CHAPTER 35

Leafstar sensed silver light all around her, encouraging her to open her eyes. She found herself sitting on the edge of the woods, bathed in the warm rays of the rising sun. Battle still raged in Dodge's camp, and on the far side of the ditch, cats were gathering around a hunched shape lying on the ground—something Leafstar couldn't see clearly. Billystorm and Cherrytail were there with Rockshade, and as she watched, Sharpclaw came racing up.

She tried to hear what they were saying, but their voices were oddly muted, and however much she strained her ears she couldn't make out the words. For some reason they seemed to be very distressed. Billystorm was crouched on the ground, his head flung back and his jaws parted in a soundless wail.

Then the crowd shifted and Leafstar gasped in horror as she saw her own body stretched lifeless in the mud at the edge of the ditch. The cream-colored she-cat was standing triumphantly over her.

No!

Leafstar jumped as she felt a tail stroke her flank. She turned her head to see a tortoiseshell she-cat sitting beside her, a look of compassion in her beautiful green eyes.

"Spottedleaf?" she rasped.

"Don't be afraid, dear one," Spottedleaf reassured her. "You are losing a life. You will return to them soon."

Leafstar became aware of another cat sitting on her other side, and glanced across to see the gray-and-white pelt of Cloudstar. The former SkyClan leader licked the top of her head as if she were a troubled kit.

"We are here," he murmured. "We will keep you safe."

"Did I do the wrong thing by bringing my Clanmates here?" Leafstar asked. "This isn't their battle!"

"But you have skills that you can give these cats to live in peace from now on," Spottedleaf told her.

"And you and Sharpclaw have fought together as a leader and deputy should," Cloudstar added, wisdom shining from his pale eyes. "Don't keep doubting him, Leafstar. He is as loyal to you and to SkyClan as you could wish."

Leafstar longed to accept their reassurances, but the anxieties of the last moon had sunk into her too deeply, like leaves trapped in the ice of leaf-bare. "It's been so hard!" she whispered. "I don't know what our destiny is!"

Cloudstar bent his head toward her. "Your destiny is what you make it, Leafstar."

Spottedleaf's sweet scent wreathed around her, stronger than the smell of blood and fury. "I gave you a life for healing wounds caused by words and rivalry," she murmured. "Use it now, Leafstar."

Her voice faded as she spoke, and the shapes of the two

StarClan cats dissolved into the surrounding woodland until they became no more than a frosty glimmer, and then were gone.

Leafstar's eyes blinked open and she saw the anxious faces of her Clanmates staring down at her.

"Oh, thank StarClan!" Rockshade's voice rose to a squeak.

"We hoped you were just losing a life," Cherrytail meowed. "It was scary, though!"

Leafstar stretched her limbs and managed to sit up. "Is the kit okay?" she croaked.

"Yes," the tortoiseshell queen replied. "My kits are all safe on the other side of the ditch."

Leafstar nodded thankfully, then looked around until her gaze met Billystorm's. The SkyClan warrior's eyes were full of love and pain; after a couple of heartbeats he turned his head away, his claws kneading the ground.

We will talk later, Leafstar promised him silently.

She became aware of the screeches of battle still coming from the other side of the ditch. Leafstar struggled to her paws. "We must help them," she wheezed.

Sharpclaw padded up and offered his shoulder for her to lean on. "Wait until your strength comes back," he meowed.

Before Leafstar could reply, there was a rustle from the trees on the other side of the ditch. Red and Harley appeared from behind a scrubby patch of bramble. Red halted, staring in horror at the battle and the wrecked camp.

"What's going on?" she gasped.

Leafstar turned to look across the ditch, trying to imagine

how Red would see the scene. The camp was in ruins, the flimsy sides of the dens squashed or torn, and smeared with blood. In the midst of the debris, Stick and Dodge still wrestled, with growls of hatred and claws clotted with each other's blood. It was obvious that the two toms were determined to kill each other.

With barely a glance at the Clan cats, Red leaped across the ditch and raced up to her father, with Harley hard on her paws. Beckoning her Clanmates with a wave of her tail, Leafstar staggered after them.

"What are you doing?" Red shrieked, standing over her father.

Without relaxing his grip on Dodge, Stick looked up; it took him a moment to focus on his daughter. "Freeing you!" he snarled.

"But I'm not a prisoner!"

All around them the other cats stopped fighting, as if they recognized that this was the heart of the battle. Stick and Dodge broke apart; Stick rose to his paws and faced his daughter, while Dodge sat up and started to lick his wounds, glaring resentfully at the cats who had attacked his camp.

"What's your problem?" Red challenged her father.

"These cats have done nothing but steal since they arrived," Stick spat back at her. "This was our home first! They have taken our prey, our dens, and now you!"

Red opened her jaws to reply, but Harley padded up close to her side before she could speak.

"No cat stole Red," the gray-black tom growled. "Do you

think so little of her? She came of her own accord."

"No," Red meowed, turning her head to gaze at Harley. "I came because of you—because I love you. No cat can make me leave."

Anger turned Stick's eyes into black pools. "This isn't love! You tricked her!" he roared as he sprang at Harley with claws outstretched.

Swift as a snake, Red threw herself in Stick's way. His claws plunged deep into her throat; at once he tried to throw his weight back, but it was too late. Red crumpled to the ground at his paws, blood welling from the wound he had opened up.

Stick stared down in disbelief, at the blood on his own claws and the gashes in his daughter's throat. "No . . . no . . ." he whispered.

For a heartbeat horror froze Leafstar's paws to the ground. Then she rushed forward to crouch beside Red. "Quick, bring cobwebs!" she ordered.

The words were scarcely out of her mouth before Cherrytail raced up to her with a pawful of cobwebs, which Leafstar slapped onto Red's wound. Shrewtooth arrived a moment later, holding out strands of sticky goosegrass from the ditch.

"Here, try this," he suggested.

Leafstar took the stems, trying to bind them across the pad of cobweb. But Red's blood kept gushing out. Her fur turned as scarlet as the sunrise behind them, as if her life were bleeding into the sky.

"Red—stay with me." Harley crouched beside her, opposite Leafstar, covering her ears with frantic licks. "Remember the kits we were going to have . . . tough little ginger she-cats, just like you? Remember how we planned our life?"

"That would never have happened," Stick snarled.

Dodge sprang to his paws. "Touch one hair on Harley's pelt and you'll answer to me."

Stick spun around to glare at him. "Then I'll kill you first."

As he crouched to spring, Sharpclaw flung himself at Stick's flank, overbalancing him and standing over him as he scrabbled in the mud. "Enough!" the SkyClan deputy hissed. "Too much blood has been shed already! You asked for our help to drive these cats out, not to kill them."

Stick stumbled to his paws, narrowing his eyes at the ginger tom. "Anything less is a sign of weakness," he spat.

Leafstar rose from Red's side and padded forward to stand beside her deputy. "Then you have learned nothing from the warrior code," she mewed. Looking around, she saw that all of Dodge's cats had been overpowered by her warriors. "This battle is over," she continued. "Dodge, leave these cats alone or we will come back and fight you again. Stick, defend your hunting places—learn from SkyClan and protect your prey as well as your dens. Use those parts of the warrior code that will help you to live without shedding more blood."

Stick said nothing, breathing hard and fixing Leafstar with a mutinous glare. But behind him Leafstar could see Shorty and Cora exchanging glances and nodding. *They have learned something, and they will use that to make their life better.*

"What?" Dodge stalked up, a truculent look in his eyes. "You're not going to get away with this!" he growled at Stick.

Leafstar turned, gesturing with her tail toward Red's body. The dying she-cat had her glazed eyes fixed on Harley; after a couple more heartbeats she gave a faint quiver and lay still, her paws and tail limp. Harley let out a groan from deep in his throat and buried his face in her fur.

"Do you think Stick can possibly suffer more than this?" Leafstar asked Dodge softly. "There is room here for all of you, if you divide it fairly. Carry on fighting to the death, and you'll only lose what you love most."

With the tip of her tail Leafstar signaled to her Clanmates, gathering them around her. All of them bore the marks of the battle, but she saw with a vast rush of relief that they were all there, all standing on their paws.

Sharpclaw padded up close to her side. She exchanged a long look with him, and he nodded solemnly.

"Come. It's time for us to return home," she meowed. With a last glance at Dodge and Stick, she led her Clanmates out of the battered camp, across the ditch, and into the woods.

While they were still among the trees, Cora raced to catch up to them.

"Thank you," the black she-cat panted, running alongside Leafstar. "For everything."

Leafstar nodded. "It was our destiny."

A pang of regret shook her as Cora turned back to return to the Twolegplace. *If things had been different, we could have been friends.* But Cora's paws lay on another path, she knew, helping her friends to rebuild their lives after the devastation of the battle. *That is her destiny. And this is ours.*

* * *

The SkyClan cats traveled slowly that day. Every cat was injured: Cherrytail was the worst, with scratches on both flanks and a wound to her neck which kept oozing blood. Shrewtooth was limping from where he had pulled out a claw, but he held his head proudly. Egg had a shredded ear, and patches of Sparrowpelt's fur had been wrenched out.

Leafstar made camp early, under the roots of a tree; with Sharpclaw and Waspwhisker, who had the least injuries, she hunted for the rest of the Clan, and found cobwebs to put on Cherrytail's neck wound.

"We'll soon have you home to Echosong," she promised.

The tortoiseshell she-cat flicked her tail. "Don't worry about me, Leafstar. I'll be okay."

The next day dawned fine, with a warm, sleepy breeze brushing the grass and ruffling the cats' fur. Leafstar glanced around approvingly as they set out again. Well-fed and rested, her Clanmates were already starting to recover. Her paws were tugging her home, but she set an easy pace, mindful of their wounds.

In the heat of sunhigh they rested beside the river where marigold grew thickly at the water's edge. Leafstar chewed up leaves to make a poultice for Cherrytail, while the rest of her Clanmates treated one another's scrapes and bruises. Egg caught another fish for them to share, and started to teach Rockshade how to do it; a close friendship seemed to be springing up between the two young cats.

SkyClan will be stronger for all we have been through together, Leafstar thought with satisfaction.

On the final day of their journey, Leafstar realized that Sharpclaw had fallen into step beside her. She had been waiting for this moment, and was mildly surprised that it had taken him so long. *Is he going to make one final challenge to my leadership?*

"I want you to know that I'll fight to the end of my nine lives to keep my position as leader," she vowed quietly, before Sharpclaw had the chance to say anything. "Not because I think I deserve it, but because I am loyal to my Clan, and to the warrior code, above all else."

Sharpclaw widened his eyes. Leafstar's voice grew sharper as she continued. "The code says that as leader my word is law, and my Clanmates must be loyal to me. If any cat cannot be loyal to me in this way, they cannot be part of SkyClan."

Sharpclaw just nodded. "I never expected anything else," he meowed.

"What?" Leafstar was outraged. "When you challenged me at every turn? When you took patrols into the Twolegplace without telling me? When—"

"But I've never doubted that you should be our leader," Sharpclaw interrupted. "I've always believed that, ever since Firestar took you to the Skyrock to receive your nine lives. I challenged you, yes, so I could be sure of your conviction that you were doing the right thing." His green eyes flashed. "What SkyClan needs more than anything else is a leader who has faith in herself. Because only then could other cats have faith in her, too."

Leafstar stared at him, stunned. *I thought he was a traitor! But all he cares about is making our Clan strong!*

"Then you have to accept the daylight-warriors," she told him, scrambling her thoughts together. "They are our Clanmates as much as any cat, and they have equal roles to play." Realizing how deeply she believed what she had just said, she added, "So Frecklepaw will be apprenticed to Echosong, just as she wishes, and we'll offer night training to all cats, not just those based in the gorge."

"Even in the Twolegplace?" Sharpclaw asked with a glint in his eyes.

Leafstar let her neck fur bristle up, but inwardly she was rejoicing at the new relationship that seemed to be unfurling between them. *Maybe I shouldn't have expected him to respect me when I didn't have enough respect for him.* "You'll have to let me think about that. But you *will* show respect to the daylight-warriors and include them in all the Clan activities. They are a worthy part of SkyClan."

Sharpclaw gave her a sideways glance. There was an edge to his tone as he murmured, "That's our destiny, right?"

Leafstar halted and faced him; the other cats gave them curious glances as they padded past.

"SkyClan's destiny is that we will never live in isolation from other cats," she meowed. "We're not like the forest Clans; we can't shut ourselves off entirely from kittypets or rogues. And visitors will be welcome."

"Just like that?" Sharpclaw queried.

Leafstar recalled the havoc that Stick and his friends had almost caused in her Clan. "No, there must be conditions." Excitement tingled through her as she realized that she was expanding the warrior code itself to fit the conditions in which SkyClan had to live. *Are these the "deeper roots" that the prophecy spoke of?*

"Visiting cats must hunt every day," she continued, "but we won't train them for fighting until they have spent one moon with us. And if they bring danger to the gorge, they must leave. SkyClan does not offer itself to the highest bidder as a fighting force." She lifted her head. "We are a proud, independent Clan with a code and honor of our own."

Sharpclaw let out a small sigh; then he nodded and touched his muzzle to the top of Leafstar's head. "I am proud to be your deputy," he murmured. He gave her a long look from sparkling eyes before turning away to pad after his Clanmates.

Leafstar stayed where she was for a moment, watching him go. Sharpclaw would never be an easy cat, she knew, blindly following her orders. He would always be a tough, challenging presence at her shoulder, with ideas of his own, and he would never be afraid to argue. *We'll have many more quarrels to come, I'm sure,* Leafstar thought. *And that's good.*

Watching her Clanmates pad away from her along the riverbank, Leafstar narrowed her eyes. *There's one more part of my destiny that I need to take control of.* With energy flooding into her paws she bounded forward until she caught up with Billystorm.

The ginger-and-white tom turned to look at her, his gaze warm with welcome. Leafstar reveled in the sensation of being close to him. *He was so strong, so brave, so loyal in the battle. . . .* She knew that he loved her, but he had accepted her destiny to be the leader of SkyClan, and nothing more. He was still prepared to go into battle beside her, and forge a path for other daylight-warriors to follow.

But Leafstar wanted more than this. If she could choose her Clan's destiny, she could choose her own. She had a deputy and a medicine cat she would trust with her eight remaining lives. Even if she had to step down from her duties while she nursed a litter of kits. In her Clan, her warrior code, there was no law against leaders having a mate, and a destiny of their own.

"Will you walk with me a while?" she asked him. "We need to talk. . . ."

TURN THE PAGE TO READ
AN EXCLUSIVE SKYCLAN
MANGA ADVENTURE. . . .

CREATED BY
ERIN HUNTER

WRITTEN BY
DAN JOLLEY

ART BY
JAMES L. BARRY

I AM *LEAFSTAR*, *LEADER* OF *SKYCLAN*.

WE'RE LOOKING FOR *TWO DOGS* THAT HAVE BEEN CAUSING A LOT OF TROUBLE FOR US LATELY.

HMMM.

I KNOW THE DOGS YOU'RE TALKING ABOUT. SOMETIMES THEY PASS THROUGH OVER THERE.

THEY LIVE IN THE HOUSE WITH THE POINTED ROOF--BEYOND THE ALLEY AND THE FENCE--AND THEY HUNT IN THE PARK AT NIGHT.

WE'RE VERY GRATEFUL FOR YOUR HELP. THANK YOU.

YEAH.

GOOD LUCK.

"ALL RIGHT...CHERRYTAIL, WASPWHISKER, MINTFUR, AND I WILL HEAD TOWARD THE TWOLEG NEST WITH THE POINTED ROOF..."

...AND SEE IF WE CAN STOP THE DOGS BEFORE THEY GET THIS FAR.

WHY NOT WAIT TO AMBUSH THEM HERE IN THE ALLEY?

TOO MANY OTHER CATS AROUND. WE DON'T WANT TO CHASE THE DOGS INTO INNOCENT KITTYPETS.

LEAFSTAR, RABBITPAW... YOU TWO SHOULD WAIT HERE AND WATCH OUT FOR ANY DOGS THAT GET PAST US, THEN FOLLOW THEM INTO THE PARK.

WAIT! WE CAN HIDE INSIDE THAT SHINY HOLLOW STUMP!

GOOD THINKING, RABBITPAW!

BILLYSTORM--I WAS WONDERING IF YOU WERE GOING TO JOIN US TONIGHT.

I AM, BUT... WHAT ARE YOU DOING *HERE?*

A KITTYPET TOLD US THE DOGS LIVE HERE!

WHAT? NO THEY DON'T! THEY LIVE IN A HOUSE BACK THAT WAY. I SAW THEM EARLIER--I WAS TRYING TO FIND YOU TO TELL YOU.

BUT...THAT MEANS...*OH NO!* COME WITH ME!

"LEAFSTAR AND RABBITPAW ARE IN DANGER!"

K-KLANG

OOWWWRROW! *MY LEG!*

RABBITPAW... WE'RE TRAPPED IN HERE, AREN'T WE?

?

NOT IF I CAN HELP IT. YOU STAY PUT...I'M GOING TO WRIGGLE OUT AND FETCH HELP.

NO! IT'S TOO DANGEROUS...AND YOU CAN'T CLIMB THE WALLS!

MAYBE NOT. BUT I CAN *RUN* AND *FIGHT*, AND I'M NOT GOING TO JUST SIT HERE UNTIL THE DOGS GET US!

WOW...LOOK AT 'EM GO!

THINK THEY'LL REMEMBER WHO WHIPPED THEM?

OH, I THINK SO.

FRECKLEWISH!

I HEARD THE MOST TERRIBLE NOISE, AND GOT HERE AS FAST AS I COULD!

IS ANYONE HURT?

COULD YOU TAKE A LOOK AT LEAFSTAR'S LEG?

WELL...NOTHING'S BROKEN. NO SCRAPES, EITHER...IT WAS JUST A BAD BRUISE.

YOU'LL BE SORE, BUT YOU'RE NOT HURT.

THANK YOU.

SKYCLAN! WE ARE TRIUMPHANT!

THOSE DOGS WON'T TROUBLE US ANY MORE!

AND THERE'S SOMETHING I MUST DO NOW...

EVERYONE! JOIN ME AT THE POOL!

TURN THE PAGE FOR A SNEAK PEEK OF

OMEN OF THE STARS #1

WARRIORS

THE FOURTH APPRENTICE

It has been foretold that Jayfeather and Lionblaze will hold the power of the stars in their paws. Now they must wait for a sign from StarClan to tell them which of their Clanmates will complete the prophecy. Soon, a StarClan warrior will visit a new ThunderClan apprentice—and the lives of the three chosen cats will be forever linked.

CHAPTER 1

A full moon floated in a cloudless sky, casting thick black shadows across the island. The leaves of the Great Oak rustled in a hot breeze. Crouched between Sorreltail and Graystripe, Lionblaze felt as though he couldn't get enough air.

"You'd think it would be cooler at night," he grumbled.

"I know," Graystripe sighed, shifting uncomfortably on the dry, powdery soil. "This season just gets hotter and hotter. I can't even remember when it last rained."

Lionblaze stretched up to peer over the heads of the other cats at his brother, Jayfeather, who was sitting with the medicine cats. Onestar had just reported the death of Barkface, and Kestrelflight, the remaining WindClan medicine cat, looked rather nervous to be representing his Clan alone for the first time.

"Jayfeather says StarClan hasn't told him anything about the drought," Lionblaze mewed to Graystripe. "I wonder if any of the other medicine cats—"

He broke off as Firestar, the leader of ThunderClan, rose to his paws on the branch where he had been sitting while he waited for his turn to speak. RiverClan's leader, Leopardstar, glanced up from the branch just below, where she was crouching. Onestar, the leader of WindClan, was perched in the fork of a bough a few tail-lengths higher, while ShadowClan's leader, Blackstar, was visible just as a gleam of eyes among the clustering leaves above Onestar's branch.

"Like every other Clan, ThunderClan is troubled by the heat," Firestar began. "But we are coping well. Two of our apprentices have been made into warriors and received their warrior names: Toadstep and Rosepetal."

Lionblaze sprang to his paws. "Toadstep! Rosepetal!" he yowled. The rest of ThunderClan joined in, along with several cats from WindClan and ShadowClan, though Lionblaze noticed that the RiverClan warriors were silent, looking on with hostility in their eyes.

Who ruffled their fur? he wondered. It was mean-spirited for a whole Clan to refuse to greet a new warrior at a Gathering. He twitched his ears. He wouldn't forget this the next time Leopardstar announced a new RiverClan appointment.

The two new ThunderClan warriors ducked their heads in embarrassment, though their eyes shone as they were welcomed by the Clans. Cloudtail, Toadstep's former mentor, was puffed up with pride, while Squirrelflight, who had mentored Rosepetal, watched the young warriors with gleaming eyes.

"I'm still surprised Firestar picked Squirrelflight to be a mentor," Lionblaze muttered to himself. "After she told all those lies about us being her kits."

"Firestar knows what he's doing," Graystripe responded; Lionblaze winced as he realized the gray warrior had overheard every word of his criticism. "He trusts Squirrelflight, and he wants to show every cat that she's a good warrior and a valued member of ThunderClan."

"I suppose you're right." Lionblaze blinked miserably. He had loved and respected Squirrelflight so much when he thought she was his mother, but now he felt cold and empty when he looked at her. She had betrayed him, and his littermates, too deeply for forgiveness. Hadn't she?

"If you've quite finished . . ." Leopardstar spoke over the last of the yowls of welcome and rose to her paws, fixing Firestar with a glare. "RiverClan still has a report to make."

Firestar dipped his head courteously to the RiverClan leader and took a pace back, sitting down again with his tail wrapped around his paws. "Go ahead, Leopardstar."

The RiverClan leader was the last to speak at the Gathering; Lionblaze had seen her tail twitching impatiently while the other leaders made their reports. Now her piercing gaze traveled across the cats crowded together in the clearing, while her neck fur bristled in fury.

"Prey-stealers!" she hissed.

"What?" Lionblaze sprang to his paws; his startled yowl was lost in the clamor as more cats from ThunderClan, WindClan, and ShadowClan leaped up to protest.

Leopardstar stared down at them, teeth bared, making no attempt to quell the tumult. Instinctively Lionblaze glanced upward, but there were no clouds to cover the moon; StarClan wasn't showing any anger at the outrageous accusation. *As if any of the other Clans would want to steal slimy, stinky fish!*

He noticed for the first time how thin the RiverClan leader looked, her bones sharp as flint beneath her dappled fur. The other RiverClan warriors were the same, Lionblaze realized, glancing around; even thinner than his own Clanmates and the ShadowClan warriors—and even thinner than the Wind-Clan cats, who looked skinny when they were full-fed.

"They're starving . . ." he murmured.

"We're all starving," Graystripe retorted.

Lionblaze let out a sigh. What the gray warrior said was true. In ThunderClan they had been forced to hunt and train at dawn and dusk in order to avoid the scorching heat of the day. In the hours surrounding sunhigh, the cats spent their time curled up sleeping in the precious shade at the foot of the walls of the stone hollow. For once the Clans were at peace, though Lionblaze suspected it was only because they were all too weak to fight, and no Clan had any prey worth fighting for.

Firestar rose to his paws again and raised his tail for silence. The caterwauling gradually died away and the cats sat down again, directing angry glares at the RiverClan leader.

"I'm sure you have good reason for accusing us all like that," Firestar meowed when he could make himself heard. "Would you like to explain?"

Leopardstar lashed her tail. "You have all been taking fish from the lake," she snarled. "And those fish belong to River-Clan."

"No, they don't," Blackstar objected, poking his head out from the foliage. "The lake borders all our territories. We're just as entitled to the fish as you are."

"Especially now," Onestar added. "We're all suffering from the drought. Prey is scarce in all our territories. If we can't eat fish, we'll starve."

Lionblaze stared at the two leaders in astonishment. Were ShadowClan and WindClan really so hungry that they'd been adding fish to their fresh-kill pile? Things must be *really* bad.

"But it's worse for us," Leopardstar insisted. "RiverClan doesn't eat any other kind of prey, so all the fish should belong to us."

"That's mouse-brained!" Squirrelflight sprang to her paws, her bushy tail lashing. "Are you saying that RiverClan can't eat any other prey? Are you admitting that your warriors are so incompetent they can't even catch a mouse?"

"Squirrelflight." Brambleclaw, the ThunderClan deputy, spoke commandingly as he rose from the oak root where he had been sitting with the other Clan deputies. His voice was coldly polite as he continued. "It's not your place to speak here. However," he added, looking up at Leopardstar, "she does have a point."

Lionblaze winced at Brambleclaw's tone, and he couldn't repress a twinge of sympathy for Squirrelflight as she sat down again, her head bent like an apprentice scolded in public by her mentor. Even after six moons, two whole seasons, Brambleclaw had not forgiven his former mate for claiming her sister Leafpool's kits as her own—and therefore his as well. Lionblaze still felt dazed whenever he reminded himself that Brambleclaw and Squirrelflight were not his real mother and father. He and his brother, Jayfeather, were the kits of the former ThunderClan medicine cat, Leafpool, and Crowfeather, a WindClan warrior. Since the truth came out, Brambleclaw and Squirrelflight had barely spoken to each other, and although Brambleclaw never punished Squirrelflight by giving her the hardest tasks or the most dangerous patrols, he made sure that their paths never crossed as they carried out their duties.

Squirrelflight's lie had been bad enough, but everything went wrong when she admitted what she had done. She had told the truth in a desperate attempt to save her kits from Ashfur's murderous fury at being passed over in favor of Brambleclaw, moons before Lionblaze and his littermates were born. Lionblaze's and Jayfeather's sister, Hollyleaf, had killed Ashfur to prevent him from revealing the secret at a Gathering. Then Hollyleaf vanished behind a fall of earth when she tried to escape through the tunnels to start a new life. Now the brothers had to accept that they were half-Clan, and that their father, Crowfeather, wanted nothing to do with them. And, on top of that, there were still suspicious looks from some of their own Clanmates, which made Lionblaze's pelt turn hot with rage.

As if we're suddenly going to turn disloyal because we've found out our father is a WindClan warrior! Who'd want to join those scrawny rabbit-munchers?

Lionblaze watched Jayfeather, wondering if he was thinking the same thing. His brother's sightless blue eyes were turned toward Brambleclaw, and his ears were alert, but it was hard to tell what was going through his mind. To Lionblaze's relief, the rest of the cats seemed too intent on what Leopardstar was saying to pay any attention to the rift between Brambleclaw and Squirrelflight.

"The fish in the lake belong to RiverClan," Leopardstar went on, her voice thin and high-pitched like wind through the reeds. "Any cat who tries to take them will feel our claws. From now on, I will instruct our border patrols to include the area around the water on every side."

"You can't do that!" Blackstar shouldered his way out of the leaves and leaped down to a lower branch, from where he could glare threateningly at Leopardstar. "Territories have never been extended into the lake."

Lionblaze pictured the lake as it had been, its waves lapping gently against grassy banks with only narrow strips of sand and pebbles here and there on the shore. Now the water had shrunk away into the middle, leaving wide stretches of mud that dried and cracked in the merciless greenleaf sun. Surely Leopardstar didn't want to claim those barren spaces as RiverClan territory?

"If any RiverClan patrols set paw on *our* territory," Onestar growled, baring his teeth, "they'll wish they hadn't."

"Leopardstar, listen." Lionblaze could tell that Firestar was trying hard to stay calm, even though the fur on his neck and shoulders was beginning to fluff up. "If you carry on like this, you're going to cause a war between the Clans. Cats will be injured. Haven't we got troubles enough without going to look for more?"

"Firestar's right," Sorreltail murmured into Lionblaze's ear.

"We should be trying to help one another, not fluffing up our fur ready for a fight."

Leopardstar crouched down as if she wanted to leap at the other leaders, letting out a wordless snarl and sliding out her claws.

This is a time of truce! Lionblaze thought, his eyes stretching wide in dismay. *A Clan leader attacking another cat at a Gathering? It can't happen!*

Firestar had tensed, bracing himself in case Leopardstar hurled herself at him. Instead she jumped down to the ground with a furious hiss, waving her tail for her warriors to gather around her.

"Stay away from our fish!" she spat as she led the way through the bushes that surrounded the clearing, toward the tree-bridge that led off the island. Her Clanmates followed her, shooting hostile looks at the other three Clans as they passed them. Murmurs of speculation and comment broke out as they left, but then Firestar's voice rang with authority above the noise.

"The Gathering is at an end! We must return to our territories until the next full moon. May StarClan light our paths!"

Lionblaze padded just behind his leader as the Thunder-Clan cats trekked around the edge of the lake toward their own territory. The water was barely visible, just a silver glimmer in the distance; pale moonlight reflected from the surface of the drying mud. Lionblaze wrinkled his nose at the smell of rotting fish.

If their prey stinks like that, RiverClan can have it!

Ahead of him, Brambleclaw trudged along next to Firestar, with Dustpelt and Ferncloud on the Clan leader's other side.

"What are we going to do?" the deputy asked. "Leopardstar *will* send out her patrols. What happens when we find them on our territory?"

Firestar twitched his ears. "We need to deal with this carefully," he meowed. "*Is* the bottom of the lake our territory? We would never have thought of claiming it when it was covered with water."

Dustpelt snorted. "If the dry land borders our territory, it's ours now. RiverClan has no rights to hunt or patrol there."

"But they look so hungry," Ferncloud mewed gently. "And ThunderClan never took fish from the lake anyway. Can't we let them have it?"

Dustpelt touched his nose briefly to his mate's ear. "Prey is scarce for us, too," he reminded her.

"We will not attack RiverClan warriors," Firestar decided. "Not unless they set paw on the ThunderClan territory within our scent marks—three tail-lengths from the shore, as we agreed when we came here. Brambleclaw, make sure that the patrols understand that when you send them out tomorrow."

"Of course, Firestar," the deputy replied, with a wave of his tail.

Lionblaze's pelt prickled. Even though he respected Firestar's conclusion because he was the Clan leader, Lionblaze wasn't sure that he had made the right decision this time.

Won't RiverClan think we're weak if we let them come around our side of the lake?

He jumped at the flick of a tail on his haunches and glanced around to see that Jayfeather had caught up to him.

"Leopardstar's got bees in her brain," his brother announced. "She'll never get away with this. Sooner or later, cats will get clawed."

"I know." Curiously, Lionblaze added, "I heard some ShadowClan cats at the Gathering saying that Leopardstar lost two lives recently. Is it true?"

Jayfeather gave him a curt nod. "Yes."

"She never announced it," Lionblaze commented.

Jayfeather halted, giving his brother a look of such sharp intelligence that Lionblaze found it hard to believe that his brilliant blue eyes couldn't see anything. "Come on, Lionblaze. When does a Clan leader ever announce they've lost a life? It would make them sound weak. Cats don't necessarily know how many lives their *own* leader has left."

"I suppose so," Lionblaze admitted, padding on.

"Leopardstar lost a life from a thorn scratch that got infected," Jayfeather continued. "And then straight after that she caught some kind of illness that made her terribly thirsty and weak, too. She couldn't even walk as far as the stream to get a drink."

"Mothwing and Willowshine told you all that?" Lionblaze asked, aware that medicine cats would confide in one another without thinking of the Clan rivalries that made warriors wary of saying too much.

"It doesn't matter how I found out," Jayfeather retorted. "I know, that's all."

Lionblaze suppressed a shiver. Even though he knew that Jayfeather's powers came from the prophecy, it still bothered him that his brother padded down paths that no cat, not even another medicine cat, had ever trodden before. Jayfeather *knew* things without being told—not even by StarClan. He could walk in other cats' dreams and learn their deepest secrets.

"I guess that's why Leopardstar is making such a nuisance of herself about the fish," Lionblaze murmured, pushing his uneasiness away. "She wants to prove to her Clan that she's still strong."

"She's going about it the wrong way," Jayfeather stated flatly. "She should know that she can't make the other Clans follow her orders. RiverClan will be worse off in the end than if they'd just struggled through the drought on their own territory, like the rest of us."

They were approaching the stream that marked the border between WindClan and ThunderClan. The water that had spilled into the lake with a rush and a gurgle just last newleaf had dwindled to a narrow stream of green slime, easily leaped over. Lionblaze drew a breath of relief as he plunged into the undergrowth beyond, under the familiar trees of his own territory.

"Maybe it'll all blow over," he meowed hopefully. "Leopardstar might see sense when she thinks about what the other leaders told her at the Gathering."

Jayfeather let out a contemptuous snort. "Hedgehogs will

fly before Leopardstar backs down. No, Lionblaze, the only thing that will solve our problem is for the lake to fill up again."

Lionblaze was padding through long, lush grass, his paws sinking into water at every step. A cool breeze ruffled his fur. Any moment now, he could put down his head and drink as much as he wanted, relieving the thirst that burned inside him like a thorn. A vole popped out of the reed bed in front of him, but before Lionblaze could leap on it, something hard poked him in the side. He woke up to find himself in his nest in the warriors' den, with Cloudtail standing over him. His fur felt sticky, and the air smelled of dust.

"Wake up," the white warrior meowed, giving Lionblaze another prod. "What are you, a dormouse?"

"Did you have to do that?" Lionblaze complained. "I was having this really great dream. . . ."

"And now you can go on a really great water patrol." Cloudtail's tone was unsympathetic. Since the streams that fed the lake had dried up, the only source of water was the shallow, brackish pool in the middle of the lake bed. Patrols went down several times a day to collect water for the Clan, in addition to hunting and patrolling as usual. The greenleaf nights seemed shorter than ever when every cat was tired out from extra duties.

Lionblaze's jaws gaped in an enormous yawn. "Okay, I'm coming."

He followed Cloudtail out of the den, shaking scraps of

moss from his pelt. The sky was pale with the first light of dawn, and although the sun had not yet risen the air was hot and heavy. Lionblaze groaned inwardly at the thought of yet another dry, scorching day.

Hazeltail, her apprentice, Blossompaw, Berrynose, and Icecloud were sitting outside the den; they rose to their paws as Cloudtail appeared with Lionblaze. None of them had been to the Gathering the night before, but Lionblaze could tell from their tense expressions that they knew about Leopardstar's threats.

"Let's go." Cloudtail waved his tail toward the thorn tunnel.

As Lionblaze padded through the forest behind the white warrior, he overheard Berrynose boasting to Icecloud: "RiverClan had better not mess with us when we get to the lake. I'll teach any cat not to get in my fur."

Icecloud murmured something in reply that Lionblaze didn't catch. *Berrynose thinks he's so great,* he thought. *But it's mousebrained to go looking for trouble when none of us is strong enough for a battle.*

To his relief, Cloudtail took his patrol to the foot of a huge oak tree and instructed them to collect bundles of moss to soak in the lake. Berrynose couldn't go on telling Icecloud what a fantastic warrior he was when his jaws were stuffed with fluffy green stalks.

When they reached the lake, Cloudtail paused briefly at the edge, gazing out across the lake bottom. It looked dry and powdery near the bank, with jagged cracks stretching across it; farther out it glistened in the pale light of dawn. As he tried to work out where the mud ended and the water began, Lionblaze spotted the tiny figures of four cats, far out across the mud. He set down his bundle of moss and tasted the air; the faint scent of RiverClan wafted toward him, mingled with the familiar stink of dead fish.

"Now listen," Cloudtail began, setting down his own bundle. "RiverClan can't object to us taking water, and Firestar has already said that he doesn't want any fighting. Have you got that, Berrynose?" He gave the younger warrior a hard stare.

Reluctantly Berrynose nodded. "'Kay," he mumbled around his mouthful of moss.

"Make sure you don't forget." With a final glare Cloudtail led his patrol out across the mud toward the distant lake.

The surface of the mud was hard at first, but as the patrol drew closer to the water Lionblaze found his paws sinking in at every step. "This is disgusting," he muttered, his words muffled by the moss as he tried to shake off the sticky, pale brown blobs. "I'll never get clean again."

As they approached the water's edge, he saw that the RiverClan cats had clustered together and were waiting for them, blocking their way: Reedwhisker and Graymist, with Otterheart and her apprentice, Sneezepaw. They all looked thin and exhausted, but their eyes glittered with hostility and their fur was bristling as if they would leap into battle for a couple of mousetails.

Reedwhisker stepped forward. "Have you forgotten what

Leopardstar told you at the Gathering last night?" he challenged. "The fish in the lake belong to RiverClan."

"We're not here to fish," Cloudtail replied calmly, setting down his moss. "We only want water. You're not going to deny us that, are you?"

"Are there no streams in your territory?" Graymist demanded.

"The streams have dried up, as you know very well." Lionblaze saw the tip of Cloudtail's tail twitch irritably as he answered; the fiery white warrior was finding it hard to control his temper. "We need water from the lake."

"And we'll take it whether you like it or not," Berrynose added, dropping his moss and taking a threatening step forward.

Instantly the four RiverClan cats slid out their claws. "The lake belongs to us," Otterheart hissed.

Blossompaw's eyes stretched wide in dismay and Hazeltail stepped forward, thrusting her apprentice behind her. Lionblaze braced himself and unsheathed his claws, ready to spring.

Cloudtail whipped around to face his patrol. "Keep your jaws shut!" he ordered Berrynose.

"Are you going to let them talk to us like that?" Berrynose challenged. "I'm not scared of them, even if you are."

Cloudtail stepped forward until he was nose to nose with the younger warrior, his eyes like chips of ice. "One more word and you'll be searching the elders for ticks for the next moon. Understand?"

Lionblaze felt a tingle of shock run beneath his fur. Cloudtail was brisk at the best of times, but he'd never seen him this angry at one of his own Clanmates. It was as if collecting water was the most important thing in the world to Cloudtail—and maybe it was, with his Clan weakened by thirst and getting weaker. Lionblaze wondered what would happen if RiverClan succeeded in preventing the other Clans from getting near the water. Would three of the four Clans die out?

Not waiting for Berrynose's response, Cloudtail swung around and addressed the RiverClan cats again. "I apologize for my warrior," he meowed. His voice was tight; Lionblaze could tell what an effort he was making to stay polite. "I think he must have caught a touch of the sun. Now, I'd appreciate it if you'd let us take some water."

For a heartbeat Reedwhisker paused. Lionblaze felt his paws itch with the urge to spring into battle. Cloudtail had warned them that they were too weak to fight, but he didn't know that Lionblaze was one of the Three and had the power to fight the fiercest battles without getting a single scratch. *But I know we've got problems enough without fighting one another.*

Finally Reedwhisker stepped back, gesturing with his tail for the rest of his patrol to do the same. "Take water, but no fish," he growled.

We're not here for fish. How many more times will we have to tell you that? Lionblaze thought.

"Thank you." Cloudtail dipped his head and padded up to the water's edge. Lionblaze followed, aware of the hostile gaze of the RiverClan cats boring into his back, watching his every move. His fury welled up again. *This is just stupid! Do they think I can smuggle a fish out under my pelt?*

He could see that his Clanmates were angry, too; Cloudtail's tail-tip twitched and Berrynose's eyes were blazing, though he had the sense to keep quiet. The she-cats' fur was bristling, and they glared over their shoulders at the RiverClan cats as they padded past.

Lionblaze soaked his moss in the lake water and lapped up a few mouthfuls. It was warm and tasted of earth and weeds, hardly quenching his thirst. He forced himself to swallow, wincing as the gritty liquid slid down his throat. The sun had risen, its harsh rays slashing across the tops of the trees, and there was no sign of a cloud from one horizon to the other.

How much longer can we go on like this?

CHAPTER 2

❧

Jayfeather picked through the herbs in the storage cave at the back of his den. The leaves and stems felt dry and crackly, and their scents were musty. *I should be stocking up for leaf-fall,* he thought. *But how can I when there's no fresh growth?*

The pressure of being ThunderClan's only medicine cat weighed like a stone in his belly. He remembered all the times he had grumbled about Leafpool telling him what to do. Now he wished that she had never resigned as a medicine cat and gone to live in the warriors' den. *What does it matter that she had kits? She still knows all about herbs, and what to do when a cat is injured.*

His pelt prickled with the bitter memory of a few days ago, when Briarpaw had pelted into the camp and skidded to a halt in front of his den.

"Jayfeather!" she panted. "Come quick! Firestar's hurt!"

"What? Where?"

"A fox got him!" The young apprentice's voice was shaking with fear. "On the ShadowClan border, near the dead tree."

"Okay, I'm coming." Inwardly Jayfeather felt just as scared, but he forced himself to sound confident. "Go find Leafpool and tell her."

Briarpaw let out a startled gasp, but Jayfeather didn't pause to ask why. Grabbing a few stems of horsetail, he raced out through the thorn tunnel and headed for the ShadowClan border. Only when he was already on his way did he remember that Leafpool wasn't a medicine cat any longer.

Before he reached the dead tree, the scent of blood led him to his leader. Firestar was lying on his side in a clump of ferns, his breath coming harsh and shallow. Sandstorm and Graystripe were crouched over him while Thornclaw kept watch from the top of a tree stump.

"Thank StarClan!" Sandstorm exclaimed as Jayfeather dashed up. "Firestar, Jayfeather's here. Just hold on."

"What happened?" Jayfeather asked, running his paws gently over Firestar's side. His belly lurched as he discovered a long gash with blood still pulsing out of it.

"We were patrolling, and a fox leaped out at us," Graystripe replied. "We chased it off, but . . ." His voice choked.

"Find some cobwebs," Jayfeather ordered. He began to chew up the horsetail to make a poultice. *Where's Leafpool?* he asked himself in agony. *I don't know if I'm doing the right thing.*

He patted the poultice onto the gash in his leader's side, binding it with the cobwebs that Graystripe thrust into his paws, but before he had finished he heard Firestar's breathing grow slower and slower, until at last it stopped.

"He's losing a life," Sandstorm whispered.

Jayfeather went on numbly fixing the poultice in place, so that when Firestar recovered he wouldn't lose any more blood. The time seemed to stretch out unnaturally, and Jayfeather's mind whirled as he tried to count up how many lives his leader had left.

That wasn't his last life, was it? It couldn't be!

He had almost given up hope, when Firestar gave a cough, his breathing started up again, and he raised his head. "Thanks, Jayfeather," he mewed weakly. "Don't look so worried. I'll be fine in a few heartbeats."

But as Firestar set off back to camp, leaning on Graystripe's shoulder, with Sandstorm padding along anxiously on his other side and Thornclaw bringing up the rear, Jayfeather hadn't been able to forgive himself. *I needed Leafpool, and she wasn't here.* His former mentor hadn't appeared until they were within sight of the stone hollow. She had been hunting on the WindClan border, and it had taken Briarpaw all that time to find her.

"You did your best," she reassured Jayfeather when he told her what had happened. "Sometimes that's all you can do."

But Jayfeather wasn't convinced; he knew that Leafpool would have saved Firestar if she had been there.

My Clan leader lost a life because of me, he told himself bitterly. *What sort of medicine cat does that make me?*

Now he finished sorting through the herbs, picked up a mouthful of ragwort, and set off for the elders' den. When he ducked under the outer boughs of the hazel bush, he found Mousefur curled up near the trunk, snoring gently, while Longtail and the old loner, Purdy, sat side by side in the shade of the rock wall.

"So this badger, see, was out lookin' for trouble, an' I

tracked it—" Purdy broke off as Jayfeather entered the den. "Hello, young 'un! What can we do for you?"

"Eat these herbs." Jayfeather dropped the stems and divided them carefully into three. "It's ragwort; it'll keep your strength up."

He heard Purdy's wheezing breath as the old loner padded up and prodded the herbs with one paw. "That stuff? Looks funny to me."

"Never mind what it looks like," Jayfeather hissed through gritted teeth. "Just eat it. You too, Longtail."

"Okay." The blind elder padded across and licked up the herbs. "Come on, Purdy," he mewed through the mouthful. "You know they'll do you good." His voice was hoarse, and his paw steps were unsteady. Every hair on Jayfeather's pelt prickled with anxiety. The whole Clan was hungry and thirsty, but Longtail seemed to be suffering particularly badly. Jayfeather suspected he was giving his share of water and food to Mousefur.

If I can get Purdy on his own, I'll ask him.

Purdy grunted disbelievingly, but Jayfeather heard him chewing up the ragwort. "Tastes foul," the old loner complained.

Jayfeather picked up the remaining herbs and padded across to Mousefur. The elder was already waking up, roused by the sound of voices. "What do you want?" she demanded. "Can't a cat get any sleep around here?"

She sounded as cranky as ever, which reassured Jayfeather that at least she was managing to cope with the heat. *When*

Mousefur sounds nice and sweet, I'll really start worrying!

"Ragwort," he meowed. "You need to eat it."

Mousefur let out a sigh. "I suppose you'll nag me until I do. Well, while I'm eating it, you can tell me what went on at the Gathering last night."

Jayfeather waited until he heard the old cat beginning to nibble on the herbs, then launched into an account of the previous night's Gathering.

"What?" Mousefur choked on a ragwort leaf when Jayfeather came to the point where Leopardstar had laid claim to the lake and all the fish. "She can't do that!"

Jayfeather shrugged. "She's done it. She said that River-Clan deserves to have all the fish because they can't eat any other sort of prey."

"And StarClan let her get away with it?" Mousefur hissed. "There were no clouds covering the moon?"

"If there had been, the Gathering would have broken up."

"What are our warrior ancestors thinking?" Mousefur snarled. "How could they stand by and let that mange-ridden she-cat decide that no other Clans can use the lake?"

Jayfeather couldn't answer her. He hadn't received any signs from StarClan recently, not since the beginning of the hot weather. *Leafpool would have heard from StarClan by now,* he thought. *They would have told her what to do to help the Clan.*

Leaving Mousefur muttering darkly over the last of the ragwort, Jayfeather pushed his way out of the elders' den and headed into the clearing. Passing the apprentices' den, he picked up a couple of unexpected scents. "Now what's going on?" he meowed irritably.

He padded across to the den and stuck his head through the bracken that covered the entrance. He could hear muffled whispering and rustling among the moss and bracken of the apprentices' nests.

"Dovekit! Ivykit!" he growled. "Come out of there. You're not apprentices yet."

The two kits scampered out of the den, stifling *mrrows* of laughter as they halted beside Jayfeather and shook scraps of moss from their fur.

"We were only looking!" Dovekit protested. "We'll be apprentices any day now, so we wanted to choose good places for our new nests."

"Side by side," Ivykit added. "We're going to do all our training together."

"That's right," Dovekit mewed. "And we're never going on patrol with any other cats."

Jayfeather let out a snort, not knowing whether he felt amused or frustrated. "In your dreams, kits. The other apprentices will tell you where you're going to sleep. And your mentors will tell you when to patrol, and who to go with."

The two kits were silent for a couple of heartbeats. Then Dovekit burst out, "We don't care! Come on, Ivykit, let's tell Whitewing that we looked in the den!"

Jayfeather stayed where he was for a moment as the two kits bundled off toward the nursery. There was an ache in his chest as he remembered when he had been a kit and believed he had a mother to boast to. Now he only had Leafpool.

As though the thought had called her up, his real mother's scent drifted toward him as she emerged from the thorn tunnel with the rest of a hunting patrol. Tasting the air, Jayfeather could tell that Dustpelt, Brackenfur, and even the apprentice Bumblepaw were carrying fresh-kill, but Leafpool had nothing.

Jayfeather's lip curled into a sneer. *All she's caught is fleas! She's a medicine cat, not a warrior. She should be helping me, not trying to pretend that her entire history vanished on the day the truth came out.*

He heard Leafpool's paw steps padding toward him, but he didn't want to talk to her. He turned his head away, and felt her sadness as she passed him. She didn't try to speak, but he could pick up her loneliness and sense of defeat as sharply as if they were his own. *It's as if she's given up every scrap of fight she ever had!*

Jayfeather could sense the awkwardness of the rest of the patrol, too, as if they didn't know how to treat Leafpool anymore. She had been their trusted medicine cat for so long that they didn't want to punish her for loving a WindClan cat once, but it seemed as if they no longer knew how to treat her as a much-loved and loyal Clanmate.

The hunting patrol started to put their prey on the fresh-kill pile. Brightheart followed them in through the thorn tunnel; Jayfeather caught the tang of the yarrow she was carrying.

"That's great, Brightheart," he called. "I wasn't sure you'd be able to find any, and we're totally out."

"There're a few plants near the old Twoleg nest,"

Brightheart mumbled around her mouthful of stems as she headed for the medicine cat's den.

Many seasons ago, a former medicine cat, Cinderpelt, had taught Brightheart the basic uses of herbs and how to treat minor wounds and illnesses. Ever since Jayfeather had become the only ThunderClan medicine cat, Brightheart had been helping him by gathering herbs and dealing with straightforward injuries. He knew she could never be his real apprentice—she was older than him, and committed to being a warrior—but he was grateful for her support.

Besides, I don't need to choose an apprentice yet. That was for older medicine cats; he felt countless moons stretching out ahead of him, thrumming beneath his paws like the ancient footprints he walked in by the Moonpool. And of course there was still the Prophecy to fulfill before it was his turn to join StarClan. *There will be three . . . who hold the power of the stars in their paws.*

The sun was well above the trees by now, beating down so that Jayfeather's fur felt as if it were on fire. *I can almost smell the smoke!*

Then his nose twitched. The acrid scent tickling his nostrils really was smoke. His pelt prickling with fear, he tasted the air for a couple of heartbeats, just to be certain, and located the smell at the edge of the hollow, close to the elders' den.

"Fire!" he yowled, launching himself toward the smell of burning.

Almost in the same heartbeat, he stumbled as Dovekit hurtled past him, her pelt brushing his as she raced out into the center of the clearing.

"Fire!" she screeched. "The Clan is on fire!"

Jayfeather was impressed that she had smelled the smoke so quickly. *I thought my nose was the best in the Clan!* But there was no time to think about that now. He had to find the fire and put it out before it spread to the rest of the camp.

More caterwauling broke out behind Jayfeather as he ran toward the hazel bush. He scented Brackenfur racing beside him and snapped, "Get the elders out of their den!"

The ginger warrior veered away to the entrance; Jayfeather raced on past the den, guided by the scent of smoke. As he drew closer to the rock wall he could hear the crackle of flames. A wave of heat rolled out to meet him and he halted. Frustration at his blindness swept over him, fierce as the fire. *I don't know where to attack it!*

Then another cat shouldered him out of the way; Jayfeather picked up Graystripe's scent, with Firestar and Squirrelflight just behind him.

"We need water," the Clan leader mewed crisply. "Jayfeather, find some cats to go down to the lake."

"That'll take too long," Graystripe yelped. "Kick dust on the fire, quick!"

Jayfeather heard the sound of vigorous scraping, but the smoke and flames didn't die down. He turned away, about to obey Firestar's order, when he heard the sound of several cats racing over toward the fire.

"Cloudtail! Lionblaze!" Firestar exclaimed. "Thank StarClan!"

Jayfeather picked up the scent of wet moss as his brother

and several other cats brushed past him. There was a loud hissing sound, and the acrid smell of smoke suddenly became much stronger. It caught in his throat and he retreated, coughing.

Moments later, Lionblaze joined him. "That was close!" he panted. "If we hadn't come just then, the whole camp could have caught fire."

"You're sure the fire's out?" Jayfeather asked, blinking eyes that stung from the smoke.

"Firestar is checking." Lionblaze let out a long sigh. "And now I suppose we'll have to go get more water. I just hope the RiverClan cats have gone."

"RiverClan?" Jayfeather felt his neck fur begin to bristle.

"There was a patrol out there when we arrived," Lionblaze explained. "We nearly had to fight for a few mouthfuls of water. If the RiverClan cats are still there, they certainly won't welcome us back." His voice grew heavy with anger. "They looked as if they were counting every drop!"

Jayfeather's tail drooped as he stood beside his brother among the sooty remnants of the fire. Around him, cats were beginning to carry the burnt debris out of the camp; the sharp scent made him cough again.

Will the end of the Clans be like this? he wondered. *Just like the lake is shrinking? So ordinary, and frustrating, and so bitterly, painfully slow?*

Lionblaze touched his nose to Jayfeather's shoulder in a gesture of comfort. "Remember, we will be Three again," he murmured. "Whitewing's kits are Firestar's kin, too."

Jayfeather shrugged. "How can we be sure? Why hasn't StarClan sent us a sign?"

"We don't know that the prophecy came from them in the first place," his brother pointed out.

"But they—"

A loud yowl from across the clearing interrupted what Jayfeather was about to say. "Hey, Jayfeather!"

Jayfeather's whiskers twitched as he recognized the voice of the most annoying cat in the Clan. "What is it now, Berrynose?" he asked with a sigh, heading in his direction.

Berrynose padded up to meet him; Jayfeather detected the scent of Poppyfrost just behind him.

"Poppyfrost is having kits," the young warrior announced importantly. "My kits."

"Congratulations," Jayfeather murmured.

"I want you to tell her she's got to rest and take care of herself," Berrynose went on. "Having kits can be dangerous, right?"

"Well . . . sometimes," Jayfeather admitted.

"Yeah, I heard that the kits can come too soon, or they can be weak, or—"

"Berrynose," Poppyfrost interrupted; Jayfeather could pick up her distress as clearly as if she had caterwauled it to the whole camp. "I'm sure I'll be okay."

"Or the kits take too long in coming," Berrynose finished, as if his mate hadn't spoken.

"There can be problems, but . . ." Jayfeather padded forward until he could give Poppyfrost a good sniff. "She's a healthy she-cat," he went on. "There's no reason she can't carry on with her normal duties for now."

"What?" Berrynose sounded outraged. "That's not good enough! Poppyfrost, you go into the nursery right now, and let Ferncloud and Daisy take care of you."

"Really, there's no need—" Poppyfrost began, but Berrynose was already nudging her across the clearing toward the entrance to the nursery.

Jayfeather stood still as the sound of their paw steps retreated. *Why consult a medicine cat if you're not going to listen, mousebrain?*

Defeat suddenly flooded over Jayfeather like a huge wave. What was the point of having the power of the stars in his paws if even his own Clanmates didn't listen to him? "I don't know if we can do this on our own," he murmured to himself. "Two or three of us . . ."